Praise for *The Washington Lawyer* by Allan Topol

"Pity the poor political novelist. After all the real-world skullduggery of recent decades—Nixon's Watergate, Clinton's intern—how can fiction possibly compete with reality? Washington lawyer Allan Topol can't beat those odds, but in *The Washington Lawyer* he's given us a lively insider's portrait of political mischief featuring a senator who is a traitor and perhaps a murderer, a nominee for chief justice of the United States who is desperately trying to cover up his own misdeeds and a gang of Chinese spies eager to bribe or, if necessary, kill our politicians to obtain the Pentagon's innermost secrets . . . Topol's version is entertaining and at times has the ring of truth."

—Patrick Anderson
"Book World," *The Washington Post*

"Archeologist professor Allison Boyd doesn't believe her beautiful twin sister, congressional aid Vanessa Boyd, drowned in the Caribbean while away for the weekend alone. Vanessa was many things but 'alone' was never one of them. Convinced Vanessa was murdered, Allison heads to Washington to uncover the truth. As she finds herself caught up in a tangled web of power players, she begins to realize how far some people will go to keep a secret. No matter the cost.

Fast-paced and action-packed, Topol's novel expertly weaves together power, murder, and intrigue to paint a chilling picture of the sinister underbelly of Washington politics. A thrill ride that doesn't let up."

—Beth McMullen
Author of *Original Sin* and *Spy Mom*

"Morals, ethics, values, and integrity often go out the window when temptations come your way. What happens when two men let their greed and desire for wealth and power overtake their moral compasses, and find that one simple indiscretion leading to one wrong choice can bring down your entire world? . . .

Once again author Allan Topol delivers a plot and storyline that will keep readers in suspense from start to finish . . . When the truth is revealed whose damage control wins out? Find out when you read this five-star novel."

—Fran Lewis
Author, creator and editor of *MJ* magazine, and host on Red River Radio Show and World of Ink Network

"*The Washington Lawyer* is a thrilling tale of intrigue and revenge at the highest levels in the American government—told from an insider's point of view. The action is nonstop, from the gripping prologue to the satisfying end. Not to be missed!"

—Joan Johnston
New York Times best-selling author of *Sinful*

THE ITALIAN DIVIDE

THE
ITALIAN
DIVIDE

A Craig Page Thriller

ALLAN TOPOL

SelectBooks

New York

Copyright © 2016 by Allan Topol

This edition published by SelectBooks, Inc.
For information address SelectBooks, Inc., New York, New York.

First Edition

ISBN 978-1-59079-366-4

Library of Congress Cataloging-in-Publication Data

Topol, Allan.
The Italian divide / Allan Topol. – First edition.
pages ; cm. – (Craig Page ; 4)
ISBN 978-1-59079-366-4 (softcover)
1. United States. Central Intelligence Agency–Officials and employees–Fiction. 2. Women journalists–Fiction. 3. Murder–Investigation–Fiction. 4. Political fiction. I. Title.
PS3570.O64I87 2016
813'.54–dc23
2015032960

Manufactured in the United States of America
10 9 8 7 6 5 4 3 2 1

Dedicated to my wife, Barbara,
my partner in this literary venture

Acknowledgments

I owe a great thanks to Kenzi Sugihara, who founded SelectBooks. This is our fourth novel together, and I could not ask for more support and encouragement from a publisher. Kenzi was enthusiastic from the first time I broached the idea of doing a book about Italy, and he offered valuable comments to help shape the concept for the novel.

Nancy Sugihara did a wonderful job of editing. Kenichi Sugihara is outstanding as the Marketing Director, and again he developed a superb cover.

My agent, Pam Ahearn, provided critical advice on the story and structure of the novel as well as editorial suggestions. It is a pleasure working with Pam.

My wife, Barbara, traveled with me throughout Italy, offering insights into the country and the people as I shaped the ideas in the novel. She then read draft after draft and offered valuable suggestions, particularly for the characters.

PROLOGUE

Biarritz, France

At two thirty in the morning, Qing Li was carrying a briefcase stuffed with 500,000 euros. He walked down three cracked concrete steps into the Volga nightclub. The lights were dim. It took a few seconds for him to see through the haze of cigarette and cigar smoke. The room was jammed with people, many speaking Russian loudly and sounding drunk.

A silver coated ball twirled from the ceiling in the center of the room. A Russian singing voice on tape blared from a loud speaker. Straight ahead was a small stage. A busty blond in a G-string went through the motions of dancing.

To the left was a bar. Qing, who was six foot four and walked ramrod straight, as they had taught him in the Chinese People's Liberation Army, headed toward the bar. He had gotten his instructions from Sergei in Moscow a few hours ago. He knew what to do.

Qing saw two empty seats at the bar. He took one of them, put the briefcase at his feet, and ordered a drink. "Macallan's 12 year old on ice."

Ten minutes later, as he was sipping his drink, Qing felt a tap on the shoulder. He whirled around to see a tall man about six-six, with a shaved head and sandpaper beard, standing behind him. The man was wearing a dark jacket unbuttoned to reveal a gun holstered at his chest over a black turtleneck shirt.

"I'm Radovich," the man said in English with a Russian accent.

"Mao's my name."

Radovich didn't crack a smile. "Come with me," the Russian said.

Qing grabbed his briefcase and followed Radovich to an office in the back. Only one man was in the room. He was short and stocky.

"This is Boris," Radovich said. "He'll be working with me."

1

Qing nodded and sat down at a table cluttered with papers and photos of strippers.

"Let's talk about the job," Qing said.

"No. First the money," Radovich said sharply.

Just like Russians, Qing thought. They don't care about the work. Only about money.

Qing pointed to the briefcase on the floor. "I have 500,000 euros in there. I'll leave it with you. The bag is a gift."

Again, no smile.

"And the second 500,000 euros?"

"It'll be wired to your Biarritz account from Moscow twenty-four hours after you finish the job."

"Show me the money."

Qing hoisted the bag onto the table and snapped it open. The euros were old and all with totally different numbers. It would be impossible to trace them.

Qing was watching Radovich. The Russian stared greedily at the money. Boris leaned over the bag, eyes wide open.

Qing guessed what Radovich was thinking: one bullet was all it would take to kill Qing. It would be easy to dump the body in the sea. No risk of getting caught. Why take a chance for another 500,000?

Qing had a switchblade knife in his jacket pocket. And a gun in an ankle holster.

Radovich lifted his hand and moved it toward his jacket. Convinced Radovich was going for his gun, Qing reached for his ankle. As Qing made contact with the cold metal, the phone in his pocket rang. Radovich dropped his hand.

Qing took out his phone. He immediately recognized the Beijing number. He had to take the call.

"Yes," he said tersely in Mandarin.

"Status?"

"Final arrangements are being made."

"Any issues?"

Qing looked at Radovich whose hands were on the table.

"None for me. Any change at your end?"

"No. Proceed."

The caller in Beijing clicked off, but Qing decided to use the call to bluff Radovich. He pretended the conversation was continuing, and he switched to English.

"Are you with Sergei now?" Qing said.

He waited a few seconds, then continued. "Tell Sergei I'm in a meeting with Radovich and Boris, his people in Biarritz. . . . No, I don't think we have a problem."

Qing stared at Radovich, hoping that invoking the name of Sergei, the Moscow crime boss, would be enough to ensure that he abandoned his intention of trying to kill Qing. "Do we?"

"Tell Sergei, no problems," Radovich said.

Qing breathed a sigh of relief. He repeated Radovich's words, then put away the phone.

"Okay, now let's talk about the job," Qing said.

"We're ready," Radovich replied.

"I want you to kill an Italian banker."

Biarritz

June 1

Alberto Goldoni stood at the window of his eighth floor suite in the Hotel Du Palais in Biarritz. A powerful storm was ahead. As he watched the angry swirling sea crashing against the rocks below, he wondered what he was doing here.

Thursday, two days ago, he had been in his office at Turin Credit bank when Federico Castiglione had called from Milan. In a frightened voice, Federico had said, "We must talk. You have to meet me in Biarritz over the weekend."

Because of their friendship and the obligation Alberto's family had to the members of Federico's family, he'd do anything for Federico. Still, he was mystified by the proposal and curious about what Federico wanted to discuss. "Why wait until the weekend? I can come to Milan today."

"No, it's better outside of the country. Please believe me. Amelie and I will get to our house in Biarritz late Saturday afternoon. You should stay at the Hotel Du Palais. We'll have dinner in the hotel Saturday evening with our wives. Then early Sunday morning, you and I can talk on the beach. No one will be able to overhear us."

From the determination in Federico's voice, Alberto realized further questioning was pointless. "I'll be there."

"Good. This is important for you, too. . . . Not just for me."

Without saying another word, Federico had hung up. Now at eight thirty on Saturday evening Alberto and his wife, Dora, having flown up in his bank's private plane early in the morning, were dressing for dinner.

Federico was the CEO and largest stockholder in the National Bank of Milan, the third largest in Italy. Alberto's bank was the largest in the country. Whatever was happening to Federico undoubtedly involved banking business or finances in Italy. Both of them had barely survived the financial upheaval of 2008. Now there must be a new threat to their survival.

Alberto would try to find out what was happening this evening at dinner. He didn't like having to wait for tomorrow morning. But he knew Federico. The man could be stubborn. If he decided on something, there was little chance of convincing him to change.

As if reading his mind, Dora called from behind Alberto. "Are you worrying about Federico?"

He whirled around and looked at her wearing a white silk bra and panties, sitting at the vanity table, brushing her long black hair. They had been married for twenty-two years, and he still found her as beautiful as the day he had met her at the University of Bologna where they were both students. He also respected her views and intellect.

"Federico sounded upset during the call Thursday."

She put down the brush. "I can't understand why he couldn't come to Turin to talk to you. Or ask you to go to Milan."

"He made it sound as if he was afraid of someone who was there."

"And he wanted to slip away from them?"

"That's what I thought. But no matter what, if Federico wanted me to do this, I had to."

"You're a good person, Alberto."

"Not really. I made you suffer through a day on one of the great beaches in Europe. And dinner in the hotel should be a hardship as well."

"The hardship will be having to put up with Federico's new French wife, Amelie."

"I know you liked Bonita, but it's not Federico's fault she died."

"He didn't even wait six months to remarry."

Alberto didn't have a retort for that. He had been surprised as well.

"And then he picks a sexy French bimbo," she continued. "A former model. Ach! You men. You're all the same."

"Hey. I didn't do anything."

The ring from Alberto's cell phone resting on the desk interrupted their banter. He picked it up and saw the caller was not identified. "Yes?"

"This is Roberto Parelli." The voice was raspy and strained. "I'm sorry to bother you on the weekend, but I've been busy with my political campaign and Luciano told me that my loans are due tomorrow."

"Actually, they were due six months ago." Alberto had spoken about it with Roberto several times. "I gave you additional time to pay them back."

"Well now, I need more time."

"How long?"

"Another six months." Parelli wasn't asking. He was demanding. "The election is on September 30. Less than four months. I expect to win. When I do, donors will step forward to pay off my debts."

Alberto's heart was pounding. This was a tough decision. The loans totaled 310 million euros. Considerably more than the value of the collateral: The Parelli farm, vineyard, and winery. The prudent thing for Alberto to do was call the loans and seize the property. That would mean not only destroying Parelli financially, but also effectively ending the heavily in debt political campaign of the controversial Parelli. The candidate was either Italy's savior or agent of the devil sent for the nation's destruction.

Alberto hated being in this position. He was a banker, not a politician. He despised Parelli's New Italy party and what Parelli wanted to achieve, but he didn't think that should influence his decision. Still, he was only human. Subject to the same passions which Parelli provoked in others.

"I'll give you one more week. That's all," Alberto said firmly.

He noticed Dora moving close to him, a concerned look on her face.

"But don't you realize what I'm trying to do for the country?"

"I'm very sorry. I can't give you preferential treatment. It's a question of fairness among all the bank's clients.

"I have promises of large contributors."

"I hope you receive them and will be able to repay the loans."

"You'll be wrecking my campaign." Parelli was raising his voice. "Think about the consequences for you."

The comment rankled Alberto. Parelli was threatening him. That only strengthened his resolve. "I have thought about them."

"Well, think some more."

"My mind is made up."

"You'll pay for this. Are you sure you want to deal with the consequences?"

"Positive," Alberto said without flinching.

Parelli hung up.

From outside, Alberto heard the sound of thunder. The skies opened. A pelting rain smacked against the windows.

"Parelli?" Dora said.

He nodded. "A very unpleasant call with an arrogant man and a not-so-veiled threat of unspecified consequences."

"Should you talk to the authorities?"

"Too risky. Some powerful people are supporting him. I gave him another week. I'm sure he'll continue pressing me for further extensions."

She sighed.

"What do you think I should do?" he asked.

"What are the latest polls showing?"

"Parelli's party is leading all the others at 40 percent. But the sharp rise he's had for weeks has ended. It seems as if he's leveled off." He shrugged. "Maybe even headed downward. It's impossible to predict. So what do you think I should do?" he repeated.

"Like you, I hate Parelli's program. I'd love to see him eliminated from the campaign, but I don't want you to be hurt."

"I've been more than reasonable, delaying the calling of the loans for six months."

"I know, but if you do, his backers will vilify you. They'll claim that a banker is deciding the fate of Italy."

"Correction. A Jewish banker."

"For sure. When all you're doing is behaving like a sound businessman."

"Besides, what can he do to me?" Alberto said pensively.

Unanswered, the question hung in the air until Alberto said, "We better finish dressing. It's almost nine o'clock. Federico is always on time."

She put on her coral silk dress and asked him to zip it. As he did, she said, "I'll bet there's a relationship between the danger Federico's facing and the Parelli loans."

He gave a long low whistle. "What makes you think so?"

"Instinct. And Federico telling you that whatever is happening to him will affect you as well. Federico may also have given loans to Parelli."

Alberto opened his mouth to argue with Dora. Then closed it. Over the years, her instincts had often been correct. There could be a link between what was happening to Federico and Alberto's loans to Parelli. Perhaps the discussion with Federico would illuminate it.

Aosta, Italy

Luigi had laid out some maps on the table in the lounge of the Hotel Milleluci. Craig Page studied the maps as if his life depended upon it, which it did. Today they had completed the second of three legs of a rally race on narrow roads in the Italian Alps. Craig, calling himself Enrico Marino, behind the wheel of a light blue 1996 Jaguar modified for racing, outfitted with a 510 horse power motor, and his navigator, Luigi, had turned in a dazzling performance so far in this race.

After the second leg, Craig was in first place. He was three minutes and ten seconds ahead of Carlucci, an experienced driver, who like Craig was based in Milan and who had won more than a dozen majors in his career. No one else was even close to the two of them.

Craig desperately wanted to win this race. It would be his first victory in a major.

This afternoon they ended in Aosta, referred to as the "Rome of the Alps," in the shadow of the peaks of Mont Blanc and San Bernardo. Tomorrow their route would carry them up into some of the most rugged roads in the Alps, to finish the race in Stresa—on the shore of Lake Maggiore.

"I think you're wrong" Luigi said.

The firmness of Luigi's tone startled Craig. In their discussion about strategy for tomorrow, Craig faced the dilemma which confronted leaders in many sports, including golf and football,. Should he play it safe, take it easy, and try to sit on his lead? Craig could do that tomorrow by driving at his average speed for the first two days, figuring it was good enough to get him into first place and should be sufficient to win. Or he could keep pushing to increase his speed, which meant a greater chance for a crash, on the assumption that Carlucci might do better today.

Luigi was arguing for Craig to play it safe. He was reluctant to reject his navigator's advice because Luigi had been in many more races. But Craig was twenty years older than Luigi. He didn't have a great deal of time to win a major.

Pondering the question, he sipped some Armagnac and looked up at the old wooden beams across the ceiling of the lounge.

The phone in Craig's pocket rang. He saw the caller was Federico Castiglione, his close friend and his largest financial backer.

"Congratulations," Federico said. "I got the results of today's race from the sports network on my computer. You had an incredible day."

"It's not over yet. Carlucci will come out tomorrow loaded for bear." Federico had told Craig he was planning to come to Stresa and meet him at the finish line. So Craig added, "I look forward to seeing you tomorrow."

"I'm real sorry. I have a business crisis. I won't be able to come."

The disappointment was evident in Federico's voice.

"Are you stuck in Milan?"

"Actually in Biarritz. I have a critical meeting here."

"Well that's too bad. "I'll do my best to win this one for you."

"I would like nothing better."

"I'll deliver the trophy to you. To put in your office or home."

"No, no. It should be yours."

"I owe you too much. I want you to have it."

"Thank you. Good luck tomorrow."

"We're revving it up," Craig said to Luigi. "We can't let Carlucci win."

"Remember Sardinia." Luigi sounded alarmed.

Craig could never forget it. Last October, Craig had started the final round, fifteen seconds behind Carlucci. In his effort to make up that time, he had pushed too hard and lost control of the car, which flipped over as it rolled down a hill. Miraculously, the car didn't explode, and Craig and Luigi had survived with relatively minor injuries. Both ended up in the hospital where they were treated for mild concussions and bruises.

"That was the rain," Craig said."

"And the prediction tomorrow is for rain as well. You'll be at a disadvantage with rear wheel drive."

"It doesn't matter. I'm going for broke."

Biarritz

"How did you happen to own a house in Biarritz?" Dora asked Federico and Amelie.

The two couples were seated in the luxurious dining room of the Hotel Du Palais, at a table adjacent to the sweeping concave window that faced the sea. Sheets of heavy rain pounded against the glass.

Looking around, Alberto saw that every table was taken. He heard the sound of voices in a myriad of languages. Loudest among them was a table of eight Russians, their decibel level rising with increased alcohol consumption.

Alberto had never been to Biarritz, the glamorous resort in the Basque country of southwest France. He was impressed with the incredible sophistication of the Hotel Du Palais and the outstanding food. The rack of lamb from the Pyrenees he was now eating following his poached sea bass was perfect and went well with the 2000 Château L'Evangile Federico had selected.

"My family is from South West France," Amelie answered. She was stylishly dressed in a pale pink silk dress and was fiddling with a ruby and diamond bracelet. "Biarritz was a whaling station until Napoleon III built a summer house here for his wife, Empress Eugenia, in 1854. That house, the Villa Eugenia, is now the Hotel Du Palais. After that, the town became hot. My family began coming here during the summers in the eighteen seventies and built a family compound. By the end of the nineteenth century, Biarritz had become the most exclusive watering hole for European royalty and the rich and famous. Princes. Artists. Tycoons. Lots of those people and my family, as well, kept their wealth and positions throughout the First World War and even during the Depression. Biarritz was the place to be in the twenties and early thirties. Then . . ."

She paused to sip some wine. Alberto glanced at Federico who seemed to have tuned out. He must have heard the story many times, Alberto thought.

Amelie said. "Then the damn Nazis came. They ruined everything."

"What happened to your family compound?" Dora asked.

"My family stopped coming. The SS took it over. Colonel Schultz used it as his headquarters to round up Jews for deportation to the camps."

"Was there much of a resistance movement in the town?" Alberto asked.

"Insignificant," Amelie replied, looking away.

When no one responded, she added, "What could they do? The Germans had overwhelming military power. They were in control until the allies began bombing which destroyed almost all of Biarritz. But not the hotel Du Palais. The allies spared that. My family compound was leveled in the bombing. Colonel Schultz was in the main house when it was bombed. He and his whole staff were all killed. So the story has a happy ending."

"Not for some," Alberto said. "Not for the Jews who were deported."

Ignoring his words, Amelie continued. "Let me tell you about the rebuilding from the ashes."

Federico interjected. "And now Europe is on the verge of its next round of destruction." He sounded distraught.

The words, coming without warning from Federico, who hadn't seemed to be listening, startled Alberto. "You mean because of our financial mess?"

Federico looked around the room nervously as if he was being pursued. Then he leaned forward in his chair and spoke softly. "That's what makes us so vulnerable. We're on the cusp of another round of conquest. Globalization is the worst thing that ever happened to Italy. Our small businesses are being destroyed. They want us to lose our character, to be like everybody else." He pointed to the table of eight loud Russian men. "In the meantime, people like that are running around Europe with suitcases of cash."

"Are you worried about the Russians?" Alberto asked in a gentle voice.

Before Federico had a chance to answer, Amelie said, "Federico has become so gloomy and pessimistic lately. I don't know why."

Rather than respond, Federico emptied his glass of wine and signaled to the waiter for another bottle. They had already finished two, a white and red after a round of champagne, with Federico doing most of the drinking. Alberto was concerned that his friend was becoming unraveled because of whatever dangers he faced.

"We French are resilient," Amelie continued, speaking nervously and sounding anxious to change the subject. "Look what happened to Biarritz. In the nineteen sixties and seventies, surfers were attracted by the great waves along the coast of Biarritz in spite of the rubble and flattened town. The wealthy followed them and began settling there about thirty years ago. My family came back and built several houses, including the one Federico bought for me as a wedding present."

"Like Napoleon the Third," Dora, said, and Amelie smiled.

"Now we have plenty of Russians," Federico interjected.

"Shh. Keep your voice down," Amelie said.

Federico ignored her. "Oligarchs arriving with suitcases filled with dollars and euros, having looted the state. Their bodyguards are former KGB agents."

Amelie turned to Dora. "There's a very fashionable boutique in town—Natashka. The proprietor carries all the top designers—including Dior, Armani, and Valentino. And she knows her business. You should let her dress you. Feel free to use my name."

Alberto could guess what his wife was thinking: *I dress myself.*

"I don't think I'll have time on this trip," Dora said politely.

"Are others of your family here this weekend?" Alberto asked Amelie.

"My brother and sister in-law and their children are down from Paris. They have their own house a block away. You'll meet them at brunch tomorrow at our house. We're at 90 Avenue Carnot, facing the public garden. Come at 11:00."

"We'd like that," Dora said.

"What does your brother do?" Alberto asked.

"He's in high tech. Computers and stuff I don't understand."

Before dessert, Amelie and Dora went to the toilette. Alone with Federico, Alberto made an effort to convince his friend to tell him what was bothering him. But Federico firmly resisted. "Tomorrow morning at 8:00, meet me at my house. We'll walk on the beach. I'll tell you everything."

His voice sounded tense.

When dinner was over, Alberto, concerned about how much Federico had to drink, suggested that he and Amelie take a cab to their house, but Federico stubbornly refused. "It's only eight blocks away. We'll be fine."

Together, the four of them walked outside. The rain had stopped.

When the valet brought Federico's car, before getting in, he moved close to Alberto. His face was a mask of fear. "Be careful, my friend," he whispered.

After they drove away, Alberto asked Dora, "How about a night cap in the bar?"

"You're on your own. I'm exhausted and going to bed."

In the bar, Alberto ordered a Sambuca, but the barman told him, "Monsieur, you're in the land of great Armagnac."

Alberto followed the recommendation, and the amber liquid was excellent. As he sipped it, he thought about Federico's behavior during the evening and his closing words, "Be careful, my friend."

Federico might be unraveling. Or he might really be in danger. Also, he must think I'm at risk as well and was trying to warn me.

Alberto was a man of action. He wanted to take control of situations, not be reactive.

Perhaps Federico had been unwilling to talk in a public place. Alberto didn't want to wait until morning to find out what was happening. It wasn't his style.

Alberto decided to walk to Federico's house, thinking they probably wouldn't be asleep yet. He'd ring the bell. In the privacy of Federico's house, he'd compel his friend to talk and let him know what was going on.

Alberto got directions from the barman. Without calling Dora, who might be sleeping, he set off, climbing the Edouard VII road, which ran from the hotel into the heart of town.

Turning the corner to Avenue Carnot, Alberto stopped dead in his tracks. Up ahead, in the middle of the block, he saw two police cars and an ambulance, flashing lights on their roofs.

Alarmed, Alberto resumed walking and checked the house numbers. The vehicles were in front of number 90, Federico's house. Spot lights were illuminating the typical Basque house built of local red stone with an overhanging tiled roof, wooden balustrades on the second floor balcony, and whitewashed walls.

Alberto ran along the cement path leading to the front door. Before he got there, a burly policeman stepped into the center of the path, blocking Alberto.

With the little French Alberto knew, he tried to explain that he was Federico's friend and he wanted to go inside.

The policeman shook his head sternly. "It's not possible."

"What happened?"

The policeman fired off a few rapid sentences. Alberto didn't understand everything he said. But enough to piece together that there had been a jewelry robbery. Amelie was okay. But Federico was dead!

Again, Alberto begged the officer to let him get into the house. "To see my friend, Amelie. To comfort her." But the policeman refused to budge.

Recalling Federico's closing words before he got into his car, Alberto realized that Federico knew he was in danger and thought Alberto might be as well. Federico had been trying to warn Alberto. After what had happened to his friend, Alberto had to take Federico's warning seriously.

He made a snap decision. He and Dora were leaving Biarritz immediately.

He turned around and scanned the area. He saw the emergency personnel and neighbors looking out of their houses. A dark blue Mercedes parked a block away on Avenue Carnot, facing Federico's house, caught his eye. Alberto couldn't tell whether anyone was inside. He took out his phone and called the pilot of his private plane, who had been sleeping. "We're flying back to Turin in an hour. I'll meet you at the airport."

In the morning he'd arrange bodyguards around the clock for him and Dora.

Then he called the hotel and woke Dora. "Start packing," he said tersely. "I'll explain when I get back in a few minutes."

"What happened?" she asked anxiously.

He recalled the policeman's words about the jewelry theft. He was convinced this hadn't been the cause of Federico's death.

"Federico has been murdered," he said.

"Oh my God!"

"I'm on my way."

Alberto walked swiftly along Avenue Carnot and turned right onto Edouard VII, retracing his route and heading down the hill to the hotel.

As he glanced over his shoulder, he saw a dark blue Mercedes approaching from behind with only the driver in the car. Alberto broke into a run. The Mercedes sped up and kept pace with him.

Whoever was in the car had to be connected to Federico's murder. As he ran, Alberto strained his eyes, trying to see the license plate, but it was too dark. Without warning, the car stopped moving. Alberto was blinded. The beam of a bright flashlight was being shined on him. He could just barely see a gun with a silencer being pointed through the open car window. That was enough for Alberto. He pivoted sharply and ran back up the hill. From behind, he heard the ping–ping of the gun being fired at him. Alberto cut sharply to the right, running across the street behind the Mercedes and out of the gun-man's line of fire.

From his afternoon on the beach, he recalled a set of about twenty cement steps that led down to the beach and a path below, straight to a rear entrance of the hotel. No car could follow him there. The driver would have to get out and pursue him on foot.

Alberto tore down the stairs so quickly he lost his balance and tripped and fell. He heard a car roar away. From the bottom of the path, he looked up. No one had followed.

He paused for a moment to dust himself off. He had torn his pants at the knee and was bleeding.

Breathless, he resumed running. He didn't stop until he entered the hotel.

He had to get out of Biarritz and damn fast. He was hoping these people didn't know who he was and wouldn't follow him to Turin.

Stresa, Italy

The light blue Jaguar barreled over the crest of a hill on the narrow mountain road at 120 miles an hour.

Craig was fatigued. Still, he kept pushing the powerful car to the limit of what it could do. And what he could do.

Having passed beneath the Matterhorn, Craig was on the final leg down the mountain to the finish line in Stresa on the banks of Lake Maggiore. At the top of the mountain, above the tree line, snow was visible on the jagged peaks. A bright blinding sun was beating down on the road. Craig was grateful for his custom made Maui Jims.

"Great view of the lake below," Luigi, his navigator, said. "But don't you dare look."

They were communicating through microphones and headsets hooked up to their racing helmets which permitted them to hear over the drone of the engine.

In rally races of this type, drivers start each day's race sequentially. This was the final day of the race and Craig, with the best time after two days, had the honor of starting last. Carlucci, with the second best time, had started right before Craig.

All that matters is how long it takes a driver to complete the course. Whoever has the shortest time is the winner. Craig knew that when they had started today, his total time for the race was three minutes and ten seconds less than Carlucci's. However, Craig had no idea how fast Carlucci was covering this final leg.

Fortunately, the rain had held off.

As soon as that thought passed through Craig's mind, he saw a dark sky ahead. With almost two hours of driving left until reaching the finish line at about four this afternoon, there was now a good possibility he'd be driving in rain.

Half an hour later, Craig was gripping the wheel hard, cutting a switchback turn a bit too closely when the skies opened up. On the left was a steep vertical drop down the side of the mountain.

"No," Craig told himself. "No." This race will end differently today. This won't be Sardinia.

They had crossed the tree line. Craig strained to see the road through his wipers which were working furiously.

"Want to ease up?" Luigi asked.

"No," Craig said tersely. "Carlucci will have the rain, too."

"I hope so."

They were constantly moving downhill, and that made the road particularly treacherous. They passed a cluster of about twenty spectators standing along the road, getting drenched to watch the cars pass their village.

"Hairpin turn on the right in one kilometer," Luigi said.

"Roger that."

"Another to the left seconds later."

"Roger that."

Through the corner of his eye, Craig saw Luigi gripping the hand support on the front dash.

Craig blasted into the first turn at full speed. The wheels spun. Craig turned into the spin to maintain traction. They were dangerously close to the edge of the road, which had no guardrail—just centimeters from a drop into the abyss.

The car bucked. Craig wasn't sure they would hold the road. He sucked in his breath. The car straightened out. Craig floored the accelerator.

"The next turn is even harder." Luigi barked. "Cut your speed."

Craig didn't listen. His guess was that Carlucci had passed these two diabolical turns before it started to rain. By easing up now, he'd lose valuable time to Carlucci.

Craig realized he was being reckless, but he pressed the accelerator to the floor. The speed increased.

"Here comes the turn," Luigi called.

Craig was gripping the steering wheel with white knuckles, perspiration dotting his forehead, as he headed into the turn. He cut it close. His tires were on the gravel at the edge of the road. The car began to spin. Craig held his breath, but kept control. They were out of the turn, heading down the mountain.

"Great driving," Luigi said in a voice filled with admiration and relief. "Those are the two toughest turns."

Craig was tempted to ease up, but he didn't.

The race finished on Corso Umberto, the main road running along the lake through the heart of Stresa. The finish line was in front of the municipal building. Crowds of people lined both sides of the road. The rain had stopped. The sun was shining.

In a matter of seconds, Craig would find out if he had a better time than Carlucci and everyone else—whether he had won the race. He was nervous and excited, the adrenalin surging through his weary body.

He passed the square in front of the municipal building and braked to a stop. He and Luigi climbed out of the car. They were heading toward the race headquarters in front of the municipal building to get the result.

There was no need to do that. People rushed up to Craig and Luigi shouting, "You won! You won!!" He glanced up and saw a scoreboard, showing he'd won by a minute and three seconds.

Craig was ecstatic. Luigi hugged him.

When they reached the headquarters desk, a man handed Craig a trophy and each of them a check. One million euros for Craig, five hundred thousand for Luigi.

Luigi hugged him again.

Photographers were snapping pictures. Video cameras were rolling.

A TV reporter holding a microphone interviewed Craig and Luigi. More reporters approached.

Craig spotted Carlucci sitting with a drink at one of the tables in a small café in front of the municipal building and walked over. When Carlucci stood up, Craig, the American hiding in Europe, held out his hand, but Carlucci ignored it. European style, he hugged Craig and smiling through crooked teeth said, "Good race. We'll see what happens in Munich."

After the reporters had their stories, Craig and Luigi went into the café where the owner cracked open a bottle of Moet and poured glasses for them. By the time they drank one glass and started another, two good-looking, shapely women, one blond, the other brunette, sat down at the table. They were matching bookends with short skirts and halter tops.

Glass in hand, Craig stood up and said to Luigi, "Have fun. I'll call you about the next race."

Craig drifted away while glancing over his shoulder. The women were all over Luigi. The crowd had thinned out. Craig planned to walk back to the Grand Hotel Des Iles Borromees where he was staying to shower and sleep for about four hours. Then he'd have a quiet dinner alone in the room.

But before he did any of that, Craig had to call Federico and let him know he'd won. Federico would be thrilled. He was surprised to reach only Federico's voice mail. He thought Federico would be waiting for his call. The banker must be in a very important meeting. Craig left a message saying, "Great news. We won. I'll deliver the trophy to you tomorrow in Milan."

As he left the café, another photographer with a video camera approached and began filming Craig. He saw the name on the camera was "International Herald" and did a double take. That was Elizabeth's newspaper.

Perhaps his tired eyes were deceiving him. He blinked and looked again. It was *International Herald*. He had seen it correctly.

Behind the cameraman, he spotted a woman holding a steno pad, a brunette in a sleeveless blue print dress with short hair. She had an athletic figure, with muscular arms and legs. In the glare of the sun from the lake, he couldn't see her face clearly. Then she moved to the right, and he saw it was Elizabeth. What the hell was she doing here?

He hadn't seen her since they broke up in their Washington house twenty-one months ago. She looked as youthful as when he first met her. Her face had a serious, intense look. He wondered why she came today. Had someone told her he'd be racing?

He hadn't thought about Elizabeth for months, but as he saw her now, all of the bitterness he felt at the time they separated welled up in Craig. To be sure, they had been through a great deal together, but he couldn't forgive her for putting her job ahead of their relationship. They had once been very passionate about each other, and even with the passage of time, he wasn't willing to forgive her.

"Any chance a hard working reporter can get an interview with the winner?" she asked while smiling anxiously. Although she had surely stared at many photos of "Enrico" she must have been stunned by his appearance and his sudden physical presence.

"I'm sure we can find a table in the café," he replied coldly.

"How about doing it at dinner this evening? 8:30 at the Grand Hotel?"

The words "No way" were almost out of his mouth when he pulled them back. Don't be a fool, he told himself, and behave like a grade school kid. Besides, he'd learned long ago never to sever a relationship. Life was long. It was impossible to know what would happen in the future.

"Fine," he told her, as he turned to leave.

*   *   *

Craig had stayed only once before at the Grand Hotel Des Iles Borromees. It was about nine months ago with Nina, a widow from Milan whom he had been seeing during the twenty-one months he and Elizabeth had been separated, except for the time he was away in Argentina. They didn't click enough for a long-term relationship, but the sex was good, and she was fun to be with from time to time.

The hotel was a magnificent stone structure with a rich history of one hundred fifty years. Immersed in a park facing Lake Maggiore, it had magnificent views of the Borromees Islands and the surrounding Alps. The seven-floor structure, with one hundred seventy-four rooms, still maintained its Belle Époque character. It had been built to last for centuries; it had survived two European world wars and was still going strong.

As he entered the marble floored lobby, Craig was greeted like a celebrity. The employees behind the reception and concierge desks, as well as guests, stood up and applauded. Shouts of "Congratulations, Signor Marino!" filled the air.

The manager led him up to the royal suite on the sixth floor with a huge living room and bedroom as well as a balcony overlooking the lake. Champagne on ice and a large vase of flowers were waiting for Craig.

Once the manager was gone, Craig, ignoring the champagne, showered, and collapsed into the bed.

Four hours later he woke up fully refreshed. While dressing, he thought about his last dinner with Elizabeth twenty-one months ago.

They had met at Tosca, their favorite Washington restaurant, following a miserable day for Craig. He had been fired by US President

Treadwell after only three weeks as CIA Director. The president had decided to sacrifice Craig at the altar of U.S.–Chinese relations.

For Craig, that had been a bitter pill to swallow. All he had ever wanted to do with his life was to serve his country, the United States he loved, although it wasn't perfect. Despite losing his wife because of poor medical care she received in the Middle East when he worked there for the CIA, he had soldiered on. Later, he had lost his daughter, Francesca, his only child. Now his country had rejected him.

Craig had come to Tosca expecting understanding and sympathy from Elizabeth. Now that he didn't have the obligations of a job, he was looking forward to planning the next phase of their life together. Though he had thought he'd never marry again after the death of his wife, Carolyn, he was beginning to change his mind.

Before he had a chance to say a word, she tossed a bucket of cold water in his face. Excitedly, she told him that the publisher of the *International Herald* had called to offer her the position of foreign news editor based in Paris. And she had been thrilled to accept it, without even discussing it first with Craig.

He was outraged. Sure, they weren't married, but they had a life together, or so he had thought.

Once she broke the news to Craig, he had understood how much his entire life was unraveling. Chinese President Zhou had a brother Zhou Yun—one of the most powerful men in China—with whom the president was very close. Craig had no doubt that Zhou Yun would come after Craig to gain revenge for what had happened to his brother.

When he was fired as CIA Director, Craig lost the protection of the US government. He would be an easy target for Zhou Yun.

That evening, Craig, realizing he and Elizabeth were finished, had developed a plan to elude Zhou Yun and to live the rest of his life. He underwent extensive plastic surgery to create a new persona for himself as Enrico Marino, a racecar driver—an adventure he had always wanted to pursue.

He had warned Elizabeth to be vigilant in Paris because Zhou Yun might have someone following her and even attack her in the hope she could lead him to Craig. She said she'd get a gun. He had no doubt she felt she could take care of herself.

They had parted, without any visible emotion, early the next morning. He was firmly convinced she didn't care what happened to him. All she cared about was her career.

Well, he had thought, to hell with her. He had plunged into auto racing with a vengeance and had been successful. He was daring, at times reckless. Luigi had once told him that he had a death wish. And maybe that was true. He didn't have much to live for.

Now, twenty-one months later, she had come in search of him. But why, he wondered, as he picked up a tan sport jacket and put it on over a light blue shirt. Then he walked out of the door toward the elevator.

The weather in Stresa was perfect that evening with temperature in the mid-seventies and low humidity. Dinner was being served in the hotel verandah, on the ground floor looking over Lake Maggiore. Stepping onto the verandah, Craig was impressed by the almost magical character of the setting. Off in the distance a few boats moved along the calm waters. The sun was setting behind the mountains, its rays still glistening on the water. The ten tables on the verandah were all taken by a dignified, mature crowd; men were wearing jackets accompanied by women in designer clothes, well-coiffed and bejeweled but not ostentatious. Elegant was the word that came to Craig's mind. Not trendy or nouveau.

Craig followed the maître d' to the table. Elizabeth was already there, dressed in a colorful print Dolce & Gabbana dress, sipping a glass of champagne. As he approached she stood up, looking nervous, he thought. But how could she not be anxious? It would take a long time to become accustomed to the fact of his altered appearance.

A waiter rushed over with a bottle of Tattinger and poured a glass for Craig.

Elizabeth raised hers and said, "To the winner."

"Whatever made you come to Stresa to see me in my new life?" he said softly.

"Your friend Betty."

"As in Betty Richards, the CIA Director."

"Yeah, that one. She called last week and told me she had a great idea for a feature for my paper: the rally race in Stresa. She said she'd seen a rally race in Sardinia last October. It was very exciting. An old friend of hers had been racing there. I recalled you once told me you had always wanted to race cars, so I figured Betty was telling me how to see you again."

"The sisterhood at work," he muttered.

"I think Betty understood how unhappy I was without you."

"Perhaps."

"I have to admit the plastic surgeon did such a good job that I wouldn't have recognized you."

"How can you be sure you're really with Craig Page?"

His voice had an edge. She ignored it.

"Your walk. Your voice. Those haven't changed." She paused for a moment, then continued. "I realize now that I made a mistake by putting my job ahead of our relationship. I've changed. I'd like to pick up where we left off. I realize how special you are to me."

When he didn't respond, Elizabeth added, "As the months passed, I missed you, and I wasn't getting the satisfaction from my work that I expected."

Craig nodded. He knew Elizabeth. It took a lot for her to say this. He wasn't ready to forgive her, but he couldn't dismiss her words. "Let's take it one step at a time. Starting with dinner this evening. How's that?"

"Fair enough."

The maître d' came over with menus and a wine list. Craig ordered black linguini with seafood and she asked for a cold crayfish salad. Craig followed with a request for a veal chop, and she ordered local freshwater cod caught in beautiful Lake Maggiore.

She handed Craig the wine list. "I would never dare to venture into your field of expertise."

He selected an '04 Turriga from Sardinia.

"Did you ever hear from Zhou Yun?" Craig asked anxiously. "Did he or his people ever make any effort to reach me through you?"

"I can't say for sure it was Zhou Yun, but for the first year after we split, I felt as if I were under constant surveillance by Chinese men and sometimes women. They would follow me much of the time that I walked or drove in Paris. They did this in other places, too, when I traveled for the paper. I thought my home phone was tapped."

"Did anyone ever attack you or talk to you?"

She shook her head. "It was all silent. I think their strategy was to unnerve me so that I would make contact with you, which I couldn't do even if I wanted to because I had no idea where you were or how to reach you."

Craig looked around nervously. No sign of any Chinese. "Weren't you concerned they would follow you to Stresa?"

She shook her head again. "The surveillance stopped exactly one year after it began. I've seen nothing since. I imagine that Zhou Yun thought it was hopeless and gave up. Still, I was careful on the way here. Walking in town, I followed the Craig Page three-left-turns technique. Nobody was tailing me."

"I'm sure Zhou Yun is still determined to kill me, to gain revenge for his brother's death."

"I agree with you. I don't know whether you're aware that Mei Ling appointed him Finance Minister."

When Craig had read about it in the *Financial Times* several months ago, he had felt betrayed. It was only because of Craig and Elizabeth that Mei Ling was the Chinese President.

"I couldn't believe it. After his brother had her husband and son killed, and tried to kill her, too"

"I asked her about it on one of her visits to Paris. She refused to discuss it. She simply said he was the best one for the job."

"He must have had something on her."

"Either that or he's leveraging the support his brother had with the powerful Chinese military."

The sommelier came over with the wine. Craig tasted it. The fruit was ripe; the color was bold, and the taste was smooth and rich.

"You'll be pleased," he told her.

She took a sip and smiled appreciatively. "You've never picked a wine I didn't like, but this is amazing."

"Turriga is a cult wine in Sardinia. Fabulous in every year."

"On the subject of wine, Zhou has gotten into the business in a big way. He's acquired DRC in Burgundy and Chateau Margaux. Both deals were made through dummy French companies in an attempt to conceal his ownership."

"You're kidding. Those are French national treasures."

"They may be, but Zhou Yun has the money and he likes good wine."

"Bullshit. He wants the prestige of owning them. He bought them because he can."

Their first courses arrived, and they paused to eat. He hadn't had much food in the last three days. He was starving.

After a minute she said, "Now that I know the name you've been using, this afternoon before we met for dinner, I went on line and checked on the results of races you've been in. You've done very well."

He had to concede she was trying hard to make up with him.

"Thanks. Did you look at the Sardinia race where your good friend Betty met me?"

"You went off the road in that one. A reporter said it was a miracle you and your navigator are still alive."

He paused to sip some wine. "Yeah. Well, Betty showed up when I was in the hospital and took advantage of my weakened condition to persuade me to help her on a job in Argentina."

"Were you involved in that matter concerning General Estrada with Argentina and Brazil?"

"You know about it?"

"Of course. It was a huge story we covered. An unidentified American agent played a role, but no one in the media was able to identify him."

"You won't out me, will you?"

She laughed. "Of course not. Besides it's old news. Where are you living?"

"Milan."

"Back to your Italian roots."

Their main courses came. Craig took a bite of the veal chop. It was superb. Then he asked Elizabeth, "What stories are you covering yourself these days?" He smiled. "Besides auto races?"

"Most of my time is spent supervising the other foreign reporters and reviewing their work. When I write myself, I've been particularly focused on Europe."

"Not on the United States, with your background there?"

"We have a reporter in Washington. I cover EU political and economic developments. The biggest story right now involves the Italian election in September and Roberto Parelli's plans for Italy."

"I can't really take Parelli seriously. Italy always has many small parties. They get a few votes. Maybe a couple of seats in the parliament, and they're finished."

"Parelli's different. He's a major force. He's striking a chord that appeals to voters."

"But his program is so extreme."

"Extremist politicians often have success in Italian elections. I've decided to see for myself. Parelli is giving a major speech tomorrow evening in Venice in San Marco Square. I'm traveling there in the morning. I intend to hear the speech. Maybe interview him afterwards. The latest polls show Parelli's moving close to the front spot. Would you like to come with me?"

He left her invitation hanging in the air.

After they finished their main courses, and before dessert, Craig excused himself to go to the men's room. When he reentered the verandah, he looked at their table. Elizabeth was talking on her phone.

Same old Elizabeth, he thought angrily. Her job always comes first. She hasn't changed at all. He'd like to take that phone and toss it into the lake.

He walked softly toward the table, convinced that she was so engrossed in her conversation she didn't even know he was approaching. He stood next to the table and stared at her. After about thirty seconds, she glanced up at him. "This is news you'll want to hear. It involves one of your sponsors who finances your racing career."

"Yeah, what?" He sat down.

"Federico Castiglione was shot and killed around midnight in a jewelry robbery at his summer house in Biarritz."

Her words rocked Craig. "What?" He leaned back in his chair. "That can't be!"

"It's confirmed. Federico's dead."

Craig put his head into his hands and lowered it to the white linen tabletop. For Craig, Federico's death was an enormous loss. It wasn't merely his financial support for racing. The two men had grown close during the last year and had spent lots of time together. Starting from scratch, in his new life in Milan and being on the road so much of the time racing, Craig had very few friends. He had been the most close to Federico—a wonderful man. And now he was dead.

"The story doesn't make sense," Craig said.

"What do you mean?"

"A jewelry robbery? Nobody—and certainly not Federico—would let themselves be killed in a jewelry robbery. They would let the thieves take the stuff. That can't be what happened."

"That's all I heard. The call came from one of my reporters in Paris. I told him to fly to Biarritz and get on the story."

"Will you let me know if he learns anything?"

"Absolutely. I'll call immediately."

"So, if I'm right that Federico would have turned over the jewels or insisted that his wife, Amelie, do it—and I know I am, that means somebody wanted to murder Federico, and they used the jewelry robbery as a cover. He must have had enemies, but I don't know of any."

"There's a great deal of turmoil in northern Italy with Parelli's campaign. I wonder if that had anything to do with it."

Craig paused to ponder her words. "I guess that's a possibility. Election campaigns like Parelli's take a lot of money and banks have it. Maybe Federico refused to lend to Parelli and—"

"Hey! Wait a minute." She sounded excited. "One of our financial reporters recently did an article about well-respected Italian banks doing money laundering for organized crime. He included the Vatican's bank, one in Naples, and Federico's bank in Milan. When I asked for his evidentiary support, he had it for the Vatican and Naples banks, but there were only rumors about Federico's bank. So I made him exclude Federico's bank from the article. Still, where there's smoke, sometimes there's fire."

"That's ridiculous," Craig said. "Outrageous. Federico wouldn't any more be mixed up with organized crime than I could fly to the moon."

"Hey, don't get pissed at me. I'm just trying to be helpful."

The waiter wheeled over the dessert card. "No dessert. I'll have the check." Craig told him.

Then he turned to Elizabeth, "I'm driving to Milan tonight."

"What'll you do there?"

"Federico was more than my sponsor. He was my friend. I want to talk to Amelie. I have to find out who murdered him."

"You could go in the morning."

"I don't want to wait."

The waiter brought the check. Craig signed it and said, "Put it on my room charge."

As he handed it back to the waiter, Elizabeth said, "I'll go with you to Milan."

"No. You should go to Venice as you planned. But call me if you hear anything about Federico."

"Whatever you want," she replied coldly and pressed her lips together.

Venice

Elizabeth was amazed as she walked into San Marco Square. A platform with a podium and huge screen behind it occupied one end of the square. In the center, chairs were arranged in rows, theater style. Elizabeth estimated there were about three thousand altogether. A multitude of signs with Roberto Parelli's picture, handsome and rugged, were tacked to posts and pillars around the square.

At eight o'clock, an hour before Parelli's speech, about half the chairs were occupied. Elizabeth made her way to the press table in front of the podium and put down her bag with a laptop inside.

At one end of the table, she saw Carlo Fanti, the political reporter for *Italy Today*. Milan based, it was one of the largest selling daily newspapers throughout Italy. His thin glasses, as usual, were halfway down on his nose and a few hairs stood up on his mostly bald head.

"Well, well," Carlo said. "The high-powered international press has arrived. Looks like our little Italian election has become a global event."

"Parelli's running an incredible campaign."

"He is, and he has an enormous number of enthusiastic supporters, but . . . please don't quote me on this."

"No, of course not."

"I think that Parelli may be peaking and spiraling downward soon."

"Why do you say that?"

"Money is running low and there are almost four months until the election."

"Are you disappointed?"

"Parelli is offering the country an alternative," Carlo said with admiration. "We have to do something to jump start our economy or we'll end up like Portugal and Greece. He's striking a sympathetic chord with voters. Young as well as old. He even has support in the south."

Elizabeth raised her eyebrows. "What do you attribute that to?"

"Both the church and Mafia would like him to win for their own reasons."

"More power for both of them?"

"Precisely. They're a formidable combination in the south."

"I've heard rumors that Parelli has links to the Mafia. Any comment on that?"

"You know the definition of rumors: something not based on knowledge."

That was a good dodge. Carlo, who was close to Parelli, wasn't talking on that topic.

"What about the allegations of Parelli's womanizing?"

"C'mon, Elizabeth. This is Italy. Men aren't perfect here." He paused for a second, then added, "They're not perfect anywhere. Look at your presidents Kennedy and Clinton. They were a mass of contradictions on personal and political issues. So don't judge Parelli too harshly."

Elizabeth couldn't argue with Carlo. She wanted to meet Parelli and form her own judgment. About six months ago, Elizabeth had done a favor for Carlo. When the Italian president was visiting Paris, she used a chit to get him an invitation to the state dinner at the Elysees Palace. Now it was time to collect on that favor. Carlo would remember. She wouldn't have to remind him.

"I want to interview Parelli after his speech this evening. Any suggestions?"

Carlo smiled, showing nicotine-stained teeth. "He's staying at the Palace Hotel. Suite 401. But you didn't hear it from me. Roberto tries to keep his locations secret. Luciano is the gatekeeper. He'll be in the suite at all times."

"What's his job?"

"He's Parelli's closest advisor and confidante. Luciano's father, Rinaldo, played that role for Mario, Parelli's father, throughout Mario's long political career. When Roberto decided to go into politics and run for office a year ago, not surprisingly he reached out to Luciano, who had been advising the People of Freedom party. Luciano dropped them like a hot potato and went to work for Roberto and his New Italy Party. He and Roberto are very close." Carlo held up two fingers and pressed them together.

People were pouring into the square. "How did you get to know him?" Elizabeth asked.

"Luciano?"

"No Roberto Parelli."

"A few years ago, I did a feature on his vineyard and his wines. It ranked him along with Gaja and Antinori at the top of the Italian wine producers in terms of quality. He's loved me ever since. We see each other from time to time."

"And he no doubt sends you wine from time to time."

Carlo smiled. "That's true. But the praise I gave him was well deserved. Have you had one of his wines?"

She shook her head.

"Try the Barolo or Barbaresco. Though his production facility is near the family vineyard in Piedmont, he also makes a super Tuscan. You should try one of them. Unless of course, you're too much of a French wine snob."

"Thank you, Carlo."

They both laughed.

Elizabeth turned to her work. As she booted up her computer, she thought about her dinner with Craig. He had behaved like a miserable prick. Sure, she had made a bad mistake twenty-one months ago, but she had told him how sorry she was and how much she missed him. In view of their past relationship and all they had been though together, he had no reason to be so cold to her. In spite of the bizarre circumstance of his completely altered appearance and his shock at seeing her again, things had seemed to go well. They could easily have finished dinner graciously and behaved as people who meant something to one another. He could have left for Milan in the morning. There was nothing Craig could do for Amelie in the middle of the night. Rushing off for that reason was bullshit.

It wasn't Elizabeth's fault that she had to answer her phone. She had even tried to help him by giving him information about Federico. Craig had been unfair. Apparently all of his racing success had gone to his head. He wasn't the same person she found so appealing in the past. He was no longer the man she wanted.

To hell with Craig. She thought wryly of the lyrics to an old song, "Got along without ya before I met you, gonna get along without ya now."

She took out her phone and called Jean Louis, the reporter she had assigned to Federico's robbery and killing.

"No information," he told her. "The police have no leads."

Good, she thought. We'll see if that self-important, big-shot celebrity Craig Page can find out anything.

Ten minutes before the start of Parelli's speech, all of the seats were taken. Crowds were standing in the back and on the sides of the square. They were both the old and the young, Elizabeth noticed. Men with children on their shoulders. Hundreds carried placards and chanted Parelli! Parelli! Parelli!"

It was a loud boisterous crowd. Dusk was approaching. Incandescent flood lights were turned on.

Parelli made his appearance to a loud, tumultuous, cheering crowd promptly at nine o'clock. The mayor of Venice introduced those on the platform, local politicians who had taken a place on the New Italy Party slate of candidates. Then he began a long laudatory introduction of Roberto Parelli.

Elizabeth studied Parelli, sitting on the platform, smiling and looking calm and relaxed, his hands folded neatly on his lap. His thick hair, still brown with only a sprinkling of gray at the temples despite his age of 71, spilled onto his forehead. He was wearing a gray suit that looked expensive. It was perfectly tailored to his body. To Elizabeth, who had covered lots of politicians over the years, the word charisma seemed apt.

Moments later, Parelli began speaking. Elizabeth was taking notes on her computer.

"Thank you all for coming." The title for my speech this evening is "History is Change."

"In 1861 Garibaldi and his followers created the present Italy. In a remarkable political feat, they fused together disparate people with little in common into a powerful nation state. In fact, prior to then, southern Italy had been a united kingdom by itself from the time the Normans seized the land from the Arabs in 1061.

"I have great admiration for Garibaldi. What he did was right for the time. But history is change. And political entities are constantly in flux.

"We recall with pride the Roman Empire. That was a glorious time with all of Europe joined under the banner of Rome. But it didn't last forever."

Elizabeth observed that the crowd was deathly still. People were hanging onto every word.

Elizabeth was, as well.

Suddenly she heard a commotion at one entrance to the square. About twenty protestors carrying signs that read: "NO PARELLI—YES ITALY" were trying to force their way into the square. They were shouting through bullhorns, "No Parelli! No Parelli!"

Parelli stopped speaking. Elizabeth saw him looking in the direction of the protestors. About two-dozen policemen swinging truncheons converged on the protestors. The scene exploded into violence. Policemen were pounding protestors in the head. Police vans roared into the area. The police were trying to overcome the protestors to get them into the van, but it was proving difficult. The protestors were throwing rocks.

Elizabeth thought about what she should do. Stay and hear the rest of Parelli's speech, or race over to cover the scuffle between the police and the protestors. Where was the better story?

Her reporter's instinct told her she'd gotten the drift of what Parelli had to say; if she could interview a couple of protestors and learn what was motivating them, they might enhance her story.

But the problem was that she found Parelli mesmerizing. She felt like Parelli was talking directly to her. And she imagined that others in the crowd felt that same way. She couldn't leave.

A few minutes later, protestors were taken away and silence reigned again in San Marco Square. Parelli resumed talking. "Here in Italy, democracy is a wonderful thing. But sometimes people misuse the democratic process. So my friends, let me return to my speech.

"In the year 410, barbarians from the north conquered and looted Rome. From that point until the unification in 1861, the land we know as Italy went through an enormous number of changes as one group and then another took control of different portions. These included Arabs, Lombards, French, and Austrians.

"However, through fourteen centuries there was one constant. Southern Italy was part of a separate political entity from the north. The border between the north and the south shifted from time to time, but it was not until 1861 when Italy was unified that north and south were joined.

"This is critical. Our history and our heritage in the north are different from that of people in the south.

"Now let's turn to our current situation in Italy. Geographically, our boundaries are essentially the same as they were in 1861. However, politically, our system is dysfunctional. Economically, we are a disaster.

"The world is changing. We have to change also.

"Globalization is killing us in Italy. Our small companies operated by skilled artisans, the makers of shoes, bags, clothing, pianos, and hundreds of other high quality items, can no longer compete because of prices on the world market. So they are going out of business.

"As a nation, we are hugely in debt. Last year it was over 130 percent of GDP, gross domestic product. And our current GDP is what it was in 1997. In other words, our economy refuses to grow.

"In northern Italy, we have so many talented and energetic people. We should be rivaling Germany as an economic powerhouse in Europe. Yet we are barely able to pay our bills.

"The reason is simple. Southern Italy is a drain on the north.

"I have thought long and hard about our economic and political situation and decided it is now time for another change in the map.

"It is time to divide Italy into one nation in the northern part of the present country. And another in the south."

The crowd was on its feet cheering wildly. This was Parelli's platform. What they came to hear. What they wanted.

Raising his voice over the crowd, Parelli shouted, "Our two economies have vast differences. Together we are not operating effectively. Divided into two, I believe we will each be able to capitalize on our respective strengths.

"We can achieve this result through the election in September. I promise that if you vote for my New Italy Party and we achieve a dominant position in parliament and in the government, I will divide Italy into two nations of the North and the South."

He stopped talking. The crowd was on its feet again giving him a standing ovation and chanting his name.

Elizabeth tuned out the noise and thought about what Parelli had said. She had been following separatist movements in Spain, one by the Basques and the other in Catalonia. There had been others in Europe as well—in Scotland and, historically, Norway and Sweden had split. Yugoslavia and Czechoslovakia had divided into three and two parts respectively. She wondered if Parelli had gotten his idea from them.

Regardless of the source of his views, although she wasn't Italian, and indeed she was still a US citizen, she found Parelli's proposal abhorrent. To be sure, the Italian economy was going through a rough patch, but so were the economies of lots of other countries. As for its dysfunctional political system, the same could be said about the United States.

With all of that, Italy was a great country. Dividing it was absurd. There was also a practical question of where to make the split.

Then she thought about the demographics of the country and the vote in the upcoming election. She would have expected all southerners to hate Parelli's program and vote against it. They would lose the support of the national government. Surprisingly, Carlo had told her that the mafia and the church were giving Parelli support. In addition, more northerners than southerners voted, and the vast majority supported Parelli. If he won, Parelli could achieve his aim.

As a journalist, she knew she should be unbiased. That was the theory of her profession. In reality, she was so opposed to Parelli's program that she'd love to find a way to stop him with her pen.

After his speech, Parelli was mobbed by supporters and the media. Elizabeth hung back and watched him bask in the glow of adoration.

*   *   *

It was almost midnight when she entered the Palace Hotel, rode up in the elevator to the fourth floor, and knocked on the door to 401.

She heard a man shout, "Come in," through the closed door.

She twisted the brass knob and pushed the wooden door in. She found herself in the large living room of a suite, furnished tastefully in heavy wooden furniture.

The scene was somewhat between disarray and chaos. Elizabeth counted ten people in the room: six men, jackets off, and four women, most with shoes off. Some were talking on the phone. Others were reading papers. Televisions were blasting with different stations. Food and bottles of wine, soda, and scotch were on the tables. Clothes, plates, glasses, and papers were strewn around.

On either side of the living room were closed doors. They must have led to bedrooms, Elizabeth guessed. It all reminded her of political campaigns in the United States that she had covered when she was working for the *New York Tribune*.

As she stood looking around, trying to decide which of the men was Luciano, no one paid any attention to her.

She noticed the door to one of the bedrooms opening. A tall Chinese man dressed in a dark suit with a white shirt and tie came out and closed the door behind him. Elizabeth had no idea who he was, but her reporter's instinct told her he might be important.

She whipped out her phone and pretended to make a call. It was a good cover while she took his picture.

Without glancing at her, he walked past and left the suite.

She waited until the door closed to approach the oldest looking man in the living room. He was seated at a table sipping water, she guessed, judging from the bottle of Pellegrino on the table and the clear liquid in his glass.

He had on a short sleeved, dark blue shirt, open at the neck and half unbuttoned to reveal curly gray hair. His eyes had a tired and sad look. His thick head of gray hair was ruffled, his face pale. He's not a well man, Elizabeth guessed.

"Are you Luciano?" she asked.

"What do you want?" he replied in a hoarse voice.

"I'm Elizabeth Crowder, Foreign News Editor of the *International Herald*. My friend Carlo Fanti from *Italy Today* suggested I talk to you. I want to interview Mr. Parelli."

She took a card from her bag and handed it to Luciano.

He studied it and stood up, looking angry and annoyed. He raised his hand, which Elizabeth noticed was shaking. "It's too late for journalists to come knocking on doors. Besides, you should call first. Perhaps in France you people have no sense about these things. Here we do."

"I'm sorry. I didn't mean to offend you. I'm doing an article on Mr. Parelli's speech tonight, which I attended. We have influential international readers. The exposure will be good for him."

"It's too late for an interview. I told you that."

"How about tomorrow morning?"

"Impossible. He's committed."

"Then when?"

Luciano was scowling. He was angry about something, Elizabeth thought. It can't be me. Maybe it had to do with the Chinese man. Luciano hadn't stood up or made an effort to see him to the door. It didn't make sense for Parelli's top advisor to behave this way with a foreign visitor.

Luciano took a card from his pocket and handed it to her. "It has my cell and office number at campaign headquarters. Call me sometime. I'll try to arrange an interview."

At that moment, the front door to the suite opened, and a man in his twenties entered. He was accompanied by a young woman about the same age with long black hair, a low cut magenta dress that revealed a generous bosom, and a black lace shawl over bare shoulders. Her face was heavily made up.

Luciano had a furious look on his face. He grabbed the man by the arm. "I told you no, Nene. Don't you understand anything?"

Elizabeth glanced at the woman who looked flustered.

"Mr. Parelli is the boss," Nene replied defiantly.

Nene pulled his arm away from Luciano. With the woman in tow, he pushed past the gray haired political advisor toward the closed door through which the Chinese man had come.

The young man knocked on the door. It opened. Elizabeth saw Parelli standing inside the bedroom in a shirt and slacks. He was looking at the woman.

"Thanks, Nene," Parelli said.

Nene gave the woman a shove into the bedroom. Parelli closed the door behind her, and Nene retreated to a corner of the living room where he poured a glass of wine and ignored the glowering Luciano.

Elizabeth left the suite, rode down in the elevator, and exited through the lobby. In the building next door along the Grand Canal, she saw a bar. She sat down at a table that gave her a view of the front of the Palace Hotel and ordered a bottle of Pellegrino.

After an hour, when the black haired woman hadn't left the hotel, Elizabeth was beginning to believe that she was wasting her time. It seemed the woman would be spending the night with Parelli.

Elizabeth was on the verge of paying the bill and leaving when she saw the woman come through the revolving door of the hotel. She placed twenty euros on the table, sprang up, and confronted the woman in front of the hotel.

"Excuse me, Signora," Elizabeth said. "I'm staying at the Grand Hotel next door. Perhaps you can spend a little time with me."

The woman flushed with delight. She could hardly believe her luck, Elizabeth imagined. Two wealthy clients in one evening. "Lead the way," she told Elizabeth.

When they were in Elizabeth's room, she asked the woman, "How much an hour?"

"One thousand euros."

Elizabeth reached into her bag, pulled out a thousand euros, and handed the bills to her. The woman began to unzip her dress.

"It's not for sex," Elizabeth said.

The woman looked frightened. She sat down. "What then, Signora?"

"I'm a French journalist." She pulled out her identification card, in French and English, from her wallet and showed it to the woman.

She probably didn't read French or English, Elizabeth thought, but still, she nodded. It must have seemed genuine to her.

"I want to talk to you," Elizabeth said.

"Talk about what?"

They were seated in armchairs facing each other. "What's your name?"

"Estelle," she replied easily. Elizabeth doubted that was her real name.

"How do you know Roberto Parelli?"

Estelle hesitated and bolted up straight. Elizabeth pulled out another pile of euros and held them up. "I promise I'll never use your name in any article."

Elizabeth handed her the money.

"I don't know Signor Parelli. The woman I work with called me early this evening. She said he was a very important client. That he will pay plenty. And that a young man, Nene, would come to my house and pick me up."

"When you left, Parelli's suite, were there any foreign men there?"

"Foreign men?"

"Chinese."

"Nothing like that. Only Nene and an old, gray haired man who was very angry."

"Did you like Parelli?"

She blushed. "He's a powerful man. Amazing in bed for someone his age."

Elizabeth decided she couldn't learn anything else from Estelle. She told the woman to go home. Then she sat down at her computer.

Before beginning to type her article, she decided to do some research on the Internet to test Parelli's claim that until 1848 southern Italy was part of a different political entity from the north.

She learned from the *Oxford Illustrated History of Italy* that the split began in 568 when the Lombards conquered the north and the Byzantines held onto much of the south, beginning the Italian divide. In the ninth century, the Arabs conquered all of Sicily and much of the south. Two and a half centuries later the Norman conquerors arrive and placed southern Italy under their banner.

In the south, the Normans gradually built up a strong state. However, over time the northern part of Italy became much more powerful than the south, which was relegated to being a provider of food and materials for the northern population and industries. This endured until Garibaldi mobilized his forces and the movement for unification in the nineteenth century.

So the basic premise of Parelli's platform was at least correct historically, Elizabeth decided. But that didn't mean it made sense to divide the country again.

As she continued her Internet research, Elizabeth discovered a startling fact. In early 2014 following the vote in Crimea to secede from Ukraine, residents in Veneto, the region of Italy with Venice as its capital, held online a referendum on secession from Italy. She couldn't find the result, but the mere fact they held the referendum lent some support to Parelli's platform.

And then she found something else striking. Recently in the northern area that included Milan, a political party received about 5 percent of the vote with a platform calling not precisely for secession, but for increased regionalization, which was a more subtle way of breaking down the unity of Italy. Supporters of the policy were upset that too much of the north's tax dollars were going to the south. So Parelli wasn't writing on a clean slate.

With her research completed, Elizabeth turned to writing the article.

She decided to write only about Parelli's speech and the crowd's reaction. She decided to leave out everything she had seen after leaving San Marco Square—the Chinese man, the prostitute, and Luciano's anger. Those would need more illumination before she could write about them.

Still, they influenced her in selecting the title for her article: ROBERTO PARELLI—SAVIOR OR SINNER.

After finishing the article, she thought some more about the Chinese man in Parelli's suite. She had no idea why he'd be secretly meeting with Parelli, but both she and Craig had been so involved with Chinese threats in the past, she had to let him know.

When he answered his phone, she said in a brusque business like tone, "Listen, Craig, after Parelli's speech in Venice, I tried to interview him in his hotel. I couldn't get past his advisors, but I saw something strange."

"What's that?"

"A Chinese man was coming out of Parelli's bedroom."

"Did you get his name?"

"That was impossible, but I took his photograph on my phone."

"Smart move. Send it to me."

"Right now."

She forwarded it. A few second later, Craig said, "Got the picture."

"Ever seen him before?"

"Negative, but it gives us something for the future."

"I'll let you know if I get anything else."

"I'd appreciate it. Any news about Federico?"

"Nothing yet."

She clicked off.

Milan

Federico's funeral was Tuesday in the Duomo di Milano, the magnificent, spired gothic cathedral in the heart of Milan. Approaching the Duomo on foot, Craig was awestruck as he always was by the splendor of its gothic architecture.

Construction had begun in the late 14th century and extended over a five-hundred-year period. The Duomo is one of the world's largest churches, second in size within Italy to St. Peters in Rome. But far more than size is the artistry and workmanship of the structure.

Constructed with brick and faced with Italian marble, its exterior with pinnacles, gables, belfries, and statues has no equal. Above the roof, a spire shoots into the air to the dizzying height of 108.5 meters. On its top is a polychrome statue of the Madonna.

This marble floored structure, built in the shape of a cross, is divided by soaring cathedrals into five wide naves divided by forty pillars. The interior contains a vast quantity of art and monuments in addition to beautiful stained glass windows. Craig couldn't even imagine the cost of the Duomo or the number of people who had worked on it over the centuries.

Walking into the cathedral, Craig reflected that over the last several decades very few people were permitted to have funerals in the Duomo. They had to be either a pivotal part of Milan's religious hierarchy, very wealthy, or exceedingly philanthropic. Federico satisfied the last two criteria.

The Duomo was mobbed with people. About 3000, Craig estimated. As he took a seat near the front, Craig recognized many of the top echelon of Milan's social elite. And since Milan was the heart and pulse of Italy, he saw so many leaders from Rome and elsewhere in the country. He also spotted some top international figures from England, France, and even the United States.

Waiting for the service to begin, Craig thought about how he'd been fortunate to meet Federico. Craig's racing coach, Paolo, had, without telling Craig, invited Federico to the track one day where Craig was training. Craig had achieved a personal-best speed that day, and when he had climbed out of the light blue Jag, Paolo had said, "We're going for coffee. I want you to meet someone who loves car racing."

When they sat down, the first words out of Federico's mouth were, "You're a helluva driver. . . . How old are you?"

Paolo had brushed aside the question, telling Federico, "In this sport, you don't win based on your age. It's how you drive. And I'm telling you that you'd be smart to make an investment in Enrico Marino. He's a natural behind the wheel."

For Federico and others who followed the sport, Paolo had almost a god-like status. Paolo's words were enough for Federico to take out his checkbook. He followed that by obtaining checks from two of his close friends in Milan who were also anxious to sponsor a driver whom Paolo was pushing.

That was more than a year ago. Since then, Craig and Federico had spent evenings together and gone to sporting events. Craig was a frequent guest for dinner at Federico's house before Bonita died of an aneurism, and again during the last few months with Federico and Amelie. Craig liked her and felt sorry for her coming into a hostile environment as Federico's second wife—and a French woman at that.

Craig had attended Bonita's funeral and Federico's wedding to Amelie. He couldn't believe he was now at Federico's funeral.

The newspapers had carried the story that Elizabeth told Craig in Stresa. Federico had been shot and killed in a jewelry robbery in his summerhouse in Biarritz.

Craig realized he should have been listening more closely to the several speakers who were eloquently praising the many philanthropic causes to which Federico had committed his time and money. "Beloved" was a word Craig heard frequently.

To Craig, that word had a hollow ring. Federico may have been beloved by many, but not by everyone. Somebody wanted him dead. For all he knew, that person was here today.

Craig's eyes roamed around the immense cathedral. He had no way of determining who was Federico's friend and who was his enemy.

But he was determined to find out who had killed Federico. He thought about his schedule. He and Luigi were planning to race in Munich next week. He'd call Luigi and cancel.

Nothing was more important than this. He had to start with Amelie. He had tried calling her twice on Monday, in the morning and in the afternoon. Both times a servant had said she wasn't taking any calls. He would try to talk to her today after the funeral.

At last, Craig saw people rising and the casket being wheeled out. Craig followed the procession outside on a gloomy day with light rain falling. Black cars were lined up on the square in front of the Duomo under the watchful eye of King Victor Emmanuel II, the onetime king of Sardinia, and then of Italy in 1861, on his horse on a statue in the center of the square. Scores of pigeons fluttered around apparently indifferent to the sanctity of the proceedings. Crowds of tourists near the arch that marked the entrance to Galleria Vittorio Emanuelle II stopped to gawk.

Craig followed the procession. After Federico had been laid to rest, he waited a few minutes, letting most of the crowd drift away before he approached Amelie, her eyes red, her face tear stained.

"I'm so sorry," he said. "Federico was a wonderful man."

"He was very fond of you. Proud of what you did."

"I'd like to come by the house to talk to you."

"Today will be a mess. Come tomorrow at two."

Craig turned and walked toward his car. As he prepared to open the door, he felt a tapping on his back. He whirled around to see Lorenzo Sapienza, Federico's lawyer standing there.

"Can you come to my office tomorrow morning at ten?"

"Of course," Craig said wondering what this was about.

Lorenzo pulled a card from his pocket. "It has my address."

The lawyer walked away without saying another word.

*   *   *

Lorenzo's law firm, which he had founded twenty years ago and ran, had twelve lawyers; it was located on via Brera in the heart of Milan's financial district. Craig felt a sense of history as he walked through the tile courtyard of what had once been the residence of a famous Milan family seeped in the arts and was now the offices of a law firm.

Craig took the elevator to the fourth floor, announced himself to the receptionist and sat down in a plush leather chair. He took out his BlackBerry and began reading Elizabeth's article about Parelli—"Savior or Sinner."

Engrossed in reading, he didn't notice Lorenzo approaching. When he heard a man coughing to clear his throat, he looked up.

Patrician and dignified were words that came into Craig's mind to describe Lorenzo. The Milan lawyer was 6´2. Around age seventy, Craig guessed; still he had a full head of thick gray hair. He was suntanned and had a dimple on his right cheek. His clothes exuded wealth and success—the carefully pressed double breasted, gray pinstriped suit, the red Hermes tie with sailboats against the background of a powder blue silk shirt, and gold cufflinks with sapphires in the center.

Craig had met Lorenzo only once before at Boeucc Antico restaurant in Milan. Craig was having dinner with Federico and Amelie when Lorenzo, who had been with three other men across the room, came over to say hello to Federico and his wife. After introducing them, Federico said to Craig, "If you ever need a lawyer in Milan, and I hope you never do, then Lorenzo's the man to see. He's the best lawyer in all of Milan."

Lorenzo led the way back to his office with a twenty-foot ceiling adorned with gold decorations from the original mansion.

"Would you like a coffee, water, or something else to drink?"

"No thanks," Craig answered. He was anxious to hear what Lorenzo wanted.

"Federico liked you and had great admiration for your driving," the lawyer said.

"I liked him as well, and I feel a great deal of gratitude to Federico. He not only sponsored me, but arranged for two of his friends to become sponsors as well."

"It meant a lot to Federico. He was reliving his dream through you. As a boy, all he wanted to do was racecars. He had a knack for it, too. But his father leaned on him to go into banking. You know how that it is."

Craig nodded. I still can't believe he's dead."

Amelie called me from Biarritz an hour after it happened. I'm still shaken from that call."

"It doesn't make sense."

"What doesn't make sense?"

"Federico would never have resisted a jewelry robbery. He would have turned over everything, filed an insurance claim, and still be alive."

"So what do you think happened?"

"Somebody wanted to kill him," Craig said, as he slumped in his chair.

Lorenzo pressed his lips together and shook his head. "I probably shouldn't tell you this, but Federico believed he was going to die."

Craig lifted his head up with a start. "What do you mean?"

"It's the reason I wanted to meet with you. Last Thursday, he came to my office. He was very upset. He refused to tell me why. He said he wanted me to prepare a codicil to his will providing that you would receive five million euros if he died. He wanted you to be able to keep racing."

Craig was flabbergasted. "What?"

"You heard me right. Five million euros. As I said before, he liked you. I told him I'd prepare it next week and send it over to him."

"And?"

He insisted I do it right then. So I did. And it's valid even though he died two days later."

Craig now understood why Lorenzo said Federico believed he was going to die. He thought about what Elizabeth had told him in Stresa.

"A reporter friend of mine said there were rumors Federico's bank was mixed up with organized crime in a money laundering scheme. Those people play rough."

"I heard those rumors as well, and I asked Federico about them a couple of times. He said there was nothing to it."

"Did you believe him?"

"Absolutely. Listen, Federico could be a frustrating client. He told me some things he was doing but not others, but he never lied to me."

"Was there anything unusual going on in connection with his bank?"

Lorenzo shook his head. "Nothing he told me about, but as I said he didn't tell me everything. Anyhow, it will be a couple of months until you receive the money. I wanted you to know about it."

"I don't want to take money from Amelie."

Lorenzo laughed. "You don't have to worry. Federico was a very wealthy man. Amelie is well taken care of."

"Have you spoken to the police? Do they have any leads?"

"I've been on the phone with every police or justice ministry official I know, and there are plenty of them. So far, they're all coming up empty—although they are at a disadvantage. This happened in France, and you can say what you want about the EU, but each country protects its own turf. We're no better."

"Well, please let me know if you learn anything."

*   *   *

Federico and Amelie lived in a huge villa in the Brianza area north of Milan. During the 1970s and 1980s it was the preferred place for Milan's super wealthy to live. But since then, with increased crime and security a decisive matter, many of the wealthy moved in closer to the center of the city to live in gated communities with armed guards.

Craig remembered Federico had scoffed at what he had called his friends' security obsession. And now Federico had been murdered.

At ten minutes to two that afternoon, Craig parked along the road at the bottom of the driveway running through thick trees up to Federico's huge, grey stone house. He expected it to be crowded with visitors. He didn't want to block the driveway.

When Amelie opened the door and he entered the house, he was surprised to see it was empty except for her and the servants. She asked him what he wanted to drink and he said, "coffee." She directed one of the servants to bring them both a cup. The coffee was left in the study, and she closed the sliding door.

"Thank you for coming," she said. "Yesterday and today. It means a great deal to me."

"Federico was a wonderful man, and I had enormous respect for him. He did great deal for my racing career."

"He would have been proud of you for winning in Stresa."

Craig was surprised she knew about the race when she was so preoccupied with her husband's death.

As if sensing his reaction, she added, "Well, you were on the front page of *Italy Today* on Monday. Opposite the article about Federico."

She paused to sip some coffee, then continued. "It's been rough for me. People can be so cruel. That's why nobody is here with me today."

He was aware she had never been accepted by Milan society where Federico's first wife, Bonita, had been a fixture for many years. Still, she seemed genuinely hurt by what had happened.

"You were in an impossible situation. You couldn't win them over."

"I'm glad to hear you say that. I loved Federico. I knew you'd understand. You're not from Milan. Are you?"

"No," Craig answered and left it at that, hoping she didn't press him about where he was from. Monessen, Pennsylvania would be hard to explain and he didn't want to lie to her.

"Federico's social group is a tight crowd. The worst part is they blame me for his death."

Craig pulled back. "I don't understand that."

"The gossips with sharp knives are claiming I urged Federico to fight for my jewelry, which is absurd."

"Of course. I know Federico. He'd never do that. It's the most ridiculous thing I've ever heard."

"Several times, Federico told me if robbers ever try to take jewelry or any other property, don't resist. 'Let them have it. That's why we have insurance. Possessions are replaceable. Human life isn't.' And I believed Federico. I would never tell him to fight for my jewelry. That's not what happened in Biarritz."

"What did happen?"

She finished her coffee and said, "Saturday evening Federico and I had dinner with Alberto and Dora Goldoni from Turin. Alberto was a banker friend of Federico's. We had dinner at the Hotel du Palais where they were staying. After dinner Federico and I returned to our house. It was ten minutes before midnight. I remember looking at my watch."

Craig leaned forward on the edge of his chair, listening to every word.

"As soon as we walked into the house and closed the door, two men came out of another room. One tall and one short. Both were wearing ski masks. The tall one gave an order to the short one in Russian."

"How do you know it was Russian."

"In my modeling days, I spent time with Russian girls. The tall Russian said to the short one, 'You take the woman.'"

Craig found himself easily falling into his prior career as an antiterrorist agent, interrogating a witness.

"What happened next?"

"The short one put a damp cloth over my nose and mouth. The smell and taste were disgusting. Later, the police told me it was chloroform. Before I became unconscious, I heard Federico say to the tall one, 'Leave us alone. We'll give you anything.' The tall one gave a sadistic laugh, raised his gun and shot Federico. That's the last thing I remember. Later, the police told me that all the jewelry from the vault in the bedroom had been stolen. Strangely, they didn't take what I was wearing."

She stopped talking and cried. Then she wiped her eyes with a napkin and continued. "Federico was prepared to give it to them. They didn't have to shoot him."

She began crying again. "Miserable fucking Russians."

Everything she had said confirmed Craig's instinct that this wasn't a jewelry theft that ended up in murder. The Russians could have taken the jewelry in the vault without Federico being able to identify them. There was no reason to kill him; and jewelry thieves typically want to avoid a murder charge that raises the stakes and expands the punishment if they are caught. Also, they didn't even take the jewelry Amelie was wearing. These two Russians came to the house to execute Federico.

"What have you heard from the police?" he asked.

She waved her hand into the air. "They're all useless. I've spoken with three different detectives. One in Biarritz, one in Bordeaux, and one in Paris. I'm convinced they have no interest in investigating Federico's murder. Perhaps they think it's simple jewelry theft. Perhaps it's because he's Italian. I've spoken to the police here in Milan. They refuse to get involved. They say it's because the murder happened in France, but I think it's because I'm French."

She stopped talking, looked at him beseechingly, then continued. "Maybe you can help me."

"What do you mean?" he asked gingerly.

"You're a celebrity in Italy. Because of your car racing, particularly after your win at Stresa on Sunday, the Italian authorities will listen to you. They'll lean on the French police to do something. They'll also investigate here. Perhaps those Russians were working for someone here in Italy who didn't like Federico. Maybe that's why they killed him, which they didn't have to do."

Craig liked what Amelie had said. After his meeting with Lorenzo, Craig was planning to get involved. Now she had given him the perfect cover. He was a friend of Federico and Amelie, and she had asked him to help.

"I'll do what I can," he said.

"Oh thank you so much."

He lifted his hand. "I don't want to raise your hopes. I've read that cases like this often take a long time to solve, but I'll do what I can to light a fire under the police."

"That's all I'm asking."

Amelie thanked Craig for coming and led him to the front door.

Walking down the driveway toward his car parked on the road, Craig was deep in thought trying to decide on his next move. He could try to enlist the help of Giuseppe who had succeeded him as Director of the EU Counterterrorism Agency, but from what he now knew, he didn't have enough information about international elements to persuade Giuseppe to become involved. He'd have to do some more digging on his own first.

Suddenly, through the corner of his eye, Craig saw a heavyset man jump out of the bushes and rush toward him. Before Craig had a chance to react, the man looped a powerful arm around Craig's neck, cutting off his air. He pulled Craig behind the bushes and to the ground. As he did, Craig raised his right foot and smashed it into the man's groin. He fell to the ground, moaning in pain.

Craig sprang up and pounced on the man, who was thrashing and scratching Craig's face while Craig punched him hard in the jaw and shouted, "Who sent you?" The man's nose was bloody, but he didn't respond. Craig was prepared to punch him again when another man ran up holding a pistol. "Don't move," he cried out.

Craig held still as the man shoved the gun barrel against the back of his neck so hard it scratched and broke the skin. Craig held his breath, not knowing if the man was planning to shoot.

They remained like that for thirty seconds. All three still. Craig wondered if the man was trying to decide to shoot. Finally, he pulled away his gun and told Craig in Italian with a Russian accent, "Get up."

"You hold him while I beat him," the man with the bloody nose said.

"Shut up. You had your chance," his colleague with the gun said. He tossed a piece of rope to the bloody nose and said, "Tie his hands behind his back."

When he was done, the man with the gun turned to Craig, "You better not help Amelie by trying to find out who killed Federico or we'll cut off both your hands. You won't be able to drive cars then Enrico Marino. And don't worry. We'll find you. We know where you live."

He recited Craig's address in Milan. "Do you understand?"

Without any warning, the man raised the pistol and smashed it against the side of Craig's head, knocking him to the ground. He lay there semiconscious, his vision blurry.

In his daze he was aware of the men running way, getting into a car, and driving off. But Craig was too weak to follow and his vision too clouded to see their plates.

In a few minutes he regained full consciousness. He put his back against a tree and rubbed the rope along the bark until he loosened the knot enough to free up his hands.

He had a giant headache, but he still thought about what the man with the gun had said. The man knew Craig was planning to help Amelie find out who killed Federico. So he must have overheard Craig's conversation with Amelie. To do that, it was likely he'd planted bugs in her house.

Craig had to warn Amelie about the surveillance. It wouldn't be easy because he realized he looked like hell with his disheveled clothes and deep scratches on his face. He felt the blood trickling from behind his ear.

He had to talk to Amelie without letting her cry out in alarm when she saw him. Once the men heard her scream on their audio receiver, they would no doubt return to kill him and perhaps Amelie as well. And he needed to get her out of danger and to a safe place.

Craig knew what he had to do.

He staggered up the driveway. Amelie opened the door. She looked horrified by his appearance. Before she had a chance to cry out or say a word, Craig put a finger up to his lips. She nodded.

He took her by the arm and led her outside the house and around to the yard in the back. Then he told her what happened and that he suspected a bug had been planted in her house.

She looked terrified. "I'll call the police."

"I have a better idea."

"What's that?"

"Where's your family live in France?"

"A small town in South West France."

"Can you go there and stay with them for a little while until this is all over?"

She nodded.

"Good. Go as soon as you can. Without telling anyone where you're going. I'll call and tell you when you can return."

"Good. I'll do it now."

She turned toward the house. He grabbed her by her arm.

"Let me ask you a few questions first."

"Sure."

"Did Federico have any enemies?"

She shook her head. "I don't know of any."

Craig needed to ask her about the possibility of Federico's bank being involved with organized crime. Russian gangs could be involved as well.

"Some Italian banks have been involved with organized crime. Do you think he—?"

"Absolutely not. I know Federico. He would never have." Then she paused in mid-sentence. "I have to be honest. He never discussed his bank business with me. Still, I find it hard to believe."

"Was his bank having any problems?"

She shrugged. "I just don't know. He never discussed his business with me. Do you really think this is about organized crime?" She looked terrified.

"I don't know."

"Will you help me find out who killed Federico by trying to persuade the Italian authorities to intervene?"

"I'll see what I can do on my own. Then I'll try to get them involved."

Craig left the house. This time he made it to his car without an incident.

As he turned the key in the ignition he decided it would be too dangerous to stay at home in Milan tonight. His Russian assailants knew where he lived. By now, they might have bugged his house. Or they might have changed their mind and decided it would be better to kill him. No, going home wasn't an option. It would be best to get out of Milan.

Besides, he wanted to get started immediately on finding out who killed Federico. He headed toward the A4 highway in the direction of Turin.

After driving an hour, he was satisfied he wasn't being followed.

He had to decide where to begin the search for Federico's killer. He recalled how angrily he had dismissed Elizabeth's story of the rumors linking Federico's bank to money laundering and organized crime. He didn't want to believe—no, in fact he couldn't believe that his friend Federico would have been involved in something illegal. Or that he could have been so wrong in judging Federico, but what if . . .

Though he found it extremely unlikely, this is where he had to begin.

Craig continued driving to Turin. There he took the first flight to London.

London

"Let me tell you a little about the Reform Club," Jonathan Abramson said to Craig.

They were walking along Pall Mall and approaching the Admiralty Arch.

Craig wasn't particularly interested in learning about the Reform Club, but he wanted to be polite to Jonathan whose help he needed.

When Craig had been Director of EU Counterterrorism, a drug cartel from Mexico was using British and Spanish banks to launder their money, Craig had enlisted the help of Jonathan who had founded a bank consulting firm based in London. He had been impressed with how well connected Jonathan was throughout the European banking business. Jonathan seemed to know everyone and everything in European banking.

For Jonathan, this was quite an accomplishment. From their time together, Craig had learned that Jonathan, now 63, grew up in a poor Jewish section of East London. He waited tables evenings at a posh Mayfair restaurant to work his way through the University of London where he graduated with honors and a law degree. After two years of grinding away at a boring law job—"what other kinds are there,"—Jonathan had told Craig, he tried to make the jump into banking. But the doors were slammed shut, and he had no doubt that it was because of British anti-Semitism. So he flew across the pond and went to work at Goldman Sachs in New York.

Ten years later, Goldman selected Jonathan to head up its European operation. He had a choice of living in London or Paris, and he selected London. "I wanted to sneer at those bastards who wouldn't let me play in their sandbox." Within fifteen years Jonathan was able to retire from Goldman with a huge bank account and open his consulting firm.

Craig particularly liked the fact that Jonathan was incredibly discrete.

As a result of the latter, Craig was willing to trust Jonathan with the secret of his Enrico Marino identity. Not surprisingly, Jonathan had done a double take when Craig entered his office along St. James half an hour ago.

"Okay, what's the Reform Club?" Craig asked.

"It looks like lots of other old, crusty, wood-paneled London eating clubs started by the powerful and wealthy in this town who didn't want to share a restaurant with people like you and me."

Craig laughed.

"But this one's special," Jonathan continued. "It was founded in 1836 by reformers who made up the leadership of the Liberal Party in England. It became their political clubhouse, and it was a palatial building when it was first opened. Now it's a purely social club, not associated with any political party. One thing that made this place famous was the James Bond movie, *Die Another Day*. They filmed the sword dueling scene inside."

Craig knew exactly what Jonathan was talking about. "They dueled up and down that gorgeous wooden staircase."

"Exactly. You'll see it as soon as we enter the front door."

That was five minutes later. The porter at the front door greeted Jonathan warmly. He stared hard at Craig. Jonathan, an intimidating presence at six-feet-six inches tall, with a neatly trimmed short salt and pepper beard, stared right back. Then with a twinkle in his eye he said, "Richard, this is my friend Enrico Marino."

"Aha. That's what I thought. I didn't want to say. I follow auto racing and belong to a club here. Congratulations on your victory in Stresa, Mr. Marino. I made a few quid betting on you."

As they sat in an isolated corner of the dining room, Jonathan said, "It's nice being with a celebrity."

"Oh shut up and tell me what to order."

"It's old style British cooking at its finest. Bland is best. Sole and boiled potatoes. Thank God for the French, Italian, and Greek chefs who moved to London."

The waiter came over. They both ordered consommé, followed by sole and potatoes. Jonathan selected a 2005 St. Emilion which he called a claret in deference to the British designation for Bordeaux.

Once the waiter was gone, Jonathan said, "Alright, what's on your mind, laddie?"

Craig laughed. "Don't be putting on British airs for me. You're only two generations removed from Lithuania."

Jonathan laughed as well. "True, but look how far I've come. Not bad for the son of a tailor."

Craig's expression turned serious. "I want to talk about Federico Castiglione who was murdered in Biarritz."

"I heard that. The papers said it was a jewelry robbery."

"As usual they had it wrong."

"What happened?"

"I don't know, but I'm determined to find out."

"Why do you care?"

"Federico was my good friend. I would never have had a career in racing without his support. I'll do anything for someone who has been good to me."

"I don't doubt that. However, is it possible that you're also itching to get back into the law enforcement game? That you've been like a fish out of water, and now you see a chance to plunge back in."

Craig thought about it for a minute. "That's possible. Still, I have strong personal motives."

"How can I help you?"

The consommé and wine arrived. They stopped talking until the waiter left.

"There are rumors that Federico and his bank were involved in money laundering. He was murdered by Russians, which adds some credibility to that scenario. I recall that you were involved with a project having to do with money laundering by Italian banks. So I thought—"

"What you're recalling is an investigation of the Vatican bank."

"Yeah. I guess that's right."

"I had only a minor role. An American outfit did the heavy lifting. It's hard to believe that a priest from God's bank could be involved in

corruption and money laundering. He and two colleagues were charged
with moving money for businesses based in Naples, a haven for organized crime, into Switzerland."

"How did it end?"

"The priest and his colleagues were arrested by the Italian police.
Then the Pope undertook a full-scale investigation, and the Vatican
instituted changes. Not a happy situation."

"People are people. I was wondering if you've ever heard anything
about the involvement of Federico or his Milan bank in money laundering—or anything else illegit?"

Jonathan paused to sip his consommé, then said, "I have heard a
rumor that Federico was involved with one of those Naples banks tied
to organized crime in a money laundering scheme. But it was just hear-
say. I wouldn't put much weight on it."

"Who would know?"

"That's a tough one."

"C'mon, Jonathan. I need help."

The waiter approached. Jonathan waved him away. "There's
a Russian, Igor Mallovich, who runs a money laundering operation using Naples banks and others in Italy. He has a big business. Russians, both expats and those still living in Russia, forward
money they've stolen from the state or made from criminal activities
in Russia to a bank in Naples, BNA. Igor controls BNA. He then
moves the illegal money from BNA via correspondent banks in Italy
who get a hefty fee to safety in a Swiss bank where he has his own
money stashed."

"Sounds like a sweet way to make money."

"Oh it is."

"Where could I find charming Igor if I wanted to ask him about
Federico?"

"Unless you're crazy, you don't want to meet with Igor. The man's a
horror. Talking to him would be bad for your health."

"I am crazy. So tell me."

Jonathan shrugged in resignation. "This time of year, he's in
Ravello, about an hour and a half south of Naples, hiding out from
the Russian government which would like to get their hands on him.

He has a palazzo there. From Swiss banks he deals with, I could get an address and phone number for you."

"That would be great."

"We'll go back to my office after lunch. I'll work on it."

*   *   *

Jonathan finished punching buttons on his computer, wrote an address and phone number on a piece of paper, and handed it to Craig. "You didn't get this from me."

Craig memorized it and tore up the paper.

"Thanks, but that one was easy. Now for the hard one."

"I'm not going to like what I hear."

"I need leverage over Igor."

Jonathan looked worried. "Why am I helping you? I must be crazy myself."

"Not really. You hate the idea of crooks like Igor corrupting the banking system in Europe."

"I guess that's it. All this proves that I shouldn't drink at lunch. It wipes out my normal inhibitions."

Craig was hopeful Jonathan would help.

"What exactly are you looking for?" Jonathan asked.

"How did Igor get his original nest egg?"

"He cleaned out a Russian bank. As a result, he and his wife and children can never set foot in that country. Russian President Kuznov would love to get his hands on Igor, but Kuznov hasn't been able to find him, and I doubt if the Italians would extradite. Also, Kuznov hasn't been able to locate Igor's accounts in Switzerland. If Kuznov could get the account info, the Swiss banks might turn the funds in the accounts over to the Russians. Since the United States lowered the boom on a couple of Swiss banks, and imposed a nine billion dollar fine on BNP Paribas, the French bank, they're all nervous as hell about aiding criminals. They're afraid the United States will blacklist them. It's a whole new world for banks since 2008."

But you could learn the number of Igor's Swiss accounts. Couldn't you?"

Jonathan nodded weakly. "I have friends in Zurich. Even with that, it would cost me some chits and take a couple of hours."

Craig checked his flight. "I'm on the last nonstop to Naples. It leaves in two hours. Why don't you send it to me electronically."

Jonathan shook his head emphatically. "Too dangerous. If Igor gets hold of your BlackBerry, he'll know where you got the info. I'll be a dead man as well as you. There will be other planes tomorrow. Go take a walk and come back in two hours."

Craig left the office. He walked only as far as the mall where he sat down on a park bench and went to work on the web. It was amazing how much information was easily available about individuals on the Internet—even scoundrels like Igor.

The Russian who had been a banker in Moscow relocated to Italy and Switzerland six years ago, Craig learned. What really got Craig's attention was that Igor had a great interest in professional sports, having bought a Manchester soccer team two years ago and a minority interest in a Brooklyn NBA basketball team. An idea was taking shape in Craig's mind.

When he returned to Jonathan's office the consultant was waiting for him. "I have what you need."

"Wonderful. Talk to me."

"Igor has his money stashed in three accounts in a Zurich bank and two in Geneva. I had my secretary type the five account numbers."

He handed a piece of paper to Craig and said, "You want to commit these to memory also and tear it up?"

"Nope. I want to keep this one. I'll be able to use it. I assume you kept a copy."

"Of course."

"In forty-eight hours, if I'm still alive, I'll call you."

"And if I don't hear?"

Craig removed a pen and pad from Jonathan's desk. He wrote a note to Russian President Kuznov explaining about the secret bank accounts where Igor had hidden the money he stole from the Russian bank. Then he handed it to Jonathan. "Put this note in an envelope with the numbers of Igor's accounts. Seal it. Write on the front: 'A gift to President Kuznov from Craig Page,' and deliver it to the Russian Embassy in London.

"How do you know Kuznov?"

"Let's just say that we saved each other's asses twenty-one months ago."

As soon as he left Jonathan's office, Craig dialed the Ravello number Jonathan had given him and asked for Igor.

"Who's calling?" a man replied in a gruff voice.

"Enrico Marino."

There was a pause. Then Craig heard a bubbly voice on the line. "Congratulations Enrico. I watched replays of your last day in the Stresa race. You did a great job of driving."

"But now I have a problem I'd like to talk to you about."

Without hesitating, Igor replied, "With Federico's death, you need a new sponsor."

The man may be a horror, but he was damn smart, Craig thought. "Exactly. I was hoping to meet with you and discuss that possibility."

"And how did you get my phone number?" Igor asked, sounding wary.

"You're a major figure in the professional sports world. We're a small community."

"Then you know where I live as well."

Craig had better be careful. "I dialed a 39 country code. That's Italy. A large country. I have no idea precisely where."

"I'm in Ravello," Igor, said seeming to be satisfied. He gave Craig an address, the same one he'd gotten from Jonathan. "I'm halfway up the mountain to Villa Cimbrone. It's a pink building. You'll have to get here on foot from the town. There are no cars permitted on the roads going up the mountain. When would you like to come?"

"How about tomorrow afternoon?"

There was a pause. Finally, Igor said, "Come at two o'clock."

Southern Italy

Craig took the morning nonstop out of Heathrow to Naples. It touched down at five minutes past eleven. Once he left the highway in his rental car, he was driving on narrow mountain roads, sometimes not even wide enough for another car to pass. He recalled what

John Steinbeck had written about this road. "It was "high, high above the blue sea, that hooked and corkscrewed on the edge of nothing."

Except for his speed, which was moderate, he felt as if he were in a rally race with the S-turns and switchbacks in the road. When he reached the coast, the Tyrrhenian Sea was off to the left, a straight plunge from the road high above.

It was a bright sunny day. Craig was constantly checking the rear-view mirror, making certain he wasn't being followed.

Of the four largest cities on the Amalfi coast—Ravello, Amalfi, Positano, and Sorrento, Craig liked Ravello the best. It had a tranquility which the others besieged by tourists didn't have. And high in the hills the air was dry and cool—the sky blue. It was no wonder that Ravello had been settled by wealthy aristocrats seeking a refuge from the hurly-burly life of Amalfi during the ninth, tenth, and eleventh centuries when the Republic of Amalfi was powerful. More recently, it had been the retreat of great writers, including D. H. Lawrence, Gore Vidal, and William Styron.

Craig parked along the road on the way into Ravello. Then to minimize the chances of being recognized, he donned sunglasses and a blue cap that said "Italia" in red letters on the front that he had purchased at Naples airport. Satisfied he looked like a tourist, he set off on foot.

In town, he walked for a while to make certain no one was following him. He found a trattoria, Sofia, on a narrow side street and ate pizza for lunch washed down by the lemon juice for which the region was famous.

After lunch, he began climbing the steps and steep road that led up the mountain to Villa Cimbrone. He passed herb, vegetable, and fruit gardens. The view of the sea off in the distance was breathtaking.

Halfway up, Craig saw a pink building—ten yards to the right. For confirmation that this was Igor's house, Craig noticed in front a powerfully built blond man in a white shirt, blue slacks, and blue blazer, whose appearance cried out "bodyguard."

Craig looked up on the roof. He saw another blond brute. The house was a perfect sanctuary for a villain like Igor.

Approaching the entrance, Craig noticed the bulge in front of the man's jacket. Undoubtedly a gun.

"I'm here to see Igor," Craig said.

"Name?"

"Enrico Marino." Craig flashed his Enrico Marino Italian passport.

"Step inside." The guard said.

Craig entered a magnificent white and black marble floored entrance hall.

The guard followed him inside and said, "Raise your hands."

Craig did what he was told and the guard patted him down roughly.

Relieved that he hadn't brought a weapon, Craig replied, "Do you treat all of Igor's guests this way?"

The guard ignored Craig's words. He took out his phone and said something in Russian. He heard a response, then told Craig, "Follow me."

The guard led the way along a marble corridor to a study with French doors leading to a patio with an amazing view of the sea.

Igor was standing when Craig entered. He motioned for the guard to leave, which pleased Craig enormously. His plan depended on being alone with Igor.

The fifty-five-year-old Russian was obese—about five ten and two hundred and eighty pounds, Craig guessed. His face was red from the sun or alcohol. His hair was thin and coal black. Craig guessed he dyed it. On his face, he had a perpetual scowl.

Igor shook Craig's hand and pointed to two leather chairs off to one side that were separated by a table with a pitcher and two glasses.

"I prefer to talk inside. It's cooler with the air conditioning."

Once Craig sat down, Igor poured two glasses from the pitcher.

"Limoncello," he announced. "The drink of the region."

Craig took a small sip. It was cold and refreshing. Also dangerous. The alcohol content was high. He cautioned himself against drinking too much.

Igor raised his class and said, "Here's hoping you have many more races like Stresa."

"I'll drink to that."

"So you're looking for a new sponsor?" the Russians said.

He certainly doesn't waste time on small talk, Craig thought. And Craig was pleased. He didn't want to have to face questioning about how long he had been racing and what he had done before that. "That's right. I've lost Federico. He had gotten two of his friends to contribute small amounts. I imagine I'll lose them as well. So I need help."

"How much are you looking for?"

"Federico and his friends were putting up two million euros a year combined."

The Russian stared at Craig. "I'll give you three, but—"

Craig laughed. "There's always a but."

"I'll want my name on your car and on the shirt you wear."

"I can live with that."

"So we have a deal?"

Craig reached out is hand.

Igor shook it. Then stood up. "I'll get the vodka. We always celebrate with that."

He brought back the bottle, a Russian brand Craig didn't recognize, and two glasses. Relaxed, he settled back into his chair across the table from Craig and poured two glasses.

"To our success," Igor said.

The Russian downed his and refilled it. Craig took a sip. As he prepared to shift the conversation, he thought about Jonathan's warning. Igor was dangerous and couldn't be underestimated. Craig didn't dare drop his guard.

"I'm happy to have your support," Craig said. "But Federico was my friend. I want to know who killed him."

"Sorry. I can't help you. Talk to the police."

"They said the killers were Russians. I thought you might know something."

Igor laughed. "You figure all Russians are one big family."

Craig narrowed his eyes and looked right at Igor. "No, but there were rumors that Federico was mixed up in money laundering, and you control that business in Italy—at least for Russians."

Igor looked alarmed. "Where did you hear that?"

"From Federico," Craig said. Dead men can't expose a lie.

"Well he was wrong."

Igor hesitated for a minute then said, "I don't like what you're saying. I'm not sure I want to sponsor you." He reached for the phone.

He's planning to call security. I can't let him do that.

Before Igor could get his hand on the phone, Craig flew out of his chair and across the table sending the pitcher, bottle, and glasses flying.

He landed on top of Igor's chest, reached his hands up, and clasped them around Igor's thick neck. The Russian was gasping for breath.

"Did you order the hit on Federico?" Craig cried out.

"No. No!"

"Who did? Tell me or I'll strangle you."

The Russian's face was turning even redder. Craig eased up a little. He didn't want to lose Igor.

"I had nothing to do with his murder."

"Was Federico mixed up in money laundering?"

"No—no," Igor stammered. "No. I tried to involve him. He refused to do it."

"Then tell me who killed him."

"I heard powerful people in Moscow arranged it. I don't know for sure."

"Tell me which people."

Igor spit in Craig's face. "Go fuck yourself."

Craig tightened his grip again. "Tell me who killed Federico."

"Take your hands off me and I'll give you some useful information."

Craig did as Igor asked. The Russian was gasping for breath. Finally he said, "Federico was clean. He didn't do anything wrong. He was a victim."

Craig believed Igor. Craig was also convinced Igor would rather die than give up the names of any of the people in Moscow who had arranged the hit on Federico. So Craig climbed off Igor. He grabbed the phone from the floor and disabled it. Then he reached into his pocket, pulled out the list of Igor's Swiss bank accounts he'd gotten from Jonathan, and tossed it to Igor.

"I don't want your thugs to bother me when I leave your house and drive away from Ravello. So I had someone put together a list of all your Swiss bank accounts with the money you stole from Russia. If I don't show up alive in Zurich tomorrow, that list will be delivered to President Kuznov along with your address here in Ravello. Russia will convince the Swiss to turn over your accounts. But you won't have much time to enjoy your new poverty. I'm sure Kuznov will send a team of assassins to kill you." Craig paused and walked toward the door. Then he added, "Sorry it didn't work out for us to be partners in racing."

Craig ran out of the room, along the corridor and through the front door of the villa, passing the guard running toward Igor's study.

Craig wasn't convinced Igor would let him escape even after Craig had threatened to forward the bank accounts to Kuznov. It was fifty-fifty at best, he thought.

Craig had to assume Igor would maximize his chances of staying alive, by sending his two goons after Craig.

Once he left Igor's house, Craig didn't take the steps down the hill. That's what they would be expecting and people would see him. Instead, he ran into the woods, which shortened the distance to the road below and his car.

As he ran, Craig tried to put himself in the minds of Igor and his guards. Though cars weren't permitted up the mountain, Craig knew that small electric carts were used to ferry up and down luggage and supplies to Villa Cimbrone, a hotel at the top. Chances were Igor's men would take one of those carts down the hill and beat Craig to the road.

Then what?

There was only a single road out of town. It would be an easy matter for the guards to find a place to park just off that road and wait for Craig. In the daylight, they could see the driver of every car that passed and ambush Craig.

With that in mind, Craig couldn't relax, even when he reached his rental car, a navy BMW. He checked for bombs and drove away from the town toward Naples. The sea was on the right, far below the cliff from which the road had been carved.

As Craig drove, he kept looking for a waiting car. About a mile out of town, he passed a gray Mercedes up ahead parked on a side road on the left. There were no cars immediately ahead or behind Craig. He increased his speed.

The Mercedes pulled on to the road and began following Craig. It had to be the Russians. They were moving up, shortening the distance between the cars.

As they neared a blind curve, the Russians pulled up on the left, alongside Craig. The guard on the passenger side lowered his window and leaned out with a gun. Craig recognized him as the man on the roof of Igor's house. He had not seen the driver before.

Craig realized their plan was to shoot him, forcing him to lose control of his car and plunge down the hill to the sea below.

He saw only one way to stop them. He slammed on the brakes and immediately threw the BMW in reverse, hoping no one was coming up behind him.

His car bucked and then moved backward.

The Russians couldn't react. Craig decided to turn around and drive in the other direction. Then he'd outrace the Mercedes. With his experience in rally races, he thought he might be able to do it.

Before he had a chance to turn around, a large truck coming from the other direction toward Ravello came around the blind corner and smashed head on into the Mercedes. The force of the impact knocked the Mercedes off the road.

Craig watched it fly through the air. It landed with a thud on rocks below and was rapidly engulfed in flames.

Goodbye Igor's guards.

The truck came to a stop, leaving a narrow opening on the road on its left side. Just enough for Craig to slip through and get the hell out of there before the police came looking for witnesses.

Fifteen minutes later, he relaxed. When he passed the truck, he had seen the driver in the cab sitting with his head in his hands. No one could tie Craig to the crash.

As he continued driving, he thought about Igor. He had offered the Russian a perfectly good deal, but Igor had failed to keep his end of the bargain. Now Craig would destroy Igor. He took out his phone and called Jonathan in London. "I enjoyed our lunch yesterday at the Reform Club."

"Did you have your meeting?"

"It's over and I survived, but I want you to deliver that letter we spoke about."

"I'll do it this afternoon."

Good old Jonathan. No need to spell things out. "Thanks."

Once Jonathan hung up, Craig thought about his next move. He believed Igor about Federico's innocence and had been relieved to hear it. He also believed that Federico had been a victim.

That still left open the question of who had wanted to kill Federico and why.

As Craig thought about his conversation with Amelie, he decided he had only one option at this point: talk to Alberto Goldoni. The Turin banker was a close friend of Federico's. They had been together the last hours of Federico's life. He was hopeful Alfredo could help him.

He waited until he was on a wider road to pull over. When he called Alberto Goldoni's office a woman with a cheery voice answered.

Craig told her he'd like to speak with Signor Goldoni.

"Who should I tell him is calling?"

"Enrico Marino. I—"

"Oh. You're the race car driver?"

"I am, but please tell Mr. Goldoni I want to talk to him about Federico Castiglione."

"Hold on for a moment. I'll see if Mr. Goldoni is available."

After a delay of almost two minutes, Craig heard, "This is Alberto Goldoni. Why are you calling me?" Alberto sounded worried.

"I just came from a meeting with Amelie, Federico's wife. He and I were friends. She asked me to help her find out who killed Federico."

"But I don't understand. You're a racecar driver. Are you a policeman, too?"

"I'm not, but I know people in law enforcement. I plan to enlist their help, but before that I want to talk to you. The more facts I give them the more likely they are to become involved. Amelie told me you and your wife Dora had dinner with them Saturday evening."

There was another long pause. Alberto's a cautious man, Craig thought. He's deciding whether he should talk to me.

After a delay, which seemed interminable to Craig, Alberto said, "Can you meet me in my office in Turin tomorrow morning at 10:00?"

"I'll be there."

As Craig resumed driving, he felt exhilarated. Racing had been a wonderful and exciting interlude. But now he was returning to his former life in the world of espionage. And that was what he loved best.

Circumstances had forced him to abandon it for twenty-one months—except for the Argentine mission—both the crummy politics of Washington and his need to hide from Zhou. Charging back into his former life carried risks. Zhou might learn who he was despite his change of appearance. He was willing to risk it.

Turin

Craig spent the night in Turin at the Grand Hotel Sitea in the heart of the city. Normally, he liked to walk around this unfairly maligned industrial city that was home to the Fiat Automobile Company. It had numerous parks and tree lined squares. He loved dining at Del Cambio with its old luxury of crystal chandeliers and large gold encrusted mirrors.

This evening, after being attacked in Milan and not wanting to be recognized, he left his car with the hotel valet, stayed in the hotel, and had room service for dinner.

The next morning, wearing sunglasses in the bright sunlight, he walked to the headquarters of Alberto Goldoni's bank. Turin Credit was located in a four-story gray stone building along the lively Piazza San Carlo. Along the way, Craig stopped and looked into retail stores, pretending to window shop. He was using his favorite technique to make certain he wasn't being followed.

Satisfied no one was tailing him, he crossed the wide boulevard to the Turin Credit headquarters. Craig saw there were two armed guards in front of the building, one on each side of the front entrance.

This wasn't unusual, Craig told himself. There was a retail branch of Turin Credit on the ground floor. It made sense to have armed guards in front.

What did surprise Craig was that inside the building, across the marbled floored lobby from the retail bank, in front of the elevators leading to the offices upstairs, were two more armed guards. And he found another two on the top fourth floor where Alberto's office was located.

When Craig entered Alberto's suite, the secretary with the cheery voice, who was a bit overweight with dark black hair and a pleasant smile, asked Craig if he would autograph a book on auto racing. "It's for my twelve-year-old son. He's crazy about the sport."

Craig signed the book for her, and she thanked him profusely. Then she led him into Alfredo's office. It wasn't particularly large and was furnished simply with handsome, decades-old wooden pieces. Nicely framed family pictures were scattered on a couple of tables. There was no "love me" wall with photos of Alberto with statesman and powerful industrialists. It was not the type of office Craig had expected for the owner and CEO of Italy's largest bank.

Alberto stood up from his desk and came forward to shake Craig's hand. Creases and lines were prominent on his face and forehead. Worry? Or just aging? Craig wondered. He had Googled Alberto that morning. The banker was 53; he looked like 63.

"You have an attractive family," Craig said pointing to the pictures.

"Thank you. Dora and I are proud of our two children. The picture on the right was taken about six months ago. Our son, Ricardo, is a student at London School of Economics. Our daughter, Ilana, is studying law at Bologna as I did."

She was a strikingly beautiful young woman, Craig thought. With her long brown hair and smile, she reminded him of his own daughter, Francesca.

Alberto led the way to two leather chairs in a corner, and they sat down, facing each other. Craig decided not to take notes for fear of spooking Alberto. With his superb memory, he'd recall what Alberto said.

"Federico was my friend," Alberto began. "Anything you can do to help find his killers would mean a great deal to me as well as Amelie."

"I appreciate that."

"What can I tell you?"

"I learned from Amelie that you and your wife, Dora, went to Biarritz to spend the weekend with Federico and Amelie. Was there some occasion?"

Alberto coughed and cleared his throat. "It was very strange. Federico called me last Thursday. He sounded frightened, almost terrified about something, but he wouldn't tell me what it was. He asked

Dora and me to come to Biarritz. He said we'd have dinner Saturday evening at the Hotel Du Palais. Then Sunday morning the two of us would go off alone on the beach and talk. At dinner, when our wives went to the ladies room, I tried again to get him to tell me what this was about, but he refused."

"How did he seem at dinner?"

"Morose. He tuned in and out. Drank a lot. He was clearly worried. He made disparaging comments about Russians. When he and Amelie were getting in the car to leave and I said goodbye, he whispered into my ear, 'Be careful, my friend.' From that, I understood he believed I was at risk from whatever threat he faced."

This would explain Alberto's anxiety, Craig thought, and the guards in the bank.

"How did you learn about his death?"

"He and Amelie left the hotel about 11:30. Dora went to bed. I was in the bar having a drink, but concerned about Federico and what he had said. I didn't want to wait for the morning to talk. So I decided to walk up to his house, hoping he would talk to me. I saw the police cars and ambulance. I tried to go into the house, but they stopped me. My French isn't too good. The most I could understand was that Federico had been killed in a jewelry robbery and Amelie was all right. I knew she had a brother in town for the weekend, and since I didn't know her that well, I decided that Dora and I should leave Biarritz immediately. As I was walking back to the hotel . . ." Alberto hesitated to go on.

"What happened?"

"Someone was following me in a dark blue Mercedes. The person aimed a gun with a silencer at me and tried to hit me. I changed direction and got out of the line of fire. Then I ran down some stairs to elude whoever was in the car."

"Did you get a look at him?"

"I couldn't see the gunman. He was driving and blinded me with a bright flashlight. I tried to see the license plate, but couldn't. I raced back to the hotel. Dora and I packed up and we came home."

"You drove?"

"No, we went by private plane. It's one of my few luxuries," he added apologetically.

"You're frightened. Aren't you?"

"Of course. After what Federico said. And of course after someone following me and trying to shoot me."

"Do you believe Federico was killed in a jewelry robbery?"

"Of course not. It's the stupidest thing I've ever heard. I know Federico. He would never fight with robbers. He'd let them take what they wanted and call his insurance company. The same as any sensible person."

"Amelie said the men were Russians," Craig interjected.

Alberto raised his eyebrows. "I didn't know that. As I said, Federico was ranting about Russians at dinner."

"Do you have any idea why Russians or anyone else would want to kill Federico?"

"None at all," Alberto declared.

"Was his bank involved in any way with organized crime?"

"Never. That's inconceivable. I think the law enforcement people you talk to should look at overdue loans. Perhaps he had some from Russians and that's why they killed him, or perhaps they had been hired by someone who did have overdue loans."

"Is there anything else going on in the Italian banking business that might have impacted Federico's bank?"

Alberto thought about the question for a moment. "Last year, two different Chinese banks bought an interest in two smaller banks in northern Italy. One in Verona and one in Bologna. I didn't find those surprising. As you know, we've had a great deal of turmoil in the Italian banking industry because of this recession which won't go way, and because of EU establishing stricter bank regulations that make it harder for all of us to do business. But I haven't heard that any foreigners were trying to take over a portion of Federico's bank."

"Is there anything else you think would be useful?"

Alberto closed his eyes for a moment and held a hand against his forehead.

"Nothing I can think of—only to emphasize that I want Federico's killers caught and brought to justice. I'll do anything I can to help. It means a great deal to me."

Alberto's last sentence seemed odd. Craig picked up on it. "You mean because he was your good friend?"

"That's part of it. But there's more."

"What do you mean?"

"Our families are bound together and each owes an enormous debt to the other."

"Could you explain that?"

"My family's Jewish. When we were expelled from Spain in 1492 by Queen Isabella, my ancestors traveled east across France and settled in a small town in Piedmont, in the area of northern Italy that welcomed Jews. This was in contrast to most other parts of Italy that severely restricted the movement and activities of Jews. Then in 1848 King Carlo Alberto and his son Vittorio Emanuele not only declared the First Italian War of Independence, . . . but also emancipated the Jews. My family took advantage of this new freedom and moved south to Turin. My great grandfather, Alberto, for whom I was named, was a hero in World War I fighting in the Italian cavalry. He could have sat out the war, but he was a patriot, so he enlisted. He received many awards from the king. After the war he founded a small bank named Turin Credit, which was the beginning of this bank.

"When Mussolini came to power, my great-grandfather walked a careful line, neither supporting nor opposing Mussolini and the fascists. He was a good man trying to protect his family and to survive in a difficult political climate. To digress for a moment, do you know the origin of the word 'fascist'?"

Craig shook his head. Alberto continued, "It's actually from a seal of ancient Rome. The Roman Empire seal had bunches of wheat joined together with a sword. Mussolini's objective was to return Italy to the glory of the Roman Empire so he took that seal and its depiction. The word for a bundle of hay was fascico and it came to mean a group or association. Political organizations in Italy were known as fasci, and Mussolini founded the National Fascist Party (partito nazionale fascista) in 1919.

"At any rate, Mussolini refused to comply with Hitler's demand to round up and to deport Jews to the concentration camps. That came later after Mussolini was deposed the first time and the Germans occupied much of Italy. However, Mussolini, a man of contradictions who always tried to play both sides, promulgated Nazi anti-Semitic regulations in 1938 that, among other things, prohibited Jews from owning large businesses like banks."

"What did your great-grandfather do?"

"He turned his bank over to Federico's great grandfather, Fabrizio, who wasn't Jewish and who worked in the bank. My great-grandfather decided to take his family to the United States until the trouble was over. He and Fabrizio had an oral understanding that when he returned to Italy, Fabrizio would return the ownership of the bank to him."

"Where did he go in the United States?"

"New York. Others in the family went as well. There he worked for the Bank of New York. As a smart man who knew banking, he rose high in the organization. After the war, they wanted him to stay, but he loved Italy and soon returned. He found that while a few of his family had been deported and executed by the Germans, most had been hidden by Italians. They helped some to escape into Switzerland."

"Did Fabrizio turn the bank back over to him?"

"Exactly as promised."

"That didn't always happen with businesses that had been turned over."

"I'm aware of that. My great grandfather was so grateful to Fabrizio that he gave him—not lent, but gave him—the money to start his own bank in Milan. This is the bank Federico ran. So you see the families owe a great debt to each other. That's why I would do anything to help find Federico's killers and bring them to justice."

"I'll do what I can. Believe me."

"I have no doubt."

Alberto was staring at Craig. "Computers and the Internet are wonderful things. Tracing Enrico Marino wasn't difficult. His life began two years ago. After our conversation today, I'm convinced you're much more than a race car driver."

Craig shifted uncomfortably in his chair.

"Don't worry," Alberto continued, "I have no intention of sharing my suspicions with anyone else. Nor am I interested in your secrets. I'm simply happy we're on the same side."

"You're a very wise man. Thank you for your discretion."

After Craig left Alberto, he went to a small, dimly lit espresso bar and sat down in a corner. As he thought about Alberto's parting words, he realized by wading into the investigation of Federico's death, Craig risked blowing his carefully constructed Enrico Marino cover. With that came the possibility that Zhou Yun with his worldwide operations and relationships would learn where Craig was and would try to kill him to avenge his brother's death. Craig had to take his chances. He was tired of running and hiding.

Besides, Zhou Yun, even more than his brother, was responsible for the death of Craig's daughter, Francesca. Zhou Yun was the one in Calgary at the time and must have given the order. Craig had his own score to settle with Zhou Yun.

However, that was all off in an uncertain future. For now, Craig had to decide on his next move.

As he sipped coffee, his phone rang. He saw it was Elizabeth calling. "Listen, Craig," she said without bothering with formalities. "I have some news for you."

"What's that?"

"I just learned that a Singapore bank—Pacific Sun—has acquired a 19 percent interest in Federico's bank. The transaction was announced a few minutes ago."

"That is really something. They didn't wait too long after Federico's death to get the deal done. It can't be a coincidence. His death and this agreement must be related."

"Exactly what I was thinking. Have you made any progress?"

"Not yet, but this will help. I also heard that two Chinese banks made investments in banks in northern Italy last year."

"That's right. One in Bologna and one in Verona. What about the money laundering by Federico's bank?"

"Neither his wife nor his lawyer knew anything about that. I've reached out to some other sources. I'm convinced Federico was a victim, not a criminal."

"If that's your conclusion, it's good enough for me. I'll let you know if I learn anything else."

Craig quickly ended the call because he was anxious to pursue what he hoped would be valuable assistance.

He put her news of the investment by the Singapore Bank together with the other pieces. Russian killers. Possible involvement of organized crime. Two Italian banks having been acquired by Chinese banks. He had been attacked by Russians.

Craig was convinced he now had enough to involve Guiseppe Mercurio, the head of EU's counterterrorism agency based in Rome. He reflected for a moment on his prior relationship with Giuseppe, who had been Craig's deputy when he held the EU counterterrorism position. He had lobbied hard for Giuseppe to succeed him when he became CIA Director for his brief stint in that job. He hoped Giuseppe would become involved in solving Federico's murder. The man was savvy as well as effective; and Craig liked working with him.

Craig decided to call him. They had spoken so often in Craig's prior life that Giuseppe's number was permanently etched on his brain.

But he hesitated for a minute. At this point only Betty Richards, the CIA Director, Elizabeth, and Jonathan knew that Craig Page had become Enrico Marino. Alberto suspected Enrico was someone else, but he had no idea that someone was Craig Page. How should he deal with Giuseppe? Try to keep his cover or not?

It only took him a few seconds to decide. Giuseppe knew how to keep secrets and he certainly had no love for Zhou Yun.

Besides, Craig wasn't good at disguising his voice.

He decided to level with Giuseppe.

"It's a colleague from your past. We worked together disarming suicide bombers in Trastevere a couple of years ago."

There was a pause. Then, "Oh really." Giuseppe sounded surprised. "That's not all we did together. It's good to hear from an old friend."

"I'll be in Rome today. How about a quiet dinner?"

"Come to my house at eight."

Craig liked that. No one could overhear them talking.

Beijing

Sitting in his corner office on the 51st and top floor of the Zhou Yun Enterprises headquarters in Beijing, Zhou Yun should have been a happy man. He was the wealthiest person in China. And according to *Forbes*, number three in the entire world. His industrial empire that began in energy and real estate now had tentacles reaching around the globe. As the Finance Minister of China, he had great political power as well.

Still, Zhou Yun was unhappy and miserable. And he knew the dual causes for that.

The first was the death of his brother, one time head of the Chinese armed forces and President of China before Mei Ling. The incredibly close bond between the brothers was demonstrated by the men displayed in the only two photographs on the walls of Zhou Yun's office.

One was a picture of a sad-looking Zhou Yun when he was only fourteen and his brother was twelve. The boys were surviving in Beijing on their own because during the Cultural Revolution Mao had banished their parents to the countryside for re-indoctrination. Their mother starved to death. When their father returned after four years, he was depressed and beaten down, a shell of the man who had gone.

The other picture was Zhou Yun again with his brother. This time Zhou Yun was smiling with pride as his brother assumed the presidency of China.

Zhou Yun had a third picture in his office. That one, he kept in his center desk drawer where only he could see it. And he did at least once each day. It was a picture of Craig Page, then CIA Director, the man whom Zhou Yun held responsible for his brother's death, as if Craig had pulled the trigger himself.

It constantly gnawed at Zhou Yun's insides that he hadn't been able to find Craig Page and to gain his revenge. For a man with Zhou Yun's money and resources, the world was small. He should have been able to locate Page. He hadn't given up. He would never give up until his last dying breath.

The other matter that vexed Zhou was the lack of respect China was receiving in the world despite its incredible economic success and military expansion. It should be ranked right up with, if not ahead of, the United States as a superpower. But people and the media, particularly in the West, still viewed the stature of China to be below the United States. Even worse, some had been discussing Russia, that economic and military pygmy, as a rival to the United States.

Zhou's thoughts were interrupted by the intercom. "Qing Li is here," his secretary said.

"Good. Send him in."

Qing was dressed in a dark suit, white shirt, and tie like Zhou. That was a shift from his former position as a military officer. Zhou plucked him out of the People's Liberation Army on his brother's recommendation to be his special assistant. Qing, as a young soldier, had been one of those who fired on unarmed protestors in Tiananmen Square in 1989. That patriotism and willingness to follow orders had appealed to Zhou.

Qing sat in a chair facing Zhou behind his huge antique desk devoid of papers. He ran a finger over this thin mustache while waiting for Zhou to begin.

"When did you get back to Beijing?"

"An hour ago. I remained in Milan until I confirmed that the acquisition of stock in Federico Castiglione's bank by Pacific Sun of Singapore had gone through. Then I left. I came here from the airport."

"I heard about the bank acquisition from one of my financial advisers. That's good. What's not good is that Federico is dead."

"As I explained on the phone, we had no choice." Qing said it in a matter of fact tone devoid of emotion. "Lin Yu, the Singapore banker did everything he could to persuade Federico to sell. The man was stubborn and the other board members stuck with him until his death. Then they saw the wisdom of selling."

Zhou was frowning. Lin Yu had failed him. "I understand everything you've said, and the acquisition is important to me. I'm not sorry I gave you the order to eliminate Federico. Still, I'm concerned this murder could be traced to us."

"Impossible. There are no loose ends. Your friends in Moscow supplied the manpower I needed. I doubt if it would even get back to them, but that's where it would stop."

"Are the French police investigating aggressively?"

"Not at all. The Russians have friends in the Biarritz Police Department. There was only one thing . . ." Qing hesitated.

"What's that?"

"Federico's widow tried to enlist the help of an Italian race car driver, Enrico Marino."

"What does he have to do with this?"

"He was a friend of Federico's, but the Russians persuaded him not to help and the widow has left town. No risk to us there."

Zhou wasn't satisfied, but there was nothing he could do about it now. So he turned to the other part of Qing's mission. "What about Roberto Parelli?"

I spoke with him in his hotel suite in Venice after a big speech he gave in San Marco Square. Parelli agreed to meet with you. He won't travel to China, but he'll meet with you at his farm and vineyard in northern Italy."

Zhou tapped his fingers on the desk. He preferred that all meetings with foreigners take place in China. Being on his home turf wasn't merely a matter of prestige. It meant that foreigners arrived exhausted from a long flight. After lots of food and alcohol they became much more malleable.

"Why won't Parelli come to Beijing?"

"He said it would attract too much publicity. Also, his campaign is at a critical point, and he doesn't want to take time away from it."

"Isn't he concerned that I'll be recognized? That there will be articles in the press reporting on my visit? Those would destroy the purpose of our meeting."

"He said that if you fly into Malpensa in an unmarked plane, he'll have someone take you from the plane that will land on a remote runway and drive you in a car with tinted windows. Complete secrecy. No one would know you were there."

Zhou nodded. He liked those logistics. Parelli was shrewd.

"There could be one problem," Qing said.

"What's that?"

"Parelli's closest advisor, a man named Luciano, was strongly opposed to the meeting. Parelli overrode him, but Luciano could be trouble in the future."

"I'll find a way to get around Luciano's opposition."

"Before your meeting with Parelli, I could go back to Italy and eliminate Luciano as an obstacle. Make it look like an accident in a car. Something like that."

Zhou shook his head firmly. One thing he didn't like about Qing was that he was too eager to kill people. Dead bodies piled up and sometimes came back to haunt and create problems. That's what happened with the death of Craig Page's daughter, Francesca.

"I'll be able to get what I want without that," Zhou said firmly.

"I understand. Would you like me to go with you to Italy for your meeting with Parelli?"

"No, it's not necessary. I prefer to do this alone."

Once Qing left, Zhou asked his secretary to arrange the plane for his trip to Italy. Then she said, "Mr. McKnight is here for your meeting."

"Good. Show him in and serve tea."

Zhou watched McKnight sipping tea nervously. The sixty-five year old pasty- faced Harry McKnight was an Englishman who had spent his entire life in Hong Kong. He was tall, with a bald head except for some gray around the sides, and blotchy, red skin on his face and neck. He wore narrow glasses that rested halfway down on his nose.

Zhou didn't like the English. He viewed them as cynical and hypocritical, pretending to follow rules of fairness while they had raped and plundered China. Their efforts to get the entire Chinese nation hooked on opium because it was commercially advantageous to them was even more reprehensible than their participation in the African slave trade. Now finally they had been relegated to their just position on the world stage—as bystanders with delusions that they would one day return to their former glory. Their future was grim. They would have all they could do to ward off internal resurrection by a hostile Muslim populace constantly increasing in size.

Zhou watched McKnight squirm in his chair, while waiting anxiously to hear why Zhou had summoned him. Though McKnight was the President of Victoria Bank in Hong Kong, he served at the will of Zhou because Zhou had engineered a secret takeover of the Victoria Bank by the Commercial Bank of China, which Zhou owned. To the outside world, Victoria Bank was independent. In reality it was a subsidiary of Zhou's bank. Chinese law permitted this deception.

Zhou glanced at the sweep second hand of his Rolex. When a full minute had passed, he began talking. "Turin Credit is Italy's largest bank. Alberto Goldoni, the CEO, is the biggest stockholder with 18 percent of the stock. I want you to go to Italy and purchase Goldoni's stock. Go up to a purchase price of 20 billion euros. I'll secretly put up the cash. Of course, I'll want final approval of the transaction, but

I want you to keep my involvement confidential. That amount of stock should give you control of Turin Credit. After you obtain it, you'll secretly transfer ownership to my Commercial Bank of China. You'll continue to serve as a front even after control is transferred. Do you understand?"

"What makes you think Goldoni will sell?"

"As we both know, everything is for sale if the price is right. Besides, I've heard, and I'm sure you have as well, that most Italian banks are struggling because of their bad loans. Some are searching for ways to get out from under this problem. An infusion of foreign capital will be attractive to Goldoni."

McKnight shook his head. "I know a little about Turin Credit. Their balance sheet is sound because of good management by Alberto Goldoni. He and I have spent time at a couple of international bankers conferences. He explained to me how much Turin Credit means to him because the bank was started by his great-grandfather."

"All I'm asking you to do is buy Goldoni's interest and you'll have control of the bank."

"I suppose that's right, but it won't be easy."

"In return for doing this, I'll pay you a bonus of 5 million yuan at the end of the year. Now do you have any questions?"

"After the investment by Pacific Sun in the Milan bank and in banks in Verona and Bologna last year by Chinese banks, I'm afraid the Italian government, the EU, or the United States may intervene to block this transaction. They'll realize that in dealing with a bank as large as Turin Credit, an 18 percent stake will give the owner effective control."

Zhou brushed aside McKnight's comment with a wave of his hand. "You worry too much. Italy knows its banks are weak. It will welcome the infusion of foreign capital. The EU is a toothless entity. As for the United States, I have leverage and a powerful voice in Washington to prevent the United States from intervening. Anything else?" Zhou's tone was dismissive. He didn't want any more questions, but McKnight wasn't finished.

"Suppose Alberto refuses to sell?"

"Remind him what happened to his friend Federico and let me know. I'll take steps to change his mind."

McKnight's arm was shaking and his gait wobbly as he left the office.

Five minutes later, Zhou's secretary buzzed. "President Mei Ling would like you to come to her office."

Zhou's face reddened with anger. He wasn't a schoolboy to be yanked around by the teacher. He and Mei Ling had regular meetings once a week. That should suffice for her. Still, he couldn't ignore the request.

"Tell her I'm in an urgent meeting which should last about another hour. I'll come then."

Zhou left his office and walked along the corridor to his private exercise facility two doors away. He changed into workout clothes and climbed on a bike.

While pedaling furiously, he cursed about that bitch Mei Ling under his breath and wondered what she wanted today.

If she raised the subject of Italy, he'd tell her as little as possible about his bank takeover plan. And in no event would he mention Parelli or his meeting with the politician.

*   *   *

Entering Mei Ling's office an hour and a half later, Zhou received a frosty greeting. She doesn't like me any more than I like her, he thought. He knew Mei Ling had made him Finance Minister with great reluctance and only because he threatened to arrange a military coup, using former colleagues of his brother, if she did not.

The two of them sat down at an octagonal conference table and glared at each other.

"You wanted to talk to me?" he said curtly.

"Yes. My financial assistant has observed large treasury outlays for banks in Italy. You never consulted me about those. I want to know what's happening."

Zhou bristled at the idea she was checking up on him. In fact, he had used treasury funds for the three Italian bank investments in Verona, Bologna, and Milan, although the purchases were being made by fronts and ultimate ownership would be in the bank he owned.

Indignantly, he replied, "I'm doing what's in the best interests of China."

"I'm sure it is. I just want to know about it."

"I have a grand strategy to restore China to its former greatness." As if lecturing a student, he continued in a condescending tone, "Many people, not you of course, are unaware of our incredible history. They believe that China stepped from nowhere onto the world stage in the twentieth century. The reality, of course, is that during the Ming Dynasty before Christopher Columbus, our ships were traveling from the South China Sea to cross the Indian Ocean and sailing as far as Africa. There is no doubt we would have gotten to the Western hemisphere before the Europeans if our narrow minded emperors hadn't decided to pull back from world exploration.

"During the Qing Dynasty we became world travelers again. China was so prosperous in the eighteenth century that some Americans proposed that the United States look to China as a model of successful development.

"At the beginning of the nineteenth century, China controlled one third of the world's total output. Our GDP and consumption of luxury goods exceeded that of Europe. Then the countries of Western Europe, led by England, conspired to weaken China while they surged ahead economically.

"Now that we are an economic power, it's payback time. We can gain a foothold in Europe from which we will exert major influence over their economies. I intend to do that by having us take over much of Italy's banking industry. In the 21st Century, whoever controls the banks controls the economy and the country."

"Thank you for that history lesson. But why Italy?" She asked nervously.

"To start with, most of the top banks in Italy are in trouble financially. That was the conclusion of an inspection last year of Italian banks by the Bank of Italy. They don't have enough assets to guard against losses on bad loans. Fifteen percent of their loans are not being repaid on time, defaults are increasing, and they don't have enough capital to cover their anticipated losses. In other words, their entire banking system was on the verge of collapse. Yet the Bank of Italy, their bank regulatory body, had a rule prohibiting foreigners from owning any portion of a bank.

Last June, at a world economic conference in Ascona, Switzerland, I spent time with the head of the Bank of Italy, called the Governatore. His organization regulates the banking industry. I convinced him that the infusion of foreign capital is critical to save their banks. He assured me that the Bank of Italy would not take any action against foreign ownership as long as their holdings were less than 20 percent. I had thought he wouldn't go above 10 percent. So I was personally surprised. Twenty percent is huge. In the case of a large bank, 20 percent ownership usually gives a shareholder effective control. The Italian government is likely to press them to put up additional capital, which they won't be able to raise. All of this makes them vulnerable to an outside takeover."

"What about other countries in Europe?"

"England, Germany, and France are too large to focus on initially. Italy is next in size right after them, and Italy is in the heart of Europe. After I control the Italian banking business, I'll move onto other countries in Europe."

"You think you'll have enough money to do what you want?"

"Absolutely. I also have the option of entering into an alliance with Qatar. I've had discussions with their Finance Minister. He's prepared to use their banks and oil money to work with me. He'd like a foothold in Europe as well."

Mei Ling looked worried. "What about the United States? Won't they intervene to block you?"

"I have leverage. I'm confident I can keep them out."

He was relieved she didn't ask him to explain his strategy for dealing with the United States. He had no intention of doing so.

Zhou looked across the table at Mei Ling. The ball was in her court. Would she dare to challenge him and try to block what he was doing?

She sighed deeply, and finally said, "I am in favor of restoring China to its former greatness, but I don't want to create enemies in Europe. So proceed carefully and keep me informed."

He barely suppressed a smile. She was afraid of crossing him. He could move ahead with his plans for Italy.

Turin

Alberto Goldoni was dreading this meeting. Parelli had called yesterday to arrange it. He had no doubt that Parelli would try to persuade him to extend the deadline for repayment of the overdue loans and mortgages on his farm and wine business.

Early this morning, sipping a double espresso at the desk in his office, Alberto had reviewed the loan sheet on Parelli. The total outstanding debt Parelli owed to Turin Credit was 310 million euros. Last week Alberto had obtained an appraisal of the mortgaged property. It came in at 202 million euros. That meant if he foreclosed now, he would lose 108 million euros.

To compound the problem, the appraiser also warned that property values in this part of Piedmont were declining, and that Parelli's winemaker, responsible for elevating their wines to compete with Gaja and Antinori, had an aggressive form of prostate cancer. The winemaker was facing death in a matter of months. That fact had been concealed from the public. So if Alberto didn't foreclose now, his losses for the bank would mount.

After he drained the rest of his coffee, Alberto closed his eyes and leaned back in his chair, recalling how he had gotten into this awful position. He owed it to two factors. The first was the business relationship between the Goldoni and Parelli families. Alberto's great grandfather lent the money to Parelli's grandfather to start the winery. Over the years, Turin Credit had made loans to the Parellis for expansion or after bad weather devastated a harvest. Those loans were small in comparison with what Parelli owed now.

The second was Parelli's charm and charisma. The man was worldly and fun to be with. Alberto and Dora had many memorable dinners at the Parelli's farm. The usually prudent banker had dropped his guard when Parelli, while vague about the platform for his New Italy Party, had asked for a large loan secured by a mortgage to launch his campaign. "Italy was once a great country," Parelli, his face flushed with enthusiasm, his voice strong and vigorous despite his age of 70, had told Alberto. "I want to restore that greatness."

Goldoni had seen the warning clouds when Parelli fell behind on his mortgage payments, but the smooth-talking candidate spoke of promises he had received of large contributions if he continued to surge in the polls, and added, "We have just bottled our best wine ever which will bring a strong infusion of capital." Alberto was dubious about Parelli's puffing. Normally prudent, he had realized there were problems with the large loan, but he had been willing to take a chance that some smaller ones would get Parelli over the hump. Now, he realized the foolishness of what he had done.

It was time to shut down a bad situation before it became worse.

Once his secretary announced on the intercom, "Signor Parelli is here," Alberto was strong in his resolve. By calling the loans, he would be a sensible businessman. Any other decision was foolhardy.

"I was sorry to hear about your friend Federico," Parelli said.

"He was a wonderful man. It was tragic."

"Unfortunately, I couldn't attend the funeral. I had campaign commitments that couldn't be canceled."

"I understand."

"When I was a lawyer in Milan, Federico took me to lunch. He told me about the relationship between your families. He also made an effort to get my business, but I declined. I told him there was no way I would ever leave Turin Credit."

What an outrageous lie, Alberto thought. Federico had called him immediately before and after the lunch that Parelli had initiated. He reported to Alberto that Parelli said he was unhappy with Alberto's bank. If Federico offered him financing at a lower rate, he would move all of the family's business from Turin Credit to Federico's bank. Federico had declined, and that's when he had explained about the relationship between Federico and Alberto's families as his justification for refusing the offer. In Federico's words, repeated to Alberto, "I could never do that to my friend, Alberto."

Alberto pointed to a small round table in a corner of the office, signaling they should sit down and start their meeting. But Parelli wasn't ready for that.

He walked over to a credenza along one wall and picked up a picture of Alberto when he was eight with his grandfather. They were both on horses. The old man was teaching Alberto to ride.

"He was a wonderful man," Parelli said. "Your grandfather—he and my father were close." He held up two fingers of his hand pressed tightly together. "Like brothers."

Alberto nodded. Parelli's charm offensive was going full force. It kept on rolling. He turned to the photo taken last year in the law school courtyard in Bologna where Alberto's daughter Ilana was a student. Alberto, Dora, and their son, Ricardo, were in the picture with Ilana.

"My oh my," Parelli said. "Ilana has become such a beautiful young woman."

"Thank you."

"Is she studying law at Bologna as she planned?"

"She is and doing quite well."

"I'm not surprised. I remember when you invited me to a religious service at the synagogue in which she spoke. Her brilliance was evident then."

Alberto was anxious to change the subject and get down to business. "Enough about my family."

They sat in chairs across the table.

Parelli had asked for the meeting. Alberto let him talk first.

"Thank you for agreeing to meet with me, Alberto."

"You owe a significant debt to this bank. Which is long overdue."

"And I've also been a good client over many years. As was my father. Indeed, your great-grandfather lent money to my grandfather when he started making wine. The Parellis have always repaid every Lira or euro to your bank."

"That's all true, but . . ."

"I've come to ask you to lend me another twenty million euros."

Alberto was dumbfounded. He had expected a plea for additional time. Instead, Parelli wanted more money. The man had incredible nerve.

"I thought you would want to talk to me about repaying what you owe."

"In due time, Alberto," Parelli's voice was soft, his tone reassuring. "But now my election campaign is gaining enormous momentum. I need just a little more cash. This twenty million will give me enough of a boost in the polls that increased contributions will flow into my treasury."

"With all due respect, Roberto, that's what you told me when I gave you the last two loans." Alberto sounded respectful but firm.

"Well, we have increased our fundraising."

"It seems to me as if you've increased your spending by an even greater amount. The latest polls show you losing ground."

"They're wrong. If I had more money, there wouldn't even be a question about where I stood in the polls."

"I'm very sorry. I can't lend you anymore. I've decided to call the loans and to foreclose on the mortgages."

Parelli's looked as if he had been punched in the stomach. He had an indignant expression on his face. Alberto wondered if he was surprised or posturing.

"Haven't I always repaid what I borrowed?"

"Yes. Until now."

"And if you give me a little more money and some additional time, I'll repay what I owe now."

"The loans are already six months overdue. Two weeks from today on June 20th, I intend to foreclose on the properties."

Parelli looked pale and terrified. It was obvious to Alberto that Parelli had never expected this. "I won't be able to meet that deadline," he stammered.

"I'm very sorry."

Parelli recovered and pounded the table. "I'll be ruined. That's what you want to do. Ruin me like my enemies."

"That's not it at all."

Parelli was on his feet and shouting while waving his arms. "The winery and the farm have been in my family for generations. I'll be finished financially."

When Alberto rose, but didn't respond, Parelli continued blustering, "It's not just me you'll be wrecking. It's this great country of Italy. My party, the New Italy Party, can provide a fresh start to this country. You'll be depriving all Italians of their future. Don't you love Italy?"

Alberto didn't want to argue politics with Parelli. His great-grandfather had been a hero in the Italian Cavalry in the First World War. Later, he came back to Italy while he could have stayed in New York and became a successful banker after the Second World War. Alberto did love Italy as his family had for generations. And that reinforced Alberto's decision refusing to extend Parelli's loans. In his view, by dividing Italy, Parelli would be destroying the country.

"Two more weeks, Roberto," he said calmly.

Parelli raised his hand and pointed a bony finger at Alberto. "You'll be sorry you did this. Mark my words. You'll pay dearly for this decision."

Parelli's words frightened Alberto, but he held his ground. "I'm sorry you feel like that."

Parelli stormed out of the office.

Rome

C raig stopped for flowers on the way to Giuseppe's house. Carolyn had once told him, "Women always like roses."

When Giuseppe opened the door of the first floor apartment in Rome, close to the Piazza Navona, his head snapped back in surprise. He waited to close the door before he said, "You sure don't look like the Craig Page I remember. My eyes must be getting weaker with age."

"I had a little work. A nip and tuck."

"You had a lot more than that."

"Well, I enjoy life, and unless I did something drastic, I figured Zhou Yun would deprive me of that."

"A very wise conclusion."

Looking at Giuseppe, Craig thought he'd aged ten years in the twenty-one months since he had last seen him. His hair, formerly a sandy brown, was now mostly gray. He had wrinkles on his face and a sad expression. He'd added about twenty pounds, which at 5' 10" made him look chunky.

Craig held out the roses. "These are for Antonia. I'm sure you never bring your wife flowers."

Giuseppe sighed deeply. "Antonia passed six months ago. She had a tough time with ovarian cancer."

"Oh. I'm so sorry. I had no idea."

Craig put the flowers down and hugged him.

"I felt bad that I couldn't tell you, but I had no way of locating you. I even tried Betty, but she was no help."

"I know. It was as if I dropped off the face of the earth. So how are you doing now?"

"A little better. I still think about her every day. But work helps. I lose myself in that. You must know how I feel."

"After Carolyn died, it was awful. Eventually, I got over it. Then I had a repeat with Francesca's murder."

"I was there when you got the news about Francesca. I'll never forget that day here in Rome. After we captured those suicide bombers."

"Seems like so long ago."

"Now, I have more bad news for you."

Craig was alarmed. "Yeah, what?"

"Instead of getting a fabulous meal from Antonia, you get my cooking."

"Should I take something to coat my stomach?"

"Not necessary. I keep it simple. We'll have some sliced tomatoes first. Then a grilled Florentine steak with roast potatoes. And I found a couple of bottles of '97 Giuseppe Quintarelli Valpolicello in the cellar that I'd forgotten I had."

"The Quintarelli. Italy's greatest winemaker. I was so sorry to learn the old man died. That sounds like a feast."

"Before we get to that, how about a drink on the patio in the back and we'll catch up."

"Fine."

"I'll get a bottle of white wine and some nuts."

"Nuts?"

"Yeah. I read somewhere that you Americans like nuts with your cocktails."

"Only on airlines."

They both laughed.

It was a crystal-clear night with a comfortable temperature and surprisingly low humidity. Seated with a glass of arneis, Giuseppe was staring at Craig. "You know whom you look like?"

"Let me guess. Enrico Marino, the race car driver."

"Have other people told you that?"

"I am Enrico Marino."

"You're kidding."

"Nope. In the flesh."

"You won the Stresa race?" Giuseppe sounded incredulous.

"Somebody had to."

"Okay. Now bring me up to date on everything you've been doing since you called to tell me that you'd been so ungraciously fired as CIA Director."

For the next half hour, Craig talked, interrupted by questions from time to time, about his plastic surgery in Switzerland, his racing, and his mission in Argentina.

"What about Elizabeth?" Giuseppe asked. "You left her out of the story."

"I don't want to talk about her." Craig sounded angry.

"Do it anyhow. For me."

Craig knew that when Giuseppe was insistent about something, he refused to be put off. And Giuseppe liked Elizabeth.

"Well, we had an argument the night I was fired. She was putting her career ahead of all else."

"How inconsiderate after you'd always relegated your career to second place in your relationship with her."

"Thank you for telling me what a shit I was."

"That's what good friends are for. Besides, somebody had to."

"Well, after that, I decided it would be safer for her if she didn't see me. Zhou Yun was likely to focus on her. We didn't have any contact until last Sunday in Stresa. She showed up after the race and we had dinner. That didn't go well. End of story."

"Sorry to hear that. I always thought you two were good together."

"Life moves on."

As soon as the words were out of Craig's mouth, he thought about Antonia and was sorry he had said them.

"So it does," Giuseppe replied glumly.

"Now, let me tell you why I came."

"Okay, but first I have to do something about a steak. And while I do, you can make yourself useful."

Craig sliced tomatoes and sautéed the potatoes. Giuseppe was watching the meat on the grill and decanting the wine.

When they finally sat down at the table, Craig took a bite of steak and said, "Hey this is great."

"Only the best for you. Now tell me why you're here."

Before responding, Craig sipped some of the Quintarelli. It was an incredibly elegant wine. "The guy was a genius. Thanks for sharing it with me."

"Okay. Now talk."

Craig told Giuseppe everything he knew about Federico's death.

At one point, Giuseppe said, "I know Alberto Goldoni. Six months ago, some suspected Iranian terrorists were using his bank to launder money without his knowledge. He was very cooperative and helped us nail them."

When Craig finished, Giuseppe asked, "What do you want me to do?"

"Investigate Federico's death. I'll work with you."

Giuseppe shook his head. "It's great to see you and resume our friendship. However, you of all people know I can't do that. You held my job for God's sake."

"I think you can."

"C'mon Craig. I know Federico was your friend and sponsor. But it was a jewelry robbery that went wrong, I have to leave it to the French police."

"You know it's more than that. There's an international component. Russians. French. Italians."

"I notice you didn't mention terrorists. I'm the Director of Counterterrorism."

"Your job description isn't that narrow. I wrote it."

Giuseppe shook his head. "Sorry, Craig, I can't do it." He sounded vehement.

Craig was surprised at Giuseppe's reluctance to become involved. "What's bothering you?"

"Twice in the last year I received a reprimand for trying to intervene in purely domestic incidents. One in France. One in Germany. I like my job. It's all I have now."

"Look at the facts."

"That's the point. You don't have any facts. All you told me is what Amelie told you."

"Fair enough. Alright, I have an idea. Tomorrow morning order the file electronically from the Biarritz police. We'll look at it and see if any facts in the file persuade you to become involved."

When Giuseppe didn't respond immediately, Craig decided he had a chance.

"Damn, you're stubborn," Giuseppe finally said.

"Coming from you that's the supreme compliment. Nobody is more experienced in solving international crimes than you are. In your gut you . . ."

"Now you're resorting to flattery to get your way."

Giuseppe pulled a white handkerchief from his pocket. "I surrender. Tell you what. Tomorrow morning I have a meeting outside the office. Before I leave, I'll get the file from Biarritz and set you up in an office with it. When I get back, we'll see if you have enough to convince me."

*   *   *

The next morning, Giuseppe downloaded and handed Craig the file from Biarritz. While Giuseppe went off to his meeting, Craig dug into it. By the time Giuseppe returned two hours later, Craig told him, "I have the facts you need."

"Okay. Go ahead."

"Amelie told me they returned to the house at ten minutes to twelve Saturday evening. Alberto, whom you know and respect, told the police that the dinner ended at around 11:30, which confirms her account."

"I have that. Go on," Giuseppe said impatiently.

"The police report shows that the house security system was disarmed at 9:53 p.m. on Saturday. That must be when the killers entered the house."

Giuseppe was listening carefully. "Agreed."

"The report also says that the house had a sophisticated vault in a bedroom closet, which was where jewels were kept, according to Amelie. The timer on the vault showed its last opening at 10:27, more than an hour before Amelie and Federico came home. The vault was left open. The police report doesn't list the jewels that were stolen. None of the jewelry Amelie was wearing was taken."

Craig paused for a moment.

Giuseppe finished his thought. "Meaning that the Russians came to execute Federico. Otherwise, they would have taken the jewels in the vault and escaped before Federico came home. And taken the jewelry she was wearing."

"Exactly."

Giuseppe rubbed his hand over his chin. The creases deepened on his forehead. Without saying a word, he closed his eyes. In silence, Craig let him digest what he'd heard.

Finally, he opened them and said, "Okay. I'm convinced. I'll work on this case."

"Good. Now, I think you and I should go to Federico's office in Milan. Interview people and check records. We should see whether the takeover by the Singapore bank had anything to do with his murder."

"We?"

"That means you and I."

"I got that much. What I'm puzzling over is how I explain your presence."

Craig thought about it for a moment and responded. "I'm a good friend of Federico and Amelie who's helping with background information."

Giuseppe smiled. "You must have passed the CIA course in deception with flying colors."

"I'm usually too modest to admit it, but I was top of the class at the Farm. . . . Let's go this afternoon."

"Whoa boy. It'll have to be tomorrow morning. I have to finish up some loose ends here. But since you want to get moving this afternoon, I have a job for you."

"What's that?"

"Get in touch with your friend, Amelie. Ask her to give you a list of the jewels that were stolen from the vault. Insurance policies always identify them in detail. If she has the policy with her in France, have her read them to you. If not, have her tell you where the policy is in her house in Milan."

"What do you intend to do with the list of stolen jewels?"

"We might be able to find the killers by following the jewelry trail. My experience is that robbers try to unload expensive jewelry as soon as possible. I have a friend, Jean-Claude, in the French National Police who has developed a relationship with the main outfits in France that fence high-end jewelry. There are only a couple of them. We'll give him the list. If any of those have shown up, the fence may be able to provide a description of whoever gave it to him."

"I like that. It could work."

"Occasionally I have a good idea. At any rate, you should stay in Milan overnight. I'll meet you there in the morning. First, I'll forward your list of stolen items to Jean-Claude. Then we'll go to Federico's bank."

*   *   *

From Linate Airport in Milan, Craig called Amelie. When she answered, "Allo," Craig detected panic in her voice. She calmed down when he told her it was Enrico Marino.

She understood exactly what he wanted and why.

"The insurance policy is buried in a stack of papers in the center drawer of Federico's desk in the study. The one with the green leather top."

"Is the drawer locked?"

"Key's in a ruby topped snuff box on the second shelf of the bookcase."

"Good. Thanks."

"But how will you get into the house?"

"Don't worry. I'll find a way."

"Are you sure?"

"Absolutely."

She seemed satisfied.

Craig had been trained well in his CIA days at the Farm. Breaking and entering was a basic course. He had finished top of the class in that one as well.

From the airport, Craig drove straight to her house, making certain he wasn't being followed.

Once he was inside, he tread softly, checking each room to make sure it was deserted and not booby trapped. Nothing here. The Russians must have moved on.

He found the policy and left quickly. It would be safer, he decided, not to stay in his own house tonight after the threat from the Russians. So he checked into the hotel Palazzo Parigi on Corso di Porta Nuova in the heart of Milan's fashion district.

From his room, he called Amelie and read off the items that were insured. Without hesitating, she told him which ones had been stolen.

They included a ring with a 12.4 carat cabochon emerald in the center surrounded by 14 diamonds, valued at 950,000 euros; a bracelet with alternating faceted sapphires (totaling 7.0 carats) and diamonds (totaling 8.3 carats), valued at 1.2 million euros; and a yellow gold necklace with clusters of diamonds and rubies, valued at 1.35 million euros. Several other less important pieces had been stolen as well.

My God, Craig thought, the woman had valuable stuff. He quickly added it up. Almost five million euros worth of jewelry had been stolen. Most were very distinctive pieces.

Craig concluded that the Russians weren't following him. So he went downstairs and had dinner in the hotel's luxurious gastronomic restaurant that had excellent food and was a favorite of many of Milan's top social set. Several people recognized Enrico Marino and congratulated him on his Stresa victory. One couple asked Craig to join them for dinner, but he declined telling them he was tired and wanted to eat quickly and leave. "I'm afraid I won't be much fun."

Over dinner, he thought some more about the jewelry. He wondered whether Federico had given them to Bonita, his first wife. Well, regardless, no mere robber would ever hang around a house once he had these in his hands. The Russians clearly had another agenda. Someone had wanted Federico dead. Craig was determined to find out who it was.

Paris

The day after Elizabeth's article on Parelli's Venice speech was published, she received a call from Jonathan Hanson, an American expat who had held her job as foreign editor of the *International Herald*. He had retired twelve years ago and was living in Provence. When she was elevated to foreign editor, Hanson came to Paris and took her to lunch. He had offered his help if she ever wanted guidance, but she had not taken him up on it and hadn't seen Hanson since then.

Today, he sounded excited when he said, "Elizabeth, it's Robert Hanson."

"Good to hear from you." She almost said Bob, but remembered he hated that so she quickly mumbled "Robert."

"Good piece you did on Roberto Parelli. First rate journalism."

Elizabeth was thrilled with the compliment. Hanson had won prizes for articles dealing with political developments in Europe. "You made my day."

"Now, I want to be helpful. I have some background info for you on Roberto Parelli. How about having lunch with me tomorrow? I'll come to Paris."

Elizabeth was delighted. She wanted to understand more about the candidate. Hanson would never have called if he didn't have something significant. "Sure. Tell me where and when."

*   *   *

For lunch the next day, Hanson selected a bistro not far from the Herald's office. When she arrived, she found him seated at a table in a corner. The place was quiet. They'd be able to talk.

Hanson was sipping red wine as she approached. The tall and trim Hanson stood up. He looked to be a model of health and vigor. He was sun tanned and had thick brown hair and a smile that turned up his mouth. He could have been an ad for the good life in Provence. She noticed a bottle of St. Joseph on the table. The waiter poured her a glass.

"Even though we're both Americans," Hanson said, "we can still drink at lunch."

"Sure. Why not?"

A portly waiter with a bushy brown mustache came to the table. Elizabeth ordered moules and frites; Hanson asked for steak and frites.

Hanson raised his glass. "Here's to your superb article on Parelli. And I loved the title: 'Roberto Parelli—Savior or Sinner.'"

His words made her feel good. "Coming from you, that compliment means a great deal. So which is he: saint or sinner?"

"Clearly a sinner. When you hear what I have to say, you'll agree with me."

"How do you know Parelli?"

"We go back a long way. Would you believe to Yale when I was an undergrad."

"The Dark Ages."

Hanson laughed. "Tell me about it."

"I wasn't even born then."

"Ouch. That hurt."

Hanson paused to sip some wine and said, "First, let's talk about Roberto Parelli's father, Mario. That becomes relevant later on. When Mussolini came to power, Mario wasn't in politics. He was operating the Parelli vineyards and winery. As I'm sure you know, Mussolini never agreed to Hitler's demands that he round up the Jews and deport them to camps like Auschwitz. Once Mussolini was deposed the first time, near the end of the war, Germany invaded Italy and the SS began rounding up and deporting Jews. Mario was outraged. Not only were some of his friends Jewish, but he was a decent and honorable person. He made his farm and vineyard a stopping point for Jews escaping from Turin into Switzerland.

"The Nazis found out about it and decided to punish Mario. They wanted to make an example of him. When the SS showed up at his farm, they gathered all of Mario's family and everyone else there into the yard in front of the house. Mario was forced to watch as they raped and then shot and killed his wife and four daughters. Roberto, his youngest, and only other child, was six months old. He survived because Mario's good friend Rinaldo held the baby and pretended it was his own. After the carnage, Mario pleaded with the Germans to kill him, but the officer in charge said that leaving Mario alive to remember what occurred would be a worse punishment."

The waiter came with the food. They stopped talking for a few minutes and ate. Then Elizabeth said, "That' a helluva story."

"Yeah. I heard it from Mario. I interviewed him a couple of times. After the war, he turned the wine business over to a man he hired away from Gaja. He devoted his life to politics to prevent atrocities like this from happening again in Italy. Rinaldo became his chief advisor—and confidante. Mario was in Parliament for many years and the minister of agriculture and finance. But of course he was never prime minister."

"So Roberto has politics in his blood."

"Yeah, but he didn't plunge in until a year or so ago. Before that he was a lawyer with a prominent Milan firm. He's very high energy. He also had a justly deserved reputation as a playboy, which in Italy isn't easy to obtain. As you're no doubt aware, marital fidelity isn't, shall we say, as widespread in Italy as in some other places. Simply put, he loves high living and he fucks anything that wears a skirt." Hanson said it with contempt.

Elizabeth couldn't wait any longer. "Tell me about Yale."

"Ah. Good old New Haven."

"I went to Harvard myself."

He smiled. "I won't hold that against you."

She ate a few mussels, waiting for him to continue.

"When I was a senior, I was Editor in Chief of the *Yale Daily News,* which I thought was a big deal."

"It was."

"Not big enough, as you'll hear. Well, anyhow, I had it all, or so I thought. I was madly in love with and engaged to a fabulous woman— smart and a drop dead gorgeous blonde with a figure that turned men's heads. Her name was Diane Taylor, a junior at Vasser. She came down to New Haven one evening for a political program in the law school auditorium about Europe's future. One of the four speakers was the US Secretary of State. Another was a graduate law student, Roberto Parelli, who was charismatic and gave a superb speech."

Hanson sounded bitter. The smile was gone. His mouth turned down. "After the program ended, I rushed up to interview the Secretary of State. Through the corner of my eye, I noticed Diane talking enthusiastically to Parelli. Before I was finished, Parelli was leaving the auditorium with Diane in tow. She called the next day and asked me to come to Vasser and collect the ring. No apologies or explanation. She married Parelli a month later and dropped out of Vasser."

"And did they live happily ever after?"

"Hardly. Ten years later and two children for her, I was still single and agonizing over what could have been. I had taken a job at the

Herald, playing a long shot that if I were in Europe I might hook up with her again."

"And?"

"Has anyone ever told you that you're impatient?"

"They do all the time."

He didn't laugh. "I heard rumors that Parelli was a playboy. Lots of affairs. So I called Diane. We had a torrid affair for about a month. She told me that she would leave him and run away with me. Then she called and ditched me again. This time, I got an explanation."

"I'll bet this was good."

"Actually, it was. Roberto had gone to dinner with his father in Rome. Mario liked Diane. He even provided the funding for Diane to open a boutique in the fashion district of Milan. He wanted to save Roberto's marriage for the sake of his grandchildren. At dinner, Mario had tried to convince Roberto to stop running around with women. They ended up in a shouting match. Roberto stormed out of the restaurant. Half an hour later, when Mario was walking back to his hotel, Libyan terrorists shot and killed him.

"Grief stricken, Roberto told her what happened with his father at dinner. He swore he was done with other women. So she took him back. She still loved him. A few months later I met Jacqueline and married her. From that point on, I tried to forget about Diane. I have no idea if Roberto has been faithful to her or not. But I doubt it. Men like Roberto are serial adulterers."

Elizabeth recalled her conversation with the prostitute in Venice. "Well he hasn't been. I can tell you that."

Hanson finished his wine and poured some more. "It doesn't matter. I got her out of my system long ago. I wanted to talk to you today because I'd like to encourage you to find a way to destroy Parelli. Not because of my personal issues with Diane. Not because he's a lying cheating scum bag. We have plenty of leaders in every country who fit that description. There's something else. If Parelli is elected, his political program would be a disaster for Italy."

"You mean because the south is so much poorer than the north and couldn't make it as an independent nation."

"That's part of it. A division between north and south would heap misery on millions of low-income people living in the south. They need the support they get from the central government. Even with that support, the south is in dreadful shape. Annual gross domestic product in the south is 21,000 per capita compared with 43,000 in the north. Sixty percent of young southerners have no job. Without it, poverty levels would rise and infant mortality as well as other health indices would go off the charts. The south lacks the manufacturing base of the north. Without it, the economy in the south would crumble. Do you think it's possible to sustain standards of living on an economy that only exports olives and olive oil. Even the best wines are in the north. But it's more than economic issues."

Hanson was sounding emotional. "I love Italy. And who doesn't? With all of its defects, and there are plenty, it is a great country. Italians are a wonderful people with a creative independent spirit. And Parelli wants to destroy it."

"He's never said where he'd divide the country."

"You're absolutely right. And for good reason. It can't be done. Would Rome be in the south? Would it be a divided city? Rome is the pulse of Italy. As much as Milan and Turino. Politicians like Parelli never worry about the practical problems. They shoot off their mouths with a grand vision. All there would be is endless fighting. Of course, there are enormous differences between people in the north and the south. That's always been the case. But so what? I know it's a trite expression that the whole is greater than the sum of its parts, but that happens to be true for Italy."

Elizabeth recalled the research she had done for her article following Parelli's speech in Venice. "On the other hand, southern Italy did exist as a separate political entity from the north for eight hundred years until the country was unified in the 19th century."

"So what? That was a different time and a different world. Massachusetts, Virginia, Pennsylvania, and other states of the United States existed as colonies of England. That doesn't mean they should go back to being separate entities."

"Do you think the people in Scotland have to stick with England if they want independence? Or in Catalonia if they want independence from Spain?"

"That's the point. You said if THEY want it. In Italy, the vote isn't just by southerners deciding to stay with the north. Northerners will be voting overwhelmingly to kick them out in order to increase their standard of living. You think that's right?"

"Polls show that Parelli has support of a majority in the south."

"Hanson sneered. "The church misleads them. The Vatican wants a real state it can dominate. Not the tiniest nation in the world."

Elizabeth didn't argue. She realized Hanson was right.

He continued, "Parelli has to be stopped, and you're an incredible reporter with a golden pen. You can do it."

The waiter cleared their dishes and asked about dessert. Hanson paused and asked for an espresso. Elizabeth had seen the waiter serving a luscious looking profiterole to a nearby table, but she had gained a couple of pounds lately. Do I or don't I?

"Just an espresso," she told the waiter.

The coffee came a moment later. "Do you have any ammunition for me to use against Parelli?" she asked.

"I'll give you two suggestions. First, develop a relationship with Luciano, Parelli's closest advisor and chief of staff. Rinaldo, Mario's best friend, was Luciano's father. Luciano is a professional political advisor. As soon as Parelli went into politics and formed his New Italy Party, Luciano went to work for Parelli. But here's the point: Luciano, like his father and Mario, is an honorable man. At some point, Parelli, the scum, will do something to alienate Luciano. That could be his undoing."

She was nodding. "That's very helpful. What's the second?"

"In his personal and business life, Parelli spends money like water. Diane told me that during our brief fling. Prior to Berlusconi's entry into politics, money was not the driving force in Italian elections. However, Berlusconi had a marketing background, and he followed the model of an American campaign with huge advertising expenditures. Parelli has taken a page from Berlusconi's playbook. So he needs lots of money. And you and I know that candidates in this type of campaign will make concessions to contributors to keep the money flowing. As they say in Washington, 'follow the money.' That may be how you can nail Parelli."

"I really appreciate everything you've told me."

"Don't thank me. Just destroy Parelli."

Milan

Craig and Giuseppe met at 9:00 in the morning in the Milan head-quarters of the carabinieri, the Italian national police. The gray stone structure the agency occupied was in the shadow of the Duomo in the heart of Milan. The director was a friend of Giuseppe's and had promised Giuseppe when he took the EU job that he'd have, "An office, a secretary, and whatever else you need. Anytime."

After studying Craig's list of the jewelry that had been stolen, Giuseppe gave a long, low whistle. "The lady has expensive taste. Those are unique pieces that will stand out."

"They could have been bought for Federico's first wife."

"Well one of them sure has expensive taste. I already spoke to Jean-Claude. He's expecting the list."

Craig liked working with Giuseppe. He moved fast and was always focused. Besides, for Craig, who except for his time in Argentina, had been racing cars for the last year and a half, it was good getting back into the groove of the hunt for terrorists and criminals he had enjoyed doing for so long.

Giuseppe grabbed his jacket and tucked a Beretta into his chest holster. "We're off to Federico's bank."

"Did you call? Are they expecting us?"

"Nope. I want the element of surprise. Man by the name of Dominic Leonardo is the acting CEO. He had been Federico's second in command."

"Good. Let's go ruin his day."

The bank headquarters were housed in a majestic stone building with four large columns in front on the square across from the La Scala opera house.

A secretary ushered Craig and Giuseppe into an ornate conference room where Dominic was waiting. Looking at the man, Craig observed he was quite short, almost bald, and very scared.

Giuseppe pulled out his ID and held it out to Dominic. With a trembling hand, the banker took it and seemed to be staring at it.

"Director of EU Counterterrorism," he said. "What's this about?"

"I'm investigating Federico's death."

"But why do you want to talk to me? Surely you don't think I stole the jewelry. I wasn't even in Biarritz on Saturday."

Craig took an instant dislike to the man.

Calmly, Giuseppe replied, "We're trying to determine if this was more than a simple jewelry theft."

Dominic handed back Giuseppe's ID and stared hard at Craig. "You're the race car driver. Enrico Marino?"

"Yeah, that's who I am."

"What are you doing here?"

Giuseppe responded before Craig could open his mouth. "He was a close friend of Federico's and is helping me with background. I'm using him as a consultant on this case."

Apparently resigned that he would have to talk to them, Dominic sat down at the heavily polished wooden table. Craig and Giuseppe sat across from him.

"You think that terrorists killed Federico and made it seem like a robbery?" Dominic asked.

Giuseppe looked sternly at Dominic. "We believe that your bank is laundering money for organized crime. That's what led to Federico death."

Dominic's head snapped back. "You're not serious."

"Why not? If the Vatican bank is doing it, so could yours. I want you to produce copies of all transactions the bank entered into in the last year for over one million euros. Also, all overdue loans."

"Do you have authority to ask for that?"

"If you prefer, I could get an order from the Ministry of Justice. Then they'll send their people to check all your records. When that happens, sometimes the media hear about it. Nobody quite knows how."

"Okay. You made your point. That won't be necessary."

"I didn't think so."

"You'll have the information in an hour."

"Now tell me about the acquisition of your bank by Pacific Sun Bank from Singapore."

"They only bought a 19 percent interest."

"Which gives them effective control."

"What would you like to know?"

Craig detected a quavering in Dominic's voice.

"Was Federico in favor of the transaction?"

Dominic looked away and responded. "Of course. As the largest shareholder, he would make a great deal of money from the sale of this stock."

"Are you certain of that?"

Before responding, Dominic fiddled with a ring on his finger for a full minute. Finally, he said, "Absolutely. We discussed it last week."

More quavering in his voice, Craig thought. He's lying. Hiding something.

If Craig were in charge, he would have sprung across the table, pinned Dominic to the back of his chair, and threatened to strangle the man with his bare hands if he didn't tell the truth. But that wasn't Giuseppe's way.

"We want to meet separately with the three highest ranking officers of the bank after you," Giuseppe said.

Dominic hesitated, then said, "I'll put you in a conference room. My secretary will have them to come to see you one at a time."

"Good. While you arrange that, I'm going to the men's room."

"I'll go also," Craig added.

Once they were both in the men's room and satisfied no one else was there, Giuseppe said to Craig, "He's lying through his teeth about Federico and the acquisition by the Singapore Bank."

"Agreed. We may have hit pay dirt."

"Perhaps one of the other top people will break."

"While you're interviewing them, I want to go to Federico's office. I'll talk to his secretary, Donna. I've gotten to know her through my relationship with Federico. Also, I want to look at his files."

"Okay. We'll split."

"What do you intend to do with the bank records he's assembling?"

"Turn them over to investigators in my office. And I'll also have them come here to make sure he's not hiding anything."

Donna looked happy to see Craig. "Oh, Mr. Marino, it's been awful."

She was a heavyset, gray-haired woman who had worked for Federico for a long time. On her desk she had pictures of half a dozen of her grandchildren—ages ten and younger, Craig guessed.

Craig wanted privacy. "Can we go into Signor Castiglione's office to talk?"

"Certainly."

She led the way. He closed the door behind them.

Craig had been in Federico's office several times before. He loved the racing memorabilia and model cars that Federico had scattered around. He also had pictures of Craig winning a race, albeit not a major, in Provence in April.

Craig sat behind Federico's desk, taking the chair of authority. She sat in what must have been her usual place, facing him.

"In view of my friendship with Federico, I'm helping the police investigate his death."

"Had he lived another week, it would have been twenty years that I worked for him. I liked Signor Castiglione. Everybody did."

Not everyone, Craig thought.

She continued. "He was a gentleman, considerate and kind. Not just to me—to everyone who worked for the bank." She began to cry. "I'm sorry. After twenty years, he was family."

Craig handed her his handkerchief. "I can understand that." He decided to jump into the key issues without any warning.

"There have been rumors of his bank's involvement with organized crime."

"That's ridiculous."

"You're sure?"

"Positive. I was aware of all of Federico's bank work. That was the nature of our relationship."

Craig believed her. "Then let's talk about the investment in this bank by the Singapore bank."

"What do you want to know?"

"Can you show me Signor Castiglione's files relating to the investment by the Singapore bank."

She looked extremely upset. "Those files aren't here any longer."

"Well, where are they?"

"I don't know."

"When did they disappear?"

She didn't respond.

"You should know, Donna, that Giuseppe has authority to go to the Justice Ministry and have witnesses who don't cooperate charged with obstruction of Justice, which is a crime." Craig had no idea if that was true, but he decided to toss it out. "Are you aware of that?"

"No . . . no."

"Then tell me what happened to the files."

She took a deep breath and let it out. "Signor Castiglione died on Saturday night. When I came into the office on Monday morning, I saw that all of his files were gone. His computer was gone as well. I have no idea who took them. You'll have to ask Signor Leonardo."

"Was Signor Castiglione in favor of selling shares to the Singapore bank?"

She didn't respond.

"Well was he?"

She linked her hands together and looked down at them.

"I don't know."

Craig was sure she was lying. He had already threatened obstruction of justice. Now he tried another tact. "You liked Signor Castiglione. I know that."

She nodded. "Very much."

"And I'm sure you want us to find out who was responsible for his murder?"

"Yes. Of course."

"Then you have to help me."

She began to cry again. "I'm frightened. Not for my job—for my life."

"I promise that whatever you tell me will never be disclosed to anyone other than Giuseppe. Not Dominic. No one."

"She studied his face, undoubtedly trying to determine if she could trust him."

Finally, she wiped her eyes with his handkerchief that she was still clutching and began in a stammering voice. "Signor Castiglione never closed the door to his office. So I heard things."

"What kind of things?"

"About two weeks ago, a man by the name of Lin Yu, the Director of a large Singapore bank, Pacific Sun, came to see Signor Castiglione."

At last, Craig felt as if he was getting somewhere.

"Lin Yu," she continued, "said that he wanted to make a major investment in our bank. Signor Castiglione told him it wasn't possible. So he raised the price. When Signor Castiglione still turned him down, he told Signor Castiglione to take his offer to the board, which he agreed to do. They scheduled another meeting the following week."

"Did Signor Castiglione take the offer to the board?"

"He did. I was at the board meeting. He argued against the transaction. The board agreed with him."

"Any dissenters?"

She shook her head. "No."

"Not even Signor Leonardo?"

"Correct. No one."

"What happened at the second meeting between Castiglione and Lin Yu?"

"There was a great deal of shouting. Signor Castiglione still refused to sell."

"What did Lin Yu say?"

"That he had powerful friends, and if Signor Castiglione didn't agree on the transaction, he would pay for it with his life."

"You heard him use those words, 'pay for it with your life?'"

"For sure. I would never forget that. I was surprised and frightened."

"Did they meet again?"

"No. But Thursday, two days before Signor Castiglione died, Lin Yu called him. I don't know what they said. Only that Signor Castiglione was very upset after the call. Then he called Signor Goldoni to meet him in Biarritz. That's all I know."

Craig thought about what she'd said. He didn't have any other questions. "You've been very helpful. Thank you."

"And you won't tell anyone other than Giuseppe what I said."

"I promise. I will not."

Craig then joined Giuseppe in his interviews with the officers. All were sticking with Dominic's story.

Afterward, the two of them left the bank's headquarters and dodged Milan's ubiquitous motor scooters while crossing the street en route to a small café two blocks away. Giuseppe was furious when he heard what

Craig had to say. "Those four were flat-out lying. I should charge them with obstruction."

"But I promised Donna we wouldn't use her."

"Yeah, I guess I can't."

"Forget them. They can't help us. Our next move is to go to Singapore and to speak with Lin Yu. Find out who his powerful friends are."

Giuseppe downed an espresso and said, "Let's wait twenty four hours to move up on Singapore. I want to give Jean-Claude a chance to locate the Russian killers from the fencing of the jewels. Also, for my investigators to examine bank files to check out the organized crime issue."

"Sounds reasonable."

"I'm going back to Rome. I'll call you tomorrow afternoon, or sooner, if I hear from Jean-Claude."

Once Giuseppe left, Craig called Lorenzo and went to see the lawyer who seemed stunned by what Donna had said about the bank takeover.

"I had no idea about any of this. I was not only Federico's lawyer, but his friend. He should have spoken to me about it."

"Do you doubt its accuracy?"

Lorenzo shook his head in dismay. "Donna is an honest woman. And Federico unfortunately sometimes confided in me and sometimes did not."

*   *   *

Still afraid of going home, Craig spent another night at the hotel Palazzo Parigi. The next morning, at five o'clock, he went running. Craig headed toward his favorite route in Milan. One of the city's most imposing sites was the Sforza Castle, a dominating brick and stone structure in the center of Milan surrounded by a moat. Construction had begun in the 15th century by Francesco Sforza whose family ruled the area. Later generations modified it. And now the castle was a major complex of museums including paintings, furniture, and archeology.

Craig liked this site for running because a vast green park area with winding paths spread out behind the castle. He had a regular route for a five-mile run, beginning at the castle and ending up there.

As Craig left the castle at the start of his run, the park was deserted and the sky was still dark. Normally when Craig ran, he tuned out whatever he was working on, but not today. He kept replaying in his mind everything he had learned about Federico's death. Donna was courageous, and she had given him his first real break, but he was still a long way from having any answers.

As he made the turn and headed back toward the castle, the sun was beginning to appear in the eastern sky. Nearing the castle, Craig, who had missed several days of running, was breathing heavily.

Suddenly, through the corner of his eye, he saw a glint of bright sunlight on his right next to a tree. Craig turned in that direction. The sun was reflecting from a gun pointed at him!

Instinctively, he dove off the path onto the grass. He hit the ground and rolled toward the rear entrance of the castle. He heard a gun being fired. A shot flew over his head.

Before the shooter had a chance to aim again, Craig raced into the castle. On the left, a wooden gate blocked the entrance to the museum. It was locked. Craig, leading with his shoulder, blasted through it, smashing the wood. He tore up the stairs to the second floor of the museum.

Glancing over his shoulder, he saw his assailant following him up the stairs. Immediately, he recognized the blond haired man: Igor's security guard who had patted Craig down when he had gone to see Igor.

A weapon, Craig told himself.

I need a weapon.

He ran through the second floor rooms until he came to the archeology section. A glass case on one side held a collection of knives. Craig grabbed a chair and used the legs to smash the glass. He reached in and pulled out a knife. Then he concealed himself, flat against a wall near the entrance to the room, the knife at his side, its blade sharp.

Gun in hand, the Russian ran in and looked around. He spotted Craig and shouted, "This bullet is from Igor."

As the Russian prepared to fire, Craig raised his right arm with the knife in his hand.

One chance is all I get.

Craig let go with the knife, aiming for the Russian's heart.

It hit the Russian in his chest, ruining his aim. The shot went up in the air against the ceiling.

The Russian collapsed onto his back. As Craig walked over, he saw the Russian was bleeding profusely.

"Help," he pleaded. "Help."

"Be glad to help you."

Craig took the Russian's gun and shot him, finishing the job.

He used his shirt to wipe the gun for prints. Then he tossed it on the ground and ran down the stairs and out of the museum.

When he was back in his hotel room and was ready to shower, his cell phone rang. It was Giuseppe.

"I heard from Jean-Claude. We caught a break."

Craig was excited. "What happened?"

Late yesterday afternoon, a Russian tried to unload some of the jewels in a shop in Marseilles where the owner buys pieces well below market value for cash. The owner recognized the pieces from the email he received from Jean-Claude so he bought them. But here's the better news."

"Tell me," Craig said impatiently.

"The owner has a hidden camera in the ceiling. He caught the Russian on video and forwarded it to Jean-Claude, who sent it to the Biarritz police. They made a match with Vladimir Radovich, the leader of a gang of Russian thugs who settled in the area when a large contingent of wealthy Russians bought homes in Biarritz. They've taken Radovich to the regional jail in Bordeaux."

"That's great. What's he look like?"

"Tall, about six-four, muscular. Why?"

"Amelie said the shooter was a tall guy."

"Sounds like our man."

"I think so."

"You and I should talk to him. I have a plane lined up to take me to Bordeaux. We'll swing by Milan to pick you up. Can you meet me at Linate at nine this morning?"

"I'll be there."

Northern Italy

Having slept three hours on the flight from Beijing, Zhou Yun arrived fully refreshed at Milan's Malpensa airport. It was ten minutes past eight in the morning. His unmarked Chinese military aircraft, with Zhou as the only passenger, taxied to a remote corner of the airfield. Through the window, Zhou saw a black sedan with tinted windows waiting.

In a show of Parelli's political clout that surprised and pleased Zhou, a crew member advised Zhou that the pilot had been informed that no customs or passport formalities would be required. The pilot and crew were directed to stay on the plane and await Zhou's return while the car took him to his meeting with Parelli.

Zhou immediately understood the significance of these arrangements. With no record of Zhou's visit, Parelli could later claim it never occurred. For the Italian political candidate, this secret meeting with Zhou was fraught with peril. At the same time, it drove home for Zhou how precarious Parelli's financial situation must be. Desperate men take high-risk chances.

Carrying a thin briefcase, Zhou bounded down the steps of the plane.

Without saying a word, the driver held open a back door for Zhou. Only the two of them were in the car when it passed through a military checkpoint at the back of the airfield.

The car made its way to the highway then sped south and west into the heart of the Piedmont region of Italy. Zhou admired the beautiful scenery, the lush, green rolling hills against the snowcapped Alps in the background.

This was Zhou's first trip to this region of Italy, and he made comparisons with China. He was struck by the relatively few cars on the road so close to major population centers, the clear blue sky without any smog, and the well-maintained roads. Along with the beauty, there was a striking tranquility he never felt in frenetic China.

Zhou thought about his brother who had a similar reaction to the south of France where he had purchased an estate. His brother would still be enjoying it if it weren't for Craig Page. He pounded his right fist into the palm of his left hand, again vowing revenge.

Perhaps, he would do something similar, Zhou thought. If his Italian operation went according to plan, he would acquire or build an estate along Lake Como or Maggiore and make that his base in the summer to escape the dreadful heat and pollution of China and all of its people. Everywhere people, people, and more people. With computers and cell phones, he could easily run his business empire from northern Italy two or three months a year.

Soon, they were in the heart of wine country. The home of Barolo and Barbaresco, two of the great wines of the world. Grapevines lined both sides of the road.

Half an hour later, the car slowed and turned right at a paved road blocked by a metal gate. On one side of the gate was a stone guardhouse. Two men in security uniforms brandishing automatic weapons stood on each side of the guardhouse. Another man was inside. As soon as the driver rolled down the window and nodded to the man inside, the gate swung open.

The road wound up a hill, slicing through vineyards. At the top, Zhou saw a two-story stone house, which had the look of a luxurious estate. This is no simple farmhouse, Zhou realized. Half a kilometer to the left was a large modern glass and steel building that had to be one of Parelli's wineries.

The car dropped Zhou off in front of the house. The door opened and Parelli, whom Zhou recognized from pictures, walked down the three stone steps to greet him.

"Welcome to the Parelli winery."

The two men shook hands, and Parelli led him into the house. Zhou saw a somber-looking man standing in a corner of the reception area, eyeing him suspiciously.

"I want to introduce Luciano, my closest advisor and confidante."

Luciano nodded without moving forward to shake Zhou's hand. He recalled what Qing had told him: that Luciano was opposed to Parelli meeting with Zhou.

"No one else is in the house," Parelli added. "I wanted us to have complete privacy."

"I appreciate that."

Parelli opened a bottle of wine and poured three glasses. He handed one to Zhou. "This is my '97 Barolo. One of the finest made in Italy during that extraordinary vintage," he said with pride.

Zhou sipped it and nodded. "It is incredible. I didn't think Barolo was capable of such finesse and elegance while having the depth and structure. I confess to being partial to great Bordeaux and Burgundy. But what you served me is in the same class."

"I appreciate that. Now I'd like you to come up to the second floor verandah. I want to give you a visual tour of the property from there."

Zhou followed Parelli up the stairs, both of them carrying their wine glasses. Glancing over his shoulder, Zhou saw Luciano remaining behind.

For the next twenty minutes as they stood outside on the stone deck, Parelli spoke enthusiastically about the property. When he was finished, Zhou asked, "Is there somewhere we can sit down to talk business?"

"My study across the hall. I'll get Luciano."

"I would prefer to talk to you alone."

"Luciano is involved in all details of my campaign."

"Afterwards, you can brief him as you believe appropriate."

That seemed to satisfy Parelli. He led the way to a study. One wall was lined with books, many of them leather bound.

Another had pictures of Parelli or his father accepting awards for their wines.

When the two men settled into leather chairs facing each other, Parelli began, "Qing Li, your associate, who met me in my Venice hotel room, said you were interested in contributing to my campaign. I told him I would be willing to listen to what you have to say without any commitments, of course."

In Parelli, Zhou recognized he was dealing with a savvy business-man. No point being vague or talking in riddles. "I'll put all my cards on the table. Your campaign is in trouble financially."

Parelli shook his head vigorously. "You have been misinformed. I—"

"If we are to do business, we must be candid with each other. Your debt to Turin Credit, Alberto Goldoni's bank, is now 310 million euros."

Parelli sat up with a start. "I can't believe Alberto spoke to you."

"He didn't. We live in the modern cyber world. Computers are not secure. There are no secrets in matters like this."

"You hacked into the computer at Goldoni's bank?"

"Hack is an awful term—with unpleasant connotations. I prefer to regard information on computers as available to those who have the technology to obtain it. So to continue, Goldoni will call those loans in a matter of days if you do not repay him. Your campaign will be finished. You will lose your farm and winery. You will be ruined."

Parelli's face was flushed. "These are only temporary obstacles." His voice displayed bravado. A false bravado, Zhou was convinced.

"Of course. Which I wish to help you overcome."

"How do you propose to do that?"

"As you're no doubt aware, I like wine and have recently acquired Chateau Margaux and Domaine Romanee Conti in France."

"I did hear that. Two of the great properties of the world."

"Now I would like to acquire the Parelli wine business."

"It's not for sale."

Zhou ignored him and continued speaking. "My financial people appraise it at roughly 200 million euros. I'm prepared to offer you one billion euros in a confidential transaction."

Parelli looked mystified. "I don't understand. You just said the property was worth 200 million."

"I want you to have the other 800 million for your political campaign. I think that should be enough for you to prevail in the election. But if you need more, I would be willing to increase the price."

Parelli was eyeing Zhou suspiciously.

"And why do you want me to win?"

"Because I believe in your cause. The New Italy Party. If you split the country as you propose, you will have a powerful economic nation in the north."

"Now it's my turn to speak candidly with you."

"Of course."

"I understand your motive. If I win, I'll be enormously grateful to you. And you would expect me to award construction and other contracts to your company and other Chinese firms. In short, you will have a foothold in the heart of Western Europe."

"I won't deny that. Friends help friends. That's the way of the world. It's a wonderful offer for you. With the money I'm providing, your New Italy Party will prevail in the election. You will be Prime Minister with the parliamentary majority you need to divide the country." Zhou paused for a minute then added, "I trust what I'm offering is acceptable to you."

Without answering, Parelli sipped some wine. He's blown away by my offer, Zhou thought. He needs a minute to think.

Finally, Parelli responded. "I am prepared to take your money. When I win, I will award construction and other contracts to your company or other Chinese firms whom you designate."

Zhou felt a surge of excitement.

"However—" Parelli sounded stern.

Zhou was worried about what was coming next.

"I will not sell the winery. Parellis have been making wine here for more than 100 years."

Zhou wasn't expecting this. "But neither your children nor grandchildren are involved in the wine business."

"Not now, but there is interest by one of my granddaughters. One day she will take control."

"Surely, you wouldn't reject all that I'm offering for that slender thread of a possibility."

Parelli looked offended. "If you truly believe that, then you do not understand me. Nor do you understand the Italian people. For us, family is above everything."

"Then I will offer a compromise."

"On this, there can be none."

"I will leave the Parelli name on the wine."

Parelli smiled. "When someone made a proposal like this to my father, he was fond of saying, 'You offer me the sleeves from your vest.' You insult me with this so-called compromise. Of course, you will keep the Parelli name on the wines. How many bottles do you think you would sell if you called it the Zhou Barolo?"

Parelli said it in a sarcastic tone. Zhou felt himself getting angry. He didn't like being ridiculed. It was so typical of the contempt Europeans displayed toward Chinese. But, he kept his wrath under control. They were close to an agreement. His primary objective, an economic foot in the door in Italy if Parelli prevailed, was within reach. Still, he refused to yield. He was determined to own the Parelli wine business. It was a matter of pride. Along with Margaux and DRC, he wanted a top Italian winery.

He decided to try another approach to persuade Parelli.

"As I have said, I am proposing a confidential transaction. However, as we both know, despite this there is always a possibility that one of your political opponents will learn that I have provided money to you. As long as it is in the context of the acquisition of your property, including the winery, that will seem justified. Without that fig leaf, we will be exposed."

Parelli shook his head. "In view of the disparity between what you will be giving me and the value of the property, that fig leaf, as you called it, will be an illusion."

"Perhaps. But it will give you something to argue about. Values are not so precise. Buyers often pay a premium. People will regard me as an eccentric. Someone from China who doesn't truly understand wine."

Zhou believed he was making a sound argument, but Parelli responded with a stone face. "I will not sell my winery."

Was Parelli bluffing? Zhou, who prided himself on reading the mind of his adversary in a negotiation, had no idea. He had never dealt with an Italian before. He didn't know how they operated. He did know, however, what he wanted: ownership of the winery. He also knew that Parelli needed a deal more than Zhou. Without it, Zhou would survive, but Parelli would be destroyed.

Calmly, Zhou stood up. "I appreciate your taking the time to talk with me, Mr. Parelli. I have enjoyed drinking your superb wine and viewing your property. It is unfortunate that we weren't able to reach an understanding. However, we're both businessmen. We realize this sometimes happens."

Parelli rose as well. When he remained silent, Zhou continued. "Now I'd appreciate it if you asked your driver to take me back to Malpensa Airport."

For a moment, Parelli stared hard at Zhou as if he were trying to read his mind from his face. Zhou showed him steely resolve. Then Parelli said, "Give me a moment to think about this."

"Certainly. As long as you like."

Parelli walked across the room to the window. While finishing his glass of wine, Zhou watched Parelli from behind as he looked out at his vineyards and the winery—the property for which he had a great attachment. He was obviously deep in thought, considering Zhou's offer.

After several minutes, Parelli whirled around and said, "How do we maintain confidentiality? If it ever came out that Chinese money was financing my campaign, even under the cover of the sale of my winery, I would have no chance of winning."

Zhou suppressed his joy at Parelli's words and responded in an unemotional tone. "I will have my lawyers draw up the agreement in the next several days. To deal with the confidentiality issue, the contract will be for the sale of the winery and other property. However, we will delay the closing of the transaction for one year. That will give you time to win the election and divide the country. Nothing will be disclosed now. And even when it is disclosed in a year, the purchase price will not be revealed."

"But I cannot wait a year for the money. I need it now."

"I understand. As soon as the papers are signed, I will place one billion euros in a numbered account in your name in a Swiss bank that has promised me complete confidentiality. You may draw on those funds immediately for your campaign. So there is no way you can be hurt by this transaction."

"You've thought of everything. Haven't you?"

"I've tried to, Signor Parelli. It is in both of our interests for you to win this election."

Parelli approached Zhou. "I don't know what the custom is in your country, but here we shake hands when parties reach an agreement."

Zhou reached out his hand. "We are in Italy. We will follow Italian customs."

Before leaving, Zhou reached into his bag to take out a cell phone, and handed it to Parelli. "This has a new encrypted technology which the NSA of the United States can't break. If you ever have to call me, use this phone. Turn on the power and press the number one. The call will go right to my matching phone."

On the ride back to the airport, Zhou relaxed, feeling very satisfied. He had gotten exactly what he wanted. With his financial help, he was confident Parelli would win.

For Zhou, this whole endeavor underscored the stupidity of Western democracy. With enough money, a candidate could get control of a country. Then he could wreck it. Or even dismantle it. Fortunately, nothing like that could ever happen in China.

Bordeaux

B efore the interrogation of Vladimir Radovich, Craig and Giuseppe met in the Bordeaux courthouse across from the prison with Jean-Claude, Giuseppe's French police contact, and Pierre Rousseau, the chief prosecutor for the District. Pierre, about forty, Craig guessed, had a beak for a nose. He was nattily dressed with a patterned silk Hermes tie, freshly pressed gray suit, and highly polished shoes. He had a haughty expression.

Craig was introduced by Giuseppe as "a good friend of Federico Castiglione and my consultant." His name wasn't given. Neither Frenchmen asked. Nor did they recognize Enrico Marino. Enrico's racing fame hadn't made it over the Alps.

As soon as Pierre uttered his first words, Craig disliked the prosecutor. Pointing to Craig, he said, "We can't have outsiders present for our internal deliberations. It violates protocol."

Craig doubted if Giuseppe would fight to keep him in the room. His fears were unjustified. "This is an EU matter. Not one governed by your Bordeaux protocol. I make the rules and I say that he stays."

Pierre turned to Jean-Claude expecting support but all he heard was, "Let's get started. Giuseppe, tell us what this is all about."

For the next twenty minutes, Giuseppe described in detail everything he and Craig had learned about Federico's murder. Pierre, taking careful notes, raised a question from time to time, which didn't add much. Craig thought he just wanted to act as if he was in charge.

When Giuseppe was finished, Jean-Claude took over, "When we arrested Radovich, I seized his cell phone and bank records. He had four calls with people in Moscow in the two days before the murder. The names of the people he spoke with had been blocked. I didn't want to involve the Russian police at that point."

"Wise decision," Giuseppe said. "With the corruption in Moscow, we can't risk tipping off anyone involved."

"Agreed," Pierre added.

"What about Radovich's Biarritz bank accounts?" Giuseppe asked.

"Patience. I'm getting there. 500,000 euros were transferred from a Moscow bank to Radovich's account the day after Federico's murder. No ID on the Moscow account."

"That's good work," Giuseppe said.

"With all of that," Pierre said, "we have a solid case against Radovich. I should be able to get him to confess to Federico's murder. So we can wrap the case up."

"That's not what we want," Craig interjected.

Pierre looked at him in surprise as if Craig had been permitted to hear the discussion but not participate.

"What do you mean?" Pierre asked.

"The endgame here isn't whether Radovich killed Federico. It's who hired Radovich to do it."

"I'll work on that as well."

Jean-Claude broke in. "I'm authorized by the minister to offer Radovich a light sentence in return for that information."

"I'll keep that in mind when I interrogate him," Pierre said.

"I'm planning to be in the room with you," Jean-Claude responded.

"No," Pierre said firmly. "I only talk to prisoners one on one. That's what works. . . . And I'm the best prosecutor in all of France with the highest conviction rate."

Craig and Giuseppe both looked at Jean-Claude. Would he dig in and argue? Even call the justice minister for support?

He didn't say anything. Craig didn't have a good feeling about this interrogation.

*   *   *

Craig, Giuseppe, and Jean-Claude were standing behind a one-way glass wall that permitted them to see into the interrogation room without the prisoner seeing them. They had ear phones to listen.

Wearing prison blues, Radovich entered the room with a swagger. He fit Amelie's description of being tall. On his face, he had what a high school friend of Craig's in Monessen, Pennsylvania described as "a shit-eating grin." No trembling or fear visible. The thought of going to prison for a long time for murder didn't seem to faze him.

Pierre came on strong. He told Radovich, "We have an eye witness who saw you kill Federico Castiglione." Without identifying Amelie as the witness, he described the crime exactly as it was committed. He also told Radovich about the Moscow phone calls and the deposit into his bank account.

Radovich showed no visible reaction.

Pierre then said, "You're going to prison for a long time. The only way you can get a light sentence is by confessing and telling us who hired you."

"I didn't do anything," Radovich said defiantly. "You have the wrong Russian. You Frenchmen always mix us up."

"Who'd you talk to in Moscow?"

"My mother," he replied contemptuously.

"And I suppose she sent you the money?"

"No. That came from my girlfriend. I'm a good fuck."

"You may be, but you're not a good liar. Where'd you find the jewels you tried to fence in Marseilles?"

"A box on the street in Biarritz."

Pierre shook his head. "That is about the stupidest story I've ever heard."

For the next half-hour, Pierre kept pressing Radovich and getting nowhere. Finally he quit.

So much for France's best prosecutor, Craig thought.

When the four of them assembled for a post mortem, Giuseppe said, "According to Amelie, there were two Russians in the house. A tall one and a short one. We have the tall one, and he won't talk. So Jean-Claude, you should have the French police in Biarritz double their effort to find the short one."

"Exactly what I was thinking. I'll let you know when we have him in custody."

Craig and Giuseppe left the others and went to a nearby brasserie for lunch, where Craig ordered a nicoise salad and Giuseppe a croque madame.

"I'm trying to raise my cholesterol." Giuseppe said.

Craig laughed. "Yeah, after the steak at your house, it should already be off the chart."

"Not with all the red wine we had. That cancels it out. It's my own Mediterranean diet."

The banter made Craig realize how much he liked Giuseppe and missed working with him.

While they were waiting for the food to come, Giuseppe's phone rang. Craig heard him say, "Yes . . . yes, I understand."

When he hung up, he looked glum. "There's nothing in the documents at Dominic's bank to suggest any involvement with organized crime."

"That's too bad. Next stop for us is Singapore to talk to Lin Yu."

"Agreed. I'll have to get approval for the trip from the Finance Department of the Italian Justice Ministry."

"But you work for the EU. Not Italy."

"Those are the new EU rules for my trips outside of the EU. I'll fly back to Rome today and try to get that approval as soon as possible."

"You won't have trouble, will you?"

"I shouldn't. This is the third Italian bank takeover by foreigners. If it continues, we'll lose control of our banking business and our economy will be in even worse shape. I don't know what's happening to my country that I love so much. Unemployment among young people aged 15 to 24 years is more than 40 percent. Almost 400,000 college graduates have left Italy to live elsewhere in the last decade, taking their degrees and education with them. Old age pensions are taking a huge bite out of our budget. Small businesses are shutting down in record numbers."

"I didn't realize it was that bad."

"Yeah. Our economy is in the toilet. We've consistently had bad leadership. And on top of all that, Parelli is an existential threat to the country."

"You're taking him seriously, too."

"The man's awful." Giuseppe was speaking with an intensity Craig rarely heard from him. "If Parelli were to win the election, it would be a disaster for Italy. Who else talked to you about Parelli?"

"Elizabeth during our brief dinner in Stresa. Speaking of disasters."

Lunch came. After eating some of his sandwich, Giuseppe said, "Listen, Craig, you can bite my head off if you want, but I have some advice for you."

"Have I ever been able to stop you from speaking your mind?"

"Okay, well here goes. I think you should call Elizabeth and have dinner with her in Paris this evening. Leave the brass knuckles and boxing gloves at home. Tomorrow, after I have my approval, I'll join you in Paris. We'll fly from there to Singapore."

This wasn't what Craig wanted to hear.

"Why are you playing matchmaker?"

"I like both of you. She was supportive and helpful to you when your daughter Francesca died. I saw how good the two of you were together, and—oh, the hell with it, that's only part of it."

A curtain of sadness descended on Giuseppe's face. Craig sat silent, waiting for his friend to continue.

"Antonia's death taught me that happiness and relationships like the one she and I had are precious. If you're fortunate enough to have one, then treasure it. You understand what I'm saying?"

When Craig didn't respond, Giuseppe added, "Don't be such a hard-ass fool. Remember, I was with you in Rome when you found out your daughter Francesca had been murdered. You couldn't help that." He sounded emotional. "You lost that relationship. This one with Elizabeth is in your hands. Don't piss it away."

"Okay. I'll call her. I hope she's still not putting her career first."

"She won't be. Trust me. I know Elizabeth. She'll be ready to start over with you. Just don't fuck it up. Oh, and by the way, tell her I sent regards."

Turin

Alberto Goldoni was wary when he received a call from William McKnight, a man he had never met, identifying himself as the head of the Victoria Bank in Hong Kong.

"I'm in Turin," McKnight said. "I'd like to meet you about a mutually beneficial business opportunity."

As McKnight talked, Alberto was working on his computer to confirm what McKnight was saying. It checked out. Victoria Bank was one of the largest in Hong Kong, and William McKnight was the President and CEO. Alberto was troubled by McKnight's call. Coming immediately after Federico's murder and the Singapore transaction with Federico's bank, this was a peculiar, Alberto thought. There had to be a relationship between these events.

He invited McKnight to come to his office in three hours. Before the meeting, Alberto had plenty to do.

He called in the head of the bank's IT department and his director of security. "Here's what I want you to do," he told the two men. "I'll be using the small conference room next to my office for a meeting. I want you to install a concealed video recorder and also concealed microphones. Can you do that in a couple of hours?"

"Definitely," one said.

"Absolutely," the other replied.

They were finished an hour before McKnight arrived.

The Hong Kong banker looked exactly like his picture on the computer. Alberto presented an amicable façade when he offered coffee, which McKnight declined, but all the while he was wary and on guard.

Smoothly, Alberto led to McKnight to one of the two chairs in a direct line of the video camera lens; he took the other one directly across from McKnight.

McKnight had asked for the meeting. Alberto let him talk first.

"As you are no doubt aware, my Victoria Bank is one of the largest in Hong Kong."

Alberto nodded.

McKnight continued. "I have had my people conduct research on Turin Credit. I'm tremendously impressed. Your bank is very efficiently run. Your percentage of under-performing loans, according to the recent study of the Bank of Italy, is one of the lowest in the country. You not only have a strong position in Italy, but you've effectively expanded throughout Europe and even into Turkey and elsewhere in the Middle East.

"On the other hand, the strength of Victoria Bank is in Asia, particularly in China and Southeast Asia. We have very little overlap.

In short, our two banks would be a perfect fit. Together, we could capitalize on global opportunities that individually would elude us."

"What is it you're proposing?"

McKnight cleared his throat. "I'd like to acquire your stock in Turin credit for 16 billion euros in an all cash transaction. I believe that's a considerable premium above your present value."

Alberto was stunned by the size of the offer, but he had no intention of selling. "I appreciate your interest," he said politely, "but my stock is not for sale. Nor am I seeking any foreign investors for Turin Credit."

"You don't think 16 billion is a generous offer?"

"The issue isn't the purchase price. My stock is simply not for sale."

McKnight smiled, showing nicotine-stained teeth. "Oh come now, Mr. Goldoni. We're both businessmen. We know that everything is for sale if the price is right. And as for my 16 billion, I have room to move. No one's first offer is ever their last."

Alberto looked squarely at McKnight. "Let me explain to you about Turin Credit. The bank was started by my great grandfather in 1920. He was a war hero of Italy in the First World War. Aside from the eight years that my great grandfather left Italy to go to New York in 1938, the bank has been in my family. My great grandfather turned it over to my grandfather, who built it into the second largest bank in Italy. My father, unfortunately, died young. So I succeeded my grandfather. With our international expansion, we have become the largest bank in Italy. One day my son, now a student at the London School of Economics, will succeed me."

"But with 16 billion euros you and your son will be able to live well."

"It's not a question of money. I promised my grandfather on his deathbed that I would never sell my interest in the bank."

"Humph," McKnight said dismissing Alberto's words. "Those promises are never intended to be taken seriously."

"Mine is. And even if I hadn't made it, I would want control of the bank to remain in the family. So I appreciate your coming, but our business is now over."

Alberto expected McKnight to rise and head for the door, but he remained seated.

"I understand you were good friends with Federico Castiglione," the Hong Kong banker said.

Alberto eyed him suspiciously. "That's right."

"Well it's very unfortunate what happened to him."

"What's your point?"

"Simply that we have a bizarre coincidence. Federico refused to approve an investment in his bank; he died in a jewelry robbery; the transaction went through; and now here I am offering to buy your interest in another bank."

When Alberto had been ten years old, his parents sent him to boarding school in Switzerland. There he had been bullied by Hans, a Dutch boy, two years older, who called Alberto "a Jew coward," beat him, and stole money from him. Alberto had been close with his grandfather. When he returned home on break, he told his grandfather what was happening. His grandfather enlisted the help of a tough longshoreman from Genoa who taught Alberto how to fight.

When he went back to school, he waited for Hans to attack him. Then he used everything he learned, effectively breaking Hans' nose, knocking out two of his teeth, and sending him to the local hospital. The school threatened to expel Alberto, but classmates came to his aid, testifying it was self-defense. In the end, they expelled Hans. No one ever bothered Alberto again. He became known as "Alberto the fighter." And right now, he was prepared to fight for what was his.

Outraged, Alberto shot to his feet. "Don't you threaten me, Mr. McKnight."

McKnight stood as well. He stared hard at Alberto, who refused to be intimidated and stared back. "I'm not threatening. Merely referring to your friend's death."

"Leave now, Mr. McKnight, or I'll call security to evict you."

McKnight handed Alberto his card. "Think about my offer, Mr. Goldoni." He walked toward the door. "Call me when you're ready to talk."

Alberto asked an armed guard to accompany McKnight on his way out.

Once McKnight left, Alberto gave an order to increase security at his home and office. Then he went home to tell Dora about his meeting with McKnight.

Her anger matched his. "This is a free democratic country. These people, whoever they are, can't force you to sell. And I assume you have no desire to accept his offer or to negotiate with him."

"None at all. I am just concerned about the danger I'm exposing us to. After what happened to Federico. I'm increasing security at home and the office. But let's be realistic. If someone wanted to kill me, they could find a way."

She tapped her foot on the floor. "I have an idea. Last year you worked with Giuseppe Mercurio, the Director of EU Counterterrorism in connection with money laundering by an Iranian."

Alberto nodded. "I liked him a lot."

"Then call him. If he'll see you now, fly to Rome immediately. Tell him about McKnight and enlist his help."

"Giuseppe's jurisdiction is in counterterrorism."

"McKnight's threats constitute terrorism. At least try to get Giuseppe's help."

"I'll do that."

Paris

Giuseppe proved to be correct. When Craig called Elizabeth from the airport in Bordeaux while waiting to board a flight to Paris and asked her to have dinner with him that evening, she said, "I'd love to."

She suggested nine o'clock at Apicius. "Jean-Pierre Vigato is the best chef in Paris. I did a profile on him for the paper a few months ago. And I've gotten to know Emanuelle. She'll give us a corner table where we can talk."

When he arrived in Paris, Craig checked into the Hotel Bristol. As he was dressing for dinner, his phone rang. It was Giuseppe.

"I just finished the most remarkable meeting," Giuseppe said. "Alberto Goldoni flew down from Turin to see me. He had a visit from William McKnight, the president of a large Hong Kong bank, Victoria. McKnight offered to buy the stock in Alberto's bank. When he refused to sell, McKnight referred to what happened to Alberto's good friend

Federico and told him to think about it. Alberto had made a secret video recording of McKnight's visit. He gave me a copy. McKnight is clearly threatening Alberto."

"What exactly did McKnight say about Federico?"

"It's very unfortunate what happened to his good friend Federico Castiglione."

"Subtle."

"Yeah. Real subtle. Then while Alberto was in the air on the way to Rome, his wife called and told him about a more explicit threat which had been left on the answering machine at home. 'Soon you'll be dead, Alberto.' This was from a man with a Russian accent."

"What did you tell Alberto?"

"To get security at his office and home. Which he had already done, and to let me know if he hears from McKnight again."

"How's Alberto taking it?"

"He's madder'n hell. Alberto's a fighter. I'm sure he's frightened, but he's not showing it."

"Do you have enough to arrest McKnight for extortion?"

"Possibly, but it won't do any good. You're the one who taught me the only way to kill a snake is by cutting off its head. Not the tail."

"I guess that's right."

"I'll let you know if I hear anything else. Meantime, what about Elizabeth? Are you having dinner with her this evening?"

"Speaking of people who don't quit—yes, nag."

"Tell her I said hello."

"Will do."

"I'm supposed to meet someone from the Finance Department of the Justice Ministry this evening to get approval for my trip to Singapore. I'll let you know what happens."

"You're not worried. Are you?"

"With those bean counters you never know."

*   *   *

Elizabeth and Craig arrived at the same moment at the break in the stone wall, which was the entrance to the courtyard on Rue Artois in front of Apicius. The restaurant was housed in an historic Parisian mansion. Determined to make this evening work, he kissed her on each cheek and said, "So glad you could have dinner with me."

She responded with a smile and took his arm as they walked along the stone path leading to the restaurant. He had to admit she looked fantastic. She must have gone shopping. She was wearing a short red, clinging sheath dress.

Inside, Emanuelle greeted them, then lead the way to a cozy and discrete corner table in the center room, right next to the floor to ceiling French windows that faced the courtyard.

Moments later, a waiter brought over glasses of champagne. "Jean Pierre wanted you to have these," he said.

Raising his glass, Craig said, "To new beginnings."

She raised hers as well and tapped it against his. "I'll drink to that."

After sipping, Craig asked, "How was Venice?"

She gave him a report of the charismatic Parelli's speech and the audience's reaction. Then told him what happened in Parelli's hotel suite when she tried to get the interview. The prostitute didn't interest Craig, but Parelli's Chinese visitor made him wonder what was happening.

"Smart move," he told her. "Taking the Chinese man's picture."

Emanuelle came over and took their order. Fois gras and frogs legs for her; crab with vegetables and rack of lamb for him. And of course a chocolate soufflé to share for dessert. He ordered a 2005 Premier Cru Chambolle Musigny from Roumier.

When she was gone, Elizabeth said, "I have to tell you about my meeting with Jonathan Hanson."

"Who is he?"

He had my job at the newspaper until twelve years ago. Another expat living in France."

As she repeated her discussion with Hanson, Craig ate a piece of bread from time to time. At the end, she said, "Hanson's convinced that Parelli prevailing in the election and dividing the country would be a disaster for Italy, and I intend to stop him."

Craig was frowning.

"You don't agree?"

"Look, I think Parelli has to be stopped because of the Chinese involvement in his campaign, but apart from that it's not for you or me to take a position. It should be up to the Italians. Perhaps dividing Italy might be best for the south as well as the north."

Elizabeth looked surprised. "You're joking. Right?"

"No. I'm serious."

"I can't believe it." She sounded outraged. "Then you must think Lincoln was wrong going to war to keep the United States together."

"Well let's put it this way. Suppose there had been a vote in the entire United States and the people in both the North and South wanted to split the country. Why not? Would the two parts of the United States be worse off than the dysfunctional political mess we now have trying to get red and blue states to work together on anything?"

"There would be slaves in the South. You think that's a good idea?"

Craig laughed. "Don't be ridiculous. Even in the South, slavery would have ended in another decade or so. The world was changing. The point is that the South could follow a conservative view of less government; and the North a liberal view of more government. Both would be getting what a majority of their people wanted. Isn't that what democracy is?"

"So you think Lincoln was a villain, not a hero?" she sounded exasperated and looked flushed.

Craig knew he should break off the discussion but he had to keep going.

"What I'm staying is that secession may not have been such a bad idea. Plenty of reasonable people said that at the time."

"For a smart man, you sometimes say dumb things. You may look different, but you have the same personality. Name three of those reasonable people."

"Truce," Craig said, gaining control. "Let's end this discussion." He didn't want this evening to conclude in disaster like the last one.

"That's okay with me."

Their first courses came. They traded tastes. Both were sublime.

After eating a little, Elizabeth asked Craig whether he had made any progress in finding Federico's killer. He described everything he had done with Giuseppe. "Who, by the way, sends his regards."

He was still talking, and they were drinking wine when the main courses came. The lamb was great and perfect with the wine.

"There's one other piece to the puzzle," Craig said. "Then you'll have everything."

"What's that?"

He told her about Giuseppe's meeting this afternoon with Alberto Goldoni and the threat McKnight made to Alberto. "What happened to Federico, and now Alberto, can't be random events. Someone must be masterminding large investments in Italian banks and using surrogates to do their dirty work."

Elizabeth dropped her fork with a clink on the plate. Other diners looked at her.

"What's wrong?" he whispered.

"Did you say that Alberto's takeover offer came from Victoria Bank of Hong Kong?"

"Correct. Why?"

"I could be wrong, but . . ." She sounded excited and pulled the iPhone from her purse. She held it up. "May I?"

"Sure."

She pushed a few buttons, then said, "Exactly what I thought. Through a long and convoluted ownership chain, Victoria Bank of Hong Kong is owned by one of Zhou Yun's banks."

He gave a long, low whistle. "Which means that Zhou's probably behind all the Italian bank transactions and Federico's murder."

"That may be a stretch, but hopefully, you'll be able to establish he was behind the transaction with Federico's bank when you and Giuseppe go to Singapore."

"But why just the banks in Italy? Zhou Yun thinks big."

"What do you mean?"

"You're the one who saw a Chinese man in Parelli's suite. You sent me his picture."

She nodded.

"Suppose Zhou is behind Parelli's campaign, making a play for political as well as economic control of Italy."

She smiled. "Same old Craig. Trying to find Zhou, like his brother, responsible for everything."

"But it is something Zhou would do. You have to admit that."

She nodded.

Craig continued, "Then, if—," raising his voice a little with excitement.

"Sh. Not so loud."

"Okay," he lowered his voice to a whisper, "then if Parelli won the election and divided the country, Zhou and China would have a strong position in Parelli's northern Italy and a foothold in Europe. That would have a devastating effect on the United States. China is now challenging the United States as the dominant world power. In many respects they are our enemy. This will give them influence in NATO and in the EU. The entire US–European alliance will be at risk—our most important relationship. We can't let this happen."

She placed her hand on top of his. "Whoa, Craig slow down. Linking Zhou with Parelli is more than a stretch. It's a leap into the unknown. How do you intend to prove it?"

"You can do it with the picture of the Chinese man in Parelli's suite on your smart phone. Suppose you sent it to your Beijing Bureau Chief and asked if he recognizes the man as somebody who works for Zhou."

"The Internet censors in Beijing would never let it go through, and I'd be putting my reporter in danger. I'll have to find another way to get him to see it. But first, I'll try to arrange an interview with Parelli. Maybe I can get him to talk about his Chinese support."

"You really think he'd do that?"

"My father taught me if you throw a rock up in an apple tree, sometimes you get an apple. If Parelli did, I could write it up in the newspaper. That would expose Zhou Yun and kill Parelli's chances."

Craig looked alarmed. "That could be dangerous. Zhou plays rough."

She reached across the table and touched his hand. "Thanks, Craig, for your concern. We don't know that Zhou's involved, but I'll be careful."

Craig was very pleased at how well the evening was going. It really did seem like old times for the two of them.

The luscious dark chocolate soufflé arrived for them to share. Jean-Pierre came out of the kitchen and added an exquisite sauce to the center of the soufflé.

Midway through the course, Craig's phone rang. He quickly pulled it from his pocket and looked at the caller. "Giuseppe," he told Elizabeth.

"You better take it."

Craig answered.

"Hope I'm not disturbing anything," Giuseppe said.

"Just a delicious dessert Elizabeth and I are having."

"I have bad news."

"What happened?"

"The bean counter in the Finance Department vetoed my trip to Singapore."

Craig was astounded. "How stupid can he be?"

"They're squeezing every euro until it bleeds. Italy. The EU. Our economies are continuing to contract. Deflation is a possibility. People are scared. They're behaving irrationally." Giuseppe sounded dejected.

"Can you appeal to his boss?"

"Unlikely to succeed."

"What do you think we should to?"

"Could you go yourself?"

"I don't know. I'm thinking. I'll let you know."

"Sorry, Craig. Really, I am."

"Yeah. I know."

He told Elizabeth what happened.

"That sucks," she said.

Craig felt a surge of anger. "I hate the damn bureaucrats in government everywhere. In Europe. In the United States. They're all the same. They're the reason I quit the CIA the first time. Some power hungry jerk gets appointed to an important job and thinks he's a statesman like Winston Churchill.

"Can you go yourself?"

"I could. Obviously, money's not the issue, and I'm not beholden to any bureaucrats, but I wouldn't be able to accomplish a damn thing. I'll need governmental authorization to see the Singapore banker. Winning the race in Stresa won't do the trick. I'm stuck."

Her eyes were closed. He guessed she was deep in thought. Craig didn't want to interrupt her. Meantime, he was thinking about Zhou

Yun. Craig was glad the Chinese industrialist was involved. Craig was now convinced that Zhou Yun, and not his brother, had been responsible for the death of Francesca, Craig's daughter. It was Zhou Yun who had been in Calgary meeting with Canadian oil companies. But his brother was in Beijing at the time of Francesca's death. Zhou Yun must have given the order to murder the nosey reporter. Now Zhou Yun had given the order for Federico's murder. And would Alberto be next?

Craig decided he had to come out of hiding. He couldn't let this evil man continue.

Elizabeth opened her eyes and said, "I have an idea for you. Use your relationship with Betty Richards. She's still the CIA director. Fly to Washington and have her authorize your trip as a US representative."

"You think there's enough United States interest?"

"I know there is. What happens in Europe and Italy always affects the United States. You just told me about the threat to NATO. Besides, they're paranoid about China in Washington. Lots of Americans fear it's only a matter of time until China overtakes the United States as the world's dominant superpower. Or at least pulls even. China's advance into Europe would feed that paranoia. Anything that would slow down China's march toward dominance would gain the approval of those people."

"I'm convinced. I love your idea. I'll fly to Washington tomorrow."

She smiled and said, "I hope you don't take an early plane."

He moved his hand beneath the table, reached under her skirt, and stroked her thigh. It was warm and soft. "I remember that Air France had a flight around four in the afternoon."

"They still do. It leaves at 4:25."

"Sounds perfect."

Craig paid the bill and they left the restaurant. Walking the six blocks back to the Bristol where he was staying, along the Rue St. Honore, they had their arms around each other, like a couple of young lovers. Alone in the elevator, on the way to the sixth floor, he pulled her close and kissed her. Her arms were tight around his back.

In the corridor, she whispered, "Oh Craig, I've missed you so much."

"And I've wanted you."

Once they were in the room, Craig kicked the door shut. He held her tight, kissing her passionately. She was clutching him. They were both on fire after twenty-one months apart. She pulled away. "Oh Craig. Oh Craig."

He ran his hand over her arm, gently caressing her skin. Then the back of her neck. He unzipped her dress and let it slip to the floor.

She was wearing a gorgeous and sensuous yellow silk bra and bikini panties. He remembered buying them for her in Corsica.

As he ran his fingers over her back, she undid his belt and unzipped his pants.

Craig unsnapped her bra and caressed her breasts. He lowered his hand down and took each of the nipples into his mouth—first one; then the other. He reached into her silk panties, to her moist folds of skin. As he touched her, she moaned, "Oh Craig, that feels so good."

His erect prick was poking out through his shorts. She slipped them down and wrapped her hand around it.

"To bed," she said with urgency. "To bed."

She stretched out on her back and he entered her, while giving her a long, deep kiss. When he pulled his head away, their fused bodies moved together. Faster and then faster.

Being inside of her felt wonderful. Fabulous.

He could sense she was on the verge of climax and he held back, waiting for her. When she cried out in ecstasy, he exploded with her.

Moments later, he rolled off and she snuggled in his arms. "I'm so happy," she said. "So happy."

"You can't believe how much I missed you."

They woke up at eight, made love again, and had room service bring breakfast.

"Don't you have to go to work today?" he asked.

"Not until you leave for the airport."

It was a gorgeous summer day. A time for lovers in the city of love. They walked through the Tuileries holding hands. They crossed the Pont Neuf to the left bank. Then walked along Boulevard St. Germain. They ate mussels, washed down by Meursault, at a small bistro near St. Sulpice.

She checked her watch. "You better get going."

They took a cab back to the Bristol where he stuffed his clothes into his wheelie suitcase.

At the front door, they kissed one more time before he climbed into the cab to the airport.

Beijing

Zhou had received a call from McKnight, still in Turin, following the Hong Kong banker's meeting with Alberto Goldoni. "I'm sorry," he had said. "I wasn't able to reach an agreement for the investment you wanted." An angry Zhou cursing under his breath ordered McKnight to fly directly to Beijing. "Don't even stop in Hong Kong. We have to discuss next steps."

Their meeting had been set for ten in the morning, but at that time Zhou was in his private gym adjacent to his office pedaling on a stationary bike. Following Zhou's instructions, his secretary led McKnight into the exercise room.

By forcing McKnight to stand in front of him to conduct their conversation while he pedaled, Zhou wanted to humiliate McKnight.

"You're a failure," Zhou shouted at McKnight. "I give you one simple job to do, and you can't do it."

McKnight stood up straight and stared at Zhou.

"Goldoni's not willing to sell. He promised his grandfather on his deathbed that he'd keep the bank stock in the family."

"I don't care about Goldoni's grandfather. How much did you offer?"

"Sixteen billion."

"I told you to offer 20."

"There was no point going any higher," he said defiantly. "Goldoni made it clear that money wasn't the issue."

"Did you let him know if he didn't sell, he'd end up like Federico?"

"I made a reference to Federico."

Zhou stopped pedaling and stared hard at McKnight. "You made a reference," he said contemptuously.

"That's right."

"You're a fool. You should have done more than make a reference. Goldoni has to understand he'll be dead if he doesn't sell."

"I thought that would be too much for our first meeting. I left him enough to think about."

"Humph. I want you to go back to Turin, meet with Goldoni, go up to 20 billion, and make it clear what will happen to him if he doesn't sell. Do you understand?"

"I doubt if it will work."

"Do it anyhow. And I'll give you an incentive to close this with Goldoni. If you don't, you'll lose your position as CEO of Victoria bank and I'll make sure that you're criminally charged with illegal currency transfer and thrown into a Chinese jail."

Zhou paused for a moment to let his words sink in. McKnight's usually ruddy face had turned ashen. "Now I think you understand what's at stake."

"I understand."

"Good. Get out of here. I want you to go back to Italy and get the job done. And to help you, I'm sending Qing Li, one of my people, with you. Talk to my secretary. She'll handle the flight arrangements for both of you."

Ten minutes after McKnight staggered out, Zhou's secretary called to say, "Arrangements have been made for Mr. McKnight and Qing to fly to Turin. Also, the United States Secretary of the Treasury, Winston Tyler, just arrived for his meeting with you."

"Fix him coffee. Tell him I'm in a meeting. I'll be there shortly."

Zhou was wondering why Tyler had wanted this meeting on short notice. He hadn't been willing to disclose a topic. He said it was better if they spoke in person.

That was fine with Zhou. He had something he wished to extract from Tyler at the meeting. Zhou finished his hour on the bike, showered, dressed, and went back to his office.

The heavyset American with a shock of gray hair and wire frame glasses, dressed in a three piece navy suit, was seated in the secretary's suite, dozing.

"Ah, Winston," Zhou said in a booming voice.

Tyler woke up with a start and sprang to his feet looking embarrassed. He straightened the gold chain running across his vest. "Long flight," he said. "I can never sleep on them. The plane was late so I came here right from the airport."

"I understand. Come in to my office. Would you like some coffee?"

"No thanks. I've had quite a bit."

When they were seated at the conference table, Zhou said, "You were very mysterious about the reason for this meeting. What do you have in mind?"

Tyler coughed and cleared his throat. "The United States has a large quantity of bonds maturing on August 1st."

"I'm aware of that. It's 3.3 trillion dollars worth, to be precise. The Chinese government owns 65 percent of those bonds."

"We plan to roll the maturing bonds over with new issues totaling the same face amount."

"I anticipated that. You've made no strides in reducing your deficit. So you have to continue borrowing to keep your government operating."

Zhou loved goading Tyler, who looked annoyed but didn't respond to the barb. Instead, he said, "I wanted you to know about our plans. I was hoping to obtain a commitment from you that China would roll over its holdings, investing the amounts coming due in the new issues."

"If we didn't," Zhou said, "your government would be in big trouble. We're by far your largest creditor. If we took the cash from the maturing issues and didn't invest in the new ones, you couldn't pay your bills."

"We'd find another purchaser," Tyler said. His words had a hollow ring.

"Perhaps, but only at a much higher rate of interest, which would damage your economy. You may act as if you're in control of your financial destiny, but we both know you're not. So let's not play games."

For a moment, Tyler looked flustered. Then he recovered. In a bold tone, he responded, "The leverage you believe you have is meaningless. Our two economies are so interwoven. I'm sure you read the book I wrote on the subject when I was still a professor at Princeton. If you damage our economy, it will boomerang back to yours. I don't have to remind you that the United States is far and away the largest consumer of goods manufactured in Chinese plants, which employ millions. If our economy suffers, your factories will have to lay off people, and you will face massive unrest. So for better or for worse, our economies are joined together."

"The difference is we could manage unrest caused by economic decline. You could not," Zhou said confidently.

"You mean with tanks in the streets again. We still remember what happened in Tiananmen Square."

"And we have gone on from there to a massive economic surge, while your economy has barely expanded. It's only a matter of time until we pass you in GDP."

Tyler coughed and cleared his throat again. "This isn't the kind of talk we should have among friends. Let's return to the purpose of my visit. I would like your commitment to invest in the new issue at the same level of your maturing bonds. It's in both of our economic self-interest."

Zhou was ready to use his leverage on Tyler who was here as a bond salesman. "On two conditions. First, your new issue must primarily be short term. We fear inflation and increased interest rates and do not want the value of our investment eroded."

Tyler hesitated for a second, and then said, "I can live with that. Most of the bonds will be five years or less. What's your second condition?"

"You may have heard about investments in three banks in Italy by foreign banks."

"Yes. The ones in Milan, Bologna, and Verona."

"Precisely. And there maybe others as well. I want you to make certain your government does not intervene or work with the EU to stop these purchases. Rather, you will let the free market take its course."

Tyler looked bewildered. "Are you behind these purchases?"

When Zhou didn't immediately respond, Tyler answered his own question. "Of course you are. Or you wouldn't have raised the issue. But these matters are outside my jurisdiction as treasury secretary. I'm not the president or the secretary of state, and I can't control them. If they decide to become involved, then—"

Angrily, Zhou pounded his fist on the table. "If you want the People's Republic of China to purchase your bonds on August 1st, then you had better make certain that the US government does not intervene in Italy. Am I making myself clear?"

Zhou was bluffing. He was well aware of the damage that would be done to China's economy and resultant civil unrest in the country if the American economy were to go into a tailspin. The consequences for China would be devastating. Zhou could never let it happen, but Tyler didn't know that. Zhou stared hard at Tyler to reinforce the bluff. He wasn't sure how Tyler would respond.

The American tapped his fingers on the table. "You have to understand how our government works. These are issues of foreign policy, and I only deal with—"

"Are you telling me, Professor, that you never meet with the president or the secretary of state?"

"Yes, but," Tyler sputtered.

"Then talk to them. Persuade them."

Tyler puckered up his lips. For a full minute he didn't respond. He's weak, Zhou decided from Tyler's anguished expression. This man is a university professor. He doesn't belong in a powerful position as treasury secretary.

"I'm not sure," Tyler finally said, "they'll listen to me."

"Then I'll give you an incentive to make them listen."

"What's that?"

"If you don't persuade them to listen, and your government intervenes in Italy, China will not buy your bonds."

Tyler looked pale. "I'll do my best to keep them from intervening in Italy."

"Doing your best is not enough. You must succeed. Otherwise you can find another customer for your bonds."

Washington

Craig met Betty in her CIA director's office on the seventh floor of the agency's Langley complex. The office Craig had occupied for a few short weeks, twenty-one months ago.

When he signed in at the reception desk as Enrico Marino and showed his ID. George Thomas, the broad-chested African American with whom Craig frequently discussed the Nationals, didn't bat an eye.

Craig had avoided saying anything for fear George would recognize his voice.

"Someone will escort you to the director's office, Mr. Marino," he said.

Craig nodded. He followed his escort along the corridor to the elevator and then to the director's office.

Betty was waiting for him at the entrance to the suite. With her secretary watching, and listening, she said, "Well, well, it's Enrico Marino. The famous race car driver."

Again, he nodded.

She led him into her office and closed the door. She was shaking her head and smiling as they sat on a sofa and chair in the sitting area in one corner.

"Listen Craig," Betty said, "I understand you had a good dinner in Paris with Elizabeth."

Craig was flabbergasted. "You already heard from her."

"To use one of your favorite expressions, the sisterhood at work. I like Elizabeth."

"I like her, too! What else did she tell you we did together?"

"She didn't. I can only imagine. What brings you to Washington?"

"I'm surprised Elizabeth didn't tell you that, too."

"Not a word. I'm anxious to hear."

"I need your help in saving Italy."

Craig felt as if he had dropped a live grenade into Betty's lap. Her expression was grim.

"I didn't know that Italy was in danger."

"Well it is."

"That's what I like about you, Craig. You never deal with the normal small issues I'm used to facing, like a terrorist planning to hijack an airplane or blow up an embassy, or the Russians spying on our embassy in Moscow. With you, it's always whole countries at risk."

"Actually, if we don't do something, other countries in Europe could be as well."

"Okay. I'm ready to listen. Start at the beginning and take it slow. After twenty-one months in this job and forty-four trips to the Hill to testify before congressional committees, my brain neurons are beginning to calcify."

"They don't calcify. They just stop reproducing."

"Thanks for pointing that out. It makes me feel much better."

Craig talked for almost an hour about Federico's murder, Italian bank takeovers, and Chinese involvement in Parelli's campaign. At the end he said, "I know Zhou is heavily involved in the bank takeovers. I suspect he may be supporting Parelli."

"But you don't have any evidence of that."

"Correct. However, based on Elizabeth seeing a Chinese man in Parelli's suite in Venice, there is some Chinese involvement."

"He could have been delivering carryout for all you know."

"No delivery man ends up in the boss's bedroom."

She sighed.

God, she seems to be tired, he thought. The job must be getting to her.

"What would you like me to do?" she asked.

"You sent me to Argentina as your special representative. Now I'd like you to send me to Singapore—as your personal representative, in order to compel Lin Yu, a Singapore banker, to tell me who was behind his investment in the bank in Milan and who was responsible for Federico's murder."

"And you don't have any personal motives here. Do you? You're not hoping Lin Yu points the finger at your old enemy Zhou Yun so you can nail Zhou for Federico's murder and gain revenge for Francesca's death and for disrupting your life."

"That thought never even crossed my mind."

"I figured as much."

"But now that you mention it, I guess it could be a by-product of saving Italy."

Betty took a deep breath, stood up, and paced around the office for a moment.

"I can't send you to Singapore without President Worth's approval. My relationship with him is different than what I had with Treadwell. Worth's a good man, although a little timid sometimes. Have you ever met him?"

"No."

"He's heard of Craig Page. And he's grateful for what Craig Page did in Argentina. So you have that going for you. Also, he's worried about increasing Chinese power. He doesn't want us to drop to second place on his watch. So that's a plus."

"You want me to go with you to meet with Worth about this?" Craig was hoping the answer was, "yes."

"That's what I was thinking. We'll have to tell him about your Enrico Marino new ID."

"That's okay with me. I'm not worried about Worth selling me out to Zhou."

Betty picked up the red phone on her desk. He was impressed at how easily she got through on a direct line to President Worth. No secretary involved. At the end of the conversation, he heard her say, "Thirty minutes is good, Mr. President. We'll be there."

They took the chopper to the White House.

Once the three of them were in the Oval Office, standing on the royal blue carpet with the presidential seal in the center, Worth pointed to Craig and said to Betty, "You told me you were bringing Craig Page with you, but he doesn't look like the pictures of Craig Page I've seen. In fact, he looks a lot like Enrico Marino, the Italian race car driver."

Worth winked at Craig and pointed to the living area where the three of them sat down.

"Would you like to tell me how Craig Page, America's super spy, became Enrico Marino, the race car driver?" Worth said.

"It's a long story, Mr. President."

"I'd love to hear it. I have a great deal of appreciation for what you did for our country in Argentina as well as in past missions."

Mindful of the time demands of the president, Craig compressed his story to a ten-minute summary. At the end, Worth said, "Are you still worried about Zhou Yun seeking revenge?"

Craig was impressed that Worth immediately cut to the heart of the matter.

"I am, Mr. President, but I don't live my life in fear. If he finds out who I am, and comes for me, I'm prepared to defend myself."

"I don't doubt that at all. Now what's this about today?"

Craig glanced at Betty to see if she wanted to make the presentation to Worth, but she nodded to him. So Craig told Worth what was happening in Italy and why he wanted to go to Singapore as an American representative. He decided to omit Chinese involvement with Parelli because, as Betty had pointed out, that had not yet been established. Even without Parelli, and merely dealing with the Milan bank transaction, Zhou and the Chinese were involved, which should be enough for Worth.

When Craig was finished, Worth was nodding. Craig took this as a positive sign.

"You've presented me with a troublesome set of facts," Worth said. "I'd like to know if you're right about Zhou and the Chinese trying to take over Italian banks. They might then try to take over other banks in Europe. We can't let that happen. On the other hand . . ."

Oh, oh, Craig thought. What's coming next.

"On the other hand, the Europeans should be out front on this. Perhaps, Craig should brief them on what he's learned."

Betty had that special look in her eyes, which Craig recognized meant that she had just been served a pitch she planned to hit out of the park.

"With all due respect, Mr. President, lately the Germans and French have been rejecting everything we suggest."

Worth ran a hand through his hair. "I guess that's right."

Craig exhaled with relief. "Thank you, Betty. Does that mean I can go to Singapore as a presidential envoy to try to get the facts from Lin Yu, the Singapore banker?"

"Absolutely," Worth said. "Pick another false name. Betty will give you an ID. I would like you to involve Jennifer Nelson, our ambassador in Singapore. Have her go with you to your meetings. She's smart, politically savvy, and knows the country."

"I'll do that Mr. President."

"Good. I want you to pull out all the stops. Threaten that the United States will blacklist Lin Yu's bank and put it on a list like Iranian banks that US firms won't be able to do business with. I want you to find out who was responsible for the transaction with Federico's bank and his murder. Was it Zhou Yun or someone else."

"I'll be firm about this, Mr. President. I promise you that."

"Good. I want you to be."

"Oh God," Betty said. "Don't encourage Craig anymore. He's generally out of control."

"I never believed that the meek will inherit the earth," Craig said. "We unfortunately live in a brutal world where might prevails. Timidity in dealing with people like Zhou Yun is a prescription for failure and disaster."

On the way to the airport to catch the flight to Singapore, Craig's phone rang. It was Jonathan, the bank consultant in London.

"Just wanted to pass along a little news."

"Sure. Go ahead."

"Those Swiss bank accounts you were interested in have been moved to Moscow."

"A real shame. What happened to their owner?"

"The news must have upset him. He had a fatal heart attack."

"Yes!" Craig cried out. "Yes."

Kuznov's people must have killed Igor and made it look like a heart attack.

Craig breathed a sigh of relief. He'd never have to worry about Igor sending someone to kill him again.

Northern Italy

In the Venice hotel suite, Luciano had given Elizabeth a card with both his cell phone number and his office number at Parelli campaign headquarters in Milan. She tried the cell first. When that kicked over to voice mail, she left her name and number and dialed the office.

A man answered, "This is Stefano." He sounded like a young man.

"I'd like to speak to Luciano, please."

"He's ill and no longer with the campaign."

Elizabeth wasn't surprised based on how Luciano had looked in the Venice hotel room.

"I'm sorry to hear that, I'm Elizabeth Crowder, foreign news editor of the International Herald. I'd like to arrange an interview with Signor Parelli."

"Please hold for a minute. I'll check his availability."

Stefano came back a moment later. "Signor Parelli said he'd be pleased to give you an interview. Can you come to his farm in Piedmont tomorrow morning at ten?"

Elizabeth was delighted. "I'll be there."

"Good. I'll email you directions."

*　　　*　　　*

The next morning, Elizabeth took an early plane from Paris to Malpensa where she rented a car. The Parelli farm was south and west of the airport in the heart of Piedmont, the most prestigious wine territory in all of Italy.

She arrived a couple of minutes before ten on a cloudy overcast day. A maid answered the doorbell and asked Elizabeth, who was holding a case with her laptop, to wait. A few minutes later, she saw Parelli charging down a circular staircase dressed in a pair of khakis and a light blue shirt open at the neck. He seemed full of energy and vitality. If she hadn't known his age, she would have guessed fifty or fifty-five.

He walked up, kissed her on both cheeks, and said, "Well, well, the famous Elizabeth Crowder. It's my honor to be interviewed by such a well-known journalist. I just didn't think you'd be so attractive."

Talk about pouring it on thick, she thought.

"I subscribe to your newspaper," he continued, "and regularly read your articles. The analysis is usually excellent—although, I thought you got a little carried away with that Savior or Sinner headline."

"I'm flattered you read it."

"The trouble with our Italian papers is they're too provincial. We don't get much news outside of Italy. For that, I need your paper."

"I appreciate your taking the time from your busy schedule to talk with me. I'd like this to be an in-depth profile."

"Excellent. That's what I was hoping for. In order to understand my motivation, you'll have to take a little walk with me." He pointed to her feet and her white leather shoes with one and a half inch heels. "Can those shoes handle a mile on a dirt road?"

"Signor Parelli—"

"Please. Roberto."

"Okay, Roberto. These shoes could handle twenty miles on a dirt road."

"Good. Let's go."

As they walked he talked about the history of the farm, how many generations of Parellis had made wine here, and how much the winery meant to the family. "It's not just a business for the Parellis. It's a source of pride. We want to make the best wine in all of Italy. The best wine in the world."

Parelli was charming. Listening to him speaking in his melodious voice, she found herself being captivated by him.

He stopped and pulled some grapes off a vine. He explained to her how the process of making wine went. "It's in my blood," he said.

"But you're leaving all this to become a politician."

"My country is very important to me. It's second after my family. Nothing is more important than family—my wife, Diane, and my children."

She thought about what Hanson had told her about Parelli's affairs and the prostitute in Venice. She didn't think that he could honestly believe what he had just said. But she had learned long ago that some Italian men always had a bizarre sense of morality. Seven hundred years ago, Boccaccio had memorialized that in his Decameron.

"You'd like Diane," he said. "She's American, too."

"Does she have a career?"

"She owns and operates a boutique on via Montenapoleon in Milan called Diane's. She carries high-end casual clothes. She started the business and made a huge success. I'm very proud of her. But her work is quite demanding. She wanted to be here to meet with you, but the business kept her in Milan."

"Why'd she want to meet me?"

"She was upset by the headline on your Venice article. She wanted to convince you that I want to help Italy. That's all. She figured she'd be able to talk to you because you're an American as well."

All of this sounded good to Elizabeth, and he was quite convincing. Still, she wondered whether Diane had said anything remotely like it, or whether he was making it up out of whole cloth.

They kept walking until they reached a small cemetery surrounded by a chain link fence. Parelli opened the gate and led her inside. "My family has been buried here since 1750."

He walked to one side and stopped at a marker that read "Mario Parelli."

"My father," he said, pointing. "We were very close. He's the inspiration for me to go into politics. I was in awe of the man."

Again, she thought about what Hanson had told her about Roberto's final blow up with his father before Mario's death.

He moved ten yards to the right. She followed him to the graves of his mother and four sisters. Parelli told her the story she had head from Hanson of what happened on that fateful day when the Nazis had killed all five.

When he was finished, with tears in his eyes, he pointed to the graves and said, "I have gone into politics for them to make life better for the Italian people. So there will never be days like that again."

He took out a handkerchief and wiped his eyes. Throughout her career, Elizabeth had seen other politicians like Parelli who were able to cry on demand.

"Let's go back to the house," he said. "There we can do the formal interview."

As they left the cemetery, he placed an arm around her shoulder. She cringed and he pulled it away. He said, "The ground's uneven here. I didn't want you to trip."

He said it smoothly. Oh, so smoothly.

He took her to his upstairs study where a maid brought coffee. She sat down at the desk and booted up her laptop while he slumped into a leather wing back chair facing her.

"Now what can I tell you?" he asked.

"You covered your reason for going into politics, which was my first question. Now, I'd like to ask you whether you conceived of splitting Italy into two nations, North and South, which is the program of your New Italy Party, or whether this was someone else's idea."

"All mine. But not original. There are separatist movements in Spain. Both in Catalonia and the Basque country. In Scotland and in Quebec. None of those have moved beyond the talking stage.

Here, I believe that I will win, and this dream of mine of a separate nation in northern Italy will become a reality."

"It sounds as if you are confident of victory."

"The latest poll in *Italy Today* shows me surging into the lead."

"I saw that. They also reported that this may be due to a recent increase in advertising by your campaign. Have you gotten an infusion of new money?"

She was looking at his face, hoping for some visible reaction. There wasn't one.

"Not new. Just a continual increase as more and more people get on the bandwagon, as you Americans say. See, I even learned your slang when I spent that year in New Haven at Yale Law School."

If he was trying to divert her into talking about his time in the United States, he failed. She returned to the campaign.

"Can you tell me who some of your largest contributors are?"

He smiled. "You really don't expect me to answer that. Do you?"

She fired back quickly. "Are you receiving foreign money?"

His eyes blinked, mouth tightened. She had hit a nerve.

"Of course not." He sounded defensive. "Who told you that?"

"Well in this age of globalization, I thought—"

"That's absurd. And I won't talk any more about the money issue. Move on to something else."

"I have been surprised that you have significant support in the south. Can you explain that?"

"Many of those people believe the current Italian government tilts its efforts and attitudes to the north. They believe they will get better treatment from their own government in the south."

"But that's not your concern because you'll be ruling in the north?"

"Correct?"

"Who would be ruling in the south?"

"The leaders whom they elect."

"Where would you divide Italy between north and south?"

Elizabeth realized that was a difficult question. Parelli ducked it.

"That's one of the details that would have to be worked out after the election."

She was ready to move into sensitive areas. She waded in slowly. "I attended your recent speech in Venice in San Marco Square. I was impressed at how you interacted with the crowds."

"Those are my people. I believe in them. They believe in me."

"After the speech, I went to your suite at the Palace Hotel hoping to interview you. Luciano said it was not possible that evening and I should call another time."

"He should have told me. I would have made time for you."

"You seemed busy that evening. I noticed a Chinese man leaving a room you were in. Who was he?"

Parelli looked mystified. "A Chinese man? I don't recall any. You must be mistaken. It was late at night. Eyes can be deceptive."

It always amazed Elizabeth how some politicians lied easily and convincingly. Was it a trait they developed running for office or were liars attracted to politics?

She reached for her phone to find the picture of the Chinese man she took in his hotel suite. Before pulling it out, she recalled exactly what Craig said about thinking Zhou was involved and warning her to be careful because Zhou played rough. But this was her only opportunity. She had to take it.

She showed Parelli the photo. "You're a busy man, Roberto," she said. "You meet so many people. Naturally, you can't remember all of them. I wonder if this refreshes your recollection about the Chinese visitor to the Venice suite."

He took the phone from her and studied the picture, or pretended to be doing so. After a full minute, he replied, "Sorry. Never saw him before."

Elizabeth realized she had no chance of getting what she wanted from Parelli. She'd have to find another way to link Parelli and Zhou. For the rest of the interview, she tossed Parelli soft pitches, letting him talk about his life and his political program. No sense alarming him any further.

*   *   *

Diane's boutique was located in Milan in prime real estate on via Montenapoleon between via Gesu and via S. Andrea, very close to Frette and Versace. It was right in the heart of the fashion capital of Italy that rivaled Paris.

Fearful Diane might refuse to meet her, and wanting to have the element of surprise, Elizabeth decided to show up without first calling.

When she asked a young sales woman, "Is Diane Parelli in?" the woman led her to an office in the back of the first floor, which was cluttered with clothes, boxes, and catalogues. Sitting behind a desk was a very attractive blonde. She looked to be around sixty, and Elizabeth concluded she had aged gracefully. Her smooth long hair hung down and framed a face bronze from the sun. She was wearing a navy skirt and pink silk blouse. A navy jacket was hanging on the wall. She had on a gold necklace. It was not ostentatious, but was in good taste like the rest of her appearance.

As Elizabeth approached, she stood up, showing a good figure. She was athletic. Ran or played tennis. Something like that.

"She asked to see you," the sales woman said and then departed.

"Elizabeth Crowder," Diane said before Elizabeth had a chance to say a word.

"Did your husband tell you I might be coming?"

Diane brushed back a few strands of hair.

"No, I recognize you from your picture which shows up in the paper and on your website. Also from television interviews you sometimes do."

Elizabeth wasn't sure she believed her.

"Actually, I've followed your career," Diane continued. "As another expat American. How about a coffee?"

"Sure."

Diane fixed two cups and cleared a chair in front of her desk so they could both sit down.

"You've become a media celebrity," Diane said. "At least you are in Paris, and I get there often."

"Speaking of Paris, I had lunch there a few days ago with an old friend of yours, Robert Hanson. I took the job he had as foreign news editor at the paper."

For a moment, Diane looked puzzled as if she were trying to recall who Robert Hanson was. She fiddled with her hair and finally said, "Oh yeah, we had a couple of dates in college. That was a long time ago—I haven't seen him in ages. How is he?"

She was another good liar, Elizabeth thought. Really good. It ran in the family. She decided not to remind Diane that she'd been engaged to Hanson.

"Oh, he's happily married to a French woman and is now retired and living in Provence."

"That's wonderful. A lot of people like Provence. I find it a bit too quiet. Anyway, I assume you interviewed Roberto at the farm." Diane said, smoothly changing the subject.

"Yes. He showed me around the farm and winery."

"I love that place. Roberto's father, Mario, lived there until his death. Then we moved in. Being there, I think of Roberto's father often. He accepted me from the time Roberto brought me home. He treated me like a daughter. I loved him. He was also a great man. I'm sure Roberto told you what happened to him with the Nazis."

Elizabeth nodded.

Diane continued, "Mario spent his life working for the Italian people. He loved his country. Now Roberto's decided to follow in his father's footsteps. It's all so unfair."

"What do you mean?"

"All Roberto wants to do is help Italy and the people but he's being ripped apart in the media." She stared straight at Elizabeth. "Roberto may or may not be the savior of Italy. But he's no sinner."

Turning the title of her article on Elizabeth stung. "I didn't mean—"

"I wasn't singling you out. You were mild, in comparison with others. It's their personal attacks that tear me apart—the false rumors that Roberto had affairs."

Did she really believe what she had just said, Elizabeth wondered.

"Politics can be rough. Here in Italy. Everywhere. You grew up in the United States. You know how the Kennedys were portrayed."

"Yes, but these unfair accusations still hurt."

"On the other hand, Roberto seems to have plenty of supporters."

"That's right. The polls are now showing him in front."

"He also seems to have increased his advertising. Has he gotten new money?"

Diane looked away. "I don't know about those things. I'm not involved in the campaign."

"Chinese money?"

"What are you insinuating?"

"I'm not. Just asking."

"That's absurd."

Elizabeth showed Diane the man's image on her phone. "Have you ever seen this man?"

Diane looked at it and shook her head. After a long pause, she said, "You'll be writing more about Roberto's campaign won't you?"

"Sure. That's why I interviewed him."

"You seem like a good person. Will you be fair?"

"I'll try to be."

Diane seemed on the verge of tears. "Don't destroy my husband, please."

Following her interview with Diane, Elizabeth tried Luciano's cell again to see if he'd meet with her. She got a recording, "This line has been disconnected."

Singapore

At nine in the morning Craig arrived in Singapore, traveling on a US passport in the name of George Moore. He checked into Raffles Hotel, a luxurious revitalized carryover from British colonial days in the heart of the business and shopping district. The bellman led Craig through the hotel's vaulted lobby to a third floor room with a patio overlooking a beautifully landscaped garden.

Though Craig thought it extremely unlikely that Zhou knew he was George Moore, he still took the precaution once the bellman was gone of checking the room and its phones for bugs. Nothing.

He showered and changed clothes. Then walked to the American Embassy. Jennifer Nelson, the ambassador, was waiting for him.

When they were seated in her office, Jennifer said, "Welcome to Singapore, Mr. Moore. President Worth called and told me you were a very important special envoy. He didn't tell me anything about your mission. Only that I was to accompany you to your meetings. But I was impressed with the personal call from the boss himself. And I'm intrigued about what you are doing here in my little back water."

Craig leaned back in his chair and sized up the ambassador. She was in her sixties, an attractive, tall and thin woman with short gray hair. Betty had given him a bio before he left Washington.

Jennifer was from San Diego and was the daughter of the founder of a real-estate empire with projects in twenty-eight states and half a dozen foreign countries, including Singapore. She had been the CEO for fifteen years before being named ambassador. Her husband was an artist whose paintings had been exhibited at some of the top galleries in New York. In return for her early support, Treadwell, Worth's predecessor, had made her ambassador. When Worth became president, he left her in place.

Betty also gave Craig a *Washington Post* article about Jennifer written when she was appointed. The words "hard-nosed, tough negotiator" from the article stuck with him.

On the long flight, he had pondered the question of how much to tell Jennifer. He decided as little as possible. She was operating in Asia, Zhou's home turf. The more she knew, the more she would be at risk.

"I'm here to interview Lin Yu," Craig said, "the CEO of Pacific Sun Bank, which I gather is one of the largest in the country."

"It is the largest. What'd Lin Yu do?"

"He just made a major investment in a Milan bank under suspicious circumstances."

"And what exactly does that euphemistic term mean?"

He liked her no-nonsense manner. He decided to respond in the same blunt way. "Lin Yu went to Milan where he met with Federico Castiglione, the CEO and largest shareholder of the bank. Federico refused to sell. He was adamant. His board supported him. Lin Yu threatened Federico. A few days later, Federico was murdered in what looked like a jewelry robbery except murder was the motive. The board reversed course and sold out to Lin Yu."

She tapped her fingers on the arm of her chair. "That qualifies as suspicious circumstances. But why are we concerned about the transaction? Isn't it a matter for the Italian authorities?"

"It's likely that Lin Yu was following someone else's orders in this."

"I won't ask you who that someone is because I can guess and you won't tell me in any event. I've learned that being an ambassador is often like being a glorified messenger. Sometimes they tell you what's in the package you're delivering; sometimes not."

"I never thought of it that way."

"I don't mind. I like the parties."

He laughed.

She continued. "Now that we've gotten that out of the way, let me tell you something about Lin Yu."

"I would appreciate it."

"Parents moved here from China when he was seven. Brilliant student. Educated at Oxford and London School of Economics. Returned to Singapore after school in England. Worked with various financial firms, including JP Morgan and Barclays. Then was appointed CEO of Pacific Sun. He's been bold and innovative. He has increased their assets several fold."

"Relations with China?"

"Close. He's lent money for numerous large projects there, and also elsewhere throughout Southeast Asia. He has plenty of money to invest. I've met him several times at social functions, and I'm impressed. He has a quick mind. Incredible memory. He's extremely well connected throughout Asia. Can't be underestimated. When do you want to meet him?"

"Today if possible."

"I'll see if I can make that happen." She reached for the phone.

*   *   *

At two o'clock that afternoon, Craig and Jennifer filed into the most ornate and luxurious office Craig had ever seen. It was furnished with English antiques. Ming vases rested on either side of a marble fireplace. On the walls hung a Renoir, Monet, Chagall, and Picasso. A grandfather clock stood in one corner, a Rodin in another. The banking business was clearly good in Singapore.

Craig thought about Alberto Goldoni's modest office in Turin. The contrast was striking and was confirmation that wealth and power had moved eastward.

Yu, in his sixties, was a tall man. He had coal-black hair parted in the center and was dressed in a perfectly tailored and pressed gray pinstriped suit.

When Jennifer made the introductions, Yu smiled broadly. His expression told Craig, "I've got the world by the balls." If Yu was worried about anything, he certainly didn't show it. Craig took a seat in front of Yu's red leather topped desk that didn't have a single paper. Behind him were three large-screened computers.

"Always a pleasure to see you Ambassador Nelson," Yu said in a very British English. "To what do I owe the honor of this visit?"

"George Moore is a special envoy of President Worth. He has a matter to discuss with you."

"I'd be happy to help in any way I can."

We'll see about that, Craig thought.

"Mr. Yu, I'd like to talk to you about your recent acquisition of shares of stock in the National Bank of Milan."

Lin didn't seem concerned. "Certainly. I have nothing to hide. We're a publicly-traded company. All details of that transaction have been disclosed to the regulatory agencies in both countries. Also, as I'm sure you're aware, shortly before we finalized the agreement, an unfortunate event occurred: Federico Castiglione, the CEO of the bank, was killed in a jewelry robbery."

"I am aware of that. What was your relationship with Federico before the agreement was reached?"

"Very cordial at all times."

"Was he in favor of Pacific Sun acquiring this interest in the bank?"

"Absolutely. He stood to make a huge amount of money from the transaction."

Craig decided he had to play rough with Yu if he had any chance of obtaining the information he needed.

Acting irate, Craig pounded his fist on the desk and shot to his feet. "Okay, now that you've had fun lying to me, why don't you tell me the truth."

Yu looked aghast. Jennifer appeared horrified.

Craig continued. "We have witnesses who told us of your angry acrimonious discussions with Federico. These were both in person and on the phone prior to the transaction, which he vehemently opposed. You told Federico that you had powerful friends and if he didn't agree to sell, he would pay for it with his life."

"That's quite impossible. I have no idea why those people told you that."

"I want to know who are those powerful friends you referred to."

"The whole story is absurd."

Craig stood up and paced around the office for a few moments like a trial lawyer conducting an interrogation. Then he bore in on Yu. "Whose idea was it for you to do this deal with Federico's bank?"

"Mine, of course. I've wanted to expand into Europe for some time. This seemed like a good opportunity."

"Who financed the transaction?"

"Pacific Sun with its own funds. Unlike your American and European banks, we have been managed efficiently and have large cash reserves."

"Could you provide records to establish that Pacific Sun financed the acquisition itself?"

"Yes, but I have no intention of doing so. You have no legal standing in Singapore."

Without pausing, Craig asked, "Do you know Zhou Yun?"

"Of course." Yu didn't blanch. "He's the Chinese Finance Minister. I have negotiated large loans in China. I have met him several times."

"He also owns a large bank in China. Doesn't he?"

"That's right."

"And it was Zhou's idea for you to do the transaction in Milan. Wasn't it?"

"Certainly not. As I told you, it was my idea."

Craig sat back down. "I'll be very frank with you, Mr. Yu. President Worth asked me to obtain answers to these questions. He told me if you weren't cooperative, your bank would be blacklisted just as the United States blacklisted Iranian banks. That means no American firm would be able to do business with your bank."

Craig paused to let his words sink in. Staring at Yu, he continued, "Do you want that to happen?"

Yu stared right back. "Let me tell you something, Mr. Moore. The manner in which you marched in here with your bluster and threats shows how little you understand about Asia and the current world."

"What does that mean?" Jennifer interjected.

"Forty years ago, I would have been terrified by your threats. The United States controlled the world then. Twenty years ago, I would have been worried. Today, I shrug my shoulders and say 'so what.' You Americans have a colloquial expression someone once taught me. 'There's a new sheriff in town.' That's the way it is in Asia. It's a whole new world here with the ascendency of China. Now we play by Beijing's rules. Not Washington's."

"Meaning you'll do whatever Zhou Yun asks you to do."

Yu gave a sardonic smile. "No. Meaning that in a conflict between the United States and China, I would be more concerned about alienating the powers in Beijing than in Washington."

"So you did follow Zhou's orders in this transaction with the bank in Milan?"

Again the sardonic smile. "No point twisting my words. Of course I didn't say that."

"An innocent man was murdered."

"I didn't kill him. I'm not a jewel thief—as you look around this office, you couldn't possibly think that I wanted to steal jewels."

"But you know who did."

Yu turned to Jennifer. "Our meeting is over. I'm a patient man, but at this point, I'm tired of listening to Mr. Moore's false accusations."

As they stood to leave, Craig said, "My investigation of your involvement will not end here today. I will continue until I establish what really happened."

Yu didn't respond. He pointed to the door.

When they were in the back of the ambassador's car, Jennifer told the driver to take them to Craig's hotel. She turned to Craig and said, "That certainly went well."

"Was I wrong?"

"It's not how I would have conducted the interview," she said tactfully.

Craig wasn't surprised to hear that. "You think he was telling the truth?"

"Of course not."

"Good. I'm glad to hear it. What do you base that on?"

"Observing his voice and facial expressions. I've become expert on that over here. In my opinion, it didn't matter how you handled the questioning. He had no intention of telling you what you wanted to know."

"Anybody we can go to in the Singapore government to bring him around?"

"I was just thinking that."

"And?" Craig held his breath.

"I've developed a good relationship with the justice minister. He might be willing to help. I'll set a meeting for the two of us tomorrow morning."

"Perhaps you should take the lead this time. You know the minister. And you'll no doubt be more tactful."

She laughed. "That's not saying much. But I'll be happy to do that. Meantime, how about having dinner with my husband, Warren, and me this evening?"

"I'd like that."

"Good. We'll pick you up at your hotel at eight."

She reached into her bag and took out a card. "It has all of my contact information, including my cell phone. Call if you need me."

*   *   *

Dinner with Jennifer and Warren, a handsome man with thick gray hair and the appearance of a successful businessman in his well-cut dark suit, was comfortable and relaxed for Craig.

The food at The Blue Ginger, according to Warren, was one of the great culinary traditions of Singapore. Known as Peranakan cooking, it was an infusion of Chinese and Malaysian styles relying heavily on exotic spices. It was superb, and they drank scotch followed by Chateau Trotanoy, one of Craig's favorites from Bordeaux. Much of the time, Craig asked Warren about how he became a painter and about what he was pursuing in his art.

"I tell Jennifer," Warren said, "that thanks to her getting this ambassadorship, and my tagging along, I'm going through my Gauguin phase."

"But not with the native girls," she responded.

"The truth is, Craig, she'd be too busy to notice if I were. And, by the way, did you know that Gauguin was a banker, married to a minister's daughter, and had four children before he began painting?"

"So why'd he do it?"

"The banking crash of 1883. I read about him and decided to follow in his footsteps. I was a banker until the crash of 2008. I had always dabbled at painting, but at that point, I dove in with both feet. I was tired of selling phony mortgage bonds. And happily, I didn't need the income—ah, the advantages of marrying a wealthy woman. It's the best move a man can ever make." Jennifer picked up her fork and playfully rapped him on his knuckles.

As they were leaving the restaurant, she told Craig, "Our meeting tomorrow morning with the justice minister is at ten. Why don't you come to the embassy at nine. We'll go from there."

They dropped Craig at his hotel at a few minutes before eleven. When he entered his room, he saw on the floor a white letter-sized envelope with the name George Moore typed on the front.

Craig ripped it open. Inside was a note neatly typed on white paper.

"Sorry I could not talk freely with you this afternoon. My office is not good for that. Could you meet me this evening at midnight at Au Jardin Les Amis Restaurant. I will give you the information you wanted."

Craig read the note twice, then tore it into little pieces and flushed it down the toilet.

He faced a dilemma. Did the note come from Lin Yu who wanted to talk or was it a trap arranged by Yu or Zhou to have him attacked or even killed? Craig decided he couldn't call Jennifer. He'd have to make up his own mind.

After thinking about it for full minute, he decided to go to the meeting point. Perhaps, he was being foolhardy; but if there was a chance of nailing Zhou, he had to take it. Besides, he had been out of the terrorism business so long that he was itching to get back into the action.

He dressed in slacks and a shirt and took a cab to the restaurant. It was a colonial style house in the middle of Singapore's lush botanic gardens, reminding him a little of Le Pre Catelan in Paris in the heart of the Bois de Boulogne.

Craig checked his watch. Ten minutes to twelve. He sat at the bar and ordered an Armagnac.

Twenty minutes later, Yu hadn't appeared. Craig was wondering if this was a wild goose chase when the maître d' came over and handed him an unaddressed white envelope. Craig opened it and pulled out a typed note. "I'm outside in the back, next to the large fountain. Go through the rear door of the restaurant, walk along the path for twenty yards, and you'll see me."

Craig wondered if he was being set up, but he had come this far. He had no intention of turning back. He paid the bartender for the drink and headed toward the rear door.

The night was balmy with only a sliver of a moon. Stepping outside into the lush garden, he saw a fountain straight ahead with water shooting up into the air. A man was standing in front of it, but in the darkness he couldn't tell if it was Yu. He headed in that direction.

Suddenly, Craig felt sick, very sick, nauseous. His eyes were blurred and he lost focus. The entire garden was spinning, around and around.

He heard voices, men speaking, "Sir, are you okay? Do you need help?"

It wasn't Yu's voice.

"No . . ." he mumbled. "No."

He felt powerful arms clutching him, around his chest and pulling him backward.

Then everything went black.

*　　　*　　　*

Craig was regaining consciousness. Every part of his body hurt. He reached up to the side of his face and felt dried, caked blood. A foul smell filled his nostrils, the odor of feces and urine.

Slowly, he opened his eyes and looked around. He was in a dingy prison cell, seated on a dirt floor, propped up against a stone wall. Seven other men were in the small cell, all wearing the same stained prison blues as Craig. He was surprised to see they had left him wearing his black pointed leather shoes.

To alleviate the stiffness, Craig stood up. As he did, he heard a shout from across the cell. "The American's awake."

Craig looked in that direction. The shout had come from a giant of a man, brown skinned and weighing about three hundred pounds.

He was walking toward Craig with a metal object in his hand.

The other prisoners cleared a path letting the giant approach Craig. Then they made a circle behind the giant.

Craig noticed the giant was holding a switchblade knife. He pressed a button and it snapped open.

"Give me some money, American," the giant called, while holding the knife in his upraised arm in a menacing grip.

"Sorry," Craig said, sounding bold. "The guards took all my money. They didn't leave me my credit cards. So even if you take Visa or American Express, I can't give you those."

A couple prisoners laughed. "Shut up," the giant shouted to them. Then to Craig, "You think that's funny. You mock me. You make jokes of me."

Craig looked around for a stick of wood, anything he could use as a weapon, but he didn't see a thing.

When the man was five yards away, Craig called out, "Listen, asshole. I wasn't making trouble for you. So piss off."

As he expected, his words enraged the giant. He kept coming. One chance is all Craig would get. He had to use it.

The giant had the knife raised in his right hand. With his left, he reached out to grab Craig. Before he had a chance, Craig was off his feet, flying through the air toward the man with those black pointed shoes out in front aimed for the giants' groin. They smashed into his balls.

The giant screamed in pain. The knife fell from his hand. They both tumbled to the ground. The giant was thrashing, grabbing for Craig. But blinded by pain, he couldn't reach Craig who spun away, grabbed the knife and sprang to his feet.

With the knife in hand, he whirled around and looked at the circle of other prisoners. "Any of you others want what he just got? Then come on."

He knew full well if they all came for him at the same time, he was dead. But he stared at them menacingly, showing no fear.

No one moved. The giant staggered to his feet, stumbled to a corner of the cell, and threw up. The others moved back, yielding one side of the cell to Craig.

About ten minutes later, two guards opened the cell door. Craig quickly closed up the knife and concealed it under his shirtsleeve. The guards motioned to Craig, who headed toward the door. As he crossed the threshold, he took out the knife and handed it to one of the guards. "I found this on the floor of the cell. Somebody must have lost it."

Craig noticed the giant glaring at him. He glared back.

The guard led him to a small room, which held a table and two chairs. Jennifer was seated in one of them. The guards closed the door and left them alone.

Craig put a finger over his lips and searched the room for bugs or a tiny hidden camera or recorder. Nothing. No one way glass.

"Okay, let's talk," he said.

"You're in a great deal of trouble and you look like hell."

"That bad."

She removed a compact from her bag and opened it to the mirror. He saw that his face was bruised. One eye was barely open. The blood was from a cut on the side of his face near his eye.

"Yeah. You're right," he said. "What did they tell you I did?"

"That you went to a brothel. You had been drinking heavily and paid to have sex with two women. You were naked in the bedroom. So were the women. You demanded anal sex, and when they refused, you became abusive and started hitting them. They screamed for the security guards. Two of them came. You began fighting with them. That's when you were beaten. The police have sworn statements from everyone involved. The women. The two security guards. Even the madam. Fortunately, the police found the card I gave you with my contact info. So they called me and I came immediately."

"What time is it now?"

"Almost ten thirty in the morning. I've been waiting here for them to bring you for the last half hour."

"They waited in order to give some monster in the cell a chance to kill me."

Her face was pale. She had deep furrows on her forehead. "This does not look good for you or for the United States."

Craig was worried she believed what they had told her. "Now would you like to know what really happened?"

"Your version."

"The truth."

"I'm listening."

He explained everything that occurred from the time he saw the note in his hotel room to his collapsing in the garden. "So they must have drugged my Armagnac," he said. "I hope you believe me."

"I've never heard of anything like this happening in Singapore. Crime rates are low, and . . ." she said hesitantly.

If she doesn't believe me, I'm really screwed.

"But," she continued. "I do believe you. I'll go to bat for you and try to convince the Justice Minster."

"You and I were supposed to meet with him half an hour ago."

"I already called and postponed that until I met with you."

Craig sighed. That meeting had been important. Yu and Zhou had totally outmaneuvered him. "Can you reset it for this afternoon?"

"I'll call him. First, I'll need him to get you out of here, which won't be easy with sworn statements from so many witnesses. It would be better for me to do it in person."

"In the meantime, what happens to me?"

"I'll convince the head of the prison to lock you up in your own cell until I return."

"You think you can?"

"He won't want anything to happen if he knows I'm meeting with his boss about you."

Jennifer proved to be correct. When she left, Craig was permitted to shower, was given clean clothes, and placed in a spotless, sanitary cell.

He didn't have a watch or clock, but it seemed as if Jennifer returned somewhere between an hour and two hours later.

"Okay. Here's the deal I cut," she told Craig. "The next plane to the United States leaves in two hours on Singapore Air for Los Angeles. If you're on that plane and out of the country, no charges will be filed."

"What about our meeting with the justice minister about Yu?"

"He'll have that meeting with me alone once you're in the air. Call me from Los Angeles, and I'll give you a report."

"But—"

Craig was preparing to protest.

She cut him off. "This is the only way to avoid a huge embarrassment for President Worth and the United States."

"I didn't do anything wrong."

"You and I both know that, but the justice minister showed me photos of you naked with two prostitutes," she said grimly. "Unless you're on that plane, he's prepared to release the photos to the media. In these wonderful days of the Internet, they'll go viral."

"Shit!"

"Exactly my sentiments."

Craig was confident her meeting about Yu with the justice minister wouldn't produce anything useful. Yu and Zhou had made his trip to Singapore a dismal failure. He was no closer to nailing Zhou for Federico's murder.

Los Angeles and Washington

Craig got off the plane in Los Angeles. After clearing customs, he had an hour before the flight to Washington.

Long enough to call Jennifer in Singapore.

"What happened?" he asked anxiously.

"Disaster averted, but you won't like the result."

"What do you mean?"

"He told me the price for his commitment not to prosecute you for what he called, 'this error of judgment' on your part."

"That's bullshit," Craig said angrily. "They set me up."

"I explained all that again. You and I are the only ones who believe it."

"Oh, c'mon. He's being paid off by Yu."

"Their town. Their rules. You know how that goes."

"All too well. What's the price?"

"The United States will drop its investigation of Yu in connection with the Milan transaction."

"That sucks."

"I also agreed we wouldn't question Lin Yu any further."

Craig was dismayed. "I'm the victim. I was attacked."

"That may be, but my job is to avoid embarrassment for the United States and keep American citizens out of jail in Singapore. Now I don't know who you really are, but I'm confident you're an American citizen."

"Thank you for helping me out of this."

"Just doing my job."

Before boarding the plane to Washington, Craig stopped in the men's room. He looked like hell, he thought as he glanced in the mirror. His face had multiple cuts and bruises.

He lifted his shirt. His back and side were black and blue and lots of other colors that nasty bruises display.

He was also exhausted. He slept all the way to Washington.

When he got off at Dulles Airport, he saw he had a message from Elizabeth to call her.

He called her back. "We need to talk," she said.

"Where are you?"

"Milan."

"I want you to go to the American Consulate and wait in the reception area. In about an hour, I'll call you."

*   *   *

When Craig walked into Betty's office at CIA headquarters, she looked at his face and said, "Same old Craig."

"Thanks Betty."

"Was it worth it?"

"I'll give you the details later, but in a word, 'no' I didn't learn a damn thing from Yu."

"Sorry to hear that."

"I have Elizabeth standing by in our consulate in Milan waiting for me to call her. Can you hook us up on a secure phone?"

"Will do."

Moments later, Craig and Betty were seated at Betty's desk; Elizabeth was in the communications room in the Milan consulate on a secure line.

"I'm in Langley with Betty. You can talk freely now."

"Hi, Elizabeth," Betty said.

"Good to hear your voice. Are you keeping Craig out of trouble?"

"I failed. He was bloodied and bruised in Singapore."

"So what else is new," Elizabeth said.

"And all for naught," Craig added.

"Oh, that's too bad—at least one of us learned something."

"Don't gloat. Just tell me."

"I think you're right, Craig, about Zhou and Parelli."

"I'm glad to hear that."

Elizabeth continued, saying, "I don't have any hard evidence. When I interviewed Parelli, I pressed him about Chinese support. He denied it, but he was so defensive. I'm convinced by his demeanor and the sudden influx of funds that he must have gotten money from Zhou. Still, that's not enough for me to use to support an article for the paper. And I can't believe Mei Ling knows what Zhou is doing."

"What difference does that make?" Craig said. "She'd never be able to stop him."

"She is the President of China."

"Look, Elizabeth. I know you like Mei Ling, and I do, too. However, I think Zhou will run all over her."

"Don't underestimate her. She may be able to stop him. At any rate, she has a right to know what's Zhou's up to."

"And how do you propose to let her know? By flying to Beijing to tell her?"

"That's exactly what I had in mind," Elizabeth replied.

"Are you crazy? That's the sort of stupid thing I would do. For God's sake, Zhou had you watched for a year. Once he finds out you're in China—and he will because their security people scrutinize the names of all arriving journalists—you'll be dead meat. They'll make you suffer torture you can't even imagine."

"Not if I come in under the radar."

"How?" asked Craig.

"As a French tourist with a false name and papers. I know people in Paris who can prepare them. Also, I'll change my appearance."

"But when you call Mei Ling's office to meet her, he'll get wind of that. He must have spies there."

"I won't do it. I'll tell Ned, my Beijing Bureau Chief, to arrange a secret meeting. He knows Mei Ling."

"This is ridiculous." Craig looked at Betty. "Tell her she's being foolish."

"Are you sure you want to do this?" Betty asked. "With the risks Craig warned you about?"

"Absolutely. Between Ned and Mei Ling, I should be able to get a positive ID for the Chinese man who was in Parelli's suite in Venice. Hopefully, he'll be somebody on Zhou's staff. Also, if I can persuade Mei Ling to shut down Zhou's Italian operation, we'll all be a lot better off."

"It's your call," Betty said.

"Thanks for the support." Craig grumbled.

"It will take me a little while to get the papers together. I'll go as soon as I can. I'll report to you when I get back."

"*If* you come back," Craig added.

After the call, Craig said to Betty, "She's insane to do this."

"She spent a lot of time with you. She learned by example."

Fearful for Elizabeth, he ran his hand through his hair. "You want to know about Singapore now?"

"Before you arrived, I received a call from President Worth. He wants to hear your report, too. Let me call and get on his calendar. We can go to the White House together."

*   *   *

When Craig followed Betty into the Oval Office, he saw two other men standing in the living area with President Worth. One was Winston ("Win") Tyler, the Secretary of the Treasury whom Craig recognized from pictures in the media. The other was Clyde Jones, the Secretary of State with whom Craig had clashed years ago when Craig was working in the Middle East for the CIA.

At the time, Jones, an African American from South Central LA and a top graduate of West Point, was a general in the Army who had achieved his rank after a meteoric rise. Jones had vetoed a couple of daring operations Craig had planned to hit terrorists at bases inside of civilian areas. Craig was dismayed by the General's super-cautious approach, afraid to take the kind of risks that were necessary to prevail in warfare. With his CIA colleagues, Craig referred to Jones as "General No."

Listening to the president introduce him, using his real name, Craig cringed. At the end, Worth said, "Craig is a true American hero. Our super spy. Recipient of the Medal of Freedom. Twice. He's changed his appearance and his name, but he's still the same Craig Page."

Jones replied, "Craig and I know each other," in a frosty tone.

Betty added, "Craig was just battered and bruised in Singapore serving his country."

"I hope you gave as good as you got," Worth said.

"Unfortunately, I didn't, Mr. President. Not this time. There will be another, I'm sure."

"Good to meet you," Tyler said.

As they sat down, Worth said, "I wanted Clyde and Win to be here because this has foreign policy and financial implications. Now Craig, why don't you begin by telling us why you went to Singapore, for their benefit, and what happened there."

Craig began by talking about Federico's murder and the sale of shares in his bank, laying out the facts that lead to Craig's conclusion that Zhou Yun was the mastermind of the whole affair. While speaking, he glanced at Jones and Tyler. The secretary of state was leaning forward, listening intently. The treasury secretary was squirming in his chair and looking uncomfortable.

He decided to leave out the Parelli discussion because Elizabeth had obtained the facts, and she was dealing with that by going to Beijing to meet Mei Ling. Craig didn't want Worth to take independent action that might jeopardize Elizabeth.

However, he described everything that happened in Singapore. At the end he said, "Your ambassador, Jennifer Nelson, was extremely helpful, Mr. President. Unfortunately, I made an error by not involving her when I went out for what I thought would be a midnight meeting with Lin Yu, the head of the Singapore Bank."

"Thanks for telling me about Jennifer. She's very impressive and competent. But the bottom line is you didn't learn anything in Singapore."

"Correct," Craig said.

"Let's try another tack," the president said. "Suppose I fly to Europe to meet with the leaders of England, France, and Germany. I'll tell them what you've learned. That Zhou Yun and the Chinese are trying to gain a foothold in Europe, starting with Italian banks. Then they can take some action to respond."

Tyler immediately pounced. "With all due respect, Mr. President, I'm sure Craig Page has done wonderful things for this country, but his claims of the involvement of Zhou Yun and the Chinese are nothing but rank speculation."

Craig responded, "Zhou owns the Hong Kong bank that's trying to take over a controlling interest in Alberto Goldoni's bank, Turin Credit, the largest bank in Italy."

"So what? International companies are constantly making acquisitions in foreign countries. That's what globalization is."

"First, the Milan bank, now the Turin Bank."

"You have zero evidence tying Zhou Yun to the transaction with Federico's bank in Milan. That's what you went to Singapore to get and you failed."

"That's why I was attacked in Singapore. Because I was getting too close to that critical information."

Tyler snarled. "You have no idea why you were attacked. And you don't have a shred of evidence to support your wild conjecture that Zhou Yun, one of the most respected Chinese business leaders and their treasury minister, wanted the Singapore bank to complete the acquisition so badly that he arranged a murder to get it done."

"Zhou is ruthless. He'll do whatever it takes to get his way."

"Sounds to me," Tyler said raising his voice, "that you and Zhou have a history."

"We do, but—"

"And that's coloring your judgment, leading you to unjustified conclusions."

The vehemence of Tyler's objections stunned Craig. "I don't think so."

"Oh, c'mon, Craig. Look at what you have. Every officer in Federico's bank told you and Giuseppe that Federico wanted the transaction, for which he stood to make a fortune."

Craig bit his lip and held his voice. He had promised Federico's secretary that he wouldn't disclose what she had told him, and he intended to honor that.

Tyler wasn't finished with his diatribe. "You may not like the Chinese, and I have problems with them from time to time over financial issues, but they're still the second most powerful nation in the world. We have to get along with them. And unfounded accusations of murder directed at their finance minister will poison our relationship with Beijing for years. I don't think you want to do that."

"I just want to see us take a stand for what's right and just."

The secretary of state broke in. "I must say, Mr. President, Win is right. We don't know enough at this point to set off alarms in Europe. In addition, you know how the Europeans are. They'll say we're trying to intervene in their internal matter."

Thanks a lot, General No, Craig thought. *I'm happy to see that you haven't changed your super cautious, gutless approach.*

Worth leaned back and closed his eyes for a minute. Then, he said, "I think the two of you have a point. Still, Craig could be right, and if he is, I hate to see us doing nothing in response to a Chinese move into Europe."

Craig saw his opening. "I have another idea, Mr. President. As I said, Victoria Bank of Hong Kong, which is a subsidiary of Zhou's bank in China, is trying to acquire the stock of Alberto Goldoni, the dominant shareholder in the Turin bank. Goldoni, does not want to sell. Threats were made against him with a reference to Federico Castiglione."

"How do you know this?" Tyler asked. "More guesswork on your part."

"Giuseppe, the Director of EU Counterterrorism, told me. He heard it directly from Goldoni. I doubt if either of them is lying."

"That's outrageous," Worth said.

"Exactly, Mr. President. What I propose to do is go to Italy under a false identity as Barry Gorman, the head of a US-based private equity fund."

"That was the identity you used in Argentina," Worth said.

Craig was surprised Worth knew and impressed that he remembered.

"Betty told me about it," Worth added.

Craig continued, "Barry Gorman will make a competing and higher offer for Alberto Goldoni's stock. Put it into play."

"And what do you hope to accomplish with that?" Tyler asked in a hostile tone.

"To smoke out Zhou. If he really wants Alberto's bank, and if he thinks he's at risk of losing it, he'll attack Barry Gorman. These attacks will be attributed to him, and this will expose his effort to gain a foothold in Italy by taking over some of its banks."

"So you'd be putting yourself in the line of fire," Worth said.

"That's right, Mr. President.

"I like the idea—as long as you're willing to take the risk."

"I am."

"What do the rest of you think?"

Betty responded first. "Excellent idea."

"I don't like it," Tyler said.

"Why not?" Craig asked.

"It puts this country in a bad position. We'd be interfering with the free market."

"There is no free market if a buyer uses murder as a weapon," Betty said.

"Suppose you outbid Victoria Bank," Tyler said angrily. "Would you expect the US Treasury to put up the money to buy Goldoni's stock?"

"It will never come to that."

The president turned to the secretary of state. "Clyde?"

"It's your decision, Mr. President."

"Okay. Let's do it. I'll trust Craig's instincts."

"But I don't think that . . ." Tyler said.

Everyone was looking at the treasury secretary. Continuing to argue after the president had decided was a breach of protocol.

"It is your decision, Mr. President," he reluctantly said.

As they filed out of the Oval Office, Craig was pleased he had gotten the president's approval for his counteroffer. Beyond the president's line of vision, Craig caught Tyler's eye. In a short rapid motion, he gave the treasury secretary the finger and smiled.

"That was smart," Betty whispered to Craig.

In the car, on the way back to Langley, Craig asked Betty, "What is it with that asshole Tyler? Why's he so intent on covering for the Chinese?"

She thought about it for a moment, and said, "Before I answer, let me tell you a little about Tyler."

"Go ahead."

"Treadwell appointed him treasury secretary and Worth kept him. He was a Princeton economics professor who became an economic advisor to Treadwell early in the campaign. He's won lots of awards for his articles, mainly on how various nations' economic policies undermined their stability."

"So now the professor gets to put his theories into practice. Is that what's driving him?"

"Actually, it's something different. Once we were both at Camp David for a two-day retreat with the president. After dinner, when he'd had too much to drink, he—"

"Made a pass at you, Craig interjected."

Betty laughed. "Has anyone ever told you that you have sex on your brain?"

"Lots of people."

"Well, anyhow, the two of us ended up alone and he confided in me why he took this job."

"I can't wait to hear."

"It irritates him that he's so much smarter than people on Wall Street, and they're raking in millions of dollars a year while he's scratching out a living on a professor's salary. So he figures if he does a good job as treasury secretary, Wall Street will come calling. He sees himself getting eight-figure offers from Goldman and Citibank. If Rubin did it, why not Tyler?"

"He really told you that?"

"Absolutely. So what it means in this situation is that he has to kowtow to the Chinese. They're the biggest buyers of the bonds and notes Tyler has to sell to keep our country afloat. If he doesn't sell those bonds, he'll seem like a failure as treasury secretary, and Wall Street won't want him."

"That's pathetic."

"It may be, but regardless, you managed to make a new and power-ful enemy. You better watch your back when he's around."

"I'm counting on you for that."

As soon as they returned to Betty's office, Craig called Giuseppe on a secure line. "I struck out in Singapore. It's just as well you didn't waste your time and the EU's valuable money by coming with me."

"So what's your next move?"

Craig laughed. "Funny you should ask. I'm planning to go into the private equity business."

"Another new ID?"

"Of course. As Barry Gorman."

"How will I keep them all straight."

"I have confidence in you."

Craig then told Giuseppe about his plan to submit a competing bid for Alberto Goldoni's stock. "What do you think?"

"I like it. Alberto promised to let me know if he heard from McKnight, and he hasn't. When are you returning to Italy?"

"I need the rest of today and tomorrow morning to get my Barry Gorman act together. I'll be on United's nonstop to Rome tomorrow at 5:30 in the afternoon."

"Good. I'll meet you at Fiumicino and hustle you through passport control which is a two hour nightmare."

"If you talk to Alberto, don't tell him about the plan. I want to break it to him myself. And if McKnight calls him, have Alberto delay his response for a week or so, in order for me to make my competing bid."

Turin

When Alberto reached his office at nine in the morning, his secretary said, "Mr. McKnight from Hong Kong called. He would like to meet with you as soon as possible today. He left a cell phone number."

Prepared to do battle with McKnight, Alberto wasn't frightened. Before returning McKnight's call, he wanted to obtain instructions from Giuseppe.

In Rome, Giuseppe's secretary pulled him out of a meeting so he could take the call. "Here's what I want you to do," Giuseppe said. "Tell McKnight you can meet him at three this afternoon in your office. I'm on my way to Turin. When I see you, I'll tell you how to play it."

At noon, Giuseppe arrived with two techies in tow. He told Alberto, "Let me know which room you want for the McKnight meeting."

"I prefer my office if that is okay."

"Sure. We'll install a hidden camera and video system that will send real-time feed to me in an adjoining office. If McKnight tries to harm you, I'll move right in to stop him. You okay with that?"

"Absolutely."

"As for your discussion with McKnight, here's what I want you to do."

*   *   *

McKnight arrived precisely at three o'clock. Alberto thought he seemed a little nervous and not as self-confident as their first meeting.

Before sitting down to talk to Alberto, McKnight walked across the office to a credenza, which had several pictures of Alberto with Dora and their two children.

"Nice family," McKnight said.

"Thanks."

"I'd hate for anything to happen to them."

Inside, Alberto was boiling, but he had to remain cool and follow Giuseppe's script. "You made your point in our first meeting, Mr. McKnight, when you told me I'd end up dead like Federico if I didn't sell."

"I'm glad you got the message."

"I did."

"Now you're telling me that you'll also harm my family if I refuse to sell."

"That's exactly what I'm telling you. I'm glad you understand. You're a very smart man."

"You're not subtle."

"I don't want there to be a misunderstanding. Are you willing to accept my offer?"

"Your 16 billion purchase price isn't enough."

"I can go to 18."

"It will have to be 20."

"Split the difference at 19."

"20 is as low as I'll go."

"I can do that. Does that mean you'll sell at 20?"

"I need two weeks to talk to other members of my family. I have cousins who also own some stock. I'll push them hard to agree. I think they will."

McKnight looked nonplussed. "We're talking about your stock. Why do you care about them?"

"If they don't acquiesce, they could make trouble by suing. That would tie up the transaction for years. Do you know what the Italian courts are like?"

"I can imagine based on how everything else in this country operates. You can have a week and no more."

Alberto sighed deeply. "I think I can do it in a week."

"You'd better. That's all the time you'll have to sell—If you don't want to end up like your friend Federico."

Their meeting was over. Before heading toward the door, McKnight held out his hand. Alberto had no intention of shaking it. He gained satisfaction from letting it hang out until McKnight stuffed it into his pocket.

"I'll see you in a week," McKnight said in his British accent.

Once security called Alberto and told him that McKnight had left the building, he summoned Giuseppe.

"Good job," the Director of EU Counterterrorism said. "You played it perfectly."

"I wanted to strangle the bastard when he threatened my family."

"I would have enjoyed watching you do that on the video, but it wouldn't have helped."

"Unfortunately, you're right. What now?"

"I want you to sit tight. You bought us a week. He thinks he has a deal. So I'm confident they won't attack you or your family during that week. I'll call and let you know what happens next."

Beijing

Zhou was in his office studying detailed summaries of banks in England, France, and Germany prepared by his staff. Once he acquired Alberto's bank in Turin, he planned to move on to ones in other countries. Mei Ling would be a problem, but he could control her for now and eventually depose her. Zhou was on his way to being the next Emperor of China, which would dominate the world.

The phone rang and his secretary interrupted his analysis. "Mr. McKnight is calling from Italy."

Zhou had given McKnight one of his new encrypted phones so he could talk to the Hong Kong banker without the risk of being overheard.

"What happened?" Zhou asked anxiously.

"Success."

Zhou pumped his fist in the air. A wide smile appeared on his face. "Alberto signed the papers selling his bank to you?"

"Not yet, but he will."

McKnight described what happened in his meeting with Alberto. By the end, the smile had disappeared from Zhou's face and was replaced by a scowl. In frustration, he pounded on his desk.

"You're a fool, McKnight," he blurted out in anger.

"But I—."

"They're playing you like a violin and you don't even get it."

"He said he needed a week to gain the support of his family members; and he expected to get it."

"I did profiles on all of the other major shareholders. He's totally in control. He wanted to buy time. That's what happened, and you gave him a week."

"I could go back to Goldoni. I could—"

"Don't you do a thing to screw this up. Just get out of Italy. Go back to Hong Kong as quickly as you can. Goldoni will contact you there when he's ready to sign the papers. I promise that will happen. You can do it all electronically from Hong Kong. I don't want you back in Italy again. Ever."

"Alright," McKnight replied weakly.

When Zhou hung up the phone, he closed his eyes and tried to figure out why Goldoni wanted to buy time. Perhaps, he had notified governmental people and they were trying to entrap Zhou. Perhaps Goldoni suspected Zhou was responsible for Federico's death and he knew the police were close to solving his murder. That would eliminate the pressure for Goldoni to sell.

Zhou couldn't answer those questions. But he had no intention of backing away from his effort to take over Goldoni's stock and control of his bank. To the contrary. He decided to intensify the pressure on Goldoni. He'd force the banker to sell.

Zhou called Qing who was in Europe.

"Can you use your Russian friends from Biarritz for another job?"

"For money they'll do anything."

"Like most Russians."

"What's the objective?"

"Alberto Goldoni has a daughter who's studying law at the University in Bologna. Here's what I want you to do."

Rome and Bordeaux

Giuseppe picked up Craig at Fiumicino Airport at eight in the morning. As they rode to Giuseppe's office, Craig listened to Giuseppe's report of Alberto's meeting with McKnight.

"Well done," Craig said. "You set the stage perfectly for my competing offer."

When they arrived at Giuseppe's office he played the video for Craig.

"Alberto was right when he said McKnight's not too subtle," said Craig.

"He's not too smart, making his threat so direct. . . . Or perhaps he's inexperienced at doing this sort of thing."

"More likely frightened and intimated by Zhou."

"Well, regardless, McKnight's given me enough to arrest the bastard for extortion. I'd like to toss him in an Italian jail and let him rot."

"But that would interfere with my plan. So you can't."

"Unfortunately, you are right. Your plan better work."

"Don't they always?"

"No!"

"That hurt."

Giuseppe's secretary stuck her head in the office and said, "Jean-Claude from the French police is on the phone."

Giuseppe put the call on the speaker. Jean-Claude sounded excited when he said: "Radovich, the Russian we arrested for Federico's murder, is now willing to talk in return for leniency."

Craig was pleased to hear that. If they got enough from the Russian to nail Zhou, he wouldn't have to make himself a target with a competing bid for Alberto's bank.

"Where is he?" Giuseppe asked.

"In the jail in Bordeaux. How soon can you get there?"

"About three hours."

"You want us to get a statement without you?"

Giuseppe looked at Craig who shook his head.

"Three hours shouldn't matter," Giuseppe said. "We'll do it together."

"Good. My chief intervened with the head prosecutor. He fixed it so all of us can participate in the interview this time."

*　　　*　　　*

Three hours later, Craig and Giuseppe were in the prosecutor's office.

"I will begin," the prosecutor said, "but the three of you can join in."

He's certainly sounding different this time, Craig thought. His boss must have leaned on him hard.

Jean-Claude looked at Giuseppe. "What do you want from Radovich?"

"We want to know who hired him to kill Federico. If we could get that, we don't care what happens to Radovich."

"You're not suggesting I let him walk. Are you?" the prosecutor said.

"No. But I would like you to offer a sufficiently light sentence that he'll be willing to tell us who hired him."

"Okay," the prosecutor said reluctantly. "I'll offer him twenty years in jail."

"I was thinking more like five," Giuseppe replied.

"I agree with Giuseppe," Jean-Claude interjected.

"Five for murder is ridiculous."

Craig decided to remain quiet. He didn't want to alienate this hard-assed prosecutor who was about to blow the deal.

Jean-Claude looked angry. "He'll never talk for twenty years. Be realistic."

"I'm the prosecutor and I'm sticking with twenty years."

Jean-Claude's face was flushed with anger. "That's ridiculous."

"Then go over my head again. You know how to do that."

Before Jean-Claude could respond, the prosecutor was interrupted by a phone call. Craig heard him say: "Yes, I see. Yes." in a glum voice.

When he hung up, he sighed deeply.

"What happened?" Jean-Claude asked.

"Radovich is dead. They think someone poisoned him. The warden is investigating."

"Oh damn it." Giuseppe was shaking his head in anger.

"I'm sorry," Jean-Claude said. "We messed up."

No one disagreed with that assessment.

"What about the other Russian who was in Federico's house?" Craig asked. "The short one."

"We've been looking for him," Jean-Claude replied. "So far no luck. We'll redouble our efforts."

When Craig and Giuseppe left the courthouse they stopped for lunch at a nearby brasserie.

"What's your next move?" Giuseppe asked.

"Let's give Jean-Claude twenty-four more hours to find the short Russian. If he doesn't, I want to meet with Alberto and move up on my Barry Gorman competing offer for the Turin bank."

"That'll be tricky. Alberto thinks you're Enrico Marino, the race car driver."

"I'll have to take him through it slowly. It'll be better to do outside of Turin in case McKnight has people watching Alberto."

"Where do want to meet him?"

"There's an excellent little place in Orta called Villa Crespi. Not far from Turin. Arrange for Alberto to meet me there for dinner tomorrow evening at eight. If Jean-Claude finds the short Russian, we can always cancel the dinner."

"Will do. I'll have one of my people drive Alberto to Villa Crespi to make sure he's not followed."

Beijing

Elizabeth was traveling on a French passport as Simone Morey, a woman with dark gray hair who wore glasses with heavy black frames. Pushing a wheelie suitcase, she smoothly cleared passport control and customs at Beijing Airport. It was 6:30 in the morning and a tired looking agent had checked the computer and asked a perfunctory question about the nature of her visit. When he heard "tourist" he quickly stamped her documents.

From the terminal, without calling ahead, she took a cab to the house of Ned Burroughs, the Beijing Bureau Chief for the *International Herald*. She hoped to catch Ned before he left for the office.

Ned was a bachelor who lived on the tenth floor of a twenty-two story new high-rise inhabited by lots of Westerners in Beijing for business.

He was in a white terry cloth robe when he answered the door.

Fearful his apartment might be bugged, she raised a finger to her lips.

Ned immediately understood. Without mentioning her name, he pointed to the kitchen table at which he had been eating breakfast and said, "Help yourself. I'll get dressed. I'd like to show you the garden outside. They did a nice job with the flowers."

Hungry, she ate a bowl of shredded wheat. Then the two of them rode down in the elevator.

When they were outside, Ned said, "We can talk here. I have the apartment swept for bugs from time to time. They keep showing up and I keep destroying them. Ditto for the office. This is a tough place to work. What brings you to Beijing unannounced?"

"It's a long, complicated story, and it's better for you if you don't know the details. I need some help."

"Sure, Liz. Anything."

Hating that nickname, Liz, she cringed. It made her feel like a reptile. In the past, she had asked Ned not to use it. Today, she decided not to correct him.

She showed him the picture of the Chinese man she had taken on her cell phone in Parelli's suite in Venice. "Do you know who he is?"

Ned studied it for a full minute. Then he responded. "His name is Qing Li. He's a special assistant to Zhou Yun, the Finance Minister."

"You're sure of that?"

"Absolutely. I've seen him with Zhou at press conferences covering economic issues. He's like an administrative aide, a sort of chief of staff, but he's also a bit of a thug. He has a military background."

Elizabeth was excited. Ned was confirming that Craig was right about Zhou's involvement with Parelli.

"What else can I do for you?" Ned asked.

"I gather that you see Mei Ling from time to time."

"Thanks to your prior relationship with her, I have the best access of any foreign journalist. She always asks about you."

"Here's what I want you to do. Try to get in to see Mei Ling this morning for a few minutes. Tell her I'd like to meet with her secretly as soon as she can, and am traveling under a French passport in the name of Simone Morey. I'll remain in your apartment until you come back with an answer."

* * *

Three hours later, Ned returned.

"Mei Ling sent a car for you," he said. "It's waiting outside. A black sedan. The driver will drive you to your meeting with her."

Elizabeth thanked Ned, took her wheelie suitcase, and headed toward the elevator.

She climbed into the back of the car. Without saying a word, the driver activated the door locks, looked around nervously, and started the engine. He drove for an hour to a grassy area on the outskirts of the city, along a lake.

When the car stopped in front of a wood-framed house, the door locks were released. "Go," he told her in English. She saw half a dozen soldiers in front of the house. They were on alert, gripping automatic weapons.

Carrying her bag, Elizabeth climbed the stairs to the house. Mei Ling was waiting inside.

"So good to see you again, Elizabeth. I use this house as a retreat from my office. We can talk freely here."

One of Mei Ling's aides fixed tea for the two of them and then departed, leaving them alone.

"Are you seeing Craig?" Mei Ling asked.

"We've resumed our relationship. He's not an easy person."

Mei Ling smiled. "You would never want 'easy.'"

"That's true. "I appreciate your meeting me on short notice."

"For you, anytime. I'm sure this is important. Do you have some information for me?"

Elizabeth told Mei Ling everything she and Craig had learned about Zhou Yun's efforts to acquire Italian banks. "I also believe, but can't prove, that Zhou is financing Parelli's campaign in order to gain a foothold in northern Italy, if the nation divides."

"What do you base that on?"

Elizabeth told her about the Chinese man, now identified as one of Zhou's aides, who had been in Parelli's hotel room. Also, the sudden increase in Parelli's campaign ads suggested he received new money shortly after seeing the man in his room. "I don't have enough evidence to write a story about it, but I'm convinced this is occurring."

Elizabeth's information seemed to shake Mei Ling, who cupped her head in her hands.

When Elizabeth was finished, Mei Ling said, "We've always leveled with each other—you and I. So I will tell you that I knew Zhou was purchasing interests in several banks in Italy. However, I had no idea a banker had been murdered and another one threatened. And I certainly didn't know about Zhou's financing of Parelli's campaign to influence the Italian election. If Zhou had revealed his plans, I would have refused to approve any of these actions. I very much appreciate your coming here at great risk to tell me about them."

"It appears as if Zhou is trying to establish a major presence for China in Italy."

Mei Ling nodded. "Which he'll no doubt use as the wedge to gain business and influence elsewhere in Europe."

"I think that's right. Is this something you want?"

"Of course I want China to be a player in Europe, but devious operations like this are not consistent with my principles. They are not how I operate my government."

Elizabeth had thought that was the case. Still, she was relieved to hear it from Mei Ling. "Can you stop Zhou in his Italian operation?"

"I don't know."

"You are the president."

"Zhou has a great deal of support among the PLA."

"Because of his brother's role as head of the military?"

"That and his brother's death," she paused for a moment. "He used to be subtle in opposing me. Recently, he's become more blatant. He's convinced some top military men that I was responsible for killing his brother."

"That's ridiculous."

"These misconceptions are hard to change—and never forget that I have my own personal issues with Zhou because of what his brother did. He not only tried to kill me, but he arranged the murder of my husband and son—my only child. I found out later General Zhou ordered the captain of the navy ship to push him off the deck into the South China Sea. The two brothers were in a joint operation. I hold Zhou Yun responsible as well. So I will do anything I possibly can to gain revenge. I am patient. One day I will get it. You can be sure of that. Meantime I'll try to persuade Zhou to call off his Italian operation, as you characterize it. And I'll get a message to you letting you know whether I succeed."

"How will you do that?"

"When is the last plane to Paris this evening?"

Elizabeth checked the schedule on her iPad. "Ten fifteen. Air France Flight 17."

"Get a seat on that plane. Before takeoff, I'll get a message to you. It will be a very simple 'Yes,' if I persuaded Zhou to stop his Italian operation. 'No,' if I did not."

"I understand."

"Before you leave, I want to ask you something."

"Sure."

"What do you think of US President Worth?"

"I've never really gotten to know him. Why do you ask?"

Mei Ling hesitated for a moment before saying, "He's reached out to me. I want to know if I can trust him."

"All I can tell you is that Betty Richards, the CIA director, feels very positive about Worth and I trust her. On the other hand, Zhou Yun's meddling in Europe will undercut any relationship you develop with Worth."

Mei Ling nodded. "That's good enough for me. Thank you."

Elizabeth was puzzled by Mei Ling's question about Worth but didn't pursue it.

Mei Ling stood. "The car's waiting outside. Go now. He'll take you to the airport. You'll be safer there."

Elizabeth understood why Mei Ling wanted her far from China. She expected Zhou to mount a major effort to find out who had supplied the information about Italy to Mei Ling and to seek retribution.

Orta, Italy

I n the persona of Enrico Marino, Craig had been to Villa Crespi twice with Nina.

It was a gem of a small inn, built in the 19th century as a Moorish palace with spires by an Italian cotton trader who had been enchanted by Baghdad. To Craig, the interior resembled the stately home of an emirate with its elegant damask engravings, horseshoe arches, and turquoise fresco painted ceilings. The effect always made Craig feel as if he was in the middle of an Arabian desert rather than on the banks of Lake Orta in the heart of northern Italy.

Besides the surroundings, something else made Villa Crespi magical for Craig. The food was incredible. The restaurant was one of the best in all of Italy, which was saying quite a lot.

Craig arrived fifteen minutes before eight. He wanted to get settled before Alberto came.

As soon as he stepped through the heavy metal and glass front door, he received a warm greeting from the maître d'. "Oh, Signor Marino, it is so good to see you again."

Craig explained that he was meeting another man for a business dinner. "We have to talk. Where do you think we should sit?"

"I'll give you the end table on the verandah and I won't use the one next to it. Would that be satisfactory?"

"Absolutely."

Craig was seated at the table with a glass of champagne when he saw Alberto approaching.

Craig stood up and they shook hands. "So good to see you again, Enrico," Alberto said.

The waiter wheeled over a cart and Alberto ordered champagne as well.

"Giuseppe was very mysterious about our meeting this evening. All he said was that I would obtain answers at my dinner with you. Even when I pressed him, he refused to say any more."

Craig waited for the waiter to leave. He had thought long and hard about how much to tell Alberto and finally decided Alberto must trust his life to Craig and Giuseppe; Craig could do no less.

"I'm not Enrico Marino," he said softly.

"You're joking."

"Unfortunately not."

Alberto looked surprised. "You're not Enrico Marino?"

"Well, I am and I'm not."

"That's a little too mysterious for me."

"Until twenty-one months ago, I was Craig Page, an American who had worked for the CIA, and then—"

"You were head of the EU Counterterrorism Agency."

"How'd you know that?"

Everyone in Italy does. You're famous here. You saved the life of the Pope and the Vatican from suffering major damage. Then you seemed to have disappeared. One of our papers—*Il Messegero* I think—ran an article in October speculating what happened to Craig Page."

Craig hadn't seen it. He must have been in Argentina at the time.

"What did they say?"

"That Muslims captured you and were torturing you in a prison in Libya."

"Someone has a vivid imagination."

"What really happened? Can you tell me?"

"A mission of mine became complicated. I was being pursued by some nasty people. To evade them, I had to change my appearance."

"Plastic surgery?"

"Yeah. And after that, I did something I always wanted to do. Race cars."

"Which you're very good at."

"I was fortunate. I had a great teacher."

"Giuseppe was your deputy when you were head of the EU Counterterrorism Agency. He worked with you in saving the Pope and the Vatican."

"He supplied most of the good ideas and the Italian relationships. Giuseppe is incredible."

"I've known him only a short while. But I agree with that."

"Let's order," Craig said. "Then we'll continue."

Alberto selected pasta with seafood and then squab. For Craig, fois gras pate followed by lamb. As he looked at the wine list, Craig had noted that they carried both the Barbaresco and Barolo from Parelli. He selected the Barbaresco, which was excellent.

When they picked up the discussion, Craig said, "I've been working with Giuseppe since shortly after Federico's death. No one in Italy knows who I really am. Please do not tell anyone, or my life would be at risk."

"You have my promise. My own life is already on the line."

"I'm aware of that."

"Giuseppe told you about the threats McKnight made to me?"

"He even showed me the video of your last meeting with McKnight."

"I could strangle the bastard."

"But it won't help you. He's only the agent of a very powerful man."

"Who's pulling McKnight's strings?"

"Zhou Yun. He's the—"

"Chinese Finance Minister, a very wealthy industrialist, and also owner of the largest Chinese bank. It figures he would be involved."

"Do you know Zhou?"

"We never met. I'd be a pretty insular banker if I hadn't heard of him. By reputation, Zhou evokes fear."

"Which is justified."

"Zhou was responsible for Federico's death. Wasn't he?"

"I'm certain of it. But so far I can't prove it."

"I want to defeat Zhou."

Their first courses came. They ate in silence for several minutes. Then Craig said, "Giuseppe and I have a plan."

He decided to omit the CIA and President Worth. "I have created a new identity for myself as Barry Gorman, the head of a US-based private equity firm with billions of dollars to invest. The firm is called the Philoctetes Group."

"After the hero of one of Sophocles less known seven extant plays."

"Exactly. I will be making a competing bid for your stock. Going head to head with McKnight. My goal will be to smoke out Zhou. As Barry Gorman, I'll make him come after me to try to kill me so he can get your stock and take over your bank. Once I can prove Zhou is the one responsible for trying to murder me, I'll seek his extradition and have him tried in an Italian court. Perhaps I'll be able to nail him for Federico's murder as well. While all this is happening, Giuseppe will provide extensive security for you and your family in case Zhou decides to come after you. Personally, I don't think he'll do that. It's far more likely he'll come after me."

"There's a defect in your plan."

"What's that?"

"When people see Barry Gorman in the press or on television, they'll recognize him as Enrico Marino."

"That's right. So I can't let them see Barry Gorman. My interviews have to be on the radio or with the press while I'm at a remote location, and they can't get a picture. I must pretend to be a kind of Howard Hughes recluse."

Alberto looked dubious. "This plan of yours seems far-fetched."

"I recognize it is a bit extreme. However, I had a good result once before with a similar Barry Gorman ploy in Argentina. And frankly, I can't think of any other way to catch Zhou."

"What do you want me to do to make it work?"

"Behave like any businessman who has competing offers for his stock. Press us both to go higher."

"I can do that—but I never want to sell my stock—You have to understand that."

"I already do. Giuseppe told me. You don't have to worry about that. In the end, like any businessman, you can say you decided not to sell. What do you think? Will you cooperate?"

Without hesitating, Alberto responded, "Absolutely."

Beijing

"**W**hat the hell does she want now?" Zhou wondered as he rode in the back of his car on the way to the president's office.

It was a miserably hot and humid summer day in Beijing. He wished he were in northern Italy.

Traffic was heavy. He was impatient. "Put on the siren and flashing lights," he barked to his driver.

Soon cars were clearing a path for them.

Mei Ling had a stern look on her face. Refusing to be intimidated, Zhou glared at her as he sat down in front of her desk.

"It has come to my attention," she began, "that you are, without my knowledge, using funds of the People's Republic of China to manipulate the election in Italy and support one candidate, Roberto Parelli."

How in the world could she have found out? Zhou didn't dare show weakness. He refused to deny her accusations. Instead, he went on the attack. "What do you mean," he said, then mimicking her, declared: "'It has come to my attention.' *Who* told you these things?"

"Who told me isn't important."

Zhou pounded his fist on the desk. "But it is. I'm seeking to restore China to its former greatness. If we have a close relationship with the new Italian leader, we'll benefit hugely. We'll get contracts for airports, roads, and infrastructure and that will just be the beginning of our control in Italy. Parelli is our vehicle to gain a foothold in Europe. Our Trojan horse. Don't you see that?"

"Those are my decisions to make. Not yours."

"Don't you realize our enemies have come to you with these stories to undermine me. Now tell me who is your source?"

"I refuse. By engaging in these acts, you have usurped the power of my office. I intend to remove you as Finance Minister and to charge you with being an enemy of the state. Tonight, I will call a meeting of the Politburo to confirm my actions."

Zhou was counting votes in his mind. There were now fifteen members of the Politburo. Mei Ling might be able to garner the support of eight. He had to play his final and best card.

Without saying a word, he removed his phone from his pocket and made a call. "General Ko, this is Zhou Yun. I am directing you to move your tanks out of their storage facility and into Tiananmen Square. Position them immediately below the president's office."

Zhou had arranged with the commander who had been close to his brother to have one unit of tanks stationed next to Tiananmen Square and ready to move if he gave the order. "Yes, sir," he said.

Zhou asked General Ko to repeat that more loudly and held the phone in the air close to Mei Ling. When Ko repeated his words, Zhou had no doubt Mei Ling had heard them.

He turned to Mei Ling. "You must know that our patriotic military leaders are still angry with you for being a party to my brother's murder. They would like nothing better than to remove you from the presidency. I have been the one urging them restraint in the interests of maintaining civilian control of our government. Now you forced my hand. You have a choice. You can ignore everything I am doing in Italy, or you can lose your presidency in a military coup that will name me as president. It's that simple. But wait. Don't answer too soon. I want you to see the tanks in the square before you make your decision so you'll know I'm not bluffing."

Zhou walked over to a window facing Tiananmen Square. Mei Ling stood at an adjacent window.

With a smile of satisfaction, he watched soldiers clear the square of civilians. Then twenty tanks rumbled into the square and took positions facing the windows of the president's office.

"Well, what's your decision?" Zhou asked.

There was a long pause. He wasn't sure what she would do. After a minute, she said, softly with reluctance, "You win."

Zhou should have been elated. He wasn't. The critical fact was that someone had told Mei Ling about his support for Parelli. He had enemies working against him. He had to find out who they were and strike at them.

Back in his office, behind his desk, Zhou closed his eyes and tore at his mind, trying to figure out the source of Mei Ling's information. Finally, he concluded it was Luciano. The political adviser had been opposed to Parelli dealing with Zhou from the beginning. He was probably prejudiced against Chinese people.

Luciano must have found his way to one of the officials in the Chinese Embassy in Rome. The information would have worked its way up to the Chinese foreign minister who considered himself a rival of Zhou.

Yes, that must be how Mei Ling found out.

Zhou had made a tactical error in not letting Qing kill Luciano when his aide had wanted to. But Zhou would overcome that. Nothing would stop him.

Zhou heard the ringing of a cell phone on his desk. It was the matching one he had given Parelli.

This can't be good news, Zhou thought. He and Parelli had reached an agreement. He had transferred the money. Why would Parelli be calling?

"Zhou here."

"We have a problem."

"What happened?"

"I was interviewed by a reporter doing a feature on me. She was pressing me hard about whether I've received any foreign money for my campaign."

Parelli sounded nervous. Zhou needed to allay his anxieties. He didn't want Parelli backing out of their deal.

"So what? That's not an unreasonable question. After all, you now have a strong lead in the polls thanks to the money I provided for your campaign."

"No. It's more than that. She had a picture of Qing on her cell phone. She took it in my suite in Venice when he met with me to set up our meeting. She's connected the dots. My meeting with Qing. My new advertising money."

"But she doesn't know we met. She doesn't know anything about our agreement. Does she?"

There was a pause. Finally, Parelli replied, "I don't think so. I guess you're right."

"I know I'm right. Who's the reporter?"

"Elizabeth Crowder from the *International Herald*."

Zhou's blood ran cold. Again, Elizabeth Crowder. That nosey bitch of a reporter.

Before focusing on her, he had to finish the call with Parelli. "You don't have to worry. She'll never get the information she needs to write an article. There won't be a leak from my side and Swiss bankers don't talk. You're safe. I assure you."

"Alright. I'm satisfied. I wanted you to know."

"Thanks for telling me."

When he put down the phone, Zhou thought some more about his meeting with Mei Ling an hour ago. He realized now he had been wrong to conclude that Luciano was the source of Mei Ling's information about Zhou's actions in Italy. It had to be Elizabeth.

That was even worse for Zhou. She was an excellent reporter. If she found out about his agreement with Parelli, she would publish it in her paper and he'd be ruined. He had to stop her from doing that. No matter what it took. That meant killing her.

That could easily be done. Fortunately, he had asked Qing Li to remain in Italy until McKnight closed the Goldoni bank deal. Qing would know how to do it without leaving a trail back to Zhou.

Zhou thought about the death of Craig Page's daughter, Francesca, in Calgary, Canada. She also had been a journalist working on a story that would have been damaging to Zhou and his effort to control Canadian oil. The truck that crashed into her car, killing Francesca, left no links to Zhou. Qing could easily arrange a similar accident for Elizabeth.

Zhou picked up a phone to call Qing. Before dialing, he realized that anger was clouding his mind. He was missing what was totally obvious.

Elizabeth couldn't have supplied her information to Mei Ling by telephone. He had a tap on Mei Ling's office phone line.

Chances were that Elizabeth had come to China to tell Mei Ling in person. She was reckless. That was the sort of thing she would do. And she might even still be in China.

Zhou personally called the head of security for all international airports. He directed him to put out the highest alert—bright red—for Elizabeth Crowder. In case she might be using a phony passport, he forwarded her picture.

Then he waited by the phone, planning what he'd do to her when he got his hands on her and how he would use her to lure Craig to China.

Turin and Paris

Alberto was unhappy. This was the last day Parelli had been given to repay his loans. Alberto had his lawyers draw up the papers foreclosing on all of Parelli's property. At three in the afternoon he planned to give them the order to file with the court. At the same time, they would serve a copy of the papers on Parelli. Alberto didn't like taking this action; Parelli had left him no choice.

For the last week, he had followed Parelli's campaign activities closely in the media. The candidate had increased his advertising.

He must have gotten additional cash from somewhere, but hadn't offered Alberto a single euro in part payment.

Alberto concluded that Parelli was playing a high-risk game. He was assuming the banker would never foreclose. Well, he doesn't know me, Alberto thought. He's going to be sadly mistaken.

The phone rang. Alberto saw the call was from Parelli. Without hesitating, he picked up the phone. He had no need to hide behind secretaries or lawyers. He would tell Parelli exactly what he intended to do at three this afternoon.

Before he had a chance to say a word, Parelli blurted out, "We have to talk. I would like to come and see you in an hour."

"You're wasting your time. I won't extend the loans."

"I won't be asking you to do that, I assure you."

"Then what do you want?"

"Only ten minutes of your time. You won't be sorry. Believe me."

Alberto wondered what Parelli had in mind. Even if he wanted to extend the loans, contrary to what he'd said, Alberto would still meet with him. After their long relationship, he didn't mind telling Parelli in person that in a few hours lawyers would be filing papers to seize his property.

An hour later, Parelli walked into Alberto's office, a smile on his face and a briefcase in his hand.

"Thank you for agreeing to meet with me," Parelli said. "I have some news for you."

I have some news, too, Alberto thought, but he let Parelli speak first. "I'm listening."

"Ten minutes ago, I wire transferred to your bank 310 million euros. The total amount I owe you. I came to tell you that."

Alberto was dumbfounded. Parelli must have gotten the infusion of cash he had been hoping for. Alberto was so surprised he couldn't respond.

Parelli continued, "I also want to thank you for your forbearance all these months. I realize it's been difficult for you. I know that because of our friendship you departed from your normal way of doing business by extending and even increasing my unpaid loans. I'm grateful to you for that."

Parelli pointed to the computer on Alberto's desk. "Check your financial accounts," he said. "Make sure the money has been received by your bank."

Alberto was itching to do that. However, his sense of propriety required him to say, "That's not necessary if you tell me something is transmitted."

"Please. I insist."

As Alberto sat behind his desk and went to work on his computer, Parelli took a chair in front of the desk.

In a few seconds, Alberto confirmed what Parelli had told him.

"Your payment has been received," Alberto said. "Thank you."

Parelli reached into his briefcase and pulled out a dusty bottle of wine. With great care, as if he were handling a fragile object, he placed it on Alberto's desk.

"It's a bottle of our legendary 1945. Bottled after the end of the war. There's never been a better vintage like it before or after. I only have three remaining bottles. I want you to have one."

Alberto was overwhelmed by the gift. "I very much appreciate it. It's something I will always prize."

"Drink it on Ilana's wedding day."

"You and I will share it together when she announces that joyous event."

"The wine is a small token of my gratitude to you for continuing to support me for so many years. I realize this went against all of your normal banking policies. By not calling the loans—even lending me more money—you put yourself in a position where you might suffer heavy losses, but because of our relationship and that of our families you still did it. And I really appreciate it."

"I'm happy to hear that. Our relationship does mean a great deal to me as well."

"I will want to ask your forgiveness for how I've spoken to you lately. I was in a desperate situation financially—which is no excuse—and I was being ripped apart by many in the media who claimed I want to destroy Italy."

"Your program is certainly controversial."

Parelli smiled. "That's a polite way of telling me you think I'm wrong about dividing the country."

"I do, but that was never the critical factor in my decision to call the loans. I was trying to operate as a prudent banker."

"I can understand why you and others disagree with me, but I want you know that it is not my intention to harm—much less destroy—Italy. I believe my program is best suited for the entire country. Both north and south. Next to my family, Italy means the most to me. When I started down this political road, I had nothing to gain financially. In fact, I gambled everything I had to win this election—I wanted to give it my best shot."

"That's why I extended your loans. I wanted you to have every chance."

"I realize and appreciate that. If I can ever do anything to repay you, I would happily do it."

"Thank you. I would just like to resume our normal business relationship."

"Absolutely, and I promise to repay every loan on time. I went through a bit of a rough patch, but my finances are alright now."

Alberto wondered where Parelli had gotten the money to repay him, but he didn't ask.

The phone rang. Alberto ignored it, letting his secretary answer. A moment later, the intercom rang. "Excuse me," he told Parelli and picked up the phone.

"I'm very sorry to disturb you, but it's Mrs. Goldoni. She said it's extremely urgent. A family matter."

Dora had never used words like that before. Something terrible must have happened. Alberto forgot that Parelli was in the office and activated the call on hold.

"Yes, Dora."

She was crying.

"Tell me what happened."

"It's Ilana. She—She's disappeared."

He was frantic. "What do you mean Ilana's disappeared?"

"Her roommate Cara called to tell me she didn't come home last night. She didn't go to class today. Last night her roommates thought she might have spent the night with a boy, although she's never done that before. And she never misses class."

"Did Cara call the police?"

"She only called me. She thought Ilana might have come back to Turin."

For an instant, Alberto was paralyzed. Oh God, no. Not his Ilana. But he had to stay in control. He understood exactly what was happening. McKnight had arranged Ilana's kidnapping to persuade him to sell. They better not harm Ilana. He'd strangle that Hong Kong banker with his bare hands.

"I'll call Giuseppe right now," Alberto said.

"Tell me what happens."

"Absolutely."

While Alberto checked his computer for Giuseppe's number, he heard Parelli clear his throat. Alberto suddenly became aware that Parelli was still in the office. Indeed, standing in front of Alberto's desk, he had heard every word that Alberto had said to Dora. He had to get rid of Parelli so he could call Giuseppe.

"I'm sorry, we have to terminate our meeting," Alberto said.

"The bastards kidnapped Ilana," Parelli said, sounding outraged.

"We don't know anyone kidnapped her. All we know is that she's gone missing."

"Who are you involved with in business conflicts at this time?"

"You have to leave, please. I must call the authorities."

"I promise I'll leave. Just answer my question."

"I can't."

"Nobody should use a person's child that way." Parelli looked indignant.

"Please leave me—"

"I will. But I'll also do what I can to find Ilana. I have friends in the Bologna area."

"No, no. Please don't do anything. The authorities will—"

Parelli turned and left the office.

Alberto immediately called Giuseppe and told him what Dora said.

"I'll get right on it," Giuseppe said. "I'll use people who are expert in matters like this. I'll also tell Craig Page. He's had experience in these situations."

"Do you think McKnight kidnapped her? To put pressure on me?"

"That thought has been running through my mind."

"I'll kill McKnight."

"Do you know if he's still in Italy?"

"I don't know."

"Please don't tell anyone else about Ilana. Tell Dora to keep it to herself as well. Secrecy is always better in something like this."

"Sorry. I already did."

Alberto told Giuseppe about his conversation with Parelli. "It was stupid of me, but I was so upset when Dora called. I forgot he was in the room."

"What's done is done. Hopefully, Parelli won't get in the way."

"Meantime, and this is critical, you have to let me know immediately if anyone tries to contact you about your daughter. We'll hook up recording devices to your office and home phones. Make sure they are plugged in. If anyone calls, keep them on the line for one minute so we can get their location."

"One minute is a long time for this."

"I realize that. Thirty seconds for sure."

*   *   *

In Paris, Craig's phone rang. He saw it was Giuseppe and answered it immediately.

"I messed up," a very distraught Giuseppe said.

"What happened?"

"Zhou and McKnight kidnapped Alberto's daughter, Ilana."

"Oh, no. Oh, no."

"I should have given her protection. It's all my fault."

Craig felt equally responsible. He could have suggested it to Giuseppe, but he had thought that after McKnight's second meeting with Alberto, the Hong Kong banker was satisfied he had a deal and wouldn't have taken any action at least for a week. Craig's guess was Zhou hadn't been content to let events play along for that week.

"I've launched a major effort to find Ilana. Alberto will let me know as soon as he hears anything."

"That's all you can do. You'll find her."

Craig didn't have much confidence in those words.

*   *   *

As soon as he finished talking to Giuseppe, Alberto went home to be with Dora and to wait for the police to install the recording device on the home phones, hoping the kidnapper would call.

As soon as he walked into the house and before the police came, his home phone rang. "Is this Alberto," he heard in a Russian accented Italian.

"Yes. Who is this?"

"You better sell if you ever want to see your daughter alive again. This is your last warning."

"If you touch her, I'll kill you."

The phone went dead.

The doorbell rang. It was the police with the recording equipment.

Beijing and Paris

Fear gripped Elizabeth. Her knees were knocking.

Two minutes ago she had handed her passport to the official seated behind the glass window at Beijing airport. He had studied it and looked at her, and then back at the passport. And then again scrutinized her. Finally without saying a word, he pressed a button next to his computer. She knew what that meant: a question had been raised about her identity and whether she should be permitted to leave the country.

Seconds later, two powerfully built men in army uniforms, guns holstered at their waists approached her. One said, "Come with us."

With one in front and the other behind, and Elizabeth pulling her suitcase, the three of them walked down a long corridor and ended up in a small dingy windowless office where a woman sat behind a desk with a computer and phone on top.

Elizabeth's supposition was that Zhou had put out an alert for Elizabeth Crowder. Her life depended on her protecting her Simone Morey identity.

The men took positions in corners of the room. The woman, heavyset and sullen looking, with cakes of flesh under her eyes, pointed to a chair in front of her desk.

"Is there a problem? I have a plane to board."

"I'm well aware of when your plane leaves. You have plenty of time. Now sit."

Elizabeth did as she was told while trying to stay calm and keep her fear under control.

"This was a short trip for you, Miss Morey," the woman said in English.

"Yes. I had a business meeting to attend."

"What's your business."

Elizabeth was ready for this. "I'm with Total. The large French oil company based in Paris. In the development department."

She hoped the woman wouldn't check, but before leaving Paris, Elizabeth had spoken with a friend at Total who would communicate with his colleagues in Beijing to support her cover.

The woman didn't reach for the phone or computer. Instead, she pointed to one of the men. "Search her bag."

The two hoisted it on a table and carefully examined everything inside. It all fit the Simone Morey cover. Total materials. A couple of French paperback novels.

"Your briefcase."

Elizabeth handed it over. Again, it was all consistent with her cover. She had packed it carefully.

"Okay. Stand up," the woman said. "Strip down to your underwear."

Controlling her anger, Elizabeth complied. The woman came out behind the desk and first checked Elizabeth's clothes, which she had tossed on the chair. Then she checked inside Elizabeth's bra and behind the front of her pants.

Appearing disappointed, she said, "Get dressed and take your things. You can board your plane."

Elizabeth kept a grim expression on her face, not daring to show the relief she felt.

Half an hour later, Elizabeth was among the first to board. She took her seat in the business class cabin, 7B on the aisle.

Still no message from Mei Ling.

She was worried but tried not to panic. What had happened? Had Mei Ling been taken into custody and couldn't even send a message?

Her leg was shaking. Her foot was tapping the cabin floor.

She checked her watch. It was ten minutes until the scheduled takeoff. As she looked up, a Chinese flight attendant, a young women, headed in her direction. She stopped next to Elizabeth's seat.

"Are you Simone Morey?"

For an instant, Elizabeth forgot that was the name she was using. She recovered quickly. "Yes," Elizabeth said anxiously, wondering if soldiers were outside the plane to arrest her.

The woman reached into her pocket and extracted a small envelope, which she handed to Elizabeth. The front of the envelope was blank.

When the woman walked away, Elizabeth ripped open the envelope. Inside was a piece of paper folded over. Typed on it was the word "No" and that was all.

So Mei Ling had been forced to yield to Zhou. That made Elizabeth's situation even more precarious.

Anxiously, she watched the minutes tick down to take off. With two minutes to go, two Chinese men in mechanics uniforms came on the plane. Soldiers in disguise?

"We'll have short delay for a mechanical problem," the captain announced. Passengers groaned. They knew that the plane could be delayed for hours while repairs were made. Elizabeth gripped the armrest of the seat with white knuckles. Was this just an excuse to hold the plane until soldiers came for her?

She kept her eyes on the open cabin door. Nobody else entered the plane. After the longest forty minutes of her life, the captain announced, "We're cleared to go. Just completing the paperwork."

Take-off followed fifteen minutes later.

It may have been an Air France plane, but she wouldn't be safe until they cleared Chinese air space. Before that, they could be ordered to turn around, and she could be pulled off the plane.

Hours later when the pilot announced, "We have now cleared Chinese air space," Elizabeth was ready to shout for joy.

She signaled a nearby flight attendant. "I'll have a glass of champagne."

*   *   *

As soon as her plane landed at Charles De Gaulle, she called Craig. "Where are you," she asked.

"In Paris at the Bristol. Waiting for you and hoping you'd call."

"Oh, Craig, I love you."

"That is music to my ears. Where are you?"

"At Charles DeGaulle. I'll be at the Bristol as soon as the cab can get me there."

That was thirty-five minutes later. When Craig opened the door to his suite, she took a look at his bruised face and blurted out, "Oh my God!"

"Some thugs in Singapore wanted me to leave with a souvenir from my visit."

"Do you hurt?"

"I heal fast."

"So I've learned. I just wish you didn't end up as a punching bag all the time."

"I'm afraid it's part of the game."

"At least the way you play it."

"What happened in Beijing?"

She threw herself into his arms. "I never thought I'd get out." She sounded distraught.

"Tell me about it."

"First, I want to soak in a hot tub for about half an hour. Then I'll be ready to talk."

"Good. I'll order some food from room service and a good bottle of wine. That'll help you make the transition."

"You think good food and wine can fix everything."

"Well, most things."

*   *   *

Half an hour later, Craig was sitting across the room service table from Elizabeth, hanging on every word as she recounted her brief and harrowing trip to Beijing.

He was so relieved she was safely back.

At the end, she said, "Bottom line: we now have confirmation that one of Zhou's aides was in the Venice hotel room with Parelli. We also know that Mei Ling was unable to control Zhou. I was happy to get out of there. And how was your day?"

He told her about Singapore and Washington. Then about his dinner with Alberto. When he began telling her about the disappearance of Alberto's daughter, Ilana, he could barely speak. It brought back awful memories of Zhou's murder of his own daughter. "Giuseppe's doing everything possible to locate Ilana," Craig said. "But it's easy to hide people. I don't have a good feeling about this. Zhou's vicious and cruel."

"Let's be optimistic. Giuseppe knows the countryside. Speaking of that, how'd you find out about this place in Orta?" she asked.

"I read about it in a guidebook."

"Liar. Why didn't you ever take me there?"

"You were pursuing your career."

"What was her name?"

He had no intention of telling her about his friend in Milan, which would have triggered more questions, such as: "What was she like? Was she better than me in bed? Was she . . .?" Now that he was back with Elizabeth, he'd never see the woman again.

"Okay. That was the commercial. Can we go back to the program?"

"I guess so. Some day when you've had too much to drink, I'll get it out of you."

"Now let's talk about my Barry Gorman ploy. As I told you before I was so rudely interrupted, Alberto is willing to cooperate. Giuseppe will help us put it together. So I'm ready to roll."

"What's your first step?"

"Going public with my competing offer for Alberto's bank. Either in a radio or a newspaper interview that won't show Barry Gorman's picture. I can touch up my appearance a little, but I want to minimize the risk of someone concluding Barry Gorman is Enrico Marino and a phony. Any ideas who could do the interview?"

"A friend of mine, Carlo Fanti, is a top reporter at *Italy Today*. He told me where Parelli was staying in Venice, so I owe him a favor I'd like to repay. He'd love to do this. I'll tell him you're giving him an exclusive."

"Would he be willing to do it without Barry Gorman's picture?"

"If I tell him that's a condition. The story's good enough."

She checked her watch. "Too late to call Carlo this evening. I'll call first thing in the morning."

"Perfect. That takes care of Zhou's bank move. Now what do we do about his Parelli operation?"

"After we cleared Chinese air space, that's all I thought about for the rest of the long plane ride."

"What'd you decide?"

"I don't have enough to write an article exposing Zhou's financial support for Parelli." She sounded dejected. "The fact that Parelli had a meeting with a Chinese man in his Venice hotel room who is an aide of Zhou's doesn't get me far enough. I know what my boss is like. He'd kill the piece. I need more evidence. Somehow I'll figure out how to get it if it's the last thing I do."

Milan

While preparing for his interview with Carlo Fanti, Craig thought about his appearance. There wouldn't be any pictures, but Craig still had to worry about Carlo recognizing him as Enrico Marino. Perhaps Carlo had no interest in racing and had never seen

Enrico Marino, but then again maybe he was an avid fan. Craig decided to do some minor touch ups and hope that was sufficient. He colored his black hair a sandy brown. He bought a pair of glasses with plain glass lenses. When he looked in the mirror, he was satisfied that he had sufficiently changed his appearance.

Craig met Carlo in the lobby of the *Italy Today* newspaper building. Elizabeth's friend was in his fifties with a stubble of a beard and a friendly smile. He shook Craig's hand firmly. "I'm pleased to meet you, Barry Gorman."

Craig, who was accustomed to making snap judgments about people, decided that he liked Carlo.

"Likewise," Craig replied. "Elizabeth said lots of good things about you."

"How do you know her?"

Craig had to be careful to stick with the Barry Gorman bio and the fake Philoctetes website. He was a Stanford undergrad and went to Harvard Business School. But they couldn't have met when she was at Harvard. He was too much older.

"We met when we were both in New York. She was working for a paper there. I was with a private equity firm based in Manhattan."

"Was it romantic?"

"Just business. She was covering one of my deals that had international implications. She's a helluva reporter."

"You can say that again. Let's go to the café down the street. I find it easier to talk there."

"Sure. Whatever you want. Elizabeth told you no pictures. You okay with that?"

"I can live with it. I was wondering why."

"Once, I was in a bidding contest for an acquisition and the principal on the other side hired someone to use a little force to get me to back off. Since then, I figure if they can't recognize me, it'll be harder to hit me."

"You're serious, aren't you?"

"Wish I weren't. Business can be like warfare."

Carlo led the way to a small café. There he directed Craig to a remote corner that was deserted. He picked up two coffees at the bar and joined Craig.

As he sat down, Carlo stared at Craig for a few seconds. Craig held his breath, hoping Carlo didn't recognize Enrico Marino.

The reporter didn't say anything. Instead he removed a pen and steno pad from his bag. "I'm old school," he said. "No computers."

"Whatever works."

While Craig sipped his coffee, Carlo said, "Elizabeth didn't tell me what this was about. She just said that her friend Barry Gorman was in private equity and he had a real scoop. So you better start from scratch."

"Okay. How much do you know about private equity?"

"It's a way for rich people to get even richer."

They both laughed. "You're close. I head up a private equity firm based in San Francisco, the Philoctetes Group. We raise money from investors. Then I travel around the world trying to find investment opportunities to put that money to work. Right now I have a fund of 50 billion I'm working with."

As Craig had been talking, he noticed Carlo writing furiously. He paused for a minute to let Carlo catch up.

"What brings you to Italy?"

"I learned that control of your largest bank, Turin Credit, is in play. I just made an offer to buy Alberto Goldoni's stock."

Carlo looked startled. "I never thought that Alberto Goldoni would sell. That bank has family history."

Craig smiled. "I don't want to appear crass, Carlo, but if the price is right, everything is for sale."

"Who else is bidding on it?"

"Victoria Bank of Hong Kong made a 20 billion euro offer. I went to 25 hoping to wrap it up quickly, but Victoria has deep pockets. They may keep bidding. That's what I like about this business. You never know what your competitors will do."

"Sounds as if you enjoy what you're doing."

"I love it."

"If you get control of Alberto's bank, will you change how it operates?"

"Absolutely not. Alberto is a superb manager. I'd like him to remain on for at least a couple of years as CEO to make sure we keep it on the tracks."

"You won't start firing employees and take all those cost-cutting measures I heard about with private equity owners?"

"I don't operate that way. People on my staff have thoroughly studied Turin Credit. We're convinced it's an excellent bank with dedicated employees. I want to keep it that way."

"Will you change the direction of the business?"

"Right now the bank is strong in Italy, Western Europe, and the Middle East. I would like to expand into Asia and Latin America. Those areas have the potential for growth."

"Would that mean transferring employees out of Italy?"

"Some perhaps, but I envision an overall gain in employment here."

Carlo looked over his note pad.

"Anything else I can tell you?" Craig asked.

"Where can I find information about the Philoctetes Group?"

Craig gave him his card. "Check our website."

He and Betty had revised it before he returned to Italy. He was confident it would withstand scrutiny.

"Elizabeth was right," Carlo said. "This is big news. It'll be on the front page of *Italy Today* tomorrow morning."

"Good. I'll look for the article."

"By the way, where will you be staying in Italy? In case I want to check any facts or talk to you again."

"I'll be moving around a lot, but when in Turin, I'll be at the Grand Hotel Sitea".

"Am I allowed to say that in the article?"

"I'd rather you didn't. Same reason I don't want any pictures. I'm afraid I may be a target. I don't want to make it easy for anyone to find me."

Craig had to stick with his story, but he realized that disclosing his hotel in the article was irrelevant. There were only a couple of luxury hotels in Turin, which was where a private equity high roller would stay. He was registered under the name Barry Gorman. By tapping into hotel computers or making a couple of phone calls, Zhou or his goons could find out where Craig was staying. That was okay with Craig. He wanted Zhou to launch his attack against Barry Gorman.

As soon as Craig separated from Carlo, he called Giuseppe.

"Any news about Ilana Goldoni?" he said anxiously.

"Not a thing. We have a large force on the case. They've combed the entire Bologna area. Absolutely no trace of her. They're expanding the perimeter of their search."

"Have the parents heard anything from the kidnappers?"

"Not a word."

"That confirms what I thought," Craig said grimly. "Zhou is waiting for Goldoni to contact McKnight who is no doubt back in Hong Kong which will never extradite him. He's waiting for Alberto to tell McKnight he's ready to sell."

"I agree with you. That means we have to move quickly. At some point, Zhou may decide Ilana's not giving him the leverage he wants and kill her."

Paris

U nless it was raining hard in the evening, Elizabeth walked from her office at the *International Herald* across the Jardin des Tuileries and across the Pont de la Concorde to her apartment just off Boulevard St. Germain on the left bank. This evening there was fog and a little drizzle. Not enough to keep her from walking.

As she cut across the Tuileries, it was a little after ten in the evening. Elizabeth was deep in thought, recalling the numerous Italian news stories she had seen today—all announcing how much of a commanding lead Parelli had. She also tried to think of how she could get the critical information she needed linking Parelli to Zhou so she could destroy Parelli's campaign.

Because it was nighttime, only a scattering of people were walking on the paths that cut across the well-tended grass. She heard footsteps behind her.

When she turned, she saw two young men who appeared to be Chinese in the dim light. They were both close to six feet tall and powerfully built, and were about twenty yards behind her. She felt a surge of anxiety, but told herself not to become paranoid. There were plenty of Chinese people in Paris. All of them weren't working for Zhou.

Still, she recalled what had happened at Beijing Airport. Zhou was definitely after her. Ever since she and Craig split up twenty-one months ago, and Zhou's men followed her, she had grown accustomed to keeping a gun with her at all times. She reached into the bag draped over her shoulder. She felt around until she clasped the .22 in her hand. At the same time, she increased her pace.

She strained her ears to listen. The two men were walking faster as well. She began to run. They were running, too. And they were faster.

She realized that with the risk of attack by Zhou she had been foolish to take such a deserted route home. She would have been better staying on wide boulevards with pedestrians. But it was too late to dwell on that.

If she made it to the Place de la Concorde, which would be brightly lit with lots of traffic and pedestrians, she'd be safe. She gauged the distance and how rapidly they were catching up.

Damn. I'll never make it.

If the two men were after her, she didn't want to give them the advantage of attacking from behind. She suddenly stopped and pivoted to face them. As she did, she saw one of them pull a metal pipe about three feet long from inside his jacket. He raised his arm with the pipe. There was no longer any question about their motives.

She guessed at their plan. One would tackle and hold her. The other would beat her with the pipe.

She glanced around anxiously, but didn't see anyone. Shouting for help was pointless. They were moving up fast. Only ten yards away now.

She yanked the gun out of her bag and aimed it at them. They stopped dead in their tracks, stunned.

Taking advantage of their indecision, she fired a round into the air. Then she lowered the gun and aimed it at them again. They must realize, she thought, if they come at her at the same time, she'd never be able to hit both of them.

She watched the men closely. Neither made a move. Close up they seemed younger, not even twenty. Perhaps they weren't hardened thugs, but students in Paris whom one of Zhou's men had recruited.

"Get the hell out of here," she shouted in French, "or I'll kill both of you."

To drive home her message, she fired two shots at the ground, one to the left the two men, the other to the right.

"The next shots will be right at you. Now run before I shoot."

She held her breath.

They turned and ran in the direction they'd come.

Elizabeth realized it wouldn't be safe to stay in her apartment. She'd have to move to Craig's suite at the Bristol. She'd have to work from there for the next few days. That was alright with her, but first she wanted to stop at home and pick up some clothes and toiletries to take with her.

Elizabeth turned around and ran across the Tuileries. As soon as she reached the Place de la Concorde, with its Egyptian obelisk in the center, she hailed a cab. Before getting in, she looked around. No sign of the two Chinese men.

She gave the driver her apartment address.

Ten minutes later, they pulled up in front of the four story old gray stone building. She asked him to wait. "I'll only be a few minutes."

When he grumbled, she handed him twenty euros and said "Keep the meter running."

She dashed out of the cab.

Climbing the steps to her second floor apartment, key in hand, she had second thoughts about the wisdom of stopping here.

I'm being stupid. Zhou might have people waiting in the apartment.

She should have gone right to the Bristol. She could have bought what she needed.

Stupid. Stupid. Stupid.

Still, she refused to turn and run away. She pulled out her gun again and dropped her bag on the floor while she unlocked the thick wooden door. It creaked when she slowly opened it. After entering the apartment, she closed the door and slipped on the chain lock.

As she looked around inside, the words, "Holy shit," came out of her mouth. Her apartment was a total mess. Drawers had been opened and the contents spilled out. The cushions on the sofa were cut, the television screen shattered.

Gun in hand, she walked into the other two rooms, her bedroom and the study. Nobody was there, but those rooms had been ransacked as well. Her computer had been destroyed. Fortunately, her laptop had been in her bag. Her clothes were strewn everywhere. Some had been ripped and cut.

The damage was a vicious act. Enraged, she wanted to shout and cry.

She forced herself to think rationally. What did Zhou and his men hope to accomplish?

It seemed unlikely they were looking for something on her computer or in her apartment. Nothing valuable was taken to make it appear that it was a break-in by burglars.

No, that wasn't it. Fearful they might not find her to kill her, the men must have done this damage to frighten and intimidate her. Well, they were sorely mistaken if they thought this would persuade Elizabeth to break off her investigation into Zhou's relationship with Parelli. It had the opposite effect, making her more determined to get the truth and publish it.

Quickly, she grabbed a duffel. Inside, she stuffed some clothes that hadn't been destroyed and some cosmetics.

She was preparing to leave the apartment when she heard men's voices speaking Chinese in the hallway on the other side of the door.

One of them inserted a key or a burglar's tool in the lock. In horror, she watched the door begin to open. Then the chain lock stopped it. They would easily smash through that, Elizabeth decided.

With her bag in one hand and the duffel in the other, she ran to her bedroom in the back, closing the door behind her. She threw open the window leading to a small verandah and tossed the bag and duffel over the railing to the grassy patch below. She took off her shoes and let them fall to the ground as well. Then she climbed over the railing and lowered herself down while holding on. Once her arms were fully stretched, she let go and jumped. As soon as she hit the ground, she rolled to break her fall. Quickly, she grabbed her shoes, the bag, and duffel, and ran to the waiting cab in front.

She told the driver to drop her at the corner of Rue St. Honore and Franklin Roosevelt. She wanted to walk the last six blocks to the Bristol, to make sure she wasn't being followed.

As she walked, she realized she would need Craig to give his authorization to the Bristol for her to use his suite, but she didn't want to use her own phone.

In the Bristol lobby she explained her situation to Eric, the front office manager. He immediately called Craig on a Bristol phone, then gave her a key, and led her up to the suite.

She had eluded Zhou again, but she realized she was pushing her luck.

Beijing

The news of Barry Gorman's competing offer for Alberto's stock hit Zhou like a ton of bricks. He never saw it coming.

He was perplexed and dismayed as he read the online version of Carlo Fanti's article in *Italy Today*, which McKnight had forwarded to him electronically.

In response, he called McKnight and screamed at him, "Why didn't you close the deal with Alberto? You're an incompetent piece of dog shit."

"I tried. Believe me," McKnight stammered. "Do you want me to make a higher offer to Alberto? Go up to 30?"

Zhou was thinking. Something didn't seem right about the Barry Gorman offer. For starters, Barry Gorman had told Carlo Fanti that Victoria Bank of Hong Kong had made the initial offer and exactly how much that offer was. Yet the offer hadn't been announced publicly. Gorman could only have gotten it from Alberto, but Alberto knew his life was on the line as well as his daughter Ilana's. Even if Alberto had gotten another legitimate offer out of the blue from Gorman, he wouldn't have given Gorman the details of the Victoria Bank offer. If he had, he would have made Gorman keep that confidential.

Alberto had to be afraid for his life, and Ilana's as well, unless . . . unless all this was being manipulated by the authorities who had offered Alberto protection and were trying to find Ilana. The more Zhou thought about what was happening the more it smelled like a fish in a house after five days. Alberto had to be cooperating with the authorities to encourage Zhou to make a mistake and to lower the boom on him.

Zhou told McKnight. "Don't make another offer right now. 'Sit tight.'"

"But—"

"Don't you question my judgment. I said sit tight."

Zhou hung up the phone and called in Chi Fan, his director of financial research. Chi was a tall, thin man in his fifties with black-framed glasses and a leathery face. "I want you to find out everything you can about a private equity firm based in San Francisco called Philoctetes Group and a principal in that firm by the name of Barry Gorman."

"How soon do you need it, Honorable Zhou?"

"In one hour."

Without hesitating, Chi replied, "You'll have it, then, Honorable Zhou."

That pleased Zhou. He liked subordinates to do what they were told.

While waiting for Chi, Zhou called Qing Li in Paris. "What happened with Elizabeth Crowder?"

"At first, my men couldn't get their hands on her so they wrecked her apartment to scare her into breaking off her investigation of Parelli. Later they found her. They planned to beat her to death, but they failed."

"What happened?"

"She pulled a gun and chased them off."

"Fools! Where is she now?"

"They lost her."

"You should toss them both into the Seine with concrete in their boots."

"I already sent them back to Beijing. They will be disciplined there. I've gotten two men from the state security branch at our embassy in Paris. They are now watching her apartment and office."

"Good. Let me know when they find her."

When Chi returned to Zhou's office, he was holding a stack of papers, as well as a small computer. Zhou pointed to the chair in front of his desk and Chi sat down.

"What did you find out about the Philoctetes Group and Barry Gorman?" Zhou demanded.

"Very mysterious, Honorable Zhou."

"That tells me a lot."

"To be more precise, there was no Philoctetes Group until twenty-one months ago."

"So what? New private equity groups start up all the time in the United States."

"I realize that. Barry Gorman's resume is the problem. It lists schools he graduated from, Stanford and Harvard Business School, and two investment banking firms, Goldman Sachs and Morgan Stanley, that he worked with before he started Philoctetes Group."

"And?"

"I had one of my people hack into the computers of Stanford and Harvard and also the employee records of the two investment banking firms. There's no record of Barry Gorman in any of those. That's why I said very mysterious."

"Well, well, well."

Zhou stood up and paced around the office thinking about what he had just heard.

After a few moments, he said, "You were right. It is very mysterious. Good work."

Chi held out his papers. "Would you like to see the results of my work, Honorable Zhou?"

Zhou shook his head and dismissed Chi.

Alone in his office, Zhou leaned back in his chair, closed his eyes, and thought some more. As he did, the cloak of mystery gradually lifted.

Barry Gorman was a fictional creation. He had an American name, spoke like an American during the Carlo interview, and had American schools and companies in his bio. Who could have done that? Had to be someone in the United States. That meant Barry Gorman was a CIA creation.

Zhou said the letters "C – I – A" aloud. Immediately, he thought of Craig Page.

To Zhou, the Barry Gorman ploy sounded like something Craig Page would have done. Elizabeth Crowder was in this up to her eyeballs. She and Page had always worked together. And Page would have done anything he could to get even with Zhou because of the death of his daughter and because he would never be safe while Zhou was alive.

Zhou was convinced that Barry Gorman was Craig Page. He had to know for sure.

He picked up the phone and called Winston Tyler, the US Secretary of the Treasury in Washington. "You must come to Beijing immediately," Zhou told Tyler. "It concerns your new bond issue."

After a momentary pause, Tyler responded. "This is not a good time for me. I am scheduled to testify before Congress."

Zhou refused to take no for an answer. Nor could he afford a delay. Establishing that Barry Gorman was Craig Page was the most important thing for him. He replied, "And it may not be a good time for me to roll over the bonds and participate in your new issue."

"Now wait a minute," Tyler said. "We agreed when I was in Beijing that—"

"Agreements are always subject to renegotiation. If selling your bond issue isn't important enough for you to come to Beijing, well, then . . ."

"How about next week?" Tyler asked.

Zhou was convinced Tyler was so anxious to sell his bonds and so gutless that he would yield. He said, "Sorry Professor, you must come now."

After another pause, Tyler capitulated. "Okay, I'll leave today."

"Excellent. Email me your ETA."

When Zhou put down the phone, he was satisfied. At least one thing was going right: he was able to manipulate Tyler. The American treasury secretary was now critical to Zhou.

While waiting for Tyler, Zhou refused to stand still. He reread Carlo's interview with Barry Gorman. Probably the man was Craig Page. Then Zhou had to kill him to avenge his brother's death. Even in the unlikely event that he wasn't Barry Gorman, he still posed a threat to Zhou. The man was an obstacle to Zhou closing the deal for Alberto's stock. Either way, Barry Gorman had to die.

Zhou summoned one of his computer experts. "I want you to find out where Barry Gorman is staying in Turin, Italy. It's likely to be one of the luxury hotels."

Ten minutes later, Zhou had the response. "Grand Hotel Sitea in Turin."

He called Qing again. "I want you to leave your people in Paris searching for Elizabeth. You should fly to Turin immediately. A man using the name of Barry Gorman is staying at the Grand Hotel Sitea in Turin. At least some of the time. If he's there now, I want you to kill him. If he's not, I want to stay there until he returns. Then kill him."

Turin and Bologna

It was noon and Alberto was pacing in the living room of his house, staring at the phone, willing it to ring with news about Ilana. He and Dora were alone in the house.

Suddenly he heard a beeping on his BlackBerry resting on the table, signaling that he had a message. Alberto grabbed it and looked.

The sender of the message was A FRIEND. The message contained an address outside Ferrara about 40 kilometers from Bologna and the words, "Come Alone. No police."

He showed it to Dora.

"Call Giuseppe right now," she said. "Have him get the police there immediately."

Alberto shook his head. "No! That would be a mistake. They said no police. I don't want to put Ilana at greater risk."

She looked flabbergasted. "What do you propose to do? Go yourself?"

"With Val, my head of security at the bank."

"Are you insane."

"Val spent twenty-five years in the military. In special forces. He was in Afghanistan with NATO troops. He's very good."

Alberto could see from the look on Dora's face that he hadn't changed her mind. Throughout their long relationship, they had rarely disagreed, and it pained him to be doing so on a subject that meant as much to them as the safety of their daughter. However, he knew he was right.

"How long have we been married?" Dora asked.

"Twenty-two years. Why?"

"Have I ever pleaded with you—begged you," she began crying, "for anything?"

He walked over and tried to put his arms around her. She pulled away.

"Well, I'm pleading with you . . . begging you."

"Please reconsider. If the police go in full force, the kidnappers will kill Ilana."

"Giuseppe and his people are professionals. They know how to handle situations like these."

"This isn't a situation. It's our daughter."

She threw her hands up in the air. "Ach, you're so stubborn."

"I'm calling Val and going."

"You're making a mistake."

He realized that once he left, she could call Giuseppe. He was confident she wouldn't.

As he headed toward the door, she called to him. "Be careful. I don't want to lose both my husband and my daughter."

They flew to Bologna in Alberto's private plane. The passengers were just Alberto, Val, and the pilot. At the airport, they picked up a rental car. Val tossed a heavy weapons bag in the trunk and got behind the wheel.

Once they were on the road, Val said, "I did some checking on the web and GPS. The address is for a two story old farmhouse. It appears to be deserted. I've had experience in Afghanistan with rescue missions like this. My thought is that I go in armed with an assault rifle and grenades at my waist. I know you're a good marksman, so I want you to grab a rifle and take cover behind the car. Watch the upstairs windows. If you see anyone, take them out. Don't approach the house until I signal you to do so. Are you okay with that plan?"

"Absolutely."

Alberto had been scared when they boarded the plane. Now the adrenalin was kicking in and boosting his courage.

"Do you have any children?" he asked Val.

"Two little girls. Five and three. If anybody grabbed one of them, I'd do just what you're going."

"You wouldn't leave it up to the police?"

"Hell, no. That's an expression I learned from my American buddies in Afghanistan."

Alberto responded with a nervous laugh. He was glad to get confirmation from Val.

After driving half an hour, Val pulled over into a clump of trees.

"House is coming up on the right in a few minutes. Let's get ready." He took weapons from the bag, also Kevlar vests for both of them.

When they were prepared, he resumed driving.

Alberto looked out of the window. Val's description was right. It was a faded and peeling white, wooden two-floor structure. In front, he saw a door and two windows on the first floor; there were two more on the second. The grounds were overgrown with grass and weeds. The fields which had once been planted looked abandoned.

Val turned in to the driveway and stopped ten yards from the house.

While Alberto took his position behind the car, rifle in hand aimed at the upstairs, Val raced toward the house brandishing an Uzi.

As he did, Alberto saw a motorcycle roar out from behind the house and across the field. The rider was wearing a black leather jacket and black helmet. His face wasn't visible. Alberto realized there was no point trying to chase him. He was too fast in this terrain. Besides, it was clear Ilana was not on his bike.

Alberto held his breath as he watched Val kick in the front door. There was no gunfire.

Oh my God, she's dead. And they left her body, Alberto thought.

He was overcome with grief. "No. Oh, no. . . . No."

He remembered that Val had told him to wait behind the car for Val to call him before coming to the house, but he couldn't help himself. With the gun in hand, he ran frantically.

When he got inside, he was blown away by what he saw. Two dead heavyset, blond young men—their faces bruised, were hanging from a beam that ran across the ceiling. Both had what looked like piano wire wrapped around their necks. Their bodies were swaying in the breeze from the open door.

"Downstairs is secure," Val said. "Follow me upstairs."

Val moved up the old wooden stairs as softly as he could. They creaked with each step. Alberto was right behind.

At the top, they fanned out, Val to the left, Alberto to the right.

In the second room he entered, Alberto saw her. Ilana was tied to a chair in a seated position. Except for the chair, the room was deserted. Ropes were wrapped around her chest. Her legs were tied to the legs of the chair. A cloth secured by masking tape covered her mouth. Her eyes were open and staring at him.

She was alive!

Thank God. Ilana was alive!

He raced over and awkwardly embraced her in the chair. A knife, he needed a knife.

Val entered the rom. "No one else is here."

Val removed a knife from his pocket and cut Ilana loose. She threw her arms around Alberto. They both cried in relief.

"I'm alive, Papa," she said. "I'm okay."

"Did they harm you?"

"Not at all. Two Russians were holding me prisoner. Beefy blond men. A few hours ago, the weirdest thing happened. Four masked men burst into the house, Italians from Naples, I think, based on their accents. They beat up the Russians, strangled them with wire and hung them from a ceiling beam. I was terrified." She paused and took a deep breath. They never touched me. Afterwards, they brought me up here. I was sure they would rape me, but they didn't hurt me at all. They tied me up and said, 'We'll notify your father to come and get you.' How strange. Who do you think they were?"

"I have no idea."

Alberto was lying. He realized Parelli was responsible for freeing Ilana. When Parelli had heard about her kidnapping, he had told Alberto he would try to find Ilana and that he had friends in the Bologna area. Also, Alberto knew that Parelli had friends in the Mafia. This was how they operated. The man on the motorcycle must have been one of theirs left behind to guard Ilana until Alberto came.

Alberto wouldn't tell anyone. The Russians were kidnappers. On the other hand, some zealous prosecutor might say, "Murder is still murder." They could go after Parelli and stories about his Mafia ties would hurt his campaign. So Alberto decided to keep this to himself.

He called Dora to tell her Ilana was alright. Then he handed his daughter the phone. While she talked to her mother, Alberto borrowed Val's phone. He went into another room and called Parelli.

"It's Alberto. Ilana's safe."

"I'm so glad."

"I can't thank you enough."

"Friends help friends. Besides, we're practically family."

Turin and Paris

A t three in the afternoon, Craig was in his sixth floor suite in the Grand Hotel Sitea, the most luxurious in Turin. After the publication of Carlo Fanti's article, he had expected Zhou to find out where he was staying and send someone to attack him. But so far nothing had happened. His phone rang. It was Giuseppe.

"We've had a major development in Federico's Biarritz murder."

"Another false alarm?"

"No. This time it's for real." Giuseppe sounded excited. "The short Russian turned himself in to the police. His name is Boris Smirnov. He was afraid the Russian gang he's with would kill him as they did Radovich. He agreed to talk in return for immunity from prosecution and resettlement in northern France where his Russian buddies won't be able to find him."

"Is Jean-Claude okay with that deal?"

"If we are. What do you think?"

"Based on what Amelie told us, he wasn't the shooter. Letting him walk doesn't bother me if, and it's a big if, he can give us enough to nail Zhou. Will that hard-ass prosecutor in Bordeaux go along with the deal?"

"Jean-Claude isn't taking any chances. He made a preemptive strike. He went right to the justice minister, who not only approved the deal but directed the police in Bordeaux to move Smirnov to a Paris prison. They're holding him under an alias to get him away from those delightful Russians in Biarritz who poisoned his buddy, Radovich."

"So you and I are going to Paris to question him?"

"Correct. Along with Jean-Claude. My plane leaves in fifteen minutes from Fiumicino. Where should I pick you up?"

"Turin Airport."

"I'm on my way. See you there in about an hour and a quarter."

Before leaving his sixth-floor suite, Craig glanced out of the window at the street below. He couldn't believe what he saw. Getting out of a cab was a Chinese man who looked very familiar.

Craig pulled up on his phone the picture Elizabeth had taken in Parelli's suite in Venice. It was a match. And the man getting out of the cab had been identified by Elizabeth's bureau chief in Beijing as Qing Li, Zhou's thug.

He had to be coming to kill Barry Gorman. Quickly, Craig bolted from his room. He took an inside staircase, racing down the steps two at a time. The day before, he had located the back exit of the hotel in case this situation should arise.

Craig guessed Qing would probably be in the hotel lobby. Craig could get from the first floor staircase landing to the rear entrance of the hotel without passing through the lobby. That back door opened onto a narrow street. Craig could race to the corner, find a cab there and escape before Qing ever even saw him.

In about a minute, Craig reached the landing on the ground floor. From there it was a short dash to the heavy metal rear door.

Craig pushed it open and stepped out into the bright sunlight. As he did, he froze.

Qing was standing there with burglar's tools for opening locks in his hand. Zhou's henchman must have been planning to break into the rear entrance to avoid the lobby. The alley was deserted.

The instant Qing saw Craig, he dropped the tools and reached for a gun in a chest holster.

Unarmed, Craig couldn't let him get his hand on that gun. In a throwback to his high school football days, he dove through the air and tackled Qing, driving him to the ground and falling on top of him. Qing tried to punch Craig in the head. Before he had a chance to make contact, Craig lifted his leg and drove his knee hard into Qing's groin. Qing groaned and stopped swinging.

Craig grabbed the gun from the holster. He smashed Qing in the side of his head knocking him out. Then he took the gun, shoved it into his pocket, and ran.

At the corner, he flagged down a cab. "Airport," he told the driver.

When he got to the airport and was waiting for Giuseppe's plane, he thought about Elizabeth. He had been afraid to call her for fear of giving her location away. He hoped she was alright in his suite at the Bristol.

*   *   *

They were in the plane over the French Alps when Giuseppe's phone rang. "Hello, Alberto," he said. "I have Craig with me. I'm putting this call on speaker."

Alberto wasn't talking. He was crying. *Oh God, no, Craig thought. Ilana's dead!*

After a few moments, Alberto got control. "Sorry. I'm just so, so happy. Ilana is free from the kidnappers, and she wasn't harmed. I can't tell you how ecstatic I feel. Thank you so much for all your help."

Craig was wondering what happened. "Did the police find her?" he asked.

"It's all very strange. Four masked men burst into the house where two Russians were holding her. They killed the Russians. Used string like piano wire to strangle them. They told me where to find Ilana."

"Who do you think did it?"

"The Russians must have had some enemies. I don't care who it was. I'm just glad my daughter is safe."

When they hung up the phone, a puzzled Craig turned to Giuseppe. "Who do you think killed the Russians?"

"The wire is a Mafia signature. Sounds like Alberto wasn't content to rely on me and the police."

"That surprises me."

"This is a wonderful country. Things surprise me every day."

*   *   *

Dressed in prison blues, Boris Smirnov was perspiring heavily when the guards led him into the interrogation room and departed. He was short and squat, with a protruding belly and a long scar along his left cheek. His hands were cuffed behind his back.

Giuseppe and Craig were in the room with Jean-Claude. They had decided the Frenchman should take the lead, which he did when the four of them were seated at an old wooden table so nicked and battered that Craig thought it must have been around for the French Revolution. Perhaps aristocrats had been decapitated on this very table. Now that was a gruesome thought.

"You're in deep trouble," Jean-Claude said. "This isn't Russia. It's France. Here, we take murder seriously."

"I didn't kill nobody." Boris said in French heavily accented with Russian.

"You can tell that to the jury. You have a problem, though. Most French people hate Russians. They don't like the crime you people bring with you."

Sweat was dripping into Boris's eyes, which were twitching. "I didn't kill the banker."

Craig liked hearing that. Boris was aware of their target. "You're telling us that Radovich killed the banker," Craig interjected.

"Uh huh," Boris said weakly.

"Louder," Jean-Claude demanded.

"Yes."

"But you put chloroform over his wife's face. Didn't you?" Giuseppe said.

"I'm not talking until you give me what I want."

"What's that?" Jean-Claude asked.

"No jail time and you give me a new identity in the north of France."

"You have to be kidding," Jean-Claude said.

"If they find out I'm a snitch, they'll kill me. Same as Radovich. Besides, I didn't kill nobody."

"But you put chloroform over the woman's face while your pal Radovich killed her husband."

"Even if I did that, chloroform don't harm nobody."

"It makes you an accessory to murder. You'd go to jail for a long time."

"If you won't give me what I want, I'll take my chances at trial."

Craig didn't think he was bluffing.

"If I agree to that," Jean-Claude said, "could you tell us who hired you and Radovich?"

"Uh huh."

"Louder."

"Yes. When Radovich brought me into this, he told me my only function was to disarm the house security system and open the safe. He didn't say anything about no chloroform. I told him I wouldn't do no rough stuff. Later, he gave me the chloroform and told me to use it on the woman."

"Who hired Radovich?" Jean-Claude asked.

"That's all I'm telling you until I get my deal. And I want it in writing."

Jean-Claude turned to Giuseppe and Craig. "It's your call. Should I give him the deal he wants?"

"Depends on what he will tell us," Giuseppe said.

"You heard him," Jean-Claude told Boris. "Let's hear what you have to say."

"Not until I have something in writing."

Jean-Claude reached into his bag and pulled out a document a prosecutor had signed. Jean-Claude had shown it to Craig and Giuseppe before they questioned Boris. It promised Boris what he wanted provided he explained fully who hired Radovich and Boris.

The Russian fidgeted in his chair. "Radovich came to my house. He asked me to join him in a meeting with somebody who wanted him to do a job. It involved a safe. That's why he wanted me in on it."

"Is opening safes your specialty?" Giuseppe asked.

"Yeah. I learned it in Moscow from the FSB. You know the successor to the KGB."

"We know what the FSB is," Craig said tersely. "Don't insult us."

"Where was the meeting?"

"In the back room of a night club in Biarritz. The Volga."

"Who was there?" Jean-Claude asked.

"A Chinese guy. He described the job. He wanted Federico killed and he wanted it to look like a jewelry robbery."

"What was the name of the Chinese man?"

"Mao."

Jean-Claude looked angry. "You think that's funny? Did you expect me to laugh?"

"No. That's what he said his name was."

"How'd you get paid?"

"500,000 euros in cash at the time of the meeting. 400 for Radovich and 100 for me. Another 500,000 after we did the job. That second 500 was wired to Radovich a day later from Moscow. He gave me another 100,000. That's all I know. The whole story. When you resettle me. I'd like to be in a town near Deauville. I want to be near the sea."

"I'm sure you do." Jean-Claude was shaking his head. "You haven't given us a damn thing, Boris, and you know it."

Boris looked alarmed.

Craig moved in to help Jean-Claude. "A Chinese man named Mao. That's a bad joke. Either he was tricking you or you're tricking us."

Giuseppe turned to Jean-Claude. "I say you send Boris back to Bordeaux. Stick him in the same prison Radovich was in and spread the word that he talked to us. So we gave him a lighter sentence."

"Okay. I'll do that," Jean-Claude said.

Boris screamed, "No. I've told you all that I know." Sweat was pouring down the sides of his face.

"It's not enough," Giuseppe added. He stood as if the interview was over. "Get this scum out of here."

Again, Boris screamed. "No. No."

"I'll call the guards," Jean-Claude said.

"Wait. I have more."

"This better be good," Giuseppe said.

"During our meeting, Mao received a call. He was talking Chinese. When he was on the phone, he seemed distracted. So I took out my own phone. Pretending to make a call, I took his picture. I'm sure he had no idea."

Craig perked up. This could be something. "Why'd you do that?"

"They taught me to do stuff like that in the FSB. You never know who will turn on you."

"Where's your phone?"

"It was in my pocket when they arrested me. It's probably with my clothes. They told me they'd lock up my clothes when they put me in this uniform."

"I'll go check," Jean-Claude said.

A few minutes later, the Frenchman returned, accompanied by a guard, with a Samsung cell phone in hand. He put it on the table.

"Is this your phone?"

"Looks like it."

Jean-Claude told the guard to take the cuffs off Boris. Then he told the Russian, "Show us Mao's picture."

Boris fiddled with the phone. Finally, he found a picture and laid the phone on the table.

Craig was staring at it. "Yes," he mumbled under his breath. "Yes. . . . Yes." The man calling himself Mao was Qing Li, Zhou's thug, the same man Elizabeth had photographed in Parelli's Venice suite. And the same man who had been entering Craig's hotel in Turino as he was leaving. Zhou's henchman. "Son of a bitch," Craig cried out in English.

Giuseppe said to Jean-Claude, "Excuse my friend. In Italy, we sometimes use that expression. We picked it up from the Americans when they liberated us in the Second World War."

Jean-Claude laughed.

On a roll, Craig said, "Now tell us how your friends kidnapped Ilana Goldoni in Bologna."

Craig was watching Boris closely. He tried to keep a deadpan expression. His eyes gave him away. They began twitching.

"Who's Ilana? What kidnapping?"

He didn't sound persuasive. Craig didn't care. He had gotten what he wanted. Zhou or one of his henchmen must have used the Russian gang in Biarritz for the kidnapping. Craig had enough on Zhou to charge him with Federico's murder. He had no need to pursue this any further with Boris. Still, he couldn't help telling the Russian, "You should be glad they didn't assign you to the kidnapping job. Your two buddies are dead. Strangled with piano wire. A painful way to die."

Boris was twitching even more.

Craig said to Jean-Claude, "If you can get a statement from Boris repeating what he told us about the Chinese man, and keep the phone, I'm okay with the immunity deal."

Giuseppe took his lead from Craig. "Okay with me, too."

Once Craig had the statement and the phone, Jean-Claude, Boris, and the guard left. Alone with Craig, Giuseppe said, "You recognized the Chinese man?"

"He's Zhou's henchman. His name is Qing Li. By establishing how close Li was to Zhou, we'll be able to build a circumstantial case against Zhou. And there's always a chance Qing will talk."

"That is good news. Except for one critical fact. We may be able to catch Qing in Europe, but China will never extradite Zhou to France to stand trial."

"That thought occurred to me."

"So we're nowhere," Giuseppe said glumly. "All this work for nothing."

"Up the creek without a paddle as we used to say when I was a boy growing up in Monessen, Pennsylvania."

Giuseppe smiled. "You Americans always have these cute little expressions."

"They help soften our misery."

"There has to be a way we can get Zhou."

"Let's sleep on it."

"Fair enough. I'm staying in Paris this evening. I want to spend some time at my office here in the morning. I assume you'll be with Elizabeth."

"For sure." He was looking forward to seeing her in his suite in the Bristol. "I'll come to your office at ten tomorrow morning. We can decide on our next move to get Zhou."

"Sounds good. Say hello to Elizabeth for me."

*   *   *

It was almost ten in the evening when Craig entered his suite in the Bristol. He saw Elizabeth seated at the desk in the living room typing away on a laptop. She had turned the living room into her office, complete with file cabinet and a printer. A table was on each side of the desk. Papers were strewn everywhere.

A room-service table with a half-eaten roast chicken dinner and an open bottle of Bordeaux had been pushed to one side.

"Hi, honey. I'm home," he said.

She kept typing, "Give me a minute, Craig. I'm completing my edits for a story."

"You mind if I finish your dinner? I'm starving."

"Help yourself."

While she edited, he ate the leftover roast chicken with mustard sauce and roast potatoes. He also finished the St. Emilion, which wasn't too bad. She had learned something about French wine.

"Done," she said and stood up. She came over and hugged him.

"Ouch," he said. His bruises from Singapore still hurt. "I was afraid to call you," he said. "For fear of giving both of our positions away to Zhou."

"I figured as much. For the same reason, I didn't call you. We can talk freely here. I searched this place for bugs."

"Now tell me what happened that made you move here?"

She described the incident in the Tuileries when she was on her way home and finding the destruction in her apartment.

"Zhou really doesn't want you to nail down his involvement with Parelli and publish it in the paper," he told her.

"For sure."

"You were smart to get the hell out of your place. I read your interview with Carlo in his paper. Superb interview."

"What are you doing in Paris?"

He described the meeting he and Giuseppe had with Smirnov. "We now have a case against Qing and Zhou," he said at the end.

"But no way to get Zhou out of China to stand trial."

"You cut to the bottom line quickly," he said glumly.

"So what will you do next?"

"Don't know. Giuseppe and I are meeting in the morning."

They climbed into the large bathtub and bathed together. She tried to be gentle with him. "Just once," she said. "I'd like to make love with you when you're not all battered and bruised."

As he led her to the bed, he said, "The pleasure will far exceed the pain."

They made love, and when they finally came together in a heart-thumping climax, he rolled off. They both fell asleep, their arms entwined.

In a deep sleep, Craig was conscious of a pounding on his arm.

"Ascona," Elizabeth shouted. "Ascona."

What the hell, he wondered as he shot to a sitting position. "What are you talking about?"

She turned on a light on the night table.

"Ascona. It's a gem of a high end resort on the north end of Lake Maggiore in Switzerland." She sounded excited.

"I know where it is." He glanced at the clock on the bed stand. It read: 4:18. "You're giving me a geography lesson in the middle of the night."

"No, I'm solving your problem."

"How?"

"Next week in Ascona, from Tuesday to Friday, will be their annual Global Economic Conference."

"What's that?"

"You've never heard of it?"

"We travel in different circles. No terrorists have tried an attack there. So it hasn't shown up on my radar."

"It's an annual summer gathering similar to Davos in the winter, except much smaller and more selective about who's invited. Also, the focus is entirely on world financial and economic issues. I've covered it the last couple of years for the paper. Only about two hundred people attended last year. Finance ministers and heads of national banks like the chairman of the Federal Reserve. Some CEOs from large multinationals are invited."

"And what do all these self-important mucky mucks do?"

"Don't be a Philistine. They discuss in workshops and panels, as well as informally, the state of the world's economy and finances. They talk about interest rates, the strength of banks—issues like that."

"But what's it have to do with me?"

"The last two years Zhou attended and spoke. He doesn't leave China often, but he comes to this to network with top finance people from around the world. So if he's coming this year, you might be able to extradite him from Switzerland."

She had Craig's full attention.

"Brilliant. I love it. How do we find out if he's coming?"

"I could check the program, right? He usually speaks. The world wants to hear what the Chinese Finance Minister has to say."

"Good. Do it now."

They both climbed out of bed and went to her computer in the living room.

Moments later, she printed the program. "Look at this." She pointed. "Friday morning at 10 a.m. Zhou Yun, Chinese Finance Minister, discusses the state of the Chinese economy."

"Fabulous," Craig said. "Do you know where Zhou stays in Ascona?"

"The last couple of years he took over a private residence outside the center of Ascona. Let me check my conference notes. I may have kept the address." She went to work on her computer. Minutes later, she said, "Number 16, via Delta. My guess is he'll use it again this year. People repeat patterns like this."

"Is there any way you can confirm that."

She thought about it, and then said, "I can email one of the women on the conference staff whom I've gotten to know. But not this early."

They went back to bed. Too excited to sleep, they made love again. Then he dropped into a fitful sleep.

At eight, they were seated at a room service table for a continental breakfast. He had a double espresso and she had a cappuccino.

Resting on the table were copies of the pale orange *Financial Times* on top of Elizabeth's *International Herald*.

While Elizabeth emailed her friend in Ascona to confirm that Zhou would be staying at the same private residence, Craig picked up the *Financial Times* and looked at the headline on the lead article in the upper right. "Parelli has opened up a 20 percent lead."

"That's a huge number," he said glumly. "He'll be hard to stop."

Craig began reading. "The *Financial Times* quotes somebody named Stefano with Parelli's campaign who said, 'It will be a new day for Italy.' So who's Stefano?"

"Some young kid who replaced Luciano. Parelli's close adviser for many years."

"What happened to Luciano?"

"He's sick. I saw him in the Venice hotel room. He didn't look well."

"What's wrong with him?"

"I don't know. Why?"

Craig ran a hand through his hair. "Sick people can talk."

"I tried calling him on his cell a couple of times. The first time, he didn't return the call. The next time, I got a recording that his phone had been disconnected."

"Do you have any other way of getting to him?"

"What are you thinking?"

"From all of the facts you've presented, it's possible that he and Parelli had a falling out—this is probably a long shot—but what the hell, we're grasping at straws."

She thought for a few seconds before saying, "I have a possible way of getting to Luciano."

"Great. What's that?"

"Your new friend, Carlo Fanti. I'll get right on it."

Elizabeth checked her email. The woman in Ascona confirmed that Zhou would be staying at Number 16, via Delta.

"Excellent," Craig said. "Now I better get moving. I have to meet Giuseppe. When should we get back together?"

She sipped some cappuccino. "I'm confident you'll be coming to Ascona next week one way or another."

"A good bet."

"I'm scheduled to arrive in Ascona on Monday around noon with a reservation at the Eden Roc. I've gotten to know the manager. I'm sure he'll let me register under the name of Simone Morey. I have a passport in that name which I used for my trip to Beijing. So you'll have a place to stay from Monday without registering."

"Sounds like a good plan."

"Since you're a hotel snob, I should tell you that the Eden Roc is up to your usual standards of luxury. It's a fabulous hotel and the best one in Ascona."

"Hey, that stung. I'd stay anywhere with you."

"I doubt that."

"Listen, Elizabeth," he said as if barking a command. "Once you get to the hotel in Ascona, stay in the room until I get there."

"Who appointed you to give me orders?" She sounded angry.

"Zhou is certain to have some of his goons with him. They've already attacked you once. If they spot you, they'll come after you again."

"Don't worry. I can protect myself. I have a job to do in Ascona for the paper, and I intend to do it."

After leaving the hotel, he took a cab to Giuseppe's office in the La Defense office complex.

Craig told Giuseppe about Ascona and his colleague reacted with enthusiasm. Together, they went to see Jean-Claude.

"Before you two tell me what you want," the Frenchman said, "I have some news for you."

Craig could see that Jean-Claude was pleased and excited. "Tell us."

"I had our Treasury people follow back to the source the money trail on the second 500,000 euros Radovich received."

"And?" Craig asked anxiously.

"From Biarritz, it goes to Moscow. From there, through a circuitous route runs to a Beijing bank owned by Zhou Yun, the Chinese Finance Minister."

"Son of a bitch," Giuseppe said. They all laughed.

Craig was thrilled. Their case against Zhou, while still circumstantial, had just gotten stronger.

Giuseppe told Jean-Claude what they wanted: the French government's extradition of Zhou and Qing Li from Switzerland the following week to stand trial for Federico's murder.

As Giuseppe was talking, Craig watched Jean-Claude screw up his face into a somber frown and negative expression, while pursing his lips together and shaking his head.

"Impossible," Jean-Claude said at the end.

Craig had learned to despise that word more than any other in the French language. He had heard French people use it for the truly impossible, like running a two-minute mile, as well as anything they just didn't want to do, like lowering the room temperature.

"Why is it impossible?" Craig asked.

"The justice minister will never approve it."

"Will you at least ask?"

"I don't know."

"C'mon, Jean-Claude," Giuseppe said. "Federico was murdered on French soil."

"That's true, but—"

"It's the only way."

Jean-Claude sighed deeply. Craig took that as hopeful sign. "Only if Giuseppe goes with me, and he does the asking. I have a family to support and I would like to keep my pension."

"That bad?"

"The idea that my government would do anything to upset, much less outrage, China, the world's second biggest economy, which is rapidly on its way to passing the United States. is too preposterous to imagine."

"But will you at least try?"

"Sure, if Giuseppe does the talking. And I would advise him to wear a bullet proof vest."

As they prepared to leave the office, Jean-Claude said to Craig, "You might as well wait here. This won't take long."

Jean-Claude was right. Thirty-four minutes later they returned, Giuseppe looking dejected.

"He turned you down?" Craig asked.

"He laughed at Giuseppe," Jean-Claude said. "He wouldn't even entertain the idea."

Craig and Giuseppe thanked Jean-Claude for his help and left the office.

They stopped at a small brassiere. "Where to next?" Giuseppe asked.

"Rome," Craig replied. "Federico was an Italian citizen. You could try Zhou and Qing in Italy. Let's ask your President Cerconi to seek his extradition from Switzerland."

"That might work. He likes you, Craig. Remember he gave you the help you needed when we were defending the Vatican."

"I know, but I'm not Craig Page now. I'm Enrico Marino."

"If you want to get this, you'll have to tell him you're really Craig Page."

Craig hated disclosing his identity to any more people, but he knew Giuseppe was correct.

Giuseppe called his pilot. "He'll meet us at Orly in thirty minutes," Giuseppe told Craig.

Rome

For the meeting with President Cerconi, Craig ditched the glasses. An hour before, he stopped in a hair salon to have his hair coloring rinsed out. He could reapply it after the meeting, but for now he was desperate to gain any advantage he could. Perhaps Cerconi was a racing enthusiast.

It was five o'clock when Craig and Giuseppe filed into Cerconi's office in the Palazzo del Quirinale, the ornate residence of the Italian president. In setting the meeting, when asked by Cerconi's secretary for the subject, Giuseppe had said that it concerns an important legal issue. Craig wasn't surprised to see that Julio Flavio, Italy's justice minister, was already in the room.

"Well congratulations on winning the race in Stresa," Cerconi said. "I was glad it was one of our boys."

Craig swallowed hard. Well not exactly. This was damn complicated. He'd better just spit it out. "Mr. President, my being Enrico Marino was sort of a ruse. I'm actually Craig Page. I think you'll remember that—"

The president's head snapped back. "I would have never thought that in a million years. Plastic surgery?"

"Yes sir."

"The surgeon did a good job."

"Thanks."

"Was he Swiss?"

"Yes, sir."

"They do the best work." Craig wondered if Cerconi had some work done or was considering it. "Agreed."

"Well anyhow, I have fond memories of Craig Page. Giuseppe explained to me that your ancestors were Italian. So I could still say one of our boys won the Stresa race."

The four of them sat down at a conference table.

"Okay. What can I do for the two of you?" Cerconi asked.

Giuseppe nodded to Craig who explained what they wanted. As he spoke, the justice minister was scowling; the president seemed intrigued.

When Craig was finished, the president said, "I like the idea of making Zhou pay for Federico's murder. He was a friend of mine, and also one of the most prominent and well-respected people in all of Italy."

"Let's not go so fast," the minister said. "You'd be damaging relations with one of our largest trading partners."

Craig responded, "I am convinced that Chinese President Mei Ling is not backing Zhou in this."

"That's good to know. I don't like being pushed around by those people," the president said. "Besides, Zhou was trying to take over a major part of our banking business."

"All of that may be true, but this is a legal issue," the minister said, trying to control the turf. "And in my opinion, the case against Qing and Zhou is insufficient for the Swiss to extradite."

"Why don't you put the case together," Craig replied, "and see what the Swiss say."

The minister looked annoyed. "Are you questioning my judgment on a legal issue?"

"I was just—"

"Do you have a law degree Signor Page?"

"No, but—"

"Then my opinion must be the opinion of this government. You do not have enough evidence to warrant extradition. So I will not seek it." His words had the ring of finality.

Craig and Giuseppe looked at the president. They were convinced Cerconi's sympathies were with them. Would he be willing to overrule his justice minister on a legal issue?

"I'm afraid, gentlemen," the president said meekly, "on an issue like this, I must defer to my justice minister."

Craig realized further argument was futile. He and Giuseppe thanked the president for his time and filed out.

Depressed, Craig accompanied Giuseppe back to his office.

Giuseppe sat down behind the desk. "What now?" he asked.

Craig was looking at a map of Europe taped on the wall. He saw Ascona in Switzerland on the northern end of Lake Maggiore. On the southern end of the lake was Stresa.

"If I could get Zhou into a boat in Ascona," Craig said. "I'd be able to bring him to Italy."

"You mean kidnap him?"

"Yes."

"But what good would that do? You heard the president's decision."

"That was only on the legal intricacies of requesting extradition. On substance, he was with us. Besides if we actually had Zhou in Italy, with Elizabeth's help, we'd use the media to trumpet the fact that Zhou killed a well-liked Italian banker and philanthropist. That Zhou was trying to take over a large part of Italy's banking business. And if Elizabeth succeeds, we'll also be able to show that Zhou was trying to manipulate the Italian election for Parelli. With all that, the Italian people would demand that he be tried. The president would then overrule the justice minister."

Giuseppe was smiling. "What's so funny?" Craig asked.

"I have to hand it to you, Craig. You're undaunted. You keep getting knocked down and you're back up on your feet."

"I take that as a compliment."

"It was meant to be. However, your plan still has one major obstacle."

"What's that?"

"Are you planning to kidnap Zhou yourself?"

Craig took a deep breath. "I was hoping you'd arrange to have three or four special ops troops from the Italian army help me out."

Giuseppe shook his head. "You're dreaming. First of all, I don't have authority to get those troops. And second, I know the minister of defense. After what happened to our troops in Afghanistan, he vowed that no Italian soldiers would ever leave Italy again as long as he was defense minister. Finally, after our meeting with President Cerconi, I couldn't possibly do that. So that's a nonstarter. You have another idea?"

Craig thought about it for a minute. "When does that United plane leave for Washington? I'll have to get my help there."

Beijing

Zhou was in his office waiting for Tyler to arrive when Qing called from Italy.

"The Russians failed us," he said grimly.

"What happened?"

"Ilana Goldoni's free. The two Russians guarding her are dead."

"They truly are incompetent. I can't believe the police found her."

"They didn't."

"Rumors are it was the mafia. They may be in a turf war with the Russians and this is one more battle between them."

Zhou didn't believe it. There had to be another explanation. He had no idea what it was. Events were rapidly spinning out of control for Zhou. Nothing was going as he planned. He wasn't used to that.

He had to catch a break. He was hoping for that from Tyler.

*　　*　　*

Moments later, Tyler staggered into Zhou's office. He must have come here directly from the airport, Zhou thought. The American treasury secretary looked weary and bleary eyed.

Before Tyler sat down, he said, "What's happening on the bond issue that you had to see me on short notice." His voice was scratchy. He sounded irritated.

Zhou decided to go on the attack. "I'm so angry that I might not buy a single bond from the new issue. That's what I wanted to tell you, Professor."

"Whoa. Can we talk about this?"

When they were seated, Tyler asked, "What happened to make you angry?"

"The purchase of Alberto Goldoni's shares in Turin Credit, the largest bank in Italy, means a great deal to me. And," he said, as he paused to point a fat finger at Tyler, "and the CIA is sponsoring a competitive bidder, Barry Gorman. You didn't even tell me about it."

Zhou was flying blind, making his accusation on speculation, hoping for confirmation from Tyler. He narrowed his eyes, looked squarely at Tyler, and pressed ahead. "Don't you lie and tell me you're unaware what your government's doing."

Tyler looked away and said, "These are issues of foreign policy. Not my responsibility."

Tyler's words delighted Zhou. The American didn't deny Zhou's charge. His shot in the dark had hit home.

"Nonsense," Zhou said, pounding on the table. "You made a commitment to me to stop action like this. So I have no intention of buying your bonds."

"But—"

"National default will happen on your watch. You'll go down in the history books as the worst treasury secretary the United States ever had."

"But—"

"You can forget about getting a high paying job on Wall Street. They might not even take you back on the faculty at Princeton."

Tyler looked miserable.

Zhou had stopped talking and waited for the American to capitulate. He was confident Tyler would. The man had no spine. No character.

"I fought against it," Tyler said weakly. "I did my best. You can't expect more than that from me."

"But you should have told me about this Barry Gorman business once you knew about it. You owed me that much."

Tyler didn't respond.

Zhou continued in a loud booming voice. "Why didn't you tell me?"

"I didn't think you'd—"

"You didn't think that I'd cancel my bond purchase. Well, you were wrong."

"That's not what I meant."

"Then what did you mean?"

"Could I get some coffee, please?"

Zhou hit the intercom, and his secretary came running. Once Tyler had a cup and gulped down half of it, Zhou said, "I will buy at least 50 percent of the bonds in your new issue if, and only if, you tell me everything about this Barry Gorman business."

Tyler began explaining this in a halting voice. "I had noth—
nothing to do with this." He was stammering. "The idea came from
Betty Richards, the CIA director."

"Who else was involved?

"I don't know."

"You're lying to me. Keep your bonds and get out of here."

"Can't we discuss the—"

"Leave now. Our meeting is over."

Tyler didn't move.

"Leave or I'll call my guards."

Tyler's hand was shaking.

After a full minute, Tyler said, "Craig Page was also involved. He
used to be CIA director."

At the mention of the name, Zhou felt a surge through is body as
if he had been struck with an electric prod. "What's Page's role in this?"

When Tyler didn't respond, Zhou said, "You tell me voluntarily, or
I'll—"

He left the threat hanging in the air.

Tyler took a deep breath and blurted out. "Craig Page had plastic
surgery to change his appearance a year or two ago. He was hiding out
in Italy racing cars. He has now surfaced again in Washington with his
old friend Betty Richards. Barry Gorman doesn't exist. Craig Page is
pretending to be Barry Gorman, the owner of the Philoctetes Group, a
private equity firm, which also doesn't exist."

"So he's using US government money to bid against me for Alberto
Goldoni's stock and control of Turin Credit."

"It's all a sham. He has no intention of buying the stock. He's trying
to trap you."

Zhou stood up and paced around the office. He had seen how
Craig Page operated in the past. None of this surprised him.

"Now you know everything." Tyler added weakly. "Will you buy
the bonds from our new issue?"

Tyler stood and Zhou walked over, close to Tyler. "Of course I'll
buy your bonds. Even though you should have come here and told
me on your own. Not wait for me to demand the information from
you."

"I'm sorry. Really, I am."

"Don't worry. I'm a forgiving person."

But not with Craig Page, Zhou thought.

Finally, with what Tyler told Zhou, killing Page had now become a lot easier.

Washington

"**R**un that by me again," Betty told Craig. "You want to have four US Special Forces troops go with you to Ascona to help you kidnap Zhou, the Chinese Finance Minister, and take him to Italy?"

They were in Betty's seventh floor office at Langley. It was eleven thirty in the morning.

"That expresses it very succinctly," Craig said. "What do you think?"

"Well, what I didn't say is you are out of your fuckin' mind."

"That's a positive reaction. Sort of."

"Okay. I'll tell you what I really think. I'm in favor of anything that brings down Zhou. The man's a horror, and bad for our relations with China. Your plan is bold and daring. Typical Craig Page. It might even work."

"What do you mean 'might.' It will work."

"I've heard that from you before. Sometimes you come up empty. There's no point you and I debating it. The critical fact is I can't authorize it on my own."

"You did for Argentina."

"A different president was involved. Also China isn't Argentina. I can and will support you. However, it'll be the president's call."

Craig had expected that response. "When can we get on his calendar?"

Betty picked up the red phone that ran to the Oval Office. He heard her say, "Craig Page is back about the China-Italy matter. We'd like some time with you. . . . Three o'clock will be great. . . .We'll be there."

She put down the phone. "We're on for three this afternoon."

"You think he'll invite Jones and Tyler?"

"Jones in Egypt. I don't know about Tyler."

"I don't like Tyler.

"Really. I couldn't tell."

"He was so damn negative."

"Sorry, Craig, even the CIA director can't tell the president whom to invite to a White House meeting. Now let's get some lunch before we go to the White House."

"I vote for Capri, that excellent Italian place not far from here."

"Aren't you tired of eating Italian food?"

"Never. Not as long as it's good."

Over lunch, Betty asked Craig, "What's happening with you and Elizabeth?"

"She's working hard to get the facts about Parelli and Zhou. She's a helluva reporter."

"No, I mean personally."

He began singing. "Matchmaker, matchmaker, make me a match."

"Very funny."

"Seriously. We're back together. The sex is as good as ever."

She blushed. "Too much information. I don't need those details. I'd like to know if wedding bells are a possibility."

"Right now both of us are trying to avoid getting killed by Zhou and his thugs. Everything else will have to wait."

*   *   *

When Craig and Betty entered the Oval Office, Craig was glad to see President Worth was alone.

As if reading Craig's mind, Worth said, "I would have included Jones and Tyler. But Jones is in Egypt having to endure violent protests and Tyler's in Beijing."

That raised Craig's antenna. "What's he doing there?"

"Something to do with a new bond issue we're putting out in a little while. He wants to make sure the Chinese buy our new bonds when we roll over the old ones."

Worth checked his watch. "We better get started."

Craig took that as a sign Worth's time was limited. So once they sat down in the living room section of the office, Craig gave a brief summary of what had happened since their last meeting. He ended with his meeting with the Italian president.

"I came away from that session feeling confident that if we could get Zhou to Italy, the Italians would try him for Federico's murder."

"And how do you propose to get Zhou to Italy?"

"Well, next week he's going to be attending a world financial conference in Ascona, Switzerland."

"I love that part of the world. I was there four years ago for a vacation. We took a boat ride on Lake Maggiore from Ascona to Stresa."

The president smiled and turned to Betty. "Craig wants to kidnap Zhou and take him by boat to Stresa. Right?"

She nodded. "How'd you guess."

"I've gotten to know how Craig operates."

"If he could do it," Betty said, "it would be good for everybody. Zhou is trouble for all of us."

"Do we know whether Mei Ling is supporting Zhou on this Italian bank business?" Worth asked.

Craig cleared his throat and answered. "Elizabeth Crowder, the—"

"Foreign news editor for the *International Herald*."

"Yes. She met with Mei Ling a few days ago. She believes Mei Ling would like to stop Zhou but she feels powerless because he has the support of the military."

"That doesn't surprise me. Mei Ling and I had a private meeting a couple of months ago. She told me about her concerns with the military. I like her. We decided to open a line of communication."

"Good to hear that," Craig said.

"So let's say I agree with you it would be a good idea to kidnap Zhou and take him by boat from Switzerland to Italy. How would you do that?"

Craig took a deep breath as if he were preparing to jump off a high board. "Well, if you let me borrow four Special Ops Forces, we could get in and out with Zhou before anybody knew about it."

"Casualties?"

"I'll develop a plan that will hopefully avoid them."

"But we both know these operations never go exactly as planned. Look at the Osama Bin Laden capture. One of our two helicopters crashed on the roof of the compound."

"They got their man. Didn't they?"

"I don't know, Craig. Switzerland is our ally. It's not Pakistan." Worth looked troubled. "The French and Italians don't want to ask the Swiss to extradite him."

"On the other hand," Betty said, "removing Zhou from the world stage would be beneficial for this country and lots of other people."

Craig was thrilled with Betty. She knew exactly when to come in.

Worth put his head into his hands and closed his eyes. At least he's thinking about it, Craig concluded.

Finally, Worth opened his eyes and picked up his head. "Okay, Craig. You have my approval on two conditions."

"Yes, Mr. President."

"First, disguise the identity of the troops. No US insignia on the shirts or anything like that. They should wear plain olive or brown so they could be from anywhere. After the operation, we can refuse to admit or deny they were ours."

"I'll do that."

"Second, when your plans are set and before you head over there, I want you and Betty to come here and brief me about the logistics. After that, you must keep Betty informed about all details of the operation, and Betty you must keep me informed in real time. I want to be able to abort this at any time before you commence the operation. Is that clear?"

Craig and Betty both nodded. "We'll do that," Craig said.

"Then don't waste your time sitting here. Get started with developing your plan. This won't be easy."

$$*\qquad*\qquad*$$

Back in Betty's office, Craig said, "I don't have a good feeling about Tyler. He was downright hostile when I proposed the Barry Gorman plan. Now suddenly he dashes off to Beijing."

"You think he sold you out to Zhou?"

"There's a good chance of that."

"I don't like disagreeing with you, but you don't have much in the way of evidence to support that conclusion. In view of Tyler's position, it's not surprising he wouldn't want to upset China. So I can't draw any conclusion from his being negative in the meeting."

He had a great deal of respect for Betty and her judgment. "Maybe you're right," he said. "Let's give it a little test."

Craig took out his phone, activated the record function, and called Zhou Yun's office in Beijing. He told the secretary, "This is Barry Gorman. I'd like to speak with Minister Zhou."

"Just a moment," she told him.

A few seconds later, he heard a booming voice, "This is Zhou. It is a pleasure to hear from you Barry Gorman. Are you the famous Barry Gorman who's the head of the Philoctetes Group?"

Craig wondered what Zhou's game was. He was determined to find out. "We have a mutual interest in a bank in Turin. Perhaps we can meet and reach a settlement."

"You're mistaken," Zhou said casually. "I have no interest in a bank in Turin, *but I know who you are, Barry Gorman*, and I would be happy to meet with such an important man. I'm sure we'll have common business interests to discuss. You tell me where and when."

"I'm going to the Global Economic Conference in Ascona next week and I saw from the program that you'll be speaking there on Friday morning. Suppose we meet 10 a.m. Thursday morning at your hotel."

"That would be good. I don't stay at a hotel. I take over a private residence on the edge of Ascona. Why don't you come there Thursday morning at 10:00."

That sounds good. What's the address?"

"I'll call you on your cell phone Thursday morning at 9:00 and give it to you."

When Craig ended the call, he said to Betty, "I recorded the conversation. You have to listen to it."

He played it for her. When it was over, he said, "What do you think?"

"He was toying with you. He knows Barry Gorman is Craig Page."

"My conclusion, too. From his emphasis on 'I know who you are, Barry Gorman.'"

"And the whole tone of the call. But how did he find out?"

"I'd bet anything Tyler told him in Beijing."

"I'm coming around to your view. Let me call Jim Burton, the head of NSA. Their routine intercepts of Tyler's calls may give us something."

She got Burton on the phone and told him what she wanted.

He called back twenty minutes later with the information. "Two days ago, Zhou Yun, the Chinese Finance Minister called Tyler and told him that he had to come to Beijing immediately to discuss a new bond issue, 'You must come to Beijing immediately,' Zhou said. In response, Tyler told him that he would come that day."

Betty hung up with Burton and called Tyler's office. She asked his secretary when he'd be returning. "Ten fifteen this evening on United from Beijing."

As soon as she reported that to Craig, he told her, "Here's what I think you should do. Undoubtedly Tyler's regular driver will be picking him up. Substitute one of your men driving Tyler's car. He can say that the regular driver got sick."

Northern Virginia

Before going to Dulles Airport, Craig called Giuseppe and woke him in the middle of the night. "Our friend will be taking over a private residence on the edge of Ascona. Number 16 via Delta. Check with the Ascona municipal officials and see if they can get the layout of the house and send it to you electronically. Then forward it to me."

"Will do. Are we still alive?"

"Absolutely. I'll explain when I see you."

Craig had an agency car take him to Dulles Airport and drop him by the side of the exit road leading out of the airport in the direction of Washington. He checked his watch. It was a couple of minutes before 10:00 p.m. This may not have been the smartest idea, Craig thought, as bolts of lightning pierced the night sky in the west and he heard rumbles of thunder. A powerful summer storm was zeroing in on Washington. Craig hoped to hell Tyler's plane landed and his car reached Craig before he got drenched.

His phone rang. He yanked it out of his pocket. Bruce, the CIA agent driving Tyler's car said, "Subject called. He's leaving the terminal. Knows I'm in the parking lot. No objection to a substitute driver."

"Good. Drive fast. The skies are about to open up."

"Will do. I noticed that."

Eight minutes later, a black Lincoln Town Car with US government plates that read "TREAS 1" came to a stop next to Craig.

He opened the back door and got in. Tyler was in the back seat. Bruce was alone up front.

"What the hell is this?" Tyler said.

"Drive," Craig told Bruce.

Bruce activated the door lock mechanism and the car pulled onto the road.

At that instant, the rain started, a fierce storm, pelting the windshield and severely limiting visibility. Bruce hunched over the wheel and struggled to stay on the road.

"What the hell is this?" Tyler repeated.

"I think you and I should have a little chat about what you did in Beijing."

"Are you crazy?" Tyler sounded indignant. "You're going to jail for this."

Tyler seized the phone in his pocket and said, "I'm calling the FBI."

Craig grabbed it from him and placed it in his own pocket before Tyler had a chance to resist. Craig then took out his own phone and laid in in his lap.

"Stop the car," Tyler shouted to the driver.

Bruce ignored him and continued driving.

"Now do you want to tell me what you did in Beijing?"

"None of your fucking business."

"We can do this the easy way or the hard. Easy, you tell me the truth about your little visit with Zhou Yun. Hard means Bruce drives straight to CIA headquarters. We have interrogation rooms in the basement. And we have drugs that cause such excruciating pain to the nerves that even hardened foreign spies will tell us what we want to know in a matter of minutes. Now you decide: Easy or hard?"

"I'm an important official in the United States government. A member of the president's cabinet. You can't do this to me."

"But I am. Now what'll it be: easy or hard?"

"We talked about a new US bond issue and I asked China to participate by buying our bonds. Zhou agreed to do that."

"What did you tell Zhou to get that commitment?"

Tyler didn't answer. He stared out of the window of the moving car into the pounding rainstorm.

"I didn't have to tell him anything. He knows it's in China's financial interest."

"But he threatened not to buy the bonds if you didn't tell him about me? Isn't that right?"

"Look, asshole. I did what I had to do to ensure the financial integrity of this country. That's my responsibility. I have nothing to gain personally. All I care about is what's good for the United States."

"So you told him that Barry Gorman is really Craig Page?"

"It's none of your fucking business what I told Zhou."

"When we get to the CIA, you'll tell me everything. We'll break you."

"Yes—I told him," Tyler sounded defiant. "I did that because it was in the best interest of the United States. It's my responsibility to make sure this country remains solvent. That means selling the bonds to China."

"Bullshit, it's your job to do what President Worth orders you to do. If you wanted to cut that deal and sell me out, you had to get the president's approval. He's the one who approved the Barry Gorman ploy."

"I did what I had to do."

"You betrayed your president and your country."

"That's ridiculous. Besides the president will support me."

"You can't possibly believe that."

"He'll know I did what's best for the country."

"We'll see about that."

Craig picked up the phone on his lap and called Betty. "The recording of my conversation on my cell phone is coming to you right now."

"Good. I'm in the White House. Worth wants me to run it upstairs as soon as I have it. Then I'll get back to you."

Craig hung up.

"You scheming bastard," Tyler shouted. "Don't you know it's a crime to record conversations without people's knowledge?"

"Treason is a worse crime."

Ten minutes later, Betty called back. "President Worth wants you to take Tyler to the CIA safe house near Charlottesville. Bruce knows where it is. I'll have guards there who will hold Tyler in house arrest, incommunicado, until this is all over. Then we'll charge him with treason."

"Can I leave once I get him there?"

"Absolutely. I'll be waiting for you in my office. We have to talk. You're taking a little trip tomorrow."

Northern Italy

Elizabeth was behind the wheel of a rental car again. She felt as if she knew the road from Milan southwest into Piedmont like the palm of her hand.

As she drove, her head ached from all that wine last evening. Even the two extra Tylenols chased by two double espressos she had this morning before leaving the Four Seasons in Milan—a luxury hotel in what once been a 15th century monastery—did little to alleviate her headache, but it had all been worthwhile.

She knew exactly how to extract from Carlo Fanti the information she needed. Carlo loved good Barolo, which he couldn't afford. She, on the other hand, had a virtually unlimited expense account with her paper. So she asked him to be her guest for dinner last evening at Principe di Savoia, a hotel near the train station, which the Nazis had taken over as their headquarters during the war.

During dinner, they talked in general about the election campaign and Italian politics. Carlo saw himself as a mentor to Elizabeth.

They began with a bottle of '04 Barolo Colonnello Aldo Conterno and followed it with a '97 Barolo Falletto from Bruno Giacosa. Midway through the second bottle, she sensed Carlo loosening up. Time to move in. She told Carlo that she was working on a feature article about Parelli. She had already interviewed Parelli, she told Carlo, then dodged his questions about what she'd learned. They were, after all, competitors as well as friends.

By the time the last of the second bottle had been poured from a crystal carafe into their glasses, Elizabeth said, "I need a favor, Carlo."

"What's that?"

"The address of Luciano, Parelli's campaign manager, and his home phone number. I want to interview him as part of my feature on Parelli." She didn't mention that she learned he was sick and had left the campaign.

He pulled out his iPad. "I can probably get that for you, but I'll want something in return."

Good old Carlo, always bargaining. A favor for a favor. "I'm sure you would. And what is that?"

"How about if we stop by your hotel room after dinner." He smiled and winked at her.

"I doubt if your wife would like that."

"You can't blame a guy for trying."

"What's your second choice?"

"You're a damn good reporter. I'll bet when you write your Parelli story, it will be explosive. I want your promise that the instant your article goes live, you'll email it to me. I'll be on line with your revelations right after you and beat all of my Italian competitors."

"That's a deal," she said.

So last evening, Carlo had given her Luciano's home address and phone number. She was betting Luciano went home when he left the campaign. She decided not to call first for fear he'd run away rather than talk to her.

She was now entering the small village in which Luciano lived, about ten miles from Parelli's farm.

She stopped at a café in the center of town for directions and another espresso.

A few minutes later, she pulled up in front of Luciano's house. It was a modest two floor wooden structure on a dirt road on the edge of the town. A heavy set gray haired woman, in her sixties, Elizabeth guessed, answered the door.

"I'd like to see Luciano," Elizabeth said.

The woman looked worried. "Who are you?"

"Elizabeth Crowder. Foreign news editor of the *International Herald*."

The woman ran her eyes over Elizabeth as if she could make a judgment about her surprise visitor. Then she motioned for Elizabeth to enter.

"I'm Luciano's wife, Maria. Why do you want to see him?"

"I'm writing an article about the Parelli campaign. I'd like to talk to him about it."

"Well good luck if you can get him to talk to you."

"What do you mean?"

"He came home several days ago. He was upset, but he refused tell me why. So he mostly sulked, sitting out on the back verandah, smoking cigarettes. I took the scotch and wine away from him. He's never been like this before. I hope he'll talk to you. That way I'll learn what's happening."

"Well, I'll try."

Maria led Elizabeth to the verandah in the back. There she left Elizabeth and retreated into the house.

After Maria's description, Elizabeth wasn't surprised to see Luciano sitting in a rocker smoking a cigarette and looking morose.

"Hello Luciano," she said. "I'm Elizabeth Crowder. We met in—"

He looked up. "I know who you are. What do you want?"

He sounded hostile. This won't be easy.

"To talk to you for an article I'm doing about the election."

"You're too late. I'm not involved any longer. You'll have to ask someone else."

"I'm confused. When I called the campaign office to arrange an interview with Parelli, a young man, Stefano, said you were sick and quit the campaign. But you don't seem to be sick. What's the real story?"

"Parelli's lying as usual," Luciano said emphatically.

"You and Roberto Parelli have been very close. Haven't you?"

"Yes, for about sixty-five years."

Elizabeth sat down in a battered wooden chair facing the rocker. Luciano put out his cigarette and lit another.

He was talking. For now, she wanted to keep it low key, not threatening, hoping he would continue. "That's a long time. Were you in school together?"

"More than that. If you interviewed Roberto, I'm sure he told you how my father saved Roberto from being killed by the Germans. He was only six months old."

Elizabeth nodded. "He told me."

"My parents lived very close to the Parelli farm. His mother and siblings had been killed by the Germans. I was an only child and Roberto and I were the same age. When he was five, Mario, his father, spent much of his time in Rome in politics, and my father began going with him as an advisor.

"As a result, Roberto and I were together almost all of the time. He was at my house for many meals. My mother treated him as if he were her child. We were like brothers. That continued until he went away to the University in Rome to study law."

"He must have been smart."

"He was and a star athlete in school, too. I loved him, but he wasn't perfect."

"What do you mean?"

"I mean the way he was with women. No matter whom Roberto dated, he always slept with others. That continued even after he was married."

She remembered what Hanson said. "His wife Diane is American. Isn't she?"

Luciano nodded. "He met her when he went to Yale Law School for a year after he graduated from the university in Rome. When he brought her home, we were appalled at the idea of him not marrying an Italian woman, but she made us change our minds. She's wonderful. We all loved her. Even after they had three children, he continued with other women, causing her so much anguish—even though he loved her, and his family meant so much to him."

Elizabeth thought about the prostitute in Venice. To this day, he hasn't changed.

Luciano paused to light another cigarette. Then he continued. "But with all of that, I felt close to him, like a brother. We saw less of each other when he was an important lawyer in Milan and ran the wine business. I had taken over my father's firm as a political consultant. Then a year ago, when he decided to go into politics and start the New

Italy Party, he asked me to work with him. I immediately said 'yes.' Even though I wasn't sympathetic with the objectives of his party."

"What do you mean?"

Luciano hesitated, and then replied, "I want your promise that if you write an article about Roberto, nothing will be attributed to me."

"Absolutely. You have it."

He stared hard at her for a minute. Apparently satisfied, he continued, "I don't like the idea of dividing Italy. I love this country the way it is. Like Roberto, it isn't perfect, and I may not have much in common with people from Calabria, Brindisi, or Sicily, but we are all Italians. Do you understand?"

"Very well. In the United States we fought a bloody civil war to keep our country together—where did he get this idea?"

"A few years ago, Roberto took a trip to Spain. First, he read about Scotland. Then he went to San Sebastian and Catalonia. He talked to people about the separatist movements in the Basque country and in Barcelona. That's when it started. I couldn't talk him out of it. I think he honestly believes dividing the country would be better for those in both the north and south. I didn't agree, but I still went to work helping him."

"So why'd you quit?"

Luciano looked away and didn't respond. Elizabeth was at a critical point in the interview. She had to convince him to continue. "I promise I will never attribute anything to you."

He still didn't say a word.

She decided to rely on what Craig had told her as a way of jarring Luciano into talking. "I'll tell you what I think."

He turned back to her.

She continued in a soft voice. "I think Roberto recently and secretly received money from the Chinese for his campaign, and you couldn't accept that."

He seemed surprised. "Why do you say that?"

"Roberto has suddenly increased his advertising in the last couple of days," she said, as she reached into her bag and pulled out her phone. She showed Luciano the picture she had taken in the suite in the Palace Hotel. "That night in Venice, this man was coming out of a meeting with Roberto. It's apparent the Chinese want to gain a foothold in Europe. Roberto has opened the gates to let the Trojan horse in. That's right isn't it?"

Luciano put down his cigarette and began crying. Finally, he looked up and said, "You're asking me to betray Roberto."

She thought that Luciano was on the verge of breaking and telling her everything. She had to give him a nudge to get him there. "I'm asking you to save Italy. Only you can do it."

"Roberto and I have been like brothers for 65 years."

"You have to do what's right. During the thirties many Italians were indifferent to the rise of Mussolini. In return they got disaster for Italy. It will be the same with Roberto. You can't let it happen."

"But loyalty is loyalty. Betrayal by any other name is betrayal."

"That's the whole point. One way you follow your obligation to Roberto. The other way, you keep your loyalty to your country. Which means more to you?"

Luciano was uncertain, hesitating. "You give me a difficult choice."

"I didn't create the situation."

"You can stop him without me."

"I can't. That's why I'm here. You're the only way."

Elizabeth had been sitting with her back to the door of the house. She heard a rustling from that direction and she glanced over her shoulder. Maria was standing at the open door. Elizabeth wondered how long she'd been there.

Maria stepped out onto the patio. "Tell her, Luciano," Maria said.

He looked at Maria. Then turned to Elizabeth.

"He wasn't merely betraying Italy, but his family, too. That farm, vineyard, and winery have been owned by Parellis for more than 150 years. . . . No longer. He sold it all to a Chinese man."

"Do you know who the buyer was?"

"Zhou Yun, the Chinese Finance Minister."

God, Craig's not as paranoid as I thought.

Luciano continued. "The farm and winery were mortgaged to their full value of about 200 million euros.

"Roberto borrowed even more than that. He needed money to pay off the loans and obtain cash for his campaign. I argued against him doing it, but he wouldn't listen. He was in a desperate situation because he had spent so heavily on his campaign. He told me he'd lose the farm and wine business regardless of what he did at that point, because Alberto Goldoni would foreclose. I argued that Alberto was reasonable and would work with him, but he said it was too late for that. So he reacted positively when a Chinese man came to the suite in Venice and said that his boss, the Chinese Finance Minister Zhou Yun, could help him financially."

Again, Elizabeth showed Luciano the picture from her cell. "Is this the man who came to the suite in Venice?"

"Yes," he said weakly.

"What's his name?"

"I don't know."

"What happened after the meeting in the suite in Venice?"

"A few days later, Zhou Yun came to the farm for a secret meeting with Roberto. I was excluded from their discussion. Afterwards, Roberto told me what happened."

Elizabeth leaned forward on the edge of her chair. She wanted to remember every word Luciano said. She didn't dare interrupt him by taking notes. Holding her breath, she waited for him to continue.

"Roberto made a secret deal with Zhou. He sold the winery and vineyard to him for one billion euros. The money is deposited now in a Swiss bank so Roberto could pay off his loans to Turin Credit, Alberto Goldoni's bank, which held the mortgages. The closing was deferred until well after the election to avoid public disclosure."

"One billion!" Elizabeth said. "I thought you told me the property was only worth 200 million."

"The transaction was all a sham—a way of disguising the Chinese contribution to Parelli's campaign. They want Roberto to win."

"What did Parelli promise Zhou if he won?"

"A voice in his government. Large contracts. The things that major contributors who decide an election regularly receive. That's it. Now you know the whole disgusting story Roberto told me about his deal with Zhou. As soon as he told me, I was sick. I walked out of his house, and I haven't seen him since. He sold out our country—Italy. He sold out his family. He was desperate for money. I know that. I can understand why he did it—but I can't condone or forgive him."

Luciano was crying again.

"Thank you for talking to me," Elizabeth said and she stood up.

Luciano stood as well. "Remember you won't mention my name."

"No. Of course not."

Maria offered to walk Elizabeth to the front door, but she said, "I'll go through the yard around the house."

She and Maria locked eyes. "Thank you," Elizabeth said.

As she walked away, she heard Maria say to Luciano, "It will be alright."

She got into her car and raced back to Milan as fast as she could drive and maintain control of the car.

Once she was in her hotel room, she began typing at her computer:

The Italian Divide
by Elizabeth Crowder

Italy faces its greatest existential threat since the German army entered the country in 1943. This time the would-be conquerors are not using soldiers and tanks. They are using money and economic might. They are coming not from the north, but from the east.

Zhou Yun, the Chinese Finance Minister, is making an effort to restore the greatness China had in the eighteenth century. He intends to repay Europe for the humiliation China suffered in the nineteenth and twentieth centuries at the hands of Europeans.

Italy is Zhou's immediate target. He has launched a daring two-part plan to dominate the government of an enormously powerful northern Italian state formed by Roberto Parelli. At the same time, he will control many of the most important banks in that new state. This is the twenty first century. Whoever controls the banks controls the economy.

Zhou has found a willing partner in Roberto Parelli, who heavily mortgaged his family's farm and winery.

Western North Carolina

Early the next morning before the sun was up, Craig, with only two hours sleep, was in a CIA plane en route to a secret Special Forces base in the mountains of western North Carolina. Betty had made the arrangements for him. Then last night around two a.m., her final words sternly delivered were, "Once you get your operation set up and before you fly to Ascona, you must stop in Washington. I have to know all the details so I can keep the president informed. No Lone Ranger stuff this time. The president has gone out on a long limb for you." Craig promised to do what she asked.

As the plane landed at a small airport in the center of a North Carolina pine forest and taxied to a stop adjacent to a small wooden building, Craig watched a tall burley man in a military uniform walk toward the plane while the stairs went down.

When Craig reached the ground, the man introduced himself. "Colonel Hal Dempsey. I'll be in charge of planning your operation."

Craig climbed into a jeep with Dempsey behind the wheel. "I'm aware of what you've done with the CIA and that you were formerly the director, Mr. Page."

"It's Craig, please."

"Okay, Craig. I don't know much about your operation. According to my CO, we're supposed to supply four of my men for an operation in Ascona, Switzerland. I was told this is high priority authorized by the president and CIA director."

"That's right. Our objective will be to kidnap Zhou Yun, an important Chinese businessman and China's finance minister. We want to get him on a boat and take him to Stresa, Italy, on the southern end of Lake Maggiore where the Italians will put him on trial for the murder of an Italian national. Hopefully, that is."

"Good. We'll be able to do that. Let me tell you how I want to plan this."

Craig took an immediate liking to Dempsey. The man had a take-charge attitude and he exuded self-confidence.

"Sure. Tell me."

"I've assembled four of my men in a conference room in our operations building. Darrell, Glen, Doug, and Tony. All near the top of my organization chart. Combined, the four have more than twenty-five years of combat experience in Iraq and Afghanistan.

"Tony is fluent in Italian—he's self-taught. His mother was born in Sardinia. She met his father when he was stationed in Italy with the Air Force at our base in Magdalena.

"I like to plan an operation like this as a group effort. The six of us will sit at a table, kick around ideas, and reject alternatives until we have something we're all satisfied with. Does that sound unorthodox to you, Craig?"

Whatever works."

"Well it does because it takes advantage of the experience my guys have had in other operations. Also, they'll be putting their lives on the line. I want them to be comfortable with whatever plans we develop."

Craig liked this approach. He also liked the looks of the four battle-hardened men seated around a conference table drinking coffee and joking about baseball teams when he and Dempsey walked into the room. All the talking stopped and the four rose to their feet.

The Colonel introduced Craig as "America's super spy and former CIA director." Craig felt himself reddening. As the men sat down, the colonel pointed to a coffee pot in the corner. Craig walked over and poured a cup.

While doing so, he looked around the room. A large screen resembling a giant television was attached to one wall. It was dark. Maps and photographs were taped to another. Craig recognized Ascona at the northern Swiss end of Lake Maggiore. Betty must have briefed Dempsey. Somebody had been busy this morning. Laptops and printers were set up on two folding tables against one wall. Duffel bags had been tossed into a corner. Craig guessed they held the four men's gear.

Dempsey had a laptop on the table in front of him. He booted it up and images flashed on the screen. First Lake Maggiore. Then Ascona.

"We obtained lots of good images from satellite and drone photos," he said. He zeroed in on the dock area in the center of Ascona near the intersection of via Albemarele, the promenade along the lake, and via Borgo, the main shopping street of Ascona. A dozen yachts were tied up.

"The objective," Dempsey said, using a laser pointer, "is to bring in a boat. Tie it up there. Then load the target onto the boat and take him to Italy. Do I have that right, Craig?"

"Yes, sir."

"Put the target's picture on the screen."

Craig did. "He's Zhou Yun, the Chinese finance minister and wealthy industrialist."

Dempsey paused for a minute to study the picture. Then he continued. "Our destination will be Stresa where the Italians have ample police and carabinieri."

"Will the Italians cooperate with us?"

"Absolutely," Craig said. "Giuseppe Mercuri, director of the EU counterterrorism agency, is based in Italy. He's been in this with me from the get go. He'll do whatever he can to help. Also, there's a reporter, Elizabeth Crowder, who will be in Ascona. She's tough as nails and she'll help us. She's also good with boats."

"I like that," Dempsey turned to Craig. "What else can you tell us to help on the planning?"

"Giuseppe should be able to arrange for Elizabeth to get a boat in Stresa. She can take it up to Ascona. I'm supposed to meet with Zhou, the target, next Thursday at 10 a.m. at a private residence outside the center of Ascona, which he's taken over. Perhaps, I could knock him out then and the five us could hustle him over to the boat."

Glen, with carrot red hair, interjected. "I prefer working at night, and I like the element of surprise. How about Wednesday evening or early Thursday morning?"

Dempsey said, "That's much better. Besides, Craig, you might be walking into a trap on Thursday morning. The target has to sleep. So he'll be at this house at some point the night before your meeting. Suppose we set the pickup for Thursday at 3 a.m. Target and much of his security should be sleeping. That'll give us the element of surprise Glen was talking about. What do you know about the house where he'll be staying?"

"The address is number 16 via Delta. I asked Giuseppe to have one of his people check it out. He sent me a schematic."

Craig forwarded it to Dempsey's computer and it went up on the screen. Three floors with four bedrooms on each of the top two floors. Dining room, kitchen, and living area on the first floor.

Dempsey pushed some buttons on the computer. "Satellite photo of the residence."

The picture on the screen showed a tidy looking three-story building with white stone walls and brown shutters on the windows. The house was isolated, set back from via Delta in front by a large grassy area; behind it was another grassy area, then the River Maggiaone. On one side were open fields; on the other, the Hotel Park was about two hundred yards away from the property. A heavy metal fence surrounded the property. It was about twelve feet high. In front was a gate that opened to a driveway that ran to the front of the house. The grounds were carefully tended with grass and an abundance of flowers.

"We have to assume," Craig said, "that the target will have bodyguards heavily armed."

"So we go in with tear gas and masks," Dempsey said.

"I like that," Craig replied.

Darrell interjected. "We'll need a vehicle to drive in and then to transport the target to the boat."

"Ambulance," Doug said.

Dempsey looked at Craig. "Do you think your friend Giuseppe could get us a Red Cross ambulance? That would also help us avoid the police."

"He should be able to do that." Craig didn't have the faintest idea if that was possible, but Giuseppe was resourceful.

"Alright, we have the broad outline," Dempsey said. "Let's focus on details. Craig, my men will be carrying lots of arms. How do you think we should get them into Switzerland?"

Craig had already thought about this question. "Equip them at the American base on Magdalena off the northern coast of Sardinia. It's Italian territory. Giuseppe will help move them into mainland Italy, then overland and give them a place to wait until Wednesday evening. They can cross into Switzerland by car at the Lake Como border crossing. Giuseppe will grease that one. I want to pick them up in the ambulance at a meeting point in the hills above Ascona Thursday at two a.m. I'll forward the exact location Wednesday during the day."

"That sounds good," Dempsey said. "Meantime, we'll maintain satellite and drone surveillance of Zhou's house. To make sure he's there at zero hour. Everybody good with that?"

"Yes, sir," rang out around the room.

"You'll split into two groups of two. Darrell and Glen are G1. Doug and Tony G2. For the assault, you'll have automatic weapons with suppressors and also tear gas and masks. G1 will take out any guards at the front gate and blast it open. All four of you race to the house. Craig will drive the ambulance in and park it in front."

Dempsey was talking fast. He paused to take a breath. Then continued. "G1 will secure and hold the first floor and the building entrance. G2 and Craig will move up the stairs to the second and third floors. Doug will secure the second floor. Tony, you'll move up to the third with Craig. We'll provide you, Craig, with a powerful sedative administered by syringe to disable the target. Speed is critical. Knock down doors that don't open quickly. You have to get in and out before the Swiss police come. Figure you'll have twenty minutes max. Less would be better. Everybody clear on that?"

All heads in the room were nodding. Dempsey turned to Craig. "It's your operation. Over there, you're in charge. That isn't something I'm used to doing. Turning command of my men to an outsider, but with your record it's justified."

"Thank you for your confidence, Colonel."

"Anybody have any questions or issues with the plan?"

Darrell spoke up. "Suppose the target eludes Craig and is escaping? Do we shoot to kill?"

Dempsey pointed to Craig.

"No. Just hit him in the leg. I need him alive."

"Anybody else?"

No one else said anything.

"Alright. Enough talking. We have plenty of work to do to nail down the operational details and not much time."

As Craig rode in a jeep back to the airport, he had a queasy feeling in his stomach. This operation in Ascona was beginning to sound a lot like the attack he had tried in Bali—when attempting to kidnap Zhou Yun's brother. There, he had led four courageous and talented young Spanish men with wonderful lives ahead of them, into a bloody ambush in which all four of them had died and Craig had barely escaped. He couldn't bear to think he'd be doing the same thing to Darrell, Glen, Doug, and Tony.

Ascona

Zhou's unmarked private jet arrived at Milan's Malpensa Airport at five o'clock Monday afternoon on a beautiful summer day with a robin's-egg blue sky and not a cloud. As he climbed down the stairs to the tarmac, he looked up at the mountains in the distance. Their peaks were still covered with snow.

Each of the past two years he had brought with him to the Ascona conference several top ranking officials in the Finance Ministry whose assignment had been to gather information about world economic developments from other delegates, particularly those from Europe and the United States. This year he brought only eight security men, whom he had borrowed from the military and were dressed in civilian clothes, and Qing. Their bags contained rifles, automatic weapons, and pistols.

Though he planned to deliver a speech Friday morning, touting China's successful investments in Africa, Zhou had no interest in economic issues at this year's Ascona conference. He had come for one reason: to kill Craig Page. After twenty-one long months, he would finally be avenging his brother's death.

Waiting for Zhou and his entourage at the airport were three black Mercedes sedans for Zhou and his men to drive. One was bullet proof. Zhou would be riding in the back of that car. One of his men would be driving. Two more would be in the car with him. His other five men would be split between the two other cars, one to ride in front of Zhou's car; the other behind.

An hour and a half later, the caravan passed through the town of Locarno, which also fronts on Lake Maggiore. Once they crossed the bridge over the River Maggiaone, they were in Ascona; then turned left onto via Delta, passed the Park Hotel and approached number 16.

The instant they were in front, the door opened. Someone inside must have seen them coming.

Zhou had taken over the house for the last two years. By now, the routine was settled. Zhou paid 100,000 euros for the five nights. In return, Hans Wilhelm, the caretaker, arranged for a team of maids and a kitchen staff to come in every day between 3 p.m. and 6 p.m. They cleaned the house. Then they all left until the next afternoon. Zhou and his group had the house to themselves.

Once Wilhelm showed Zhou the food, he and his staff departed.

Zhou, as he had in the past, took the master suite, the largest room on the top floor facing the river on one side and Lake Maggiore in the distance. The head of Zhou's security group assigned the other rooms, except for the room next to Zhou, which would be occupied by Qing Li.

As Zhou got off the elevator on the top floor, he saw Qing waiting for him. "I've swept your room for bugs," Qing told Zhou.

"And the other rooms?"

"Also clean. We have to go to your room to talk. I have something to tell you." Qing sounded worried.

Once they were in Zhou's room, Qing took out his hand held computer and turned it over to Zhou. "Look at this article that just went up on the *International Herald* website."

In stunned disbelief, Zhou read Elizabeth's article, exposing in detail his agreement with Parelli.

Her source? He asked himself. Who was her source?

Then it struck him. There was only one possibility: Luciano. Zhou had made a critical error not having Qing kill Luciano.

At the end of the article, he saw a news flash stating that Parelli would be giving a speech at seven this evening. He checked his watch. That was in a couple of minutes.

Zhou turned on the television across the room to CNN. Moments later, he saw Parelli's picture on the screen. He grabbed the remote and turned up the volume.

Parelli was speaking to the media with a cluster of microphones in front of his face. Zhou listened intently.

"It is with the deepest regret," Parelli said, his expression grim, "that I have decided to withdraw from the election and terminate my New Italy Party. I do so because the disclosure of the sale of my farm and winery to a Chinese man has caused a backlash among my supporters. Unfortunately, many of them have withdrawn their support even though everyone recognizes I did nothing illegal or inappropriate. It was my property and I was free to sell to whomever I wanted. I am truly astonished in this age of globalization that some people should be so narrow minded to believe that Italian property must be sold to an Italian.

"I feel dismayed because I wanted the best for the people of Italy and my New Italy Party would have done that. The Chinese man involved, a very respected international business figure, purchased my farm and winery, just as he purchased two top wineries in France. He did not want—nor did I promise him—any influence in the new Northern Italy nation should I have been elected.

"However, I realize that in politics perception often trumps reality. And that is all I have to say."

Reporters fired questions but Parelli ignored them. Holding his head high, he turned and walked away.

Zhou wasn't surprised by Parelli's withdrawal. He didn't have any choice after the publication of Elizabeth's article. She had destroyed his campaign.

As for the monetary consequences for Zhou, they wouldn't be significant. His lawyers hadn't yet forwarded the agreement to Parelli for his signature; now they wouldn't. Parelli had no doubt spent on his campaign some of the money in the Swiss account, but in such a short period it couldn't have been that much. Zhou had set up the account with a provision permitting him to take back the funds at any time until the agreement was signed. Nor was he disappointed that he wouldn't own Parelli's winery and vineyard. If he made a move into Italian wines, and he might very well do so, he'd go after the more prestigious Gaja or Antonori.

Zhou called his Swiss banker to transfer back the bulk of the one billion euros from the Parelli account.

There was a moment's pause. Zhou expected to hear the banker say the transfer was made. Instead, Zhou heard, "I can't do that."

"Why not?"

"Parelli took it all except for 1,000 euros and moved it to a bank in Palermo, Sicily. It's gone."

"Make a claim to the bank in Sicily. Demand the money."

"Unfortunately, the Palermo bank is controlled by the Mafia. They don't respond to demands from other banks. Doing business in Sicily is a challenge."

Zhou knew he had a lost cause. "That thief, Parelli," he wailed in frustration and hung up.

So Parelli would be able to pay off his debts and turn a nice profit when all this was over. Zhou swore he'd gain revenge, but right now he had to concentrate on closing the deal for Alberto's bank. That would be a success Zhou could point to with the Central Committee if Mei Ling came to them with the loss of one billion euros to Parelli. It was about all Zhou could salvage from his Italian operation that was going from bad to worse. He had to gain control of Alberto's bank.

Zhou had to move on from the Parelli fiasco. He had no choice. He explained to Qing what Tyler had told him about Barry Gorman, and about the meeting he had set with Barry Gorman, who was really Craig Page.

"I'm not surprised," Qing said. "I could never understand what Barry Gorman was doing. That made me suspicious. For example, his press interview."

"Thursday morning, we're going to kill Craig Page," Zhou said coldly.

"How do you plan to do that?" Qing sounded excited.

"Let's start with the fact that I have a great advantage. I know that Barry Gorman is Craig Page, but Page isn't aware that I know."

"Are you certain of that?"

Zhou didn't like being questioned. "Yes, I'm quite certain. I have to assume Page is planning to kill me when he comes Thursday morning. He's still trying to avenge his daughter's death."

"That's a reasonable assumption."

"So I have to kill him before he gets here at ten Thursday morning and make sure it can't be attributed to me. I don't intend to give him the address here until an hour before our meeting so Page won't be able to plan a move against me."

Qing was nodding. "Do you know where he's staying in Ascona?"

"I've had someone hack into the computers of all the leading hotels in the area, but none of them have a reservation for Barry Gorman. My assumption is he won't be staying here Wednesday evening. He'll come into Ascona in the morning of our meeting. Via Delta is the only road leading to this house. I want you to work with the eight security men I've brought. Thursday morning, I want four of them placed on via Delta close to this house's driveway. Two on the north and two in the south because we don't know which way he'll be coming. One as spotter. One as a shooter."

"I'll do it. What about the other four?"

"Station one along the driveway, leading to the house and one in the back between the house and river, in case the first four miss. And leave the last two with me in the house, in the event Page, who's tricky, finds another way to get inside. Once Page is shot, it will be up to the killer to escape. You explain to all eight men that if they do the shooting, or if they're the spotter, they can't be taken alive under any circumstance. Tell the others to fasten weights to Page's dead body and dump it into the river downstream from the house where the river flows into the lake."

"I understand," Qing said. "Do you have a photograph of Barry Gorman?"

Zhou reached in to his bag and extracted a dozen copies. "This was taken from the Philoctetes website."

"What will you do until Thursday morning?"

"What I would normally do at this conference. I want to hear some of the speeches, particularly that of Jane Peterson, the chairman of the US Federal Reserve who will be talking tomorrow morning about their view of interest rates. Also, mix around with other delegates. Attend receptions."

Zhou could tell that Qing wanted to say something, but he was hesitating.

"What are you worrying about?" Zhou demanded.

"I think you should stay here in the house until Page is dead. He knows what you look like. He may try to kill you before Thursday morning. At the conference, we may not be able to protect you."

"Never," Zhou said emphatically. "I refuse to hide in a cave like a sniveling coward. I'm the finance minister of the world's most powerful nation and I intend to conduct my business. Craig Page will not upset my activities. Do not suggest that again."

"Yes, sir."

As Zhou thought about his plan some more, he realized it had one weakness. By killing Barry Gorman so close to the house he was staying in, he would be drawing suspicion to himself with the Swiss authorities, who would eventually learn that Barry Gorman was involved in a struggle for control of the Turin Bank to which Zhou had ties. The Swiss were good at cutting through bank chains of ownership. Their banks created enough of them. And if Page's killer were captured either alive or dead and he were Chinese, or Craig's body was discovered in the river close to Zhou's house on Delta Road, that would heighten their suspicions. Zhou was confident he could buy his way out of being implicated, but he didn't need the aggravation. It would be neater and cleaner to kill Page before he ever got to Ascona.

He told Qing that was what he wanted to do.

"Work with my computer people in Beijing." Zhou told Qing. "Find out when Barry Gorman is scheduled to fly into any airport in Italy or Switzerland. Once we have a flight, we can send a couple of my men to meet that flight. Then follow Page as he leaves the airport and kill him before he ever reaches Ascona. That'll be much better."

Qing raced off to his own room to hook up with Zhou's computer people. Half an hour later, he returned looking dejected. "No flights for Barry Gorman into any European airport. They will keep checking every few hours and let me know if that changes. They said he might be flying under another name."

"I thought of that," Zhou said. "We could station a couple my men at each of the two Milan airports and Zurich. We could give them Barry Gorman's picture and tell them to wait for him near the exit for customs."

"I'll arrange it," Qing said.

"Only for tomorrow and Wednesday during the day. I want them back here Wednesday by midnight. We'll need everybody here to carry out our attack on Thursday morning."

"Understood."

"Also, tomorrow and Wednesday I want the other two men at the house at all times—one in front and one in back. You'll accompany me to all events at the conference, armed at all times."

Qing was holding up a picture of Barry Gorman and staring at it.

"Does he look familiar?" Zhou asked.

"On Italian television, I saw a man who looked exactly like Barry Gorman."

"Who was he?"

"An Italian race car driver named Enrico Marino."

Zhou gave a long low whistle. "Check your computer. Find out how long Enrico Marino has been racing."

Qing dutifully complied. After a moment, he said, "The earliest article in which Enrico Marino was mentioned was published a little over a year ago in connection with a race in Southern France."

Zhou now understood how Page had spent his time after disappearing. First plastic surgery. Then rebirth as Enrico Marino, a racecar driver. Now death in Ascona.

Washington

Monday afternoon, Craig flew from North Carolina back to Washington to brief Betty. When he arrived at CIA headquarters, she said, "No sense doing it twice. President Worth wants to hear all of the details straight from you. The chopper is waiting."

Craig was surprised. He would have expected Worth to rely on Betty for a briefing. He was also surprised when he spoke in the Oval Office an hour later. Worth asked probing questions getting into the minutia of the operation. He even wanted to know where the boat would be waiting for Zhou.

Craig decided that as long as Worth had ultimate responsibility he had to know what he was authorizing. And after all, Switzerland was an ally and China was the second most powerful nation in the world.

"What about the risk of civilian casualties in Zhou's house?" Worth asked.

"It's a small place. Zhou told me he would be taking it over."

"There may be local people. Maids. Cooks. That sort of thing."

"Correct."

"Minimal at 3 a.m. We'll be careful."

"How are you careful with tear gas?" Betty interjected.

"I mean we'll only fire our weapons at enemy combatants."

"Be realistic, Craig. In the fog of tear gas, it will be chaotic. Civilians are likely to be hit."

No sense fighting against the obvious. "You're right, Betty. As in many other operations, civilian casualties are a risk."

Worth was tapping his fingers on the edge of his chair.

"And that's not your only problem," the president said.

"What else?"

"You'll have the Swiss police to deal with."

"We'll get in and out before they arrive."

"And after that?"

"The ambulance will help. I really think we can avoid a confrontation with them."

President Worth stood up and paced around the office. The moment of truth had arrived. Would he sign off on the operation?

As Worth paced, Betty fiddled with a package of cigarettes.

Finally, Worth said, "You're good to go. Remember, both of you, what I told you said at the last meeting. Craig, you must keep Betty informed of everything in real time. And Betty, you'll have to do the same for me. I want to be able to abort until the last moment. Are you both clear on that?"

"Yes, Mr. President," they replied together.

"You did a good job interrogating Tyler," the president said. "I'm furious at him. When this is all over, I'll discuss with the AG what steps we should take. He's endangered your life."

"At least I know about it. I'll act accordingly."

"Then I guess we're finished. How are you getting to Ascona?"

"There's a late evening plane on United into Zurich. It'll get there midmorning tomorrow. I'll drive down to Ascona from Zurich."

Betty was shaking her head.

"What's wrong?"

"Too risky. Suppose Zhou wanted to take you out in a preemptive strike. Which airports would he be watching?"

Craig thought about it for a minute before saying, "The two in Milan and also Zurich."

"Correct."

"So what do you recommend?"

"Go into Munich. Then drive to Ascona."

"Good idea. Thanks. Also, the Chinese are great at hacking into online computers. So if we're really playing it safe, I better not fly as Barry Gorman. How about getting me a false ID?"

"That's easy enough to do."

Two hours later, when Craig and Betty were ready to separate in her office, she gave Craig a hug—something she had never done before. "Be careful, Craig. We've been through a lot together. I don't want to lose you."

"You're working too hard. You don't have to worry. You'll have me to deal with for a long time."

"I don't have a good feeling about this one."

Ascona

Tuesday morning, Elizabeth decided to attend the plenary session at which Jane Peterson, the Chairman of the Federal Reserve would be talking about interest rates.

The Global economic conference was being held at the Monte Verita conference center on top of a mountain on the outskirts of Ascona. Usually Elizabeth ran in the morning to stay in shape, but when she was in Ascona, she found another way to work out—the ultimate stress test—climbing the one hundred thirty-eight steps from via Borgo in the heart of the shopping area to the top of Mount Verita and the convention center. And they weren't straight up the mountain. Instead, the stairs had lots of bends and turns.

At eight in the morning following breakfast, dressed in shorts and a tee shirt and carrying a duffel bag with a change of clothes, her iPad, reporter's steno pad, and pens, Elizabeth set off from the Eden Roc.

Fortunately, there was cloud cover when she started the climb. Midway up the mountain, the sun was beating down on her. Crossing the road that ran from the town below up to the conference center, she was tempted for an instant to take the road the rest of the way up. Instead, she took a couple of deep breaths and quickly banished that thought.

By the time she reached the top, sweat dotted Elizabeth's forehead and her shirt was soaked. When she first attended the conference two years ago, she made friends with the director of the conference center who also operated a sixty-room hotel on the site. He let her use a hotel room to shower and change clothes.

The morning session was scheduled to start at ten in the auditorium with Jane Peterson's speech. Before that, Elizabeth walked around, talking to finance people she knew while keeping an eye out for Zhou Yun. No sign of him.

At ten minutes to ten, she entered the auditorium, which resembled a large classroom with rows of desks gradually elevated until the last row had a steep view of the speakers below. The press table was in the first row on the left side facing the podium. Elizabeth greeted a couple of her press colleagues and sat down facing the stage and podium.

*   *   *

At five minutes before ten, Zhou Yun and Qing, who crossed the parking lot from the car Qing had driven up the mountain, entered the conference center. Qing remained outside the auditorium while Zhou took a seat reserved for him in the last row on the right side facing the stage.

The Finance Minister of Russia approached Zhou, said hello, and sat down next to him. The auditorium doors closed and the conference director introduced Jane Peterson.

In her speech, Peterson began, "The Federal Reserve is facing an dilemma. We can keep interest rates low in an effort to stimulate the economy; but we risk creating asset bubbles, which in the long run could endanger prosperity. We're trying to walk a tight rope and . . ."

Zhou looked around the auditorium. From his vantage point, he could see most of the others in the room.

There were so many familiar faces from the world of finance who had come to meet him in Beijing, hoping to gain Chinese investment in their countries.

As he looked at the press table, he could hardly believe his eyes. *Elizabeth Crowder!*

She had to know Zhou was here. After the attack on her in Paris, she was foolish, even reckless to be here.

Or more likely, it was something else. When Craig intended to kill Zhou Thursday morning, she might be planning to help him.

For Zhou, her being here was a stroke of good fortune. Qing could grab her and take her back to the house on via Delta. Zhou would be able to use her as bait in luring Craig and make it easier for Zhou to kill Craig.

Zhou had to tell Qing what to do but he didn't want to leave the auditorium for fear this would cause a commotion, and Elizabeth would spot him.

He reached into his pocket for his phone to send Qing a text message. A break was scheduled for 11:15. Delegates typically left the hall for coffee and to mingle. There was an exit close to Elizabeth's seat at the stage level. She would undoubtedly leave through that door. It might be tricky, but Qing was resourceful. He would follow her and snatch her. Zhou told all of that to Qing in his text message. He couldn't wait for 11:15.

*   *   *

As the Federal Reserve Chairman neared the end of the question and answer session following her talk at twelve minutes past eleven, Elizabeth was writing furiously on her steno pad, not wanting to miss a word.

In a concluding sentence, Jane Peterson said, "We at the Federal Reserve are well aware of the enormous repercussions for the world's economy of the actions we take on interest rates. You can be sure we will do everything possible to act prudently. Thank you for your attention and for your thoughtful questions."

The audience stood and applauded the Federal Reserve Chairman. On her feet, Elizabeth looked around the auditorium. Up the rows on the right side at the top was Zhou Yun.

He was staring at her.

Their eyes locked. She saw him pressing keys on his phone. She guessed what he was doing: alerting one of his men outside the hall to seize her at the break.

This was precisely what Craig had warned her might happen, and she had brushed that off. She had been kidnapped by Zhou's brother in Paris, and that had ruined everything for Craig. She couldn't let that happen again. She had to find a way to elude Zhou's men and get out of the convention center.

While the audience was still clapping and the conference director was thanking the Federal Reserve Chairman, Elizabeth knew what she had to do. It was likely that whomever Zhou sent to grab her would be waiting outside the door closest to her on the lower level.

For a few more seconds the center aisle consisting of stairs leading up to the doors in the back of the hall were still clear while people were applauding and before they began heading toward the exodus. That was her best chance to get away.

She stuffed her iPad into her duffel and bolted for the aisle and up the stairs. She made it to the top just as the exit began from the auditorium. She hoped that by moving fast, Zhou would never have a chance to alert whomever he had sent to grab her.

She rushed through the front door of the hall and out into the air. The skies had opened and a summer shower erupted. She tore down the driveway. Then she took off her low beige heels, placed them in the duffel, and raced barefoot down the steep one hundred thirty-eight stone steps, cutting through the woods.

The steps lacked a railing, and they weren't straight. From time to time, they turned ninety-degree corners. Rain-slickened, they were treacherous. Elizabeth had to watch her footing to avoid slipping

After going down about twenty steps, she thought she was alone and safe, but then she heard footsteps racing behind her.

Oh no!

A quick glance over her shoulder confirmed it was Qing—the Chinese man who had been in Parelli's suite in Venice.

She picked up the pace running as fast as she could. It wasn't good enough. Qing was gaining. If she could get to the road midway down the stairs, she might be able to flag down a passing vehicle. It was a good idea, but at this rate, she'd never make it.

She saw a sharp turn to the left approaching. Elizabeth made the turn, then ducked down and moved in close to the wall so the approaching Qing couldn't see her.

The instant Qing passed her step, she sprang up, swung her duffel, and smacked him in the back of his head. The blow knocked Qing off balance. He fell against the side of the low wall, over it and into the bushes.

He was dazed but still conscious. She ignored him and continued running, realizing she only had a couple minutes head start until he resumed his chase.

Her feet were hurting, but she kept going. At last she reached the road. The rain had stopped. The sun was shining.

She spotted a white van coming down from the conference center. She ran into the center of the road and waved her hands. The van stopped. Something indicating "Eco Friendly Products" was painted on the side. Only a driver was in the van. Well, we'll see if these environmentalists have any compassion for a human being, she thought.

The driver rolled down his window and called to her, "Do you need help?"

No, I'm out here, getting a sun tan, she thought. What do you think? "Oh, please help me," she cried out. "I need a ride into town."

"Climb in," he said.

Those were the most wonderful words she'd ever heard.

As he pulled away, the driver asked, "What happened to you?"

"Fight with my boyfriend."

That shut him up. He dropped her at the end of the promenade, two blocks from the Eden Roc. She had no intention of telling Craig what had happened.

Meantime, she'd have to be more vigilant. She was sure that Qing would try to find her; and Ascona was a small town.

Ascona

It was a long, torturous ride for Craig from the airport in Munich to Ascona. Traffic was heavy, and he was constantly encountering road repairs. Craig also made a couple of sudden stops and detours to satisfy himself that he wasn't being followed. At five minutes past eight on Tuesday evening, he reached Ascona.

After parking in a public lot on the edge of the Ascona shopping area, just across the bridge from Lecarno, he strolled around the town as a tourist might on a comfortable summer evening, following his three left-turns rule to make certain he didn't have a tail. Satisfied no one was following, he walked on the via Albemarele promenade along the lake lined with open-air restaurants one next to another, about twenty altogether. Most of them were crowded. The promenade was also jammed with pedestrians. A few ducks were swimming in Lake Maggiore. No one paid any attention to Craig.

He checked his watch. It was nine o'clock. Hopefully, Elizabeth was in her hotel room at the Eden Roc. Craig walked along the lake to her hotel. From the outside, it looked simple, not elegant. That changed the moment Craig entered the polished marble floor lobby and a smartly dressed concierge asked, "May I help you?"

Craig glanced around at the freshly painted beige walls, glass cases filled with luxury goods, and guests dressed perfectly in expensive clothes, the women with striking jewels. All of that confirmed what Elizabeth had said about the Eden Roc. It had a quiet, dignified elegance.

He told the concierge he was here to see Simone Morey. The man picked up a phone, dialed, and handed it to Craig.

"I'm downstairs," he said. "What's your room number?"

"404."

"I'm on my way up."

Once he got into her room, he took out a piece of paper and pen from his pocket, and wrote, "Have you checked for bugs?" and handed it to her.

She looked annoyed. "That's insulting."

"Okay. Okay. I've trained you well."

"You're infuriating. My life didn't begin with you."

"Sorry. It's just that—"

"You never give me any credit."

"Only trying to be careful. I'm sorry. I spent a long day in the car."

"Wow, you're strung really tight. Are you hungry?"

"Starving."

"I'll order some food from room service. Meantime, go stick your head under a cold shower. It'll relax you."

"Before I do that, I want to congratulate you on your Parelli article. What fabulous journalism, and you completely devastated Parelli. I'm in awe of that. Truly I am."

She smiled. "Thank you. Now go shower."

While they ate, and drank Rion Chambolle Musigny, Craig asked her about her interview with Luciano—and complimented her some more on the article.

Until they finished eating, Elizabeth refused to talk to Craig about Zhou. "You need an hour off."

By then, he was feeling more mellow. Craig moved away from the table and walked over to the window. The curtains were drawn tight. He opened them a crack and peeked out at the swimming pool below and the lake stretching out as far as he could see.

He cut across the room to the door, opened it and glanced into the corridor. It was deserted.

"Let's talk about Zhou," he said.

Elizabeth picked up her wine glass and moved away from the room service table. They settled in comfortable orange leather chairs facing each other.

"I assume you have a plan to kidnap Zhou," she said.

"A good one, but it could get a little dicey. Zhou knows that Barry Gorman is Craig Page."

She looked chagrined. "How in the world does he know that?"

Craig explained about Tyler.

"What a traitor," she said.

"Well, anyhow, I called Zhou from Washington and spoke to him as Barry Gorman. We set a meeting at his house Thursday morning at ten."

"Where he'll no doubt have a handful of assassins on hand to kill you."

"For sure. So I have to grab him before he can kill me."

"From his house?"

"Exactly."

"How much do you know about the layout of the place?"

"Now who's being insulting?"

"Touché."

"I had Giuseppe send someone to visit the place. He gave me the layout of the whole inn. Zhou will no doubt be staying in the largest room on the top floor. Hopefully, there won't be an locals in the house when we move in, but we don't know for sure."

"So what's the plan?"

"Gee, you're impatient. President Worth and Betty gave me four special ops troops for this operation. The strange thing is that Worth wanted to know all of the details of the operation, and he wants Betty to keep him informed, even on minute details in real time."

"So he can abort?"

"That's what he said, but it's more detail than I've had to give other presidents about an operation. I guess each one's different," he added thoughtfully.

"You still haven't told me the plan."

"I'm picking up the four special ops troops Thursday morning at 2 a.m. somewhere outside of Ascona. Tomorrow, I'll find a good place to meet them. We're moving in on Zhou an hour later. Zero hour is 3 a.m. The five of us go into the Zhou's house, and use tear gas, and grab him."

"It'll be risky for you," she said grimly.

"I know that. If I don't make it, I want to be buried near Francesca and her mother."

"You're going to make it, Craig. You never talked like that before. Don't do it now."

"Okay."

"Will I have a role in this?"

"A major one. I remember you know a lot about boats. So here's what I want you to do."

Stresa

When Elizabeth woke up at 7 a.m. Wednesday morning, Craig was already out of her bed and gone from the hotel. She had breakfast from room service.

As she ate, she thought about everything Craig had told her last evening. Suddenly, she understood what was happening. She was convinced that between Craig and Zhou, only one of them would get out of Ascona alive. She didn't dare call Craig to tell him what she thought for fear Zhou would pick it up and that would spoil everything. Besides, nothing Craig could do about it. She just hoped Craig was the one who survived.

She put on a tourist outfit of khaki shorts, New York Yankees tee shirt, sneakers, and a wide brimmed hat.

From the moment she left her room, she looked around anxiously. No sign of Qing or anyone else Chinese.

At the dock, in the center of the promenade, she boarded a public ferry to Stresa at the southern end of the lake.

As they cut across the lake in the cool morning air, under a blue sky, a young couple from New York tried to strike up a conversation with her.

She said, "Yes, I'm from New York. But I'm getting too much sun."

She left them to go to another part of the boat. Over her shoulder she heard the stringy blonde say to her husband with a sandpaper beard and stomach hanging over his belt, "Some people sure aren't friendly,"

Elizabeth didn't care. She didn't want to make any new friends today.

When she got off, she wandered around the dock for a while until she saw a large white sign with red letters, "Marcello's boats. Short-term and long-term rentals."

"I'm looking for Marcello," she said to a short squat man in his sixties with a leathery weather beaten face. He was wearing a sea captain's cap, jeans, and black leather boots.

"I'm Marcello." "Who are you?"

She recalled what Craig had told her to say and she repeated it, "Giuseppe rented a boat from you, the Matterhorn, for twenty-four hours. He asked me to pick it up."

Marcello was snarling. She had a pretty good idea what was bothering him. She had to play it tough.

"You have a problem?"

"I didn't know I was going to turn my best and fastest boat over to some girl."

Exactly what she suspected. The men who operated on the seas were convinced you needed a penis to operate a boat. It was the same in New York or Italy.

"Giuseppe paid you a lot of money to rent that boat. He won't be happy if you don't give it to me."

"Too fuckin' bad. Let him get his ass down here and take the boat himself."

"You figure I won't know how to handle it. That I'll ruin your boat."

"Never met a girl yet who knew how to control a boat."

She took a deep breath. Marcello wasn't easy. Craig had given her Giuseppe's phone number in case of an emergency. She considered calling Giuseppe, but rejected it. She'd be damned if she'd do that. This was her part of the job. And she intended to do it herself.

She reached into her bag and pulled out a wad of euros. "Tell you what. I've got 5,000 euros here. You take the Matterhorn and you give me your next fastest boat. We'll race across the lake and back. If you win, you get the 5,000 euros and I don't get the Matterhorn. If I win, I keep the money and I get the Matterhorn for twenty-four hours just as you promised. How's that sound?"

He puckered up his lips and eyed her with hostility.

Finally, he smiled.

"You got balls, girl. I'll say that for you. Let's race."

He gave her the black Laguna. It looked like a powerful boat, but it didn't seem as if it would be a match for the sleek white Matterhorn. He pointed to the town of Pallanza on the other side of the lake. That would be the midpoint of the race.

"Over and back," Marcello said.

As they climbed into their boats, Elizabeth was wondering if she'd done something stupid. She could not only lose 5,000 euros, but she might not get the Matterhorn. What's more, she was afraid that it would be too late to call Giuseppe. Male pride would prevent Marcello from relenting after he whipped her in the race.

This is great, she thought. She would be blowing Craig's operation before it even got out of the gate. And all because of her own vanity.

"Start first," Marcello called to her and she took off.

By the time she was midway across the lake, passing the three Borremei islands, she had the Laguna opened up to full throttle. Glancing over her shoulder, she saw she was leading by a couple boat lengths. She was pushing her boat hard. It was vibrating but keeping up the speed.

By the time the two boats reached Pallanza, turned around, and headed back to Stresa, people in other boats and on the shore were watching them. She was still in the lead by a couple of lengths. She glanced over her shoulder at Marcello. He looked relaxed, a cigarette dangling from his lips.

A sick feeling hit her in the pit of her stomach. What if Marcello was toying with her? What if he could pull ahead any time he wanted to?

She tried to banish those thoughts and gripped the wheel hard. As they reached the middle of the lake, passing Isola Bella, she still had the lead.

Suddenly, she heard a roar behind her. Marcello had opened up the Matterhorn. As he passed her, he tossed away his cigarette and laughed.

She had been right. He had been playing with her. She felt miserable. Craig would never forgive her for blowing his operation. She would never forgive herself.

When she eased into the dock, Marcello had already tied up the Matterhorn and had a cigarette dangling from his lips. She tied up the Laguna. Humiliated, she took the five thousand euros and held it out.

He shook his head. "Keep your money, girl. You never had a chance. I equipped the Matterhorn with engines that could outrun the carabinieri. She's my pride and joy. So you better take good care of her."

"Do you mean I—"

"You proved you can operate a boat. So take the Matterhorn and get the fuck out of here before I change my mind."

She never expected this. "Thanks Marcello. I really mean that."

"Don't get sappy."

She pulled away from the dock. As she passed the Borremei islands, her speed was up, but she had plenty left. She realized Marcello wasn't kidding. This beauty was one helluva boat. Marcello had said it could outrun the carabinieri. The question she wondered was whether it could outrun the Swiss police as well. She hoped she wouldn't have to find out.

Ascona

At four in the afternoon, she pulled into slip number nine, which Craig had reserved for the Matterhorn, in the dock at the intersection of via Albemarle and via Borgo. The galley had plenty of food, so she decided to follow Craig's instruction and remain in the boat until Craig came with his package.

She looked out of the back of the boat. It was about ten yards along the wooden dock from the road to the boat. Craig had told her to be at the wheel at 3 a.m. ready to take off. Once he covered those ten yards with his package, he'd yell, "Go."

Then she'd open up the Matterhorn on the way to Stresa.

*   *   *

At five minutes before eleven p.m., Wednesday evening, Craig parked his rental car on the side of a deserted dirt road outside of Losone, Switzerland, a few miles from Ascona along the Maggiore River. He got out of the car, looked up at the full moon in a clear sky, and cursed. He would have preferred a dark sky, but he didn't have a choice. This was the only night to get Zhou.

Five minutes later, Craig saw a red and white ambulance approaching. On the side were the words Red Cross. It stopped next to his rental car. Giuseppe climbed out.

"This ambulance looks like the real thing," Craig said.

"It is."

"How'd you get it?"

"When you're in law enforcement, your files contain the names of all kinds of characters."

"Let me guess. You brought a car thief with you into Switzerland to steal it from the Red Cross."

Giuseppe laughed. "I wouldn't put it that way."

"Then how would you put it?"

"We borrowed it for a few hours from a Red Cross facility in Locarno. They won't miss it. However, I'm not expecting you to damage it. The Swiss can be finicky about stuff like that. They're meticulous people. Even a scratch on one of their vehicles gets them upset."

"I'll be real careful."

"Oh, and there are five uniforms in the back for EMS personnel."

"I'll tell my men to keep them clean."

"Don't worry about that. I'll launder them in Italy and send them back."

"Thanks for everything. The keys are in the rental car."

"I'll drive it to the dock in Locarno and park it there. I have a boat waiting to take me to Stresa. See you there in a few hours."

Giuseppe looked nervous. "Be careful, Craig."

"I will. Believe me."

Giuseppe gave Craig a hug. He started toward the rental car, then turned and said, "I got a call from Marcello, who rented the boat."

Craig was concerned. "Is Elizabeth okay?"

"Yeah. She got the boat okay. The Matterhorn. Marcello called to tell me that girl I sent has balls the size of melons."

"Marcello has that right."

Then Giuseppe said, "You sure you don't want me to come with you tonight."

"You can't possibly. In your position."

"Good luck then."

"Everything is on schedule. A little while ago, I heard from my people in North Carolina running the air surveillance. Zhou returned to the house about half an hour ago, apparently for the night. He has eight men with him. Also Qing. Some of them have left for periods of time the last couple of days, but all are back now. They look like tough military types. We have to assume they're armed to the teeth. One is standing guard at the front gate. Another behind the house. Hopefully, the others will be sleeping. I guess I'll find out."

Craig drove about fifty yards down the road and pulled into a clump of trees. He had a view of the road. For the next two hours, he didn't see another vehicle.

"Show time," he said aloud. He started the engine of the ambulance.

As he drove thirty minutes to the rendezvous point outside of the village of Arcegno, in the hills above Ascona, he thought about what lay ahead.

Zhou would have crack troops with him. Even with the element of surprise, Craig and his four men would be in for a ferocious battle.

He remembered his unsuccessful effort to kidnap Zhou's brother in Bali. All of the troops with him had been killed. He had barely escaped with his life. This would be as risky. If he failed, he had told Elizabeth that he wanted to be buried next to Francesca and her mother. But regardless of what happened tonight, this would mark the end of his long running battle with Zhou and his brother. If he succeeded, at long last he would finally be avenging the murder of his daughter Francesca.

What would he do with his life after that? Race cars? Return to the espionage game? In the US? In Europe? He didn't know, and he didn't want to think about it. All he cared about right now was getting Zhou.

At the rendezvous point, a dark blue BMW minivan was parked alongside the road. Craig stopped the ambulance in front of it.

Immediately, Darrell, Glen, Doug, and Tony scrambled out of the BMW and climbed into the back of the ambulance. They were all in full battle gear with bulky back packs.

Once Craig heard the rear door slam, he slid open the glass partition that sealed off the back.

"Ready?"

"Go," Darrell replied.

Craig pulled the ambulance onto the road. He drove for ten minutes. Then he stopped in an observation area that was separated from the road by a clump of trees.

"Do you have everything?" Craig asked.

"We're good to go," Darrell said.

"Okay. Put on the EMS uniforms and toss me one."

*   *   *

Craig drove to via Delta along back roads which fortunately were deserted. The last thing he needed now was to be stopped by a policeman or anyone else.

As Craig turned on to via Delta, he pulled over and called Dempsey in North Carolina.

"No change at the target house," Dempsey confirmed.

Craig glanced quickly in the rear view mirror at Darrell, Glen, Doug, and Tony in the back. Two on each side of the gurney.

All were in pale green EMS uniforms. Underneath they had Kevlar vests, as did Craig. They were wearing helmets and gas masks, outfitted with night vision goggles. Each man was gripping an automatic weapon with a suppressor. They had grenades in a belt at their waists. No one was talking.

Craig's gas mask was on the front seat of the ambulance along with a Beretta. The needle and syringe were in a small case hooked to his belt.

We'll have the element of surprise, Craig thought. Hopefully, Zhou, Qing and the security people will be sleeping. Time was critical. They had twenty minutes to get Zhou. Any more and the police might come.

Craig drove along via Delta, past the Park Hotel, which looked dark. Two hundred yards ahead, he saw Zhou's house. Standing just inside the wrought iron metal gate was a lone sentry. He didn't have a gun in his hand. Craig stopped the ambulance.

"Go," he shouted.

While Craig remained behind the wheel of the ambulance, his four men scrambled out of the back and ran toward the gate. Darrell was in front. He got off a single suppressed shot that took down the sentry. Glen blew the gate open with a muffled explosion. They were inside the grounds, racing toward the house, Craig behind them in the ambulance.

So far, so good, Craig thought. He parked in front of the house. Then he put on his gas mask and helmet and grabbed his gun.

Glen ran toward the back of the house to take out the other sentry. Darrell, Doug, and Tony were scrambling toward the front door. Craig was right behind them.

The front door was locked. Without hesitating, Darrell fired a suppressed round blasting off the lock. He kicked the door open.

The house, which smelled from garlic, was quiet. The first floor deserted. Darrell cut off the phone line and then took a position near the front door.

Tony and Doug were heading up the heavily polished wooden staircase, running up from the center of the reception area. Craig was following them.

Craig was convinced that after everything they had done, the Chinese troops would know they were coming and had plenty of time to grab their weapons. Once they reached the second floor, Tony stopped and tossed one tear gas grenade to the left and another to the right. Craig and Doug kept climbing to the third floor.

Behind him, Craig heard firing of Tony's suppressed gun and other non-suppressed weapons that had to be the Chinese.

On the third floor, Doug tossed tear gas grenades in both directions, then stood gun in hand ready to fire. Craig ran to the right to the master suite at the end of the hall. He heard Doug firing suppressed rounds behind him.

There was only one door between Craig and Zhou's room. Suddenly, it opened. A man stumbled out gun in hand. In the tear gas haze, Craig recognized Qing. Craig dropped him with a single shot to the chest.

The door to Zhou's room opened. In blue silk pajamas, Zhou staggered out into the corridor. He was gagging and choking.

Craig forced Zhou back into his room and slammed him to the floor. He straddled Zhou and removed the case with the syringe from his belt. Quickly, he injected Zhou with the drug that would render him unconscious.

In the instant in which Craig was inserting the needle into Zhou's arm, he saw terror on Zhou's face. "Fuck you, Craig Page," he blurted out. Then he was unconscious.

Craig picked up Zhou like a sack of potatoes and tossed him over his shoulder. Heading back to the staircase, he watched Doug shoot one more gagging Chinese security man. The third floor was quiet. Craig followed Doug down the stairs. On the second floor, Tony, with blood dripping from his leg, was firing at an enemy combatant at the end of the hall. He hit the man who stopped firing.

Midway down the stairs leading to the first floor, Craig had to step around a Chinese soldier who was stretched out not moving. Tony was covering Craig from the back, Doug from the front. The house was quiet.

Out in front of the house, Craig saw Darrell with his gun raised looking around.

"Where's Glen?" Craig asked Darrell.

"In the ambulance. He killed the sentry in the back, but he took a bullet in the arm."

"I'll go tape him up," Doug said.

"You better do Tony's leg also," Craig told him. We have plenty of supplies in the back."

After Doug opened the rear door of the ambulance, Darrell helped Craig toss Zhou onto the gurney. As Darrell was covering Zhou with a blanket, Craig ran around to the driver's door.

He heard the rear door slam. Once he started the engine, he glanced at the clock on the dash. Eighteen minutes. Pretty damn good.

He decided not to turn on the siren and flashing lights unless he saw a police car. That would give them legitimacy, but no need drawing extra attention.

Craig drove toward the dock along back roads to avoid the center of town and promenade as much as he could. He approached the dock on via Borgo without seeing another vehicle. Craig drove along the cobblestone road that led to the dock.

Only one more step to go, Craig thought. Just have to get Zhou into the boat.

The instant the ambulance stopped moving, Darrell and Doug opened the back doors. By the time Craig ran around the ambulance, they were wheeling Zhou out of the vehicle on the gurney heading toward the Matterhorn.

Glen and Tony were taped up. They looked okay. "You two get on the boat." Craig told them. The two of them ran ahead of the moving gurney.

Craig was walking alongside the gurney that Darrell and Doug were wheeling. Craig looked ahead to the end of the dock and the Matterhorn. Nothing suspicious. Elizabeth was at the wheel, ready to go.

Craig couldn't believe it. At long last, he would be gaining his revenge for Francesca's death.

Right before hoisting the gurney on the boat, Darrell and Doug stopped it.

"Wait a second," Craig said. He wanted to do one more final I.D. He pulled the blanket away from the still body. It was definitely Zhou Yun. Looking at Zhou's face, Craig found it hard to believe that this man was such a monster.

Craig's eyes were on Zhou when he heard a gun fire. Zhou's body jerked as a bullet hit him in the center of his chest. Then another.

"No," Craig cried out. "No!"

A third struck Zhou in the head. Zhou's body shook in the throes of death.

Craig immediately looked in the direction from which the bullets had come, to the rooftop of a yellow four-story apartment building.

Darrell checked Zhou for a pulse. "He's dead."

"Leave him here," Craig shouted to Darrell. "You and Doug get in the boat with Glen and Tony. Tell Elizabeth to get all of you to Stresa. Giuseppe will take care of you from there."

Craig was racing away from the dock toward the yellow building. Behind him, he heard the Matterhorn pull out into the lake.

At breakneck speed, he ran up a cobblestone road toward the back of the yellow building, guessing the sniper would exit there.

Craig saw the sniper from ten yards away, on the path behind the yellow building. The man didn't have a gun. He must have left it on the roof, Craig decided, hoping to get away without arousing suspicion.

The sniper ran up the steep cobblestone road away from the lake. Craig was giving chase. The sniper must have realized that because he increased his speed and wove around parked cars to get away. But Craig was closing the gap.

They were coming into a grassy square. With a burst of speed, Craig caught up to the sniper. He dove, catching the man around his ankles and pulling him down.

As Craig raised his head, he saw the sniper preparing to put a pill into his mouth. Cyanide, Craig guessed. With a swat of his hand, he knocked it away. The man was on his back. Craig straddled him and wrapped his hands around the man's throat. "Who sent you?" Craig shouted.

The sniper didn't respond. "If you tell me, I'll let you go. I promise. If you don't, you'll spend the rest of your life in a Swiss jail."

The sniper still didn't respond, but stared at Craig.

"The police will be here in a minute," Craig said. "It's now or never. Tell me and I'll let you go."

"Mei Ling," the sniper blurted out.

Craig released his grip. He helped the man to his feet. "Go. Run for it," he said.

Washington

President Worth's secretary led Craig through the French doors to the rose garden. Then she retreated into the White House.

He saw that President Worth was alone, sitting on a rocker. He seemed to be deep in thought. The garden was bathed in an eerie silence. Craig thought of a line he had once read in a book about Washington. "It's lonely at the top."

Craig coughed and cleared his throat, letting Worth know he was there. The president immediately stood up.

"I hope I'm not disturbing you, Mr. President," Craig said. "Kathy told me to come out here."

"No. Not at all. I like to grab a few quiet moments when I can. It helps with the pressure of the job. Glad you could come. I wanted to talk to you. To thank you for the outstanding and heroic job you did in Ascona. There wasn't a single civilian casualty and only two slightly wounded among our troops."

"I feel as if I failed, letting Zhou be killed before I could get him to Italy where he would stand trial."

"Amazing how things sometimes seem different then they are."

It was a peculiar statement. Craig waited for the president to explain. When he didn't, Craig said, "We had a mess with the Swiss authorities. I appreciate your smoothing it over."

"Oh, I called in a few chits which you don't have to know about. They were willing to sweep it under the rug and blame unidentified terrorists for Zhou's death."

"Mei Ling sent the sniper who killed Zhou," Craig said. "I wanted you to know that."

Craig expected the president to be surprised. Instead, he said, "She had good reasons for wanting Zhou dead. On a personal level, he was responsible for the death of her husband and her son—her only child. On a national level, she believed that Zhou was not only undermining her presidency, but the integrity of China and its prosperity in the world. She and I have developed a very close relationship. We talk often on a dedicated secure line."

Suddenly, Craig understood.

"You gave Mei Ling all of the details of our operation which you received from Betty and me. That's how the sniper knew precisely where to be. Isn't it?"

The president's forehead wrinkled. He walked over and placed an arm around Craig's shoulder. "As you know very well, Craig, we live in a rough world. The US and China are the two most powerful nations. We have to cooperate and help each other to whatever extent we can. It's mutually beneficial for both of us."

Craig pulled away and stared at Worth. "You had this in mind from the moment I came to you with my plan to kidnap Zhou and take him to Italy. Didn't you?" Not wanting to sound disrespectful, Craig added, "Mr. President."

"I never liked the Italy trial idea. I thought it would get too messy for us with Italy, Switzerland, and China."

"You could have told me that. I would have accepted your decision."

"And perhaps I should have."

"But you were concerned I might not have carried out the operation as efficiently. So you . . ."

"Used and manipulated me, are the words you'd like to use if you weren't respectful of my office."

"Something like that."

Worth looked into Craig's eyes. "By way of explanation, let me say this. I've studied your background and everything you've done for our country. In my opinion, you are among the most loyal and patriotic Americans this country has ever produced. I felt as if I could give you any assignment in our national interest and you would do it. That's what I did here."

*   *   *

Craig left the White House grounds through the west gate. He walked to 17th Street where Elizabeth was waiting behind the wheel of a car. He had wanted her to come with him to his meeting with Worth but she had refused. "This is your show," she had told him.

As he climbed into the car, she pulled away from the curb.

"Do you need directions?" he asked.

"I've only been there once. It's not a place I'll ever forget."

She headed toward the Theodore Roosevelt Bridge to cross into Virginia.

"How did it go with Worth?" she asked.

"He used me. It was all a set up. Worth and Mei Ling orchestrated Zhou's death."

He was astounded that she didn't respond. "Well, aren't you surprised?"

"No. It's what I thought."

"Why didn't you tell me?"

"I didn't figure it out until after you left me in the hotel in Ascona. Calling would have put you even more at risk if Zhou picked up the call, and besides there was nothing you could do about it."

They were crossing the bridge. "How did you figure it out and I didn't?"

"When I was in Beijing, Mei Ling spoke to me about her relationship with Worth. That was the piece you didn't have."

They rode in silence for another half hour. Finally, Elizabeth pulled into the entrance to the cemetery.

She drove slowly on the winding roads until she reached Francesca's grave.

Then she parked and they both got out. Craig, mourning for the daughter whom the Zhous had murdered, his only child. Elizabeth, mourning for the loss of her lover's daughter and her friend who was also her star young reporter.

Approaching the grave, it was hard for Craig to believe that it hadn't even been three years since Francesca died.

During the whole time, he and the Zhou brothers had waged their unrelenting warfare.

In front of the grave, he moved away from Elizabeth and dropped to his knees. He lowered his head and wept for his beautiful talented daughter.

When he had no more tears, he picked up his head. As if talking to Francesca, he said, "It's over. It's finally over. Both of the Zhou brothers are dead. Your murder had been avenged."

Elizabeth helped him to his feet. Arms around each other, they walked back toward the car.

"Where would you like to go now?" she asked.

"Dulles Airport. You and I have a plane to catch."

"We do?"

"Yes. Air France to Paris. If you'll have me, I'd like to move back in with you."

She smiled. "I'd love it, but my place is a mess."

"We'll clean it up together."

"I'd quit my job if you have other ideas for us."

"Thanks. I appreciate that. But, no. I want you to keep it."

"What'll you do?"

"Race cars. I'll move my base from Milan to Paris. There's a big race next month in the French Alps. I want to get ready for it."

She threw her arms around him. They held each other tightly.

About the Author

Allan Topol is the author of eleven novels of international intrigue. Two of them, *Spy Dance* and *Enemy of My Enemy*, were national best sellers. His novels have been translated into Chinese, Japanese, Portuguese, and Hebrew. One was optioned and three are in development for movies.

In addition to his fiction writing, Allan Topol co-authored a two-volume legal treatise entitled *Superfund Law and Procedure*. He wrote a weekly column for Military.com and has published articles in numerous newspapers and periodicals, including the *New York Times*, the *Washington Post*, and *Yale Law Journal*.

He is a graduate of Carnegie Institute of Technology who majored in chemistry, abandoned science, and obtained a law degree from Yale University. He became a partner in a major Washington law firm. An avid wine collector and connoisseur, he has traveled extensively researching dramatic locations for his novels.

For more information, visit www.allantopol.com.